D0370895

Juicy
Mangos

Juicy
Mangos

erotica collection

edited by

michelle herrera mulligan

ATRIA BOOKS

New York   London   Toronto   Sydney

ATRIA BOOKS
1230 Avenue of the Americas
New York, NY 10020

"Diamondback" © 2007 by Mayra Montero
"Diamondback" translation © 2007 by Simon & Schuster, Inc.
"Juan and Adela" © 2007 by Michelle Herrera Mulligan
"Faith in Disguise" © 2007 by Mayra Santos-Febres
"Sensually Yours" © 2007 by Sofía Quintero
"Don't Be Mad at Me" © 2007 by Adriana López
"A Kiss From Lares" © 2007 by Elisha Miranda
"The Lunalía" © 2007 by Yxta Maya Murray

First Atria Books trade paperback edition July 2007

10 9 8 7 6 5 4 3 2 1

ATRIA BOOKS is a trademark of Simon & Schuster, Inc.

Manufactured in the United States of America

For information about special discounts for bulk purchases, please contact Simon & Schuster Special Sales at 1-800-456-6798 or business@simonandschuster.com.

Library of Congress Cataloging-in-Publication Data
Juicy Mangos : the best Latina erotica / edited by Michelle Herrera Mulligan.—1st Atria Books trade pbk. Ed.
     p.   cm.
   1. Erotic stories, American.   2. Hispanic Americans—Fiction.   I. Herrera Mulligan, Michelle

PS648.E7J85 2007
813'.608035380868073—dc22   2006101303

ISBN-13: 978-0-7432-9444-7 (trade pbk.)
ISBN-10:   0-7432-9444-0 (trade pbk.)

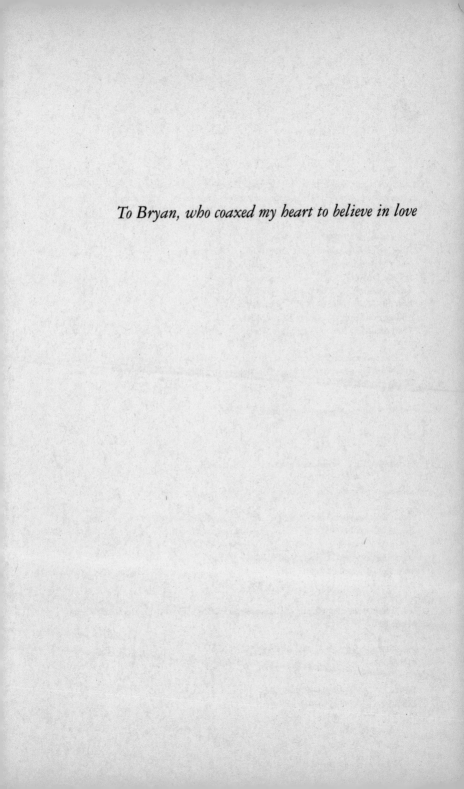

To Bryan, who coaxed my heart to believe in love

Contents

Editor's Letter

Sweet, juicy mangos. The soft sound of Spanish drifting from glossed lips . . . congas pulsing on a crowded beach . . . women drinking passion-fruit margaritas as they shake their generous curves in time . . . exposed backsides of wet, tanned flesh. The word Latina *seems almost synonymous with* erótica, *as naturally connected as bodies that stick together on a dance floor.*

When Johanna Castillo, an editor at Atria Books, called to ask me to coordinate the first-ever English-language Latina erotic fiction anthology, I responded as any self-respecting Latina would: I pumped up my sex appeal—even though I consider myself a major nerd. "Erótica? *Claro que sí,*" I whispered into the phone in Spanish, my hand tucked seductively around my mouth, so my co-workers wouldn't hear. "I could definitely do that. I love *erótica.*" I made sure to use the Spanish pronunciation of the word, exaggerating the *r* in erotica so that my sexy Ecuadorian editor would know I was the real thing. Then I hung up the phone, went to the ladies room, and broke into a cold sweat. "Erotica, what was I thinking?" My head was spinning. "All I know about erotica can be summed up in the three dusty books I store behind the Harry Potter series on my bookshelves. How am I going to be able to attach my name to a cover that could possibly feature a naked body? What if my *abuelita* finds out?" When I went to bed that night, an even more serious concern dawned on me. "What the hell am I supposed to write about?"

I resolved that night to call the editor first thing in the morning and tell her, sheepishly, that I wasn't the right one for the job.

The next morning I woke up ashamed. How could I doubt a great opportunity like this? Wasn't it passé for the post *Sex and the City* generation to even blink an eye over erotica? But I knew I wasn't worried about the response from my trendy, cynical Anglo friends, who joke easily over the right brand of vibrator and wild nights at strip clubs. This book would be for Latinas, the women who are capable of shaking their asses to the latest merengue one night and casually considering re-virgination surgery another.

No matter how deep our cleavages or short our skirts, Latinas don't like talking about sex. Years of Catholic and other strict upbringings have taught us that being labeled a *sucia*, despite what bestselling novels will tell you, is definitely a bad thing. And yet our images everywhere smack of sex: Even the latest cover of *Maxim* looks like it's for a children's book compared to the front pages of our racy Spanish-language magazines (not to mention the amped-up swimsuit segments of our mega beauty contests—the Sports Illustrated Swimsuit Calendar's got nothin' on *Cosmo en Español*). A lot of my *feminista* sisters have criticized our obsession with beauty and seeming sexual objectification, and I've enthusiastically agreed with them in the past. But as I see a tide of fundamentalism take over the headlines around the world, I can't help but feel that our bold, clothes-shedding ways are a good thing—an in-your-face reminder of our strength.

But the world of our own Latina desires and fantasies has lived in a shroud of silence for too long. It's as if, when the men who shoot the photos and the women who judge the contests look away, our sexuality evaporates, leaving innocent, stuttering schoolgirls in their wake. It's high time we shattered our silence and talked about what sex is like from our own *perspectivas*. What is the temptress on the cover of *TV y Novelas* magazine fantasizing about as she pouts for the camera? What's it like for us when we leave the lights on?

In *Juicy Mangos*, seven award-winning Latina writers tell hot erotic stories featuring strong Hispanic women—and delve deeply into the inner worlds of their characters.

Each story revolves around a holiday theme—from Valentine's Day to Christmas—honing in on the charged emotions and new and daring personas the characters take on during these special times of year. As the writers explore the mysterious moments in life when we are not our ordinary selves, their characters discover secret places where they can explore their darkest impulses.

Let's make one thing clear right from the start: these stories are explicit, and not just sexually. In "The Lunalía," by acclaimed author Yxta Maya Murray, a married Chicana librarian struggles with her mortality and her frightening desires until her sexual experimentation leads her to a dark supernatural realm. Murray creates an enticing fantastical world that stretches her readers' imaginations yet never loses sight of her character's emotional center. Her epic story proves that erotic writing can be as raw psychologically as it is physically, taking its reader on an intimate tour of one fictional Latina's soul.

As does good sex, each writers' prose wholly captures every moment—emotionally, spiritually, and physically—injecting depth and range into their stories, often describing how a characters' sexuality reveals a painful truth about herself. Author Elisha Miranda, who recently published her debut novel, *The Sista Hood: On the Mic* (as E-Fierce), explores a young Nuyorican film director's discovery of her unhealthy addiction to sexy Latina women and her longing for family acceptance in "A Kiss from Lares."

In these erotic stories, the writers challenge the way we think about sex, making it not just an element but a character itself, infusing each action in the story with its own intoxicating spell. In one, journalist Adriana López puts at stake the very sanity of her character, Anna, a sophisticated Colombian-American editor at a literary magazine who succumbs to the force of her insatiable and jealous love for a young Spanish author with a troubling past.

The writers also reveal the playful side of sex, taking their characters to exotic locales, ranging from the hot springs of southern Puerto Rico to the streets of Barcelona during the sexually charged *Diada de Sant Jordi*. Their travels are reflected in experiments with the language itself, playing with Spanish, English, and the controversial Spanglish and the mixed cultural idioms of their characters' backgrounds. Two stories were originally written in Spanish and translated, giving us a glimpse into the exciting realm of contemporary Latin America. The esteemed poet Mayra Santos-Febres, who translated her own story from Spanish, takes her readers from colonial Brazil to modern-day Chicago in a startling tale about a sexy historian possessed by the powers of an antique dress. Award-winning author Mayra Montero, translated by the legendary Edith Grossman, opens our collection with a poignant story of an aging Puertoriqueña's dangerous dalliance with her sister-in-law over a Christmas visit. Transformational moments like these make all the stories memorable on many levels.

The characters regularly and unabashedly take the reins in their sex lives, daring to make the first move to satisfy the *deseo* that burns within them. In "Juan and Adela," a middle-aged Mexican maid acts on her attraction for her thirty-two-year-old son's Dominican stockbroker friend, even though he's more than twenty years younger. Inspired by my own mother's scandalous marriage to a much-younger man, I focus on how Adela's leap of faith into an unlikely love affair inspires her to take risks in other aspects of her life.

All the writers share an important quality: the ability to have loads of fun telling their stories. Sofía Quintero, who wrote chica-lit favorite *Divas Don't Yield*, offers us "Sensually Yours," the story of a sex-toy saleswoman who takes on a business partner with benefits to boost her dipping sales. The story offers an exciting and sexy glimpse of the world of Latina passion parties and sex toys, introducing us to wonders such as "four-ounce bottles of Chipper Dipper Erection Crème, an array of edible panties, little paddles in black and red leather, and assorted palm-sized vibrators that the company has discontinued—for those ladies who can't wait two weeks for their goodies and want something to take home tonight."

With love interests such as a horny entomologist, a Dominican who is a former gang-banger, a full-time male stripper, a luscious and curvy Puerto Rican television producer, and an insubordinate male intern—placed in love scenes involving the beach, music, and lots of fruit—this book is definitely one you'll want to read at home, with the shutters closed.

As the first Latinas to tread these erotic waters, we've made sure to be as tantalizing, titillating, and sexually outrageous as we've ever been, only this time we'll be the ones getting off on it. *Que lo disfruten!*

—*Michelle Herrera Mulligan, September 2006*

Juicy
Mangos

Diamondback

Mayra Montero
translated by Edith Grossman

W hen she raised her arm to put the star in place, I knew that, for the first time, I wanted to kiss a woman.

"Is it all right here?" she asked me, and I didn't look at the star but kept looking at her white underarm, blaming myself for this discovery, this hypnotizing taste that filled my mouth, a noise like glass breaking at the horrified back of my skull.

"Emilia, does it look straight to you?"

I kept looking at her, not saying a word, and I wanted to burst into tears. Something rose from my feet to my throat, a quick mouthful that wasn't anything, or was like an attack of vertigo. I staggered and looked at the sofa. I wanted to fall onto the sofa, and then Walter, who was observing us, hurried toward me and gripped my arms.

"The wine must have made you dizzy," he said, and he helped me to sit down.

Marzena climbed down the ladder. I looked at the star, which was a little crooked. We had spent the entire afternoon trimming the tree. She and I hanging the balls and some porcelain angels, and Walter organizing the rest of the decorations, the fake snow and angel hair, and pouring glasses of wine.

"It probably would do you good to get into the water for a while," Marzena suggested and pointed toward the ocean. Then she laughed and I looked at her lips, and for the second time in less than a minute I was horrified at my own desire to kiss her. Walter brought me a glass of water and asked why I didn't go for a walk along the beach and get some fresh air. He asked his wife to go with me.

"Go with my sister," he said to Marzena, and he leaned over to give me a kiss. "You must be thinking about *Mamá*."

I nodded in agreement. "About Mamá," I murmured and began to think about all the years that had gone by since I first met Marzena; about the first time my brother brought her home; about the first night she had supper with us, with my mother and me, when I was recently divorced with two little boys who sat on her lap and asked why her name was so funny. Marzena replied that it was the name they give little Polish girls who were born with an extra toe. She took off her shoe and raised her foot. My mother and I looked with as much astonishment as my two children: Marzena showed us the miniature toe, immobile and kissable, a tiny worm of flesh growing out of the little toe on her right foot.

Walter had graduated by then and been hired as a veterinarian on a farm, on several farms to be exact. Marzena was studying entomology, and we had to explain it twice to Mamá. "Bugs," I remember Walter telling her, "she works with insects." Mamá made a disappointed face, and Marzena glanced over at me; I responded immediately and found her gaze unfathomable: she had chestnut-colored hair and changeable eyes; I couldn't say if they were large or small, green or brown. Her mouth was the most ordinary kind of mouth, but her eyeteeth protruded a little, just a little, and the spell consisted in that. I don't know if it was a spell or what; it was a piece of carnivorous information that fascinated me.

"Why don't you come with me to the lab?" she asked in a quiet voice, leaning over my chair but looking at her husband. When she leaned over, I could see her breasts. After so many years—how many years had she been married to my brother: fourteen, maybe fifteen?—I had never seen her breasts; I hadn't even seen her nurse her daughter, my niece, a ten-year-old girl, the one who had insisted that we spend Christmas Eve at the beach, my first Christmas Eve without Mamá and without my own children, who were with their father, and without a guiding principle in my life, without a refuge, only this dismay that suddenly overwhelmed me.

Marzena leaned closer. I smelled her perfume, a vegetal scent, like watercress juice.

"I have to identify some fungi—it'll only take a few minutes."

I wanted to know Walter's reaction, but my brother was ahead of me: when I raised my head, he was staring at me.

"It'll probably make you sick to go to the lab," he said. He was only two years older than me. "Her stomach's upset," he added, looking at his wife.

What happened next, what I said, was not the work of my mouth or my brain; my voice didn't come from either of those places but from lower down. I said that for my whole life, ever since I'd met Marzena, I had wanted to see her in the lab. Marzena laughed, gave instructions to her husband about when to turn off the oven and about which bottles he had to chill. Walter walked with us to the car, opened the door, and saw me sit down with my legs very close together and my shoulders tense; he must have seen something forced in my expression.

"If you feel sick again," he said, taking my arm, "tell Marzena to bring you back."

I agreed and watched Marzena adjust her seatbelt. She said it wouldn't take us very long to get to the university because there was hardly any traffic on Christmas Eve. Without taking her eyes off the road, she extended her hand and pressed the play button for a cassette. The music came on immediately, and she turned up the volume.

"Do you know that song?"

I didn't know any songs, I wasn't very interested in songs. Marzena was; she knew a lot of them, in English and in Spanish, and she often sang with her daughter.

"That's Billy Joel," she said, laughing, and she began to sing along: "Don't wait for answers, just take your chances . . . Don't ask me why."

I closed my eyes: a small, miraculous emotion began to move around my head. I didn't want to become dizzy, and I opened them again and looked at Marzena. She was wearing shorts, the fronts of her thighs were reddened by the sun, and I wanted to put my hand there, on that hot, tender skin. My hands were cold; not only my hands but my feet, my forehead, my cheeks. I noticed that sometimes she forgot some of the words, and then she sang tra-la-la. When she sang tra-la-la I could see the tip of her tongue; I'd never wanted to take in a woman's tongue before, never in my blind, uninspired, wasted life.

"There's my lair," she said when we reached the university. I saw a gray building with closed windows; we got out of the car and went in along a side corridor that led to a staircase, and the staircase to a basement. The doors downstairs seemed to be made of iron, and some had little signs with the names of their occupants. We came to Marzena's. It pleased me to see her name giving a name to her lair. She took out the key and we went into the darkened lab; she waited a few seconds before turning on the light, and for those few seconds we were very close, unintentionally brushing against each other. Then the lights went on and all around me I saw fish tanks without water and without fish; some were empty and others were occupied by insects.

"I'm going to look at those fungi," she said. "They're probably filled with spores by now."

I said I always thought she worked only with insects. She said with insects, of course, and with everything that made them sick. She explained that her work was searching for pathogens, and my reaction was idiotic:

"You really *look* like somebody who searches for pathogens."

It wasn't only the words but the way my voice came out, the sodden intonation, that vulgar hint of masculinity. She gave me an indecisive look, hesitating between accepting the joke without saying anything or asking me what I meant by that.

"I *do* look like somebody who searches for them, don't I? Yes I do."

She took off her blouse in front of me, and I saw that she wasn't wearing anything underneath it. She walked to a coat rack and took down a blue lab coat, held it for a moment, and then put it on without buttoning it.

She sat down on a stool and asked me to have a seat on another, but I said I preferred standing and watching her work.

"Do my bugs make you sick?" Marzena asked after a while, pointing to a kind of immobile butterfly.

I came up behind her to see. I couldn't help thinking about her open lab coat, the profile of her breasts, the tongue with which she tra-la-laed songs.

"They eat cabbages," she said, laughing. I didn't see the joke or the humor. I saw her hands adjusting the microscope and noticed a faint smell of sweat, a gentle odor that made me shiver. I didn't move, but she gestured in a kind of invitation for me to look more carefully, and when I came closer my chest and belly rubbed against her back and buttocks. My chest, my erect nipples, pressed against her back; my belly, which was the same height as her backside, felt that eternal pressure. I looked over her shoulder, I still couldn't make out the precise form of the insect that was on the table, and I pushed against her a little more. Marzena didn't move an inch; she didn't do anything to withdraw from the proximity of my body, a hot, sly body overwhelmed by the afternoon's new development, a new development that wasn't completely new: for how long had I liked women?

"It's called a cabbage moth," she said in a confessional, slightly husky voice.

For a moment I rested my chin on her shoulder. We were sisters-in-law, almost sisters, this wasn't the first Christmas we had spent together, and it surely wouldn't be the last. I moved my left arm forward and leaned it on the table; I did the same thing with my other arm. In front of me, her back turned to me, Marzena was trapped. And with just a gesture from her, the slightest attempt to escape, I would have withdrawn. But she didn't do anything, Marzena remained still and pliant, and over her shoulder, instead of looking at the insect, I lowered my eyes and looked at her breasts.

"It's also called the cabbage nymph, the cabbage worm, the green cabbage caterpillar."

What she said about the caterpillar filled me with heat. Heat at the back of my neck, and an absolute heat in my throat; that impatience to get away from there, or perhaps just the opposite, to keep anybody from getting away. I was still pressing against Marzena's back, but then I also put my arm around her waist. She kept silent, she didn't move, but her body stiffened. With the other hand I began to take off her lab coat while at the same time I kissed her on the neck. She heaved a great sigh, which was both a sigh and a moan.

"I like what it's called in Mexico," she whispered in my ear. "*Palomilla dorso de diamante.*"

I remembered that once, years earlier, Marzena had come to visit my mother and me and spent the entire afternoon with us. Then my brother had come to pick her up, and when he greeted his wife, he kissed her on the neck. It was a long kiss that made me sad and caused a certain resentment I couldn't explain then. I could explain it now, a few hours before Christmas, in the half light of a laboratory that smelled of formaldehyde, old paper, fingernail clippings (that's the smell of insects), and a strange vegetal perfume. Marzena turned around and the lab coat slipped to the floor. I didn't say a word, first I kissed her mouth, a hurried, cold kiss, and then I sucked her nipples. I looked at her face and saw that it was pale and had a hostile expression, and I expected to be shoved away. But instead she moaned, a loud moan that somehow brought me back to life but condemned me to death.

I don't know where I found the strength: I'm a small woman, but Marzena is very tall, with meat on her bones, to use the expression my mother liked so much. I took her in my arms and practically lifted her into the air; then I made a rapid movement and lay her on the floor. She was compliant, still, in distress. When she was on the floor, lying on her back, Marzena moaned again. She closed her eyes, and I took the opportunity to remove my blouse. I tore my clothes off as clumsily as if I were a child, a baby who can't bear to be confined any longer. The two of us were sighing and I pulled off her shorts; my hand, that had once been a woman's hand, had turned into a claw, an instrument for scratching or wounding, tearing apart whatever got in its way. Finally it appeared, floating on that white flesh, Marzena's dark sex. I leaned over it; I still didn't dare to press my face, my nose, my lips into it. Marzena arched her body and offered me her belly. It was a signal and I lowered myself to her flesh, I buried my head, I breathed as if I had discovered it was possible to live under water, breathing gently in the deep. I raised my face only to see if after that discovery I was also capable of living outside, and then I saw the landscape of Marzena: her breasts, her chin, her face as intense as if it were being lapped by the sea. I was certain I was amphibian; it was a certainty that signified a great blow: I lost my memory but recovered my entire life in that absurd, solitary moment.

Marzena was desperate. I was absorbing, sucking all knowledge there, but I forgot to absorb and suck her. She put out her hand and placed it on my head—it was the first time I received her orders, the first time I let myself be governed by a real lover: another naked woman. She pushed my face against her sex and I began to devour it as if it were cabbages, with small, disorderly bites. I was the insect, the conscientious moth; I calmly swallowed and regurgitated my food, which in turn was nourishing another creature, cruel and in love, her autonomous vulva that breathed independently.

Then I moved up and placed my face on Marzena's face, and she wrapped her legs around my waist. She searched for my ear, asked for my fingers, begged me to bury them between her buttocks; she repeated this as she rubbed her sex against mine. We pushed against the table unintentionally and something rolled, things fell to the floor, and glass dropped, perhaps one of the fish tanks, and shattered very close to my legs. I felt the shards of glass piercing me but I didn't care, instead I bit my sister-in-law's lips; I told her she was my woman and she burst into laughter; I said it again, I said "my woman," and then she ordered me to move up and sit on her face; I'd never sat on anybody's face, man or woman. Not even the father of my children ever put his lips on my sex, or the man who came after him, or the one after that. In some obscure way, redemptive in its instincts, I had been keeping myself, saving myself for Marzena. She needed me there, on her lips of a Polish woman searching for pathogens. And there I fell, there I wanted to die, but I wanted her to die too. Later I asked her to turn over, and I moved down slowly, kissed the nape of her neck and licked her back. She sighed when I embraced her waist.

"In English," she murmured, "do you know what it's called in English?"

I stopped for a moment, I had no idea what she was asking me.

"Diamondback moth." She spoke too loudly. "Don't you think it's a pretty name?"

I sank my teeth into her and she shouted a curse. I bit the back of her thighs and returned silently to her buttocks; I spread them with both hands and sank down without fear, I thought I couldn't do it but I did, out of fury, out of hunger, out of love. Marzena kept shouting and I was afraid someone would hear her. I raised my head and looked toward the door, and she was like a madwoman and begged me, condemned me not to stop. Then my fingers searched her out in front. We pushed the table again but this time nothing fell: everything that could roll had already rolled. When I sat up to look at her back, I noticed that she had perspired a great deal; I was convinced that this, and not the one on the insects, was the genuine diamondback. Then I understood her question, her science, her perversity: all the frenzy that trapped me under the halftone of no light.

When I stood up I discovered that my legs were bleeding. All around me was broken glass, and Marzena looked for absorbent cotton and alcohol. As she cleaned my legs she said:

"You'll be injured this Christmas Eve . . . imagine what your brother will say."

And when I heard that word *brother*, I felt a wave of shame and guilt. I'd just made love to his wife, I'd had her nipples in my mouth, and her sex, her navigable back, and the burning world of her buttocks and what lay between them. I'd devoured his wife, who in a certain sense was also mine. Marzena kept looking at me. I lowered my eyes, rejected her with a small gesture, a gesture so useless I'm sure it hurt her.

"What am I going to say to my brother?" I stammered.

Marzena still didn't do anything. She had the cotton in one hand

and the bottle of alcohol in the other. She was naked, and I felt cold for her.

"Shall I tell you what you have to say to him?" She stepped forward and threw the cotton in my face. It was an act of fury. She shoved me as she passed and murmured an insult. When I looked at her again, she had an ironic smile on her face, and she dressed, wearing that smile. We left the lab and got into the car in total silence. She played the song again—"Don't Ask Me Why"—but this time she didn't sing it. I listened to the lyrics, trying to retain some phrase, and I saw her yawn; she yawned several times on the way back, not saying a word for the entire trip.

When we reached the house, my niece was watching television. She said that her *papá* was taking a nap. Marzena went straight into the kitchen and stayed there a long time; we heard her singing and the girl looked at me in amusement:

"Mamá likes Billy Joel so much . . ." and she began to sing too, accompanying her mother from a distance.

I didn't move from the sofa, as lifeless as if I had died, and I stayed that way, even when Marzena came into the living room to say she was going to take a bath. When she said this she kept looking at me, the two of us looking at one another with curiosity.

"You ought to take a nice shower too," she said to me. "It's Christmas Eve, Emilia." Then she turned toward the tree. "I have to straighten that star."

The girl approached her mother and put her arms around her waist, a waist that was part of the family now: it belonged to my brother, my niece, and especially to me. Marzena climbed the ladder again, extended her arm, and I could see her underarm. It was an underarm as white as a small dove. She moved the star back and forth, looked at her daughter, and gestured toward me:

"Will somebody please tell me if it looks straight?"

Juan and Adela

Michelle Herrera Mulligan

a loud clanging startled Adela out of her sleep. She'd been dreaming about working on a farm, dressed in a leather outfit with a whistle around her neck. A ring of bare-chested laborers stood in front of her, waiting for her command. She was just about to tell the tallest one, a hard-faced *morenito*, he could start by peeling off her skintight *vaqueros* when a noise nearly knocked her out of bed. *Joder.* What was that? A cowbell? "*Ay,*" she yelled to the empty house. "*Qué pasó?*" It took a moment for her to remember she was alone. Then she placed the sound: the high-pitched chiming piercing her brain was the doorbell.

She'd just moved in a few weeks ago. It was a small casita in stately Floral Park, a residential neighborhood in the hills of Santa Ana that pretended that the dirty city full of Mexicans that crowded its borders didn't exist.

So far, she enjoyed the solitude of her little casita, tucked away behind a larger house at the end of a long road lined by walnut trees. But now someone was invading her doorstep at what felt like what her *mamá* called *la hora de la muerte*. She looked around the darkened room, kept pitch black by dark canvas curtains she'd attached to the windows, the first thing she'd assembled when she'd moved in. The glaring red numbers on her digital alarm clock said 9:15. She dragged herself out of bed and put on the bright red silk robe hanging on the back of her bedroom door. On the way, she tripped over the clothes she'd thrown aside the night before.

She and her best friend Marisol had been hitting the ranchero clubs. Adela could still feel the strain of too many low *quebradita* dips in her back. She stumbled to the front door and peeked through the peephole. "*Ay, carajo,*" she whispered. It was the Hour of Powers: the cable television evangelicals that had been prowling the area, looking for lonely people to pester. They would pay for this.

She jerked open the door. A blinding light flooded her field of vision, and she put her hand up to her face to block it. Slowly, a slim blonde wearing a pastel blue skirt suit and a teenage boy so tall he looked like he'd been stretched came into focus. "Hola, señora," started the blonde, in a high, nasal voice, the Spanish struggling to be released from her taut lips. "*Venimos para compartirle un mensaje de salvación.*" Oon Maynsahey Dee Salvayseeon, eh?, thought Adela, Well, I have a *mensaje* for you.

"You take you brochures and all of you boolshit," she said slowly, to make sure the girl understood, "and you shove 'em up into you ass." The girl's powder blue eyes widened. Adela slammed the door before the girl, or her gangly companion, could think of a response. Adela had wasted a lot of her childhood reciting the Lord's Prayer and making confessions under her parent's watchful eyes. She wasn't going to start entertaining hypocrites now.

She headed back to bed. With my *boca sucia*, you'd think I got more *acción*, she wondered. As she stretched out on the stiff new mattress, she pondered how long it had been since someone had shared a bed with her. *Podría yo dormir con otro?*, she asked herself. Would I even know how to make room for anyone else? Before and after her divorce, she'd had many lovers. She'd even found work as a paid escort, justifying her exploits in the beginning on the thrill of adventure. What the hell, she'd figured, you go out, you have a great time with some *rico*, and you ended the night with hundred dollar bills in your pocket. It had been fun until she started getting regulars. They stopped bothering with *saludos* and dinners after the first few dates. They would just take her to bars to parade her in front of their friends until they took her home. The last straw was Rafael Garcia, the exporter with the dead eyes. He would stare at her so coldly she shivered the whole time she was with him, even while he was pumping away at her. She could smell his thick spicy cologne on her for days after their dates, no matter how many times she showered. After her third month with him, she couldn't take it any more. She quit the business forever. She'd picked up where she left off, dating for fun without too much commitment. She preferred it that way.

But she hadn't been with anyone for a long time. Though she was still beautiful at fifty-five, Adela hadn't even considered bringing a man home in years. Somewhere along the line, she'd lost the energy for the theatrics of romantic life. But that didn't stop her desire. Adela was a lusty woman. She didn't only fantasize about men in her dreams. On Saturdays, she would head to the Albertson's downtown at 8:40 a.m., twenty minutes before they opened. She told herself it was to avoid the crowds or to get the best produce as it came in. She would park near the back entrance and watch the *obreros* bring in the carts of freshly picked fruit. She loved the way their sinewy muscles spread the worn cotton of their T-shirts thin, a sliver of their *panzas* visible through the rips and fissures that gathered around the edges. A sliver just big enough for her tongue to slide into.

Once, while looking for a discount mart on the outskirts of Santa Ana, she'd seen men in the fields picking grapes from long rows of brush under the scorching sun. She pulled over across the street, telling herself she had to check the map she kept in her glove compartment. She put on her sunglasses and cracked the window; her map spread uselessly across the dashboard. The sweet smell of rotting grapes mingled with the stale air in her old Toyota as she watched the workers toiling in the fields. They seemed to move in time as they bent over to slash and pick the brush, then slash and pick again. One of the stockier guys stepped out of the field to get a drink from his cooler. He threw his machete in the grass, and rolled the sleeves of his T-shirt to his shoulders. He dipped his hand in the cold water to fish out a drink. She watched his arm as it reached inside; she took in his large, callused hands and massive biceps. After he took a sip, he spotted her looking. He smiled and took a step toward her.

She pulled back onto the road immediately and drove away. When she got home she went straight to her bed. She imagined herself bent under him in the field, on the receiving end of his forceful hips, as he ripped off her clothes with his machete. She ran her fingers over her round breasts and the soft folds of her stomach, then down below, imagining that it was his coarse fingers that slipped deep inside of her.

Despite the occasional lonely moment, she was happy with her life. She enjoyed working at El Colonial, an old hotel where most of the staff were regulars and knew her by name. She had plenty of *compañeras* to spend time with on the weekends. Her children made their own lives when they left California years ago for fancy jobs back East. They rarely came back for visits.

The call that came the morning after the *invasion evangélico*, while she was pressing her uniform before work, was a total shock. It was her eldest son, Gabriel, a thirty-two-year-old investment banker who'd managed to hold on to the small fortune he'd made on the Internet in the '90s. She hadn't heard from him for months. And now, speaking with the confidence he'd acquired with wealth, his smooth voice shattered the silence that followed her through her casita. "Hey Ma, guess where I'm spending Christmas this year?"

"Dónde, mijo?" she said. Gabriel was the only child she spoke to in Spanish. She spoke English with her daughter, Anjélica.

"Your new house! I'm coming home to spend Christmas with you, and I'm going to bring my friend, Juan. He's a broker trainee in the office with me, and he could use some of your cooking. Is that cool?"

"Te vienes a Los Angeles para visitarme a mi?" she asked doubtfully. He hadn't even seen her last house in the Valley, and she couldn't imagine what would bring him out now.

"Well . . . actually, Juan and I won this sales initiative at the office, and we have a free luxury hotel for the week after Christmas. I've always wanted to teach Juan how to surf, and since I haven't seen you for so long . . ." Gabriel babbled on.

Ah, *por éso*, she thought. He wants to be with his friend, the same one he wants to bring here. Then it hit her. Christmas was only three weeks away She wanted to yell, *"Qué? Qué!?!"* It was already December 3, and she still had unpacked boxes stacked everywhere. *"Pero por qué lo tienes que hacer tan pronto?"* she almost whispered, talking as much to herself as to him. "Well, we just kinda decided to do it at the last minute," Gabriel said in his usual breezy way. "If it's not a good time for you, I could just stay in Malibu and catch you at a better time." She was ready to take his out, to tell him it was impossible. But a longing was taking over. She hadn't realized how much she had missed him. Both her children had acknowledged her recent move with cards that sunnily wished her a happy housewarming. The kind that gringos sent each other instead of visiting, she'd thought as she tossed them in the trash. But she'd never believed either of them would offer to see it in person. She had to say yes.

It meant a lot that Gabriel wanted to see her casita, even if it was attached to some last-minute vacation. "*Pues . . . si te vienes, te vienes. No te preocupes.* I can't wait to see you, *mijo.* I hav' to go right now, ok? *Hablamos después,*" she said, in the quiet, lilting accent that emerged when she was nervous. "But, Mom, don't you want to know when we're—"

"No, *es* ok," she said quickly, "We'll talk about it soon, *me hablas mañana.*" After she hung up the phone, she kneeled over the sink, overcome by a sudden cramp in her stomach. She wasn't ready.

Adela had only visited Gabriel once, when he'd called two years ago and told her he'd bought her a ticket to New York City. She'd barely had time to see her daughter on the trip, and Anjélica never offered to visit. She was married to a doctor now, and she was busy with the new baby. Adela heard from her so infrequently she didn't want to impose.

Adela had been planning on having yet another tamales-and-Tecate Christmas Eve with the señoras from La Tienda Morelos, the store downtown where she picked up her chiles and Mexican *quesos* on the weekends. Marisol would cook a big pot of her arroz con pollo and they would meet everyone in the big room in the back where they had parties. Adela enjoyed being away from family on the holidays, anyway. Her parents had passed away a few years back, and one thing she hadn't missed was explaining her life to extended family members who didn't know how to relate to her now that she was a *soltera*, without children or a husband in the house to fuss over. The señoras, on the other hand, made a special effort to make her feel welcome. Their get-togethers were casual gatherings where everything was served on paper plates and the conversations revolved around how Isabella, that *rica atrevida*, would dispose of her latest lover on *El Cuerpo del Deseo*.

She went about her business and ignored her son's impending visit until the Saturday before Christmas, when she awoke in a panic. *Tu hijo viene*, a voice said in her mind. And he's bringing someone with him. She stopped in at different stores every night after work to go and buy what she needed to make her place look livable: sheet sets, throw rugs, bright red plates for their dinner. She had no idea how she would be ready in time. Both Anjélica and Gabriel had indulged the fantasy that she had been like Doña Maria, the señora featured on the can of frijoles she reheated for them when they were children. With elegant Spanish curls tumbling down her shoulders and a round, open face, that *mamá* would have worked day and night to make sure her children had only the best.

This was unlike Adela, who worked mornings and evenings, and barely had time to slap tin containers of tacos and rice from the *taqueria* on the table and head to her next job. She tried to picture Gabriel's friend as she went grocery shopping a few days before their visit. No doubt he was one of those brokers that wore those *joto*-style body-hugging silk shirts that looked like they cost a hundred dollars. He would probably be a liberal, boring her all night with talk about immigrants' rights. A *mamón*. She packed her carts with the thickest steaks and cuts of pork she could find, along with too many bags of rice, beans, and frozen hot peppers. She decided to make a *morisqueta*, a big manly dish that involved big slabs of beef and pork, slathered with a heavy sauce over a bed of white rice. I'll make something that tastes hot and sweaty like when he was little, and we used to visit his *abuelos* in Michoacán, she thought. If that *mamón* is a vegetarian, he can deal.

The day before they arrived, Adela gave the house an expert cleaning, the kind that left her knuckles raw and chapped when she was done. Gabriel had called. They were going to arrive on the day before Christmas, at some point in the afternoon. She woke up early that day and started cooking, filling the house with the comforting smell of frying onion and meat, a smell that hadn't filled her home in a long time. When she finished, she put the food in the oven to keep it warm.

Then she looked around to find something else to clean, to arrange, to avoid the moment she had been dreading. At around three, she knew she couldn't put it off any longer. It was time for her to get ready. She put on the outfit she'd splurged on at an elegant boutique in Garden Grove. Then she faced herself in the full-length mirror behind her door, the one she usually tried to avoid.

She was wearing a stiff, cream lace bra that held in her generous breasts, pushing them up until they spilled over her D cups and into the subtle dip of the silk cream blouse she had chosen. The blouse had long, straight sleeves, so it would cover the tattoo one of her *galanes* had bought for her after her divorce, a thick black snake that wound up her arm. She paired it with a tight pencil skirt that hugged the round shape of her behind. She lightly brushed on her makeup. Her high cheekbones and naturally plump lips gave her the sensuality of a younger woman. The combination of her small features and her wide, cat-shaped eyes (*Ojos del Diablo*, her mother had called them) guaranteed that she would never blend in a crowd. She ran her tongue over her glossed lips. Her upper lip covered the chip in one of her front teeth, a flaw she'd never had time to correct. Her hand drifted to the thick curve of her belly, which remained despite all her diets and *ejercicios*. "Ni modo," she said out loud, "I look like a *mamá*. I hope he can be proud of me." She sat at the window seat in her kitchen and waited for them.

They didn't arrive until it was starting to get dark. Adela was starting to worry until she heard Gabriel roaring into her cramped driveway. It was seven o'clock, and the sun was setting. "Ay, *pero que sinverguenza*!!" She yelled in his direction, shaking her head. But the minute she saw his skinny body jump out of the car, her anger evaporated. She ran outside to greet him. She saw the two years that had passed between them, in the gray streaks in his jet black hair and the tiny lines starting to form around his eyes. He smelled as light and citrusy as ever, no trace of sweat despite his long flight over. Nothing dirty ever stuck to Gabriel.

He wore a lime green T-shirt and low-slung jeans; his hair sprayed into a deliberate mess, as if it couldn't choose a direction. Then she saw the car he was driving. It was a cherry red Ferrari whose smooth, racy lines seemed to mock her small driveway. She was just about to ask why he paid so much for a rental when she heard the car door slam and the words stalled on her lips.

The first thing she saw were the stranger's round, black eyes, glittering in the twilight like the sheen of Olmec statues. His high cheekbones and angled face were softened by his full lips, which opened into an easy smile. He walked toward her. She noticed that his flimsy, polyester suit was cheap. He must work for Gabriel, she thought. His broad shoulders made a V down to his waist; his body was sharp all over, like a man who had to work hard to survive. He was just under six feet tall but towered over Gabriel. Her son looked like an awkward teenager next to him. She met the stranger's eyes immediately and couldn't look away. They penetrated hers, sending a shiver down her spine. He had a scar along his jaw, a dark line in a creamy bowl of chocolate.

When he saw her he smiled. She quickly turned to Gabriel. "Mom, you look great!" he said. "I want to introduce . . ."

"Juan," the man said, stepping up and taking her hand. Adela simply nodded in response, managing a tight little smile. "You two must be starving. *Vengánse ya,*" she said, leading them into the house. "The food is heating up . . . I'll show you the house *por mientras,*" She hurried up the stairs to show Juan and Gabriel the bedrooms. Suddenly shy and nervous, she didn't want to catch Juan's eye again. "This is my bedroom, sorry 'bout de mess," she said, opening and shutting the first door quickly. Then she led them to the two doors down the hall, which opened to guest rooms she'd just outfitted with brand-new furniture and sheets. She opened the door to the first one, and saw Juan nudge Gabriel as they walked in. "You better watch out, señora," he said. "This place is so nice Gabriel might

want to move back in." He called me señora, she thought. I'm probably just some old *madre* to him. A twinge of disappointment tightened within her.

Gabriel rolled his eyes. "Please, bro. Cali's way to slow for me, as
my mom already knows. The only thing I'm still into here, besides
my mom, of course, are the waves. Right, ma?" he said, as he
feigned balancing himself on a narrow surfboard, jumping on the
wooden shelf that jutted out of the brand-new bed. Adela glanced at
him. He still looked so young to her, like he was when he was a
teenager bringing a friend home to stay overnight. "Yeah, you're a
real surfer dude," Juan responded. He wandered over to the window
to look out on her backyard, Adela dared to look in his direction. "*Si
me hubieras dicho que tenían lugar para hacer barbacoa afuera, yo te
podría hacer úna bien rica,*" he said, meeting her eyes. She didn't
even own a grill, and she hadn't barbecued in years. Why would he
say that it would be a good place to barbecue? "*Y por qué dices eso, si
ni tengo yo parrilla para hacer barbacoa?*" she asked. "*Pues, no se
necesita parrilla para calentar las cosas,*" he said, and winked, breaking into a smile. His face looked open and young, punctuated with
deep dimples. Adela blushed and lead them out of the room.

"Let's eat, no? Before the food get burned."

Gabriel looked between them, confused. "What are you guys
talking about?"

"Nothin' bro, Nothin'," Juan said, glancing at Adela. His hand
brushed against hers on his way out of the room. She felt lighter as
she rushed down the steps. She went straight to the kitchen and
started bringing tortillas fresh from the stove onto her gold tinfoil-
covered dining room table. Gabriel roamed through the rest of the
casita, as Juan lingered by the table. As she pulled one of the chairs
out of her way, she noticed Juan's eyes stall on the hem of her skirt.
"Something smells great in here," he said, giving her his wide smile.
He walked over to the large artificial tree she'd bought and assembled in a corner of the living room at the last minute. It was covered with cheap decorations that sparkled with the reflection of
countless strings of lights hung hastily on the walls. He examined it

closely, as if it stood in the lobby of a grand hotel. His eyes followed the lights then came back to her skirt. "And it looks great too."

"Oh, it's nothing big, I . . . ," she turned to say to him, then stopped.

Jésucristo en el cielo. She quickly stepped away, feeling his stare as she bustled between the kitchen and dining room. She busied herself putting meat, rice, and drinks on the table. Then they all took their seats. She let her son do the talking, mostly about all the crazy things a Ferrari could do these days. "It can even get to know your voice now!" he said. "Oh, *por favor*," she teased, "you are such a show off." She turned to Juan to roll her eyes and found him looking straight at her. She looked away. His fingers were tracing small shapes from spilled salt on the tablecloth.

Gabriel kept on. "Anyway, I wouldn't even know about it if it weren't for Juan here, " he said. "He keeps up on all that stuff and lets me know what time it is when it comes to new cars, stock tips, what I should wear at the office . . ."

Juan's head snapped up, his eyes boiling with a sudden intensity. He slapped the table with his hand, and Adela felt electricity blow through her. She shot a surprised look at Gabriel.

"No, man, you got it twisted," he said. "You're the one that tells me what time it is at the office. You got me the job. I was just messing around at school, man, I wasn't even going nowhere," he said, his jet black eyes now on Gabriel. "Most of the time I don't even know what I'm doing there." Then he stopped abruptly and looked down, as if he hadn't spoken at all.

Adela wondered what his story was. Her eyes stayed on Gabriel. On the spot, he looked uncomfortable for half a second then snorted out his *risa del chango*, his monkey laugh, is what Adela always called it. "Oh, Juan's just exaggerating. I met him when I was giving a talk about the world of finance at Lehman College, and he came up and asked me a ton of questions. I knew he had potential. He's just finished school and he's starting the trainee program; it can be a tough transition."

Juan was still looking down. "I know, you keep saying that, but I don't fit in there. I just took the job because I want to see my baby girl again. My ex took her back to Santo Domingo; and without my papers, I don't know how I'm gonna get her back. I keep trying to make a good impression, so they'll sponsor my visa, but they just look at me sometimes like I should be pushing a mop around." He stopped suddenly, glancing quickly at Adela, "I didn't mean anything's wrong with that, it's just that . . ." He fell silent again.

Adela remembered her first job as a maid. She'd thought the hulking women that worked at the hotel looked like American *luchadoras*. They had deep, harsh voices, as if they'd smoked since the day they left the womb. Trailer trash, she had heard one of the customers call them. They had a name for her as well. "At my first job, a woman call me Maria José, *como una de esas* maids they saw on television," she said softly. "Whenever anyone ask my name, they answer for me."

The first time the woman had said it in a flat tone, not even looking as she'd pointed Adela out with a jerk of their thumb. "Her name's Maria somethinorother; they're all called that. I just call her Mary J, after my favorite medicine." The woman had snorted in laughter with her customers over their little joke, and before Adela had realized what they'd meant, it was settled. Her name was Mary J until the day she left the chintzy hotel lobby for the last time. "Nobody there ever knew my real name." She glanced at Juan and met his round eyes. She knew he understood.

Gabriel looked at a loss for a moment, then shrugged. He raised his glass in a toast. "But look at you now, mom, the head of your department, and you got this nice new house. Here's to new beginnings!" He adeptly switched subjects again. "Speaking of new beginnings, have you guys heard about that corn oil they are trying to pass off as gas these days, as if that's going to work?" From that point on, the dinner conversation was smooth. Gabriel kept his steady stream of conversation going.

Occasionally Juan would interject, usually to make fun of her son the *tonto*. Adela sat back and enjoyed the sound of Juan's deep voice. When he smiled she noticed that his whole face opened up, as if nothing bad had ever happened to him; his dimples gave him a touch of innocence. She caught herself wondering what his face would look like if she were to slip his *palo* in her mouth. She blushed and reached for another glass of the thick yellow Dominican eggnog that Juan had brought all the way from The Bronx. She was so flustered she almost knocked it over.

Juan caught her eye again, "*Que pasó, te 'borachaste'?*" he said, in his clipped Caribbean Spanish. His thick New York accent ignited a fire in her nether regions, which were pulsing with alcohol and her dirty thoughts. "Oh," she laughed him off, her English and Spanish blurring. "*No tomo tanto* lately." Everyone laughed, especially Gabriel. "Yeah, you're a real lightweight, Mom."

After they'd all had seconds, Gabriel rubbed his stomach. "Wow, Ma, that was amazing, " he said, pushing away his half-empty plate. "I am so wiped out from the trip over." He picked up his plate and put it in the sink. "I think I'll hit the sack. Hey Juan, should we take our stuff upstairs . . . ?"

"Nah, bro," Juan said, keeping his eyes on Adela. "I'll get my stuff later. I'll stay here for now and help your moms clean up."

"Wow, what a nice boy," Gabriel said sarcastically, mouthing the words, "Kiss-ass" to his mother. Adela started quickly gathering up plates and taking them to the kitchen. "Well, I'll let golden boy here clean up, and I'm going to bed; I'm knocked out," she heard Gabriel say. Then she heard his steps up the stairs.

For a moment, there was silence. Maybe he changed his mind, she thought, as she stood paralyzed in the kitchen. "Maybe he woke up and realized 'helping' a *vieja* like me is no way to spend Christmas." Then she heard the kitchen door behind her. *Santo Dios.* She couldn't bring herself to turn around and look at him. She just kept scrubbing ferociously at the plate, as if it were the dirtiest thing she'd ever seen. He stood behind her. She could feel the heat from his body. He brushed a wavy lock of hair off her neck and leaned into her. "I like you, Adela," he whispered into her ear.

Adela's whole body trembled. No one had been this close to her in four years. Had he known what she was thinking all night? It was ridiculous; she was old enough to be his mamá. But she wanted him. She stayed glued to her spot, the dish frozen in her hand. He gently took it from her, placing it back into the sink.

He touched her hip, and she turned around to face him. She opened her mouth to say something, anything to him, but his black eyes silenced her. She felt her arms slipping around him, and his lips touching hers. She tasted the tough meat and the sweet eggnog on his lips and wanted to bite him, to taste his tongue around her own. He pulled away and looked at her for a moment, as if wondering what she would do next. She traced his scar from his cheek to his mouth with the tip of her finger as he slowly started unbuttoning her blouse, cupping her breasts through the stiff cotton of her bra. She let her hands slide down his shoulders, then to the hard muscles on his back, down to his ass. Finally, she reached for the stiffness in his pants.

He took her hand and led her to the living room. Gabriel, and whatever he may have seen or heard, evaporated from her mind. She lay on the couch and Juan hovered over her, his tongue tracing the line of her collar bone. He gently slipped off her blouse and her bra, and then his tongue grazed the tips of her nipples. They hardened in his mouth, and he pushed them together, switching between them as he sucked them harder. She arched her back, pushing herself closer to him. His tongue traveled lightly down her body, like a breeze that drifts through the soft waves at sunrise. When he reached her belly, he paused, kissing it as if to venerate her loose skin, to declare her ripples beautiful. She felt like he already knew her body, like no man had before. She fought the urge to cling to him tightly. She felt vulnerable, like a swimmer lost at sea. His tongue made tiny circles on the outsides of her thin cotton panties, teasing the fabric, then slipping through the elastic at her crotch. She felt her whole body vibrating. She stayed absolutely still, afraid she'd open her eyes and he'd disappear. Then he stopped. "What do you want, *nena?*"

She slid off her panties and pulled her skirt up, pulling him toward her by his neck, until his tongue plunged deeper, teasing her clit as it rode the wave of flesh between it's tip and her opening. Her body shook harder. Then he took her clit and the folds beneath in his mouth and sucked her, until she almost felt faint. She pushed him away.

She longed to taste him. She pushed him down and unzipped his pants, taking his thick *palo* in her hand. She bent her head and slipped it in her mouth. He tasted like the green salsa her mother made, sweet with the sharp bite of *chile* underneath.

She hovered over him. She rubbed his *palo* against her opening. She no longer recognized herself, she was some kind of wild *vieja* possessed by a demon even her mother would not have been able to resist. She thrust him inside as far as he would go. She rode him quickly then slowly, moving with him in a fevered shake as if they were dancing to the wild congas of a fast merengue song. As she was about to come their eyes locked, and she slowed the desperate motion of her hips. She felt as if a huge block of ice had melted inside of her. He came seconds before she did. He pulled her hips hard against him and held her there. Her body shook as if it was erupting from its skin as she came all over him.

She immediately pulled herself off of him and jumped off the couch. What did she just do? She looked at Juan in shock. He was still lying there with a smile on his face. What would he say to his friends about this trip? Did he think she was just one of those horny *madres* that uses her son's friends for fun on lonely nights? Could Gabriel have possibly slept through this insane *pornografía*? She pulled down her skirt, and sat on the other side of the couch. She primly locked her knees together. She felt humiliation burn inside her.

"You mus' be tired, " she said formally, not recognizing her own voice. "Would you like a *té de manzanilla* to help you sleep?"

At first he just looked flabbergasted, his pants were still open, the aftermath of their adventure still covering his stomach. Then he pounced on top of her, pushing her back down on the couch as if she hadn't said anything, his wide, easy smile filling up his face. She couldn't help but giggle at his blatant shamelessness. "You know," he said. "This ain't going to be no one-time thing."

Adela finally pulled down the heavy, poppy red curtains she'd bought over Christmas. She'd kept all her decorations up for way too long, long past Three Kings Day and the easing into the next year. It was Valentine's Day, and over a month had passed since she'd seen Juan. She needed to do something physical to get him out of her mind. She didn't want to forget their night together, but she had to do something to get herself back into reality. *Es un niño*, she kept telling herself. He has no idea what he's doing. She had been amazed when an invitation had arrived in the mail two weeks after he and Gabriel had headed back home. He'd written it freehand. His scrawl was careless, like a *chavalito* who'd stolen his mother's good stationery. "Meet me at my place for Valentine's Day," the note read; a ticket from LAX to Newark for the following weekend was shoved inside. He had carefully typed out directions and a telephone number and folded them into the letter. She'd called him right away. She was surprised at how clearly she remembered his voice, how deep and confident it sounded.

"Yo," he said.

"That how you answer, Yo? Yo *que?*," she teased.

"Adela, *mi vida*,"

"Ah, so you still remember my voice. Juan, I'm sorry to have to tell you that I can't use this ticket," she'd started again, formally.

"I'm sorry to haf to tehl you," he mocked. "Where'd you learn English, from Salma Hayek?"

"Ay, Juan," she said, laughing. "Stop it. Anyways, I was trying to say," she started again, "You know I can't go there!"

"Why not?"

"Because, I have work, and what we do when I got there?"

"Oh, I could think of a few things . . ."

"Ay, please. What about Gabriel, you gonna tell him you asked his mamá on a date?"

"Gabriel ain't invited, and besides you weren't worried 'bout that the last time I saw you."

"Well, I couldn't control myself then; a wild *muchachito* from El Bronx was seducing me."

"Yeah, well you ain't seen nothing yet."

"How old are you, anyways?"

"Don't worry, I'm old enough, believe me, I'm startin' to feel all thirty years in my back."

"All thirty huh. Well I'm goin' to have to take a rain check, *viejito*, because I'm not going to be able to make it."

"Yeah, I'll see you then. Be sure to pack your swimsuit, a slammin' dress, and flip-flops. I got crazy plans for you."

Juan hung up before she could tell him no again.

She put down the phone. How was she going to make him understand that this was it? She knew she had to end it, but she couldn't remember the last time she'd felt so light. He made her feel like a teenager.

He'd called and left a few messages in the last few weeks, but she hadn't called back.

She'd have to learn to stuff thoughts of him in the back of her mind, just like the decorations she was finally packing into boxes on a sunny Saturday morning.

The phone broke her reverie.

"Guess where I am," a familiar voice asked.

"Juan?"

"I'm in a car, on the way to your place, You say you ain't comin', so I'm goin' over there."

"What!" *Él no me puede ver así*, she thought. What will I wear when I see him?

"*Donde estás?*" she demanded, trying to sound firm. "How long until you get here?"

"I'll be there in fifteen minutes. Pack your fanciest dress, and bring that bikini with flip-flops."

"Juan!"

He hung up before she could ask him what he was talking about. A dress and bikini? Was he taking her to some country club breakfast? How did he get here? Was this a dream? All she knew was that she was deliriously happy. She was going to see him again. She quickly jumped in the shower and got dressed, barely having time to throw a long polyester dress she'd sewn herself, a pair of cheap earrings, and a free makeup bag she'd won at Macy's West into a duffel bag. She squeezed herself into the first bikini she found in her dresser and put on a T-shirt and sarong to go over it.

When she saw him standing in her driveway again, in a light brown guayabera and cutoffs, his easy smile on his face, all her fear and doubt melted. "Where we going?"

"Happy Valentine's Day. You'll see," he said, as he planted a light kiss on her lips and pulled her close. She took in his scent, a warm mix of moist wood and something fresh and sweet, like the *mango con lima* she used to buy on the beach in Mexico. He opened the door for her and she slid into the front seat of the small two-seater.

He started north on the little roads that waved through Santa Ana, avoiding the highway.

"I asked you where you're taking me! Why would I need to be ready to go to the beach and get dressed up at 10:30 in the morning?" she demanded. "You'll see, *mi reina*," his hand brushed against hers, and everything felt easy, as if they'd never left each other. "I got a tux in the trunk. I'm taking my *nena* to the beach then dancing tonight."

His *nena*? Dancing? Adela's mind raced. She burst out laughing, her heart beating faster at the thought of getting on a ballroom floor again. In Mexico this had been her greatest pleasure, to dress elegantly and pretend she was royalty on the dance floor, instead of some *ruca* from the concrete maze of southern Mexico City.

"How you learn to dance, anyways?"

"My mother. She taught me how to dance nice, like *los blancos* do in the fancy ballrooms back home. She always wanted me to be a *caballero*."

"Where you mother now?"

"She died." Juan's jaw tightened, and Adela tensed to see a dark cloud pass over his face. "Got shot by some punks in Santo Domingo two years ago."

"*Lo siento*," she said, quietly.

"Don't worry about it, they got theirs anyway." The cloud cleared abruptly. "Anyway, I'm gonna show you her moves later."

"How you know I can dance?"

"I just knew," he said, and he looked over at her. In the bright morning light, Adela could see that his face was slightly off-kilter, as if someone had removed it and replaced it fifteen degrees off center. Was it his cheekbone? Yes, he must have broken it. It gave his face an uneven tilt, like the *cubista* Diego Rivera paintings she'd seen in the Arte Plástico exhibit near her parent's house in Mexico City. It made him all the more beautiful.

"But where we going? I haven't dance in years."

"You'll see when we get there, ok? No more questions," he said, and squeezed her hand tightly. After that she was silent. Her index finger stayed looped around his for the rest of the trip. About an hour had passed on the road, and Juan finally turned onto the Pacific Coast Highway, which opened up to them like a revelation of endless blue sea and cliffs. They drove miles north until she finally knew where they were. Malibu. Juan and Gabriel had left her house to surf these waves just after their adventure at Christmas. She wondered what Gabriel would think now, if he saw the two of them driving along the highway like teenagers on a summer vacation, his mother's hand wrapped around his friend's muscular brown arm. Adela shuddered as she thought of his reaction. If she let herself dwell on it, she'd make Juan turn the car around.

Instead, she stared out of the window. The first time she'd seen Malibu, it had almost looked fake, like colorized Vicente Fernandez movies, bleeding into the edges of her television screen. They drove on and on. White sand spread infinitely against the canyons, like the arms of an elegant lady gathering warm mounds of earth. Finally, he pulled off the highway and into the parking lot of a charming brick hotel high on a cliff. She could see a courtyard beyond the scripted hotel sign: La Hacienda Malibu.

He pulled a large picnic basket and their luggage out of the trunk. She waited outside while he checked in. The beach below was empty.

They headed down and stripped to their bathing suits. Juan opened the picnic basket. He spread open a thin cotton blanket that was on top and pulled out its contents: a rosé wine, still slightly chilled, two glasses, two small tins of guava juice, and two warm Cuban sandwiches.

"Where you find all this so early in the morning?" She asked, amazed.

"I found a little Mexican place downtown that was open early," he said.

She couldn't think of a single place downtown, or anywhere else, that would open this early. He must have driven miles to find their lunch. She ate every last bite of her sandwich. The savory slabs of pork and fresh pickles blended perfectly in her mouth. The warm white cheese melted on her tongue.

When they finished, they waded into the ocean together. Adela hesitated. She wasn't a strong swimmer. Juan dived underneath her over and over again, pretending to try to knock her over. When she eventually did fall in, she didn't mind. His hands achored her and she felt safe. She hadn't felt the salt water and the sun on her skin for almost a year, despite how close she lived to the sea. Juan's arm never left her side. She felt like they were already moving in time.

After they got out, they lay on their stomachs, drying in the sun. Adela stretched her long legs out behind her. "You're wearing me out," she said, laughing. "My legs are already sore."

"Maybe you need a massage."

"Mmmm, *éso sí*," she said.

He swept back her hair and untied her bikini top. He rubbed her neck, her shoulders, then down her back until she forgot that she had ever been sore. His hands drifted lower, keeping their rhythm as they traveled down her back, until he reached the bottom of her bikini and pulled it down, massaging the round curves of her ass. Then he slipped his fingers underneath and rubbed her through the wet material. She felt herself throbbing against the wet lycra, the heat spread quickly through her body. He whispered, "I'm thirsty, are you?" She nodded. He pulled one of the tin guava juice cans and took a sip, then he put it to her lips and she sipped obediently. He poured a thin line of juice on her back; it felt cool on her hot skin. He started at the top, making figure eights with his tongue, licking and nibbling her skin until he reached the crevice in her flesh. He pulled her suit completely off.

He grabbed her wrists with one hand, holding them behind her to show he was in control. He spread her ass cheeks, and plunged his tongue inside until she opened to him like a flower. He entered his finger into her slippery *concha*, gently pulling in and out as his tongue pressed harder into her ass. She bucked against him. "Do it now," she whispered. "*Métemelo.*"

He shook his head again. He drew his fingers out and slipped his hands underneath her stomach. His hands covered her breasts, rubbing her nipples until nectar poured from inside of her and onto her thighs. Waves of pleasure ripped through her as she pressed her ass against him. She reached for his cock and he pushed her hand away again; this time tugging a lock of her hair in punishment. "I told you," he whispered. "I'll fuck you *a la hora que yo digo.*"

She ached for him. He rubbed his dick against the opening of her ass, down to the hole of her sex, teasing it, slipping his *pinga* in and out.

"*Te suplico,*" she said, "Now." He gently held her hands back, holding her there. "He whispered in her ear. "How do you want it?" "*Duro,*" she whispered. "What?" he said.

"*Duro.*" She yelled it, as loud as she could. "*Lo quiero duro.*" He entered her fiercely, his hands covering her breasts underneath. She felt as if she were holding her breath, coming up for air each time he plunged into her. They climaxed together, not moving for a long moment afterward, as if the force of their lovemaking had welded them at the center.

Afterwards, they collapsed on the blanket. They lay there watching each other until the light from the sun faded away. Their knees were shaky as they climbed up toward the Malibu hotel to change for dinner.

After they bathed and dressed, they headed to the Olympia Supper Club on Wilshire Boulevard. Juan wore a tailored black suit and Adela donned her long, emerald polyester dress. It gathered in elegant folds under her breasts. It wasn't her best, but she knew it flattered her, even though she had chosen it quickly. She wore her hair in a high ponytail and had popped in cheap, dangling glass earrings at the last minute, as they were heading out the door of their hotel. Juan looked awed when he saw her, as if she were outfitted in diamonds and silk. He kept looking her up and down. He whispered to her that he couldn't believe his good luck. As they walked into the club, she hung on his arm. She walked comfortably in stride with him, as if they'd been lovers for years. A white-haired man looked them over at the door. "A table for two for the lady and her . . ." he frowned as his eyes followed the path of Adela's arm around Juan's. He probably thinks I hired Juan for the night, she thought.

"Date," Juan finished the man's sentence. "A table for two for the lady and her date." The white-haired man led them to a long empty table for six. Adela laughed. Only a few other couples were scattered throughout the club. When they sat down, Adela was still thinking about the white-haired man's response. "*Sabes qué*, Juan," she said. "I think we should keep this a secret, you and me." She was worried about his response.

He reacted quickly. "No problem, *nenita*. From this point forward, what happens between you and me is between you and me."

After their dinner of bland enchiladas *verdes* with lumpy frijoles and rice, a portly Mexican man wearing a beige suit and an enormous cowboy hat stepped onto the stage. He followed the band, four *jóvenes* in matching suits looking down looking down at their congas and keyboards as they waited for their cue. They sat in cheap folding chairs. The man started playing a mournful note on his electric blue accordion. At first the sound echoed through the nearly empty club, the accordion's graceful gills waning in and out as everyone wondered what would come next. Then the young men stood up and blasted a brassy polka and pounding *bajo sexto* into the rhythm. Everyone stepped onto the dance floor. It was a *cumbia*.

Adela tugged Juan's sleeve. She needed to dance. When they reached the shiny marble floors, they immediately starting moving together, as if they'd danced together a hundred times. The song's deep bass swayed them back and forth. Juan had never heard a *cumbia* before, so he pulled Adela close and followed her wide hips through the song's low shakes and slow rhythms. He kept his eyes on hers, always, bringing her back into place effortlessly after every turn. She felt as if she were flying; she'd forgotten the freeing sensation of her dress whipping against her ankles. They didn't see the waiters in their stained tuxedos or the faded velvet curtains tied clumsily at the sides of the stage. They didn't even notice the cheap ivory statues of Athena and Thor that towered in the club's empty corners, keeping vigil over their hedonism.

The next day Juan woke up and wandered into her backyard. Adela hadn't been back there much since she moved in; she knew it would just remind her of all the mowing and *limpieza* she hadn't started yet. He offered to barbecue, kicking dust in the empty square pit that she thought was a dirty hole. "That's what that *porquería* is for," she said, laughing. "I was going to put a complaint to *la dueña*." She called him back into the house, vetoing his plan. "I told you this would be a good place to barbecue," Juan said. "I should get this shit started up right now."

"'You not going anywhere. *No te permito.*" She pulled him back into bed, where he laid his head on her chest. She traced the scar along his cheek.

"How did it happen?"

"In Santo Domingo, in the barrio where I grew up; everybody's got one of these somewhere," he said. "I took mine on my face. If it weren't for my ma, I probably woulda been dead by now."

"She send you here?"

"Yeah, she thought I was the smart one in our family," he said, smiling. "If you could believe that. She sent me here to live with my aunt, while I went to school. It was hard, but I was so proud when I got into Lehman." He paused for a moment, as if he wanted to say something more. She watched him. He stared out her window. She thought his eyes looked like deep dark pools she could dip herself into and never feel the end, like the *cenotés* where the Mayans used to hide their treasures.

"How you have a daughter?"

"I met Silvia at Lehman," he said, lacing his fingers into Adela's. "She was younger than me, and she looked up to me. When I got her pregnant, I didn't want to let her down. I had to drop out and get a job contracting with my uncle. It was all right for a while until she started traveling back and forth from D.R."

"Why you not still together?"

"She finally met some playah out there that could keep up with her. I was happy, in a way, to not have to deal with her anymore. Then she said she wanted to move my baby girl back there. I tried to stop her, but I wasn't paying full child support. I found a lawyer, and he said if I paid up I'd have more rights. Now I got the degree, 'business management,' and I still can't do shit about it." He's older than me when I had Gabriel and Anjélica, Adela thought. But he still looks too young to have a daughter.

"My little girl is in Santo Domingo. I love her but part of me wishes I'd never met Silvia. If I hadn't of messed with her, l woulda finished school sooner. I could have gotten a good job sooner too, then I could have been able to bring my ma back before . . ."

He stopped there, shaking his head in frustration. Adela pulled her hand out of his and rubbed her fingers through the stubble on his scalp; when she'd seen him last his head had been completely smooth.

"Did you go to school to do what Gabriel does?" He turned and looked her in the eye. "Honestly, no disrespect to him, but I'm not into that. It's like I was telling you last time, I hated that office."

"What you mean, you hated? You no work there anymore?"

"Oh, I quit that place." Adela tensed. *Carajo.* She didn't need another man without a job. He'll find another one, she told herself.

"I can't stand to be inside all day. The real reason I studied business was so I could get a small loan. I want to start my own contracting business some day. I like to be outside, building things. When I was out there right now I was looking at your yard, and in my head I can see all these things we could do with it." Juan got out of bed, found a discarded envelope on the nightstand. He started scribbling a basic rectangle that represented the tangle of weeds and grass behind her house. "If we take all the grass out, we could build a deck and one of those reflecting pools. We could plant some eucalyptus trees in the corner. That and some potted plants, and it would look dope. Listen to me, I sound like one of those *pato* designers you see on TV," he said, laughing.

He said *we*, she thought. She sat up in bed and looked at his drawing. He had talent. "I know what you mean," she said, excitedly. "I been trying to get a loan, too. I want to start my own *tienda de boda* downtown, for the Mexicanas that plan their weddings and *quinceañeras* around here and don't think they can afford it. The kids don't know, but I went to classes to learn how to start a small business. It was a three-class program *que te enseñaba todo.*"

She applied for it three years ago, after she had seen an advertisement one spring day on a bulletin board at La Tienda Morelos for an adult education course at Santa Ana College. By the time she received the notice she'd been accepted she'd forgotten she'd even applied, and it filled her with panic to even imagine it. She didn't want to ask Gabriel or Anjélica for help. She could just hear them laughing at her. Why would you start now, mami, after all these years? they would ask. She'd never catch up with them. *Éran tan inteligentes.* On the first day she had to force herself to leave the house. She circled the pristine college parking lot at least twenty times trying to get the nerve to park. She'd pictured a bunch of young Gabrieles and Anjélicas inside the classroom, making fun of an old lady for trying to act like a college girl.

When she'd finally made it inside, she'd been relieved to see the class was almost entirely filled with people around her age, from all kinds of immigrant communities. They were all trying to find a way to fund diverse new businesses. It had been difficult to struggle to fill the holes in her English and follow the assignments. Everyone in the class helped. They showed her how to follow the book and fill out the paperwork. It turned out that she wasn't as *burra* as she thought she was. She passed the class. She was so excited when the report card came in the mail, the first ever with her name on it. She took out all of her

friends from La Tienda Morelos as if she were celebrating a gradua-
tion. Right after that she was offered the head maid job at The Colonial Inn. She had to take it because the money was so good. She didn't
take the next class in the series, but she still had her plans.

"I even made a drawing of the store," she said. "I know what I
want it to look like."

"Yeah?" Juan asked. "Let's see it." She jumped up and ran to get
the special art drawing pad she'd bought at the university bookstore.
It was expensive, way more than it would have cost at Target, but she
wanted to buy something at the store, which was so fancy even the
plastic bags they gave out came with an embossed crest. She'd
plunked down her credit card to cover the fifty dollars, along with
the twelve-dollar soft brown pencil she bought to go with it. When
she put the drawing in front of Juan, he stared at it a long time, making her nervous. She waited for his reaction. She was starting to love
the way he made her heart race, as he sat there looking over the
pages like her father used to study her catechism homework.

"I could build this thing," he said, muttering, turning the pages of
the notepad, and starting to draw furiously.

They spent the rest of the day drawing and talking, ordering in
Chinese takeout when they got hungry. They never left her bedroom, as if it were the safest place in the world. When they went to
bed that night, he wrapped himself around her like a lifeboat. For
the first time since she'd moved in, she slept through the night.

They spoke every morning before work and every night before
bed. It became her ritual, the buzz of the alarm clock then the
sound of Juan's voice. The days passed. She dusted, scrubbed, and
smiled in people's faces, going through her routine just to get to the
point where she could hear Juan again, the perfect end to her days.
She saw less of her friends.

She invented an upcoming trip to see Anjélica and her granddaughter, Jessica, who would soon turn two, to explain herself. Everyone commented on how the excitement brought color to her cheeks
and how young she looked. She couldn't even bring herself to tell
Marisol about Juan. She felt as if talking about it could ruin the spell,

like a big *calabaza* at midnight. She was surprised at how easy it had been to lie to everyone, including Gabriel, when he called to check up on her. It was like she was living in an alternate reality.

She was headed East, but this time she wouldn't attempt to see either of her children. Juan had invited her to stay a long weekend in New Jersey, over the Easter holiday. He said he had big news, and something to ask her. She assumed his ex was sending his daughter, Araceli, back for the summer, and he wanted them to meet. It was a big step, but she was thrilled.

She couldn't wait to celebrate, to see the shadows that lingered under his eyes finally disappear. She also had a surprise for him. She had asked an architect, one of the hotel's regular visitors, to do a professional rendering of the shop, from his drawings.

She couldn't wait to show it to Juan.

The days passed like years but finally it was time for her to fly to New York. She wore a suit when Marisol dropped her off at the airport, then changed into a low-cut long sleeve blouse and skintight dark jeans on the plane. She couldn't wait to see him. Her body longed for his hands, his lips everywhere. She'd packed a blood red chiffon gown, with razor slits along the bottom that left her legs free to move on the dance floor. He was taking her out to dinner and to the Copacabana, and this time she was prepared. She'd brought at least five pairs of earrings. They were all long and sparkled, bringing out the flecks of green in her eyes.

The last time she'd visited New York, she'd gone to the Broadway shows and museums that Gabriel had planned for her, but hadn't felt the excitement that people had about the city, the *chispa* of Nueva York. Juan was going to cross the George Washington Bridge with her to Manhattan, and she was hoping he would show her the wild side of the city, another crazy thing she wouldn't be able to mention to Marisol. When she was searching for his place in her rented Toyota, she'd identified it by what it didn't have: no big wheels or bicycles tossed absentmindedly in the yard, no grass growing into the next yard or flickering neon beer logos that screamed *soltero*. His house was the only one on the block that still had its original paint job. It was a dull gray color that faded into the street, like a gap in a crowded row of teeth. It looks like mine, she thought.

When she pulled up and knocked on the door, he opened it right away, as if he'd been waiting right next to the door for her. She walked into his small, sparsely decorated home. She saw a framed photo of a little girl on his desk and went over to look at it. Araceli. Juan suddenly came up behind her and put his arms around her back. "It's so good to see you." He gathered up some papers that were on his desk and put them in a drawer, shoving one in his pocket. Before she could ask him what it was, he was rushing her to his room. They had reservations to make.

That night they went to Son Cubano, an upscale Latino restaurant in the Meatpacking district, where young women who looked like models glided by them as they stood on the street, glued to the earpieces on their cell phones. She'd heard that just ten years before, it would have been *putas* that paced here, offering themselves to butchers as they ended their shifts in the huge, dark warehouses that lined the street. Now the warehouses housed trendy restaurants and clubs. As they entered the painted white door of their restaurant, a trio played "Lágrimas Negras" on their *tambores*.

After their guayabera-clad waiter sat them, they immediately started ordering one neon-pink drink after another. Juan's eyes darted around nervously as pushed his pineapple-infused pernil around his plate.

After her third drink, Adela grabbed his hand across the table.

"*Qué tienes?*" she asked. "What, you going to tell me you're getting back together with your ex-*novia*? Spit it out." She was joking, but her words scared her.

He jumped out of his chair suddenly, pushing it back then kneeling before her. Diners gave them curious sidelong glances.

"I know this may sound crazy to you, especially since we've only known each other a few months," he started.

"Juan," Adela interrupted, trying to stop him, her heart rattling her chest and all the bones connected to it in her body.

"Please, let me finish. When I think about you, *nena*, it makes me so happy. Not because of what we do together, or even what we talk about. It's just . . ." he said, struggling for the words. "When everything's fucked up I picture your face; it makes me feel completely happy. I'm so proud to be with you. I feel like bragging to all my friends about how classy my girl is, with her brand-new house and beautiful clothes. I always stop myself before I even tell them though, 'cause I don't want it to be cheap like that. I want to be real. I want to see you in the mornings when I wake up. I want to call Gabriel to tell him how much I'm in love with his mother." She saw his eyes moisten. Despite herself, her wide hazel eyes clouded in response.

"I know you're going to tell me that I'm nuts, and I'm just a stupid kid," he said. "I've been so alone; no one's felt like family to me besides my daughter since my mother died. There's been nobody I could trust like that. And now I've met you, and I know you'll be blood for the rest of my life. I want to make it official." He took her hand, his tears spilling unselfconsciously.

"Will you marry me?" He said it. She was speechless. Other boyfriends had done it. They would get high on sex and partying and bend a knee, begging her to be their bride. She would gently convince them that it was the tequila talking, that the Juan Gabriel song the mariachis were singing had gone to their heads. She would tell them to sleep it off. They could ask in the morning, if they still felt like it. They never did.

But this was different. Juan was serious. His shaved head was glistening with sweat, and there wasn't a shimmer of doubt in his eyes. He was earnest as a man about to take his vows. He opened a velvet box that seemed to come out of nowhere. A small sapphire sparkled in a circle of tiny diamonds. What was she supposed to say to Gabriel and Anjélica? *Me enamoré de alguien* the same age as you? Yet how could she say no? She felt herself bending toward him, like a reed in the wind. I may be a *vieja tonta*, but don't I deserve another chance? she thought to herself. She pulled back into his seat, circling him in her arms.

"Yes," Adela said.

Drunk on their emotional high and too many passion-fruit margaritas, they jumped into a cab and headed to the Copacabana. She'd always wanted to see it in person. It was smaller than she'd imagined it, and a lot of the crowd looked younger and less sophisticated than what she'd pictured. But its decadence was unmistakable. In line she saw a frosted-haired transvestite applying layers of makeup, her porcelain skin more flawless than a Hollywood star's. The girls' faces in line may have been younger than what she'd imagined, but they still wore dresses made of gold sequins and mascara so thick their eyes looked painted on.

They ordered more drinks and slipped into a dark booth to the side of the dance floor. Adela felt dizzy and reckless. She was suddenly starved for him. She rubbed his soft wool suit at the crotch. She whispered that she was going to unzip his pants and suck him under the table. She had five drinks and she was flying.

"You're a freak," he said, playfully.

"What do you mean, like in the circus?" she said. She made a clown face.

"No, like a sex*adicta*," he said, mocking her way of combining English words with Spanish.

"You have no idea," she whispered, suddenly tempted to tell him all the details of her perverse past.

"Oh yeah," he said, "Are you going to show me?"

She heard the first bars of "*Devórame otra vez*," a song she'd loved when she was a new divorcee, and she heard it blasting through the massive speakers above the dance floor. She'd first heard it when she'd started to hit the dance clubs with her friends. The plaintive verses reminded her of the first time she found the nerve to dance, the surprise of a stranger's hips against her own.

She was just about to drag Juan out onto the dance floor when she saw a man walking toward their table, and her veins filled with ice. He was thicker than he was when she saw him last; the weight disguised him like a rubber suit. His black hair was as oily as ever, slicked back to reveal his doughy face. It was Rafael Garcia, the exporter that had ended her life as an escort. He'd taken her to dance clubs like this many times when she was seeing him. He'd loved the way her body moved on the dance floor as much as Juan did. She saw that he still wore terrible brown suits, his tie bound so tightly the skin on his neck slightly peaked over the edge of his collar. He leaned over to plant a noisy kiss on her cheek. His familiar scent flooded her senses, the same mix of coconut pomade, that spicy cologne, and sweat.

"Adela, I knew it was you," he said in his gruff voice. "I see your beauty has not faded with time."

"Juan," Adela said, dread weighing her down like a block of concrete, "*Te presento al Sr. Garcia*, one of our hotel's regular business clients."

Juan nodded at Garcia, his eyes flashing between the man and his young, bored companion, whose enormous breasts were pouring out of her glittery blue dress.

Garcia let out a crude laugh. It came from somewhere inside his giant *panza*. "I see that the times have changed," he said. "You have your own *compañero* now, just as I have mine." The young girl rolled her eyes, and Garcia automatically reached to pinch her ass, without blinking an eye. A light of understanding came over Juan's face.

"Well, you're a lucky *cuate*," Garcia said, winking at Juan. "I've always said that Adela is the very best." Adela could not look at Juan. He looked like he could strangle Garcia right there. "Yeah, I'm lucky, but I ain't nobody's *compañero*. Juan said, restraining himself from saying more. She kept a plastic smile on her face as she silently willed Garcia to leave. Garcia let out another of his belly laughs. Juan needed no other confirmation.

"Well, it was nice to meet you," Garcia nodded condescendingly to Juan. "The senorita and I have dancing to do." And then he disappeared into the tangle of bodies that surrounded them.

"I thought you said you wanted to dance," Juan said a moment later, jerking her up roughly and pulling her through the crowd. He moved quickly; the tenderness that had guided him earlier in the night had disappeared. They went into the DJ room. It was so packed, the entire room seemed to be dancing with one another. Juan clamped his mouth on her neck, marking his territory. She didn't complain. His hands moved up and down her hips while the next song came on, a *reggaetón*. It slammed its animal bass line into the crowd and took it back: Thump thumpthumptha—Thumpthumptha. He moved her back and forth with the dirty rhythm of the street that didn't leave half an inch between them.

Juan's eyes were a black curtain, obscuring his feelings as he grinded against her on the dance floor. *Ni modo*, she thought, we'll laugh the whole thing off in the morning.

He was silent all the way home. They were barely in the door when he lead her into the bedroom. He lifted up the back of her dress and put his hand on her back, pushing her down over the bed without a word. She was unnerved but went along. This was her penance for the man with the slicked-back hair. Then he entered her roughly from behind. The dancing and craziness of the night had her underwear soaked, and she could play his game. She reached behind her to stroke him as he pumped against her. Afterwards they passed out.

At around 3 a.m., she shot up in bed. She saw a presence hovering over her. She screamed, and fumbled for the lamp on the night stand.

It was Juan. He didn't move at the sound of her scream. His eyes were bloodshot and cold, and she knew he hadn't slept.

"How could you do that man?"

"Jesus, Juan, *me asustaste*. What are you talking about?"

"Wat are ju talking about," he mocked. "I'm talking about fucking that nasty fat ass just for money, when you had kids at home and everything." The veins in his neck were pulsing with fury. Adela stared at him, a chill ripped through her. "You coulda done something else, you didn't have to ho yourself out."

Adela was about to deny it all, telling him he was crazy and jumping to conclusions, when something stopped her tongue. She just stared at him. Shame, then fury, started to boil inside her. She never relied on escorting for a living; she didn't even really know the reason why she'd done it. But she certainly wasn't going to let this little *idiota* tell her what she was.

Suddenly he looked ridiculous in his cliché wifebeater stance, flashing his muscle to scare her when he was nothing but a good-for-nothing little *chavalito* having a tantrum like a baby. She had faced much worse in her life.

She pulled off the engagement ring and threw it at him, shaking with rage. "You can take your *pinche* ring back, and all of you bool-shit with it," she yelled. "You don't know anything about what my life was like then or now.

"How dare you talk to me about how I raised my kids when you haven't even seen your daughter in how long? I may have worked as a *puta* in my life, but at least I've always had a job. I don't blame my problems on some girl in Santo Domingo." She knew she went too far, but she needed to tear him to pieces.

She jumped out of bed and pulled her dress, crumpled at the foot of the bed, back on, throwing her things wildly into her bag. Juan just stared at her, his hand forming a fist. "Fuck this!" he screamed, punching the wall, leaving a hole like a gaping wound, "Go then. You can take your ho ass and get the fuck out!"

He stormed out of the room. Adela jumped a little at the sound of his fist hitting the wall, but she didn't look up. She knew how to deal with angry men. Like dogs, you couldn't let them think you were scared. She focused on making sure she had everything, that all her papers were gathered and put away. She grabbed any stray paper she saw on the floor. I don't want him seeing that beautiful rendering, she thought. She picked the ring off the floor and put it on the night stand. She put on her heels, pulled her brand-new rollaway to the door, and left.

She told the woman at the United ticket counter that she needed the "first ticket out of here to Los Angeles, I don't care how much it cost." She fought back the tears threatening to roll down her face, the alcohol still throbbing in her head. She saw her reflection in the airport's merciless stainless steel columns. She looked like an overaged beauty queen, the plunge in her dress now a sign of desperation.

The next morning, back in Santa Ana, the whole scene played back in her mind. She remembered what she had said to Juan. Whenever she closed her eyes, she saw the gaping hole in his bedroom. It flooded her brain like a bottomless pit. It was her fault. Seeing Garcia had overwhelmed him. She should have comforted him, found some way to explain right then, instead of saying those nasty things. But it was all such a shock.

She would apologize. She would show him the professional rendering and cover his face with kisses as only she could do, and he would forgive her. She looked for her notepad in her bag. As she was shuffling, an unfamiliar sheet of paper slipped out on the floor. It was folded in four parts, as if someone had carried it in their back pocket. The house was silent as she kneeled to lift it; she could hear a child playing in the distance through her window. She held the paper in her hand for a few moments, afraid to open it. Then she did.

It was written in capital letters, a plain website that didn't bother with graphics. It delivered it's message clearly and unceremoniously. HOW TO PURSUE RESIDENT STATUS THROUGH MARRIAGE TO A NATIONAL, IN FOUR EASY STEPS.

The paper, along with the rendering, went into the unused barbecue pit in her backyard later that day, an occasion to finally fire it up.

As she watched the fire burn, the wind scattered scraps through her empty yard, separating the block letters into odd disjointed messages: marriage, easy, resident, sue, how. She focused on the words as they swirled into the air, feeling like they made more sense than what had just happened.

When Adela couldn't sleep or was particularly bored, she would flip to television *en inglés*. She favored semi-intellectual true-crime dramas, the kind that appeared on Court TV or A&E. She became transfixed with the show's sober reenactments of the crimes themselves, which didn't appear overdramatic or campy in any way to her. She enjoyed the way the somber voiceovers would recount the forensic details of the case. The voiceovers had a remarkable distance in their analysis of horrible things. "It was a seemingly random crime," the somber voice would begin. "Something must have snapped when he saw her struggling with a stroller in the parking lot."

She tried to channel that voiceover's deadpan now, as she stood in her yard watching the beautiful drawing of her store burn. Had he originally planned to troll the bars until he found some fat gringa who was willing to trade her marital status for a good fuck Dominicano or a few bucks? Did a light bulb flash in his head when Gabriel told him about his lonely little *mamacita*? Or was it spontaneous? Did he see some sad *vieja* who didn't have a date for Christmas dinner with her son, someone who clearly hadn't gotten laid in years? Did he think she was pathetic, that she'd do anything to keep a nice piece of ass around to make her feel young?

Hot tears burned on her cheeks. She couldn't help replaying every moment she spent with him. It all seemed like an elaborate humiliation. He went to so much trouble, all those trips, the *chilladera* at the restaurant. Why did he bother? How long would it have taken before he finally left me? One year, maybe two? However long it took to get one of those envelopes with perforated edges and an inset American flag, informing him that he was now a legal resident of *Los Estados?* He would have made sure he had legal permanent status before he walked out the door with his young ex-*novia?* Adela pictured her as one of those *niñas* who runs her finger through her wet hair, puts on a half shirt and some lip gloss, and boom, she's ready to go.

The thoughts were coming rapidly now, overwhelming her brain with blurry images, like a tattered film reel off its axis. "It's not you, Adela," he would have said, when he finally got his green card and packed his bags. "It's just that Silvia and Araceli need me, and I just need to be close to them again, blah, blah, blah."

At least he'll never have the chance to say any of it to me, she thought. *Nunca le vuelvo a hablar.* I'll erase him from my life as if he'd never been here in the first place.

After she cleaned the charred paper out of her barbecue pit, she composed a speech that would flatten him when he finally called to apologize about his outburst in New Jersey. She knew he would call to make up with her. He had to grease the wheels for his immigration papers. In her mind, he'd barely have a chance to say hello before she doused his hopes with her icy tongue. She could be a cold *bruja* when she had to be.

The next morning she stayed in bed, close to the phone, now plugged into the outlet behind the nightstand. She turned her back to it and stared at the wall, trying to picture what he would be doing at that moment. He must be awake by now, she thought. In New Jersey, it's twelve o'clock. He'll already have cleaned up the rubble wreaked from the argument on Friday night, the plaster dust from the walls, the twisted sheets thrown in accusation. He's probably wondering where that paper got off to, whether it slipped out of his back pocket to some spot behind the couch or under the bed. He's just realizing that she has it. He'd be trying to find the words to apologize, to win her love back.

She couldn't bring herself to turn around and face the red numbers on the clock. Instead she saw the hours pass in the shadows on the wall, the reflection of the sun fading into darkness.

The stupid *maricón* is afraid to face me after all that, she thought. When she finally got up to make herself a sandwich, she noticed that it was 11 p.m., way past the time for groveling. She knew it then. He wasn't going to call that night. She would have to wait. She tossed the ham-and-cheese sandwich she'd just made in the trash. She was too upset to eat.

The next morning she got up at her normal time and went to work.

She told everyone things had gone well with her daughter, blaming the bags under her eyes on jet lag. She still didn't mention Juan to anyone, even Marisol. The whole week she told herself he was still contemplating his words. She saw him writing out anguished letters and tossing them in the trash, as she mechanically replaced soiled sheets with fresh ones. By the second week, the thought that he may not ever call entered her mind like a tiny worm, wriggling its way through her sanity.

The next month, when Gabriel called for Mother's Day, she asked casually if he'd heard from his friend.

"Na," he'd said. "Ever since he left Goldberg Sanderson, he hasn't been in touch." The disappointment dried her throat like a cup of sand. She hung up quickly, citing a lingering cold.

Months passed. She barely noticed the pounds that started to weigh down her center or the new small lines in her face that she didn't bother to smooth with makeup. One day she looked in the mirror and was surprised to see a roll of fat pushing her shirt over the top of the strained cotton of her white flowing skirt, which she'd chosen for it's looseness, the free way it swayed as she walked. Her eyes looked small and retreated into her face, and her fly-aways formed a frizzy halo in the back of her head. She looked her age. She took on extra shifts, avoiding the moment she got home and realized she wouldn't hear Juan's voice on the answering machine. She also avoided looking at any surface that offered her reflection.

Perplexed by her friend's depression, Marisol insisted on dragging her to the clubs. Adela went at first, eyeing the crowds for a man worthy of a distracting fling. But when they returned her stare, she looked away. She was afraid she'd see Juan's face in her mind the moment she closed her eyes for a kiss. She avoided fantasizing for the same reason.

One night, after an especially intense double shift at the Colonial, she fell into a deep sleep. In her dream she was lying in a cornfield, completely naked. A wrinkly *viejo* she'd seen panhandling outside the hotel was looking down at her, his huge cowboy hat blocking the sun. He was wearing the same ancient plaid shirt and torn jeans he wore every day. He stepped beside her and squatted down. His dark, wrinkled copper hands reached for her breasts and rubbed them lightly. A rustling came from the fields. He pulled his hands away and looked at the corn expectantly.

A lithe, naked young woman walked out of the rows. She had long, wavy blond hair pulled up in a ponytail that cascaded down her back. Her eyes were a liquid black, and she watched Adela with a smile on her curvy lips as she walked toward her. She had small, round breasts with large, pale pink nipples Adela was suddenly desperate to taste. She knelt in front of Adela.

The old man stepped back, and watched them with his hungry eyes. The woman pulled a silk fabric out of her long hair, which now flowed down both their faces. It smelled sweet and intoxicating, like the first bite of a ripe raspberry. The woman placed the silk fabric on Adela's chest. Suddenly it grew into an ultrathin sheer blanket. It felt as soft as a feather sweeping down Adela's body, and her nipples hardened under its touch. The woman kissed Adela's body through the silk, running her small tongue over Adela's lips, nipples, and belly. Adela reached for the woman. She wanted to feel her high white buttocks, but she couldn't touch her. The blanket became small again.

The woman placed it over Adela's concha, rubbing her own against it until a soft electric current bound them together. They rocked against each other until Adela felt as if she were about to explode. The woman moved off, kneeling over her again. Her fingers were on the fabric, pushing deeply inside of Adela until she came. Then the woman stood up. She placed the fabric over Adela's face.

Adela could smell her own musky scent, mixed with the beautiful woman's sweet essence. She took a deep breath and drank it in. Then she pulled the fabric off. Now Juan's face stared at her, filling in around the woman's shiny black eyes. It was him the whole time. It would always be him.

When she woke, she was soaked through her white T-shirt and underwear. A dull sadness throbbed in her head. She knew no one could satisfy her the way he did.

After that, she vowed to keep a tight lid on herself, squashing all sexy thoughts as if to prevent her body from responding to him again, even in her dreams. Her life became a litany of rituals and routine. She even visited the señoras at Tienda Morelos' *iglesia pentecostál* a few times, glad for the interruption of rousing *cánticos* and healing *gritos*.

An entire year passed. Then one day she was driving downtown on a Saturday and saw that a dusty little sporting goods store on a deserted stretch of Bristol Street had shut down. The owner had written, *"Se vende, buen precio"* on the window. She called the number immediately, and by the fall, she had the capital and the plans together. She was finally ready to open her *tienda de bodas*. The project reinvigorated her. She started waking up early to take long walks before work. She began to feel lighter.

She contracted a local Chicano artist to work with her on a new design. When she visited before they started working on it, she saw how small it was, and how easily it could drown on the avenue; there wasn't much but a deserted wholesale party favor store to it's right and a strip club to it's left. All she saw was potential. She had beautiful arches made on the outside and had the exterior painted a deep rose. She wanted her customers to feel elegant but comfortable, as if they'd finally found a place that catered to them. She called the shop La Boda Linda, The Beautiful Wedding. At her grand opening, the store was packed with Mexicanos from the local churches and restaurants; she had even advertised on Spanish radio. She hired a conjunto band and had her friends walk through the crowd with plates of taquitos and quesadillas from the Tienda Morelos for everyone who wandered into the store. The smell of cinnamon and hot chocolate *mexicana* wafted through the air. She'd designed the dresses herself, hiring a small team of skilled Mexican seamstresses to help her. They had a small room in the back where they sewed mantilla veils and layered *quinceañera* dresses.

She kept her prices low. She wanted the *jovencitas* that were fingering the embroidered organza and lilac chiffon, wondering how they would afford dresses for their *primas*, *hermanas*, and *madres* on their big day, to think of her as a resource. She saw how successful her design had been in the girls' eyes, as they shyly peppered her with questions and compliments as if she were a *doña alta*. She was glad the store looked nothing like Juan's drawings. She'd built shelves and artful hangings where the girls were scooping up the crystal rosaries, lassos, and porcelain quinceañera dolls displayed there. She was doing well. She quit her job at the hotel.

A couple of weeks after the opening she was doing inventory in the back, when Carla, one of the girls she'd hired to help her, interrupted. Her almond eyes were wide as she told Adela a man was looking for her in front. "I think he might be *borracho*," she whispered, her full shiny lips pausing on the *o*. Adela was stunned, but she kept her face stern. She told Carla to stay by the phone, ready to call the police if needed. When she walked out onto the floor she was shocked to see a skeletal version of Juan. He wore a faded pair of carpenter pants and a dirty white T-shirt, as if he were sleeping on the streets. He stood next to the counter. His black eyes were dull and his face drawn sharply as if he were suffering from some mysterious illness. She almost felt sorry for him; instead, she was filled with a sudden rage. How dare he come in here and mess with my *tiendita*! she thought. Without a single word of greeting, she said, "Please see me in the back, sir," waving a hand at a concerned-looking Carla. She didn't want anyone she knew to drop by and see him there.

"What are you doing here?" she asked, as they stood in the airless back room.

"So, that was it," he said. "You were just never gonna call me again? What, did you go back to being a ho to pay for all this shit?" Adela saw that Juan was teetering. He did look drunk.

"What!" she hissed. "Keep your voice down! How dare you come in here *para acusarme*, after you try to sell me out for your *papeles*. I should call the *migra* on you right now. Get out!"

"What the fuck are you talkin' about, *la migra*," he said. "I'm not even . . ."

She didn't let him finish. "If you don't leave, *en diez segundos* I'll have *la policia* boot you ass out," she said, her words sputtering from her like grease on a hot grill.

To her surprise, she felt elation mingling with her many emotions. She straightened the blazer she was wearing, and stepped calmly back to the floor. "An old friend of Gabriel's, he's going through a tough time," she said to Carla, whose wide eyes continued to follow her through the store.

The next day a bouquet of calla lilies and yellow roses were waiting for her on the counter in the shop, wrapped in a cream tissue paper and thin, shiny plastic. It matched the *tienda*'s ivory paint and yellow trim. Even in his *borrachera*, he must have noticed it the day before. "It says it's from Juan," Carla said, her eyebrows raised. "Ah, *sí*," Adela said, maintaining her composure. "He's one of our main investors. He probably wants to congratulate us on our opening weeks sales." Carla nodded and went back to her magazine. There was a small note sealed in an envelope attached to one of the lilies' stems. It read, "I'm sorry about yesterday. Meet me at Luna's tomorrow at 8. Let me explain."

She kept her face stoic as she read the note, but her heart pounded rapidly.

She barely slept that night, and she took the next day off of work. He said he'd meet her at the restaurant, a new upscale Cal-Mex place that opened up in the southern part of Santa Ana, near Costa Mesa. He didn't even call to see if she was coming. He would just wait for her there. She knew she should just stay at home. What could he possibly say to make up for what he'd done to her? But she couldn't lie to herself. She missed him, and there were times at night when her body still ached for his hands. She had to know what had happened. She would go to find out. She pulled out twelve outfits from her closet and tried them all on, unsure of what message she wanted to send. He'd looked so dirty when she'd seen him at the store, like some homeboy *de la calle*. Maybe he's lost his mind, she thought. Maybe he'll be asking for money. I'd better sit somewhere close to the door, to keep my distance at the restaurant. She chose a subtle business suit, a low-cut blouse with a blazer over a skirt. She wore a lacy pair of panties and a push-up bra underneath, despite her doubts. She couldn't help herself.

When she arrived, she took a long look at the restaurant before she saw Juan. The seats were vinyl and there was a frosted plastic panel in the back, to conceal the area where waiters ordered the food from the cooks that worked behind it. The place wasn't as nice as what she had pictured. The only thing that made it upscale were the white faces that poked out of the vinyl booths. She spotted him sitting in the back. He was dressed better than anyone else there, in a fine charcoal linen suit with a slim bouquet of flowers in his hand.

He was handsome enough to own the restaurant. He stood up when he saw her walking toward the table.

"*Gracias por venir*," he said, kissing her briefly on the cheek. Adela glanced at their reflection in the mirrored panel behind the booth. She thought they looked like passing business acquaintances. She took her seat across the booth from him. Her hands lightly tapped the table.

She nodded. "What happened the other day? What are you doing here now?"

"I came to see you. I'm sorry I was so drunk that day, " he said, looking down. He looked uncomfortable, as if he didn't know what tone to use with her. He looked down. Then slowly and carefully, he started to speak, as if he were talking to a reporter. "I've actually been in town for a few weeks, doing some work out here. I looked you up and found out about your store, but I didn't know how to talk to you after all this time. I passed the store for days and saw you in there talking all professional to people. One day, after working on this guy's house all day I got drunk by myself, trying to think of what I would say to you. I've been thinking about you nonstop, and I couldn't help it. I just walked in. Then you seemed all crazy mad, and we got into it. I knew I had to do it over, to do it right. So here we are." His hand was in his coat pocket, where he twisted something over and over again.

"I seemed crazy?" Adela said, and straightened in her chair. She took a deep breath and promised herself she wouldn't allow *la emoción* that clawed at her throat to break free. She kept her voice low. "You're the one who proposed to me, acting all romantic, when all you wanted were your stupid *papeles*. Then you freaked out over nothing and never called me again. *Y yo soy la loca.*"

"What are you talking about, for my *papeles*?"

"I saw the paper Juan. How to Be a Resident in Four Easy Steps? I'm not stupid."

"That thing I got online," he said, his voice slowly rising. Anger transformed his eyes to an all-too-familiar darkness. "That's what you think this is about? I forgot all about that. I don't even know how you could even think about that after what you did. I only printed that shit out to have it on file, to see what my options are after we got married, so I could make plans for the future. I bought the ring before I found that shit online. I even told Araceli about you. I was so ready to bring you into our lives, so she could have someone to look up to . . . I mean, never, in a million years, would I have thought that someone like you . . ."

Todavía está con éso, she thought, anger starting to bubble. The revelation about the ring hadn't changed anything. She was ready to run out.

He reached his hand across the table, brushing his finger against hers, his voice now barely a whisper. "I know this isn't coming out right, but I wanted to tell you I'm sorry. I went crazy when I saw that *comemierdas* at the Copa. It was too much for me. But I don't care about what happened before. We could just forget about it, we never have to mention it again. Don't worry about the green card shit, either, I got a plan for all of that. All I want is to be with you again, if you'll take me back." To her shock, he pulled out the object he'd been fiddling with in his pocket. It was the ring, shining in the center of the table like a spotlight.

She stared at the ring. The *rabia* that had just consumed her slipped away, like air leaking out of a balloon. Instead, a different feeling was washing through her. It was like the slow numbing of novocaine. She couldn't share his excitement, despite his declarations. She looked at his face. His skin was clean and smooth, like the inside of a sea shell. He was untouched by the heaviness of age, the disappointments that set in with jowls, deep lines, and creaky bones. She checked the booth's mirrored panel again. They didn't look like business acquaintances after all. They looked like *familiares*, like *madre y hijo*.

"*Escucha bien*, Juan," she said. "I can't marry you. This is all my fault. I never should have let myself see you again."

She got up to leave, and he caught her hand, pulling her back to the table. "No, I'm just a fucking *pendejo*. I should have called you, and I should have come right away. That Garcia thing . . ."

"It's no Garcia I talking about, Juan," Adela said quietly. "It's me. I'm fifty-five years old. We've never talked about it, but I'm old enough to be your mother." He opened his mouth to speak, but she stopped him. "I know what you're going to say, *que no importa. Pero si importa.*"

She looked into his eyes now. "I be sixty in five years. I can't give you no more children. *Y no quiero que me cuides*, like some helpless *viejita*, when I'm too old to take care of myself."

She fought hard to blink back tears. Before Juan could say anything, she left. But when she pulled her car into the driveway, he was already there. He was standing outside, leaning against his rental. His eyes were red around the rims.

"You think you gonna get rid of me just like that?" he said. "Just because I'm younger? You know this goes deeper than that. I felt it since the moment I left your house last Christmas. I got about halfway to the airport after Malibu with Gabriel, and I just wanted to drive back, because being with you was the only place I felt at home. I was going to tell him right there. I didn't feel right again until I came back. That's why I kept coming back, no matter what you said. It's because I knew. I still know. We're meant to be together."

"What if you change you mind when I get older?" she said. "*No te puedo despedir otra vez.*"

"I don't want to say goodbye," he said. "I want to start over."

He took her hand, and she let herself believe him.

She put her head on his chest. His arms wrapped tightly around her. She breathed in his scent: moist wood and fresh mango. Tears started pouring from deep within her, a place she had thought was too deep to reach. He brushed hair back off her face and combed his fingers through it, massaging her scalp the way her mamá used to when she would get upset. It was the only thing that used to calm her down, and he did it naturally, as if she'd whispered her secret to him in a dream. He opened her door and they went inside. He gently pulled off her blazer and folded it, placing it on the couch. Then he unbuttoned her blouse slowly, never taking his eyes off of her. She turned away at first, embarrassed. She moved away from him, sitting at the far end of her couch, with a frown on her face, as if they'd been transported back to the moment after they'd made love for the first time. She hadn't lost all the weight she'd gained since they'd last seen each other. He read her thoughts again.

"*Eres bella,*" he whispered, as he sat beside her, erasing the rift between them. He unhooked her bra, and pulled off her *calzones*. "*Bella, bella, bella.*" He repeated it over and over again, as he kissed her cheeks, her earlobes, and her neck, all the way to her heart. He released her long curls from the ponytail that held them up, and took her face in his hands. "I love you." Adela's tears didn't stop, even when he slipped the ring onto her finger. "*Yo te amo, también,*" she whispered, and enveloped his lips with her own. Their tongues intertwined like lines of silk.

He took his kiss down her body, entering the deep groove between her breasts with his tongue, biting the points of her breasts, circling them with his tongue. He opened her legs and kissed her inner thighs, nibbling her until she arched her back and pushed herself up toward him. He reached inside her with his tongue, deeper and deeper until she felt like he'd joined her body, and they formed one shivering blade of grass together. Then he flicked the outsides of her opening with his tongue, weaving it around all her flower until he reached her clit, which he drew completely into his mouth.

When he entered her, he moved as deeply inside as he could, remaining there for a moment. He looked into her eyes, and she imagined he saw his barrio in Santo Domingo in the shifting hazel, the soft brown cotton skirts of the girls in the schoolyards.

She felt as if her whole life she'd been waiting for this moment, when she finally saw the point where the legions of random stars and the cold earth connect, and the world came together. She knew Juan was right. They were a perfect fit.

Faith in Disguise

Mayra Santos-Febres
to Mario Santana Ortiz

n ow that I think about it, it's not surprising that Faith and I always meet on this day. All Hallow's Eve. Holy Eve. The Eve of All That Is Sacred. October 31 is the chosen date for our meetings. I get ready for our encounter. Today is my turn again to transform into the slave, or better yet, become the lover of Faith the slave. I have been meeting with this enigma a while now. It has been two years since our first secret encounter, which happened on an October 31.

If I am lucky, this may be our last October.

I follow the instructions that Faith has given me. I should wait until sundown. Then, and only then, will I proceed to carefully bathe myself, dedicating special attention to my face, my nails, my nether regions. My beard should be trimmed closely, my face neatly shaven, and my teeth gleaming. I should also get rid of my extra hair, especially around my private parts. However, I cannot mask my natural, underlying scent with colognes or creams. Faith is fastidious. Faith does not like intrusive essences. She does not want perfumes or sweat to burn or infect our exposed flesh tonight.

I pull back my foreskin, which I clean throroughly with water and soap. Today it is my turn to become the lover's slave. The slave lover. Tonight my white skin, clean and shiny, translucent like paper, will tell the story of my one and only disguise.

To disguise oneself is to put on another face, to change one's skin, if need be. Thus, to wear a disguise is a complicated matter, because skin is not merely a covering for the flesh, but an essence. I know this, now that I look at myself, naked, freshly bathed. Watch and recognize what stirs under this whiteness that is both my skin and my disguise. It is the disguise of privilege, if you want to think of it that way, the disguise of a transparent identity. But Faith has toppled it all. Never before her have I thought of myself as being marked by this skin, nor by the piece of flesh that dangles between my legs and makes a male out of me. Faith made me look closer. For two years now I have been looking closer; looking at me, at her, at our skins and our disguises, merging into one. I look at myself, carefully. I pause to write these impressions down. It is important that I talk about Faith's disguise. Faith in disguise. To tell her story and the story of that dress.

It is not surprising that I offer my body in sacrifice each October 31. The body of Martín Tirado, historian and researcher, who has painstakingly tried to interpret the meaning of this, a story that dissolves in midair. The meaning of my encounters with Faith, which I want to remember and record. I have lost count of the nights without sleep, of days that I remain awake, writing. Time has stopped. My story will remain as testimony, in case I cannot return from this Eve of All That Is Sacred. *Víspera de Todos los Santos.* Or in case the one who cannot return turns out to be Faith.

I started working with Faith five years after she organized that famous exhibit on emancipated Brazilian slaves of the eighteenth century. I was new to Chicago and had never lived outside of Puerto Rico. But the Center took care of every detail, setting me up, finding me an apartment near work, and introducing me to Faith.

Previously, she had worked wth two collaborators, Álvaro Marqués and Figurado Ortiz. They were both historians, quite well known in their respective fields. But Faith was the star, mainly because there are not many like her in our discipline. No, there are not many women who can boast degrees from Florence or México, internships in Washington's Museum of Natural History or the New York's Schomburg Center. There are not many academic stars with such preparation, let alone her skin tone. Faith is black. White, male historians like Figurado Ortiz or Álvaro Marqués can be counted by the hundreds. Like me: men with extensive academic backgrounds, pale as the documents with which we choose to surround ourselves in order to hide our inadequate presence in the world of the Present, the world of the living.

They had hired me to oversee the electronic archives of the Historical Research Center. My specialty is in the restoration, care, and preservation of old historical documents and their transposition, storage, and display by electronic means. I am what you could call a virtual historiographer. I recompose fragments of the past and carry them to the present in our preferred time capsule—computers—which can win the war against the death of everything organic: the death of paper, the death of memory, or so we think. I was chosen from among many due to my impeccable background as a researcher and my vast knowledge of computer languages. But the results of my training are the same as ever: I live surrounded by the past.

I started working for Faith after the two historians that preceeded me had vanished, changing their addresses, moving away from the city, never again working in the subtle discipline of history. I do not know how they managed to escape Faith's wicked game, nor how they managed to compensate for the passion she offered to them. I wish I knew how they did it, poor lonely men lost in history, just like me. It is a well-known fact that a passion such as Faith's easily eludes men such as ourselves.

So I arrived at the Research Center without knowing that I would become Faith's third victim, or her third accomplice. It is all the same to me now. I am too embedded in this game, in the sweetly disguised life of museum curator and historian Faith Verdejo. And, despite the risk, I do not want to get out, not without Faith. I'd rather burn in her flames.

I should start from the beginning, or at least try to find a suitable beginning among many.

When I finally joined Faith's team of researchers and began my assignment at the Center, I experienced a fleeting period of glory.

The Center was abundantly funded. It had the means to pay for the digitalization of rare historical archives. It offered illustrated talks and museum exhibitions to researchers and students alike. I was a young and promising researcher, and could not believe my luck. But, once I started working with Faith I discovered that in the years before the famous exhibit, the Center had come very close to closing its doors forever. No funds, no name, a small, unknown research facility lost in a poor Latin community on the outskirts of the city.

That was when Faith decided to play her wild card. She started by herself cataloging and digitalizing the Center's oldest documents, which were already starting to rot in paper. It so happens that while sorting through these documents, she found the key to solving the Center's dilemma. Nobody knows how or when exactly, but the Center at some point came into possession of a number of important documents about emancipated slaves in eighteenth-century Brazil. Faith decided to put together an exhibit featuring these documents, accompanied by rare artifacts also from the period of the Portuguese Empire. This exhibit focused on the lives of Xica, Diamantina, and Mariana—three of the emancipated slaves mentioned in the documents—placing them in a historical context.

Faith had decided to concentrate on the Brazilian region of Minas Gerais, specifically on Tejuco and its diamond mines. Paying her own way, she traveled to Minas. There, she found a way to secure permits to further her research and bring back to the Center the original emancipation documents for the slaves and the baptismal registrations of the sons and daughters they had borne to their owners/lovers, all of them rich Portuguese officials of the Crown. She also brought back jewelry made with *mineiro* diamonds, as well as photos of these women's descendants. But what astonished everyone was the dress she managed to find and keep for the Center. Nobody knows where she found it. Only I and the two historians who vanished before me know its story.

I was at the center for six months before Faith selected me as her "accomplice." Without a doubt, it was she who made the choice. It had to be. I would not have been able to be so bold, even had I wanted to. At that time I was working on one of the most boring aspects of my duties. The research division of the Center was selecting new material to round out the files of our already famous electronic archives and web page. My job was to design a new electronic link and to go through the scanned texts to make sure they were correct. I also had to compose the titles that specified the virtual content of each. All that to say I was working as a sort of virtual monk, the same as in medieval times, only the technologies differed. In total silence, bent over the board, I copied and read.

So, I did not notice the day, the week, when Faith Verdejo chose me. I only know that one afternoon I sensed her presence behind me. It was late. There were only two or three shadows roaming the Center. Faith materialized as an apparition behind me and suddenly I knew it all. I got up from my desk and followed her through the empty hallways. Past the elevators, the employees' bathroom, we entered the coffee room. Faith lit the lights. She served two cups of coffee. She handed me one.

"I wanted to ask you a favor, Martín. That's your name. Martín, right?"

My name took form between her lips. I felt conjured. Faith continued. "I need you to go over something I'm working on. It's for a conference next month at Salzburg. I've read it to so many times I cannot find my own mistakes."

I could not listen to a word she was saying. I could only watch her luscious, full lips moving. They were slightly moist.

"I'll send you my files by email, so that you can look at them when you have the time." Faith turned around and then gave me the gift of her full, round hips pulsating under the dark cloth of her skirt. I wanted to bite her flesh and her coffee lips. I wanted to bite her so badly that I had to bite down on my own lips hard, until they hurt, just to appease that hunger. My frown then helped me to regain control of myself and to appear concentrated and serious about the proposition. "Of course, Faith. I'll be waiting for the files," I answered, while writing my email address on a piece of paper. I stepped closer to hand it to her. Then, while she took the note from my hand, she gave a look, one that I still cannot interpret correctly. I do not know whether it was filled with shyness, or a provocation to shame.

"Are you coming?"

"Haven't finished my coffee yet."

"I should get back to my article."

"I'm burned out. Can't go any further."

"Then you should go home now. It's late, they'll be waiting for you."

"I live alone."

"Historian's luck."

And then she left. Faith Verdejo disappeared in the hallways of the Center.

That night, as soon as I got to my apartment, I opened my computer and read the files she had sent. Her words entranced my eyes and fired up my fingertips. I was in heat; my arms, my chest, my whole body fell under her spell. I bit my lips as I had done in the coffee room, but this time I drew blood. Meanwhile, without my even noticing it, my hands slid down my chest, pinching my skin and my nipples.

Don't ask me why, I cannot understand it myself. But that was the beginning of my obsession. The files read: "Born in 1731 or 1735, exact date cannot be determined. Daughter of a black slave and a Portuguese merchant—Hija de María da Costa y Caetano de Sá, respectively."

I scratched my chest while pulsing the mouse with my hand. My eyes could not be torn away from the computer screen as I continued reading. "Slave to Arraial de Tejuco's physician, Don Manuel de Pires, who took her as a lover by the early age of eleven." My fingertips continued directing the mouse. But my other hand finally dove inside my pants, like a cannibal hungry to find his catch: my own penis, already erect and moist. I kept on reading, like someone possessed. My mind was completely riveted by the story and my chest filled with an incredible hunger to break, to tear, to bite. I kept on stroking myself. "As a result of his excesses, Pires received a reprimand from the Church in the person of the vicar. When young João Fernandes de Oliveira came to Tejuco to take possession of his father's estate and mines, the physician sold her to him as a concubine for the price of 800 réis. Thus Xica became her new master's lover." I finished reading the article, but my other hand continued its obsessive task. I couldn't stop it. But then I found the attachment. It came at the end of the file, in a JPEG format. I opened it. It contained a close-up photograph of Faith's disguise, of Xica's dress, I should say. The dress she had recovered for the famous exhibit. Only then did I come.

From that day on, I became an expert on Faith. I analyzed her every movement and little quirk. Needing to explain what had happened to me, I turned to the only thing I knew that worked: research. And so I researched Faith, watched for proofs, collected data. I used every free minute I had in the Center to study her until I learned her by heart; learned, for instance, how she arrived at the Center at nine o'clock each morning. She was never late, even on days of extreme traffic or when it was raining. Faith went directly to her desk and worked nonstop until 10:30 a.m., when she took a break for breakfast. A cup of coffee, black, no sugar, freshly brewed in the Center's coffee machine. I watched her bite on fruits, pieces of cheese, a slice of whole wheat bread. She was careful with what she ate; no wonder she had such a lean figure, tight and strong under her garments, always black and white. How can that be, with a job so sedentary, of such long hours? It must be because she was one of those early morning workout women. So I imagined Faith in the gym, taking yoga classes, kickboxing, pilates. Her long, lean muscles proved me right.

She smoothed back her wavy hair with odorless gels that kept it close to her head. Faith never wore makeup and never had nail polish on her fingers. She always wore leather pumps, so her toenails were invisible. They remained a mystery to me until much later. She didn't smell of any perfume, but a subtle aroma always surrounded her. She smelled of coffee, of the warm essence of wood, of fruit trees. Her lips were frequently dry. Every two or three hours, Faith took out a lip balm that she applied with her fingertips, first to the lower lip, then upper. Afterwards the lips met. Faith corrected any excess with a handkerchief. Sometimes she licked them a little. Sometimes, when concentrating, she bit on them. She was elegant and sober.

It drove me crazy, watching her sit at that desk chair, smoothing her dress, running her hands lightly over her hips. Then she would adjust the chair to the correct height and pull herself closer to the computer screen, rolling her neck, once, twice, to each side. She repeated this operation several times a day. There were days (depending on stress levels) in which she would do up to four neck rolls by lunchtime.

I accessed the Center's employee files to investigate our star curator's records. Impressive. A Guggenheim fellowship, a Ford postdoctoral—the same one that Secretary of State Condoleezza Rice received at the beginning of her career. Four years ago, she received a Fulbright to further her research on the relationship between slavery and titles of nobility in the Antilles, Brazil, and Portugal. Her conferences and achievements are too many to list in this relation of the facts. Besides, there are other achievements of hers that caught my interest.

I studied her, thoroughly, exhaustively, without touching her. That was the ritual conjured by her distance and her silence, for Faith had not approached me, not even once, since she had announced that she'd be sending her files to my computer. Faith pulled back and I used that time to read her, hidden, unnoticed, like only a pagan shaman knows how. At night I retired to my monastic cell and continued studying Faith in my computer, interpreting the smoke signals of her fires. There she reappeared: doubled, fractured, reunited, under the names of the slave ancestors that she had picked for herself—Diamantina, Francisca, Mariana. Faith. I then took out my hunger and became slave to Faith's masters, slave to Faith's desires, which were now my own.

• • •

Xica Da Silva, la Diamantina, Mariana. Her file list grew in my computer. Each night Faith sent me a new file, and each night she awakened the beast in me. Don't ask me why because I can't explain it myself, nor can I explain the man I became during that time, and in this. A man of hunger. I honestly do not know how I, the pale, shy historical researcher Martín Tirado, turned into that awful animal whose agitated hands and bared fangs probed both Faith's files and its own appetites. I divided in two—one read, the other touched himself. But both remained obsessed: always wanting more; more files, more Faith.

Now that I think about it, I can honestly say that those nights in my room, in front of the computer screen, were the first in my life that I did not feel alone. On the other side of it was Faith with her slaves; Faith accepting the offerings of my lust. And I swear to God, to all gods, I could hear her saying, "It will soon be time." Soon I would gain access to Faith's body, soon bite her nipples and her lips, soon be inside her, opening her flesh at last. Soon she would allow me to probe her surfaces, to lick her all over, to taste the juices be-tween her legs; obedient, quiet, wide open. And I would at last close my eyes at the sound of her joyful screams; controlling their sym-phony. Faith would scream her hunger, her pain, her anger. She would give herself to me, I could tell. The only thing needed was my initial submission.

I finished reading all of Faith's files, editing her Salzburg paper. By email, I offered to organize a multimedia presentation for her. She ac-cepted my offer, but I had to wait for an entire week to show it to her. She did not answer my emails or phone calls. Many nights I mastur-bated in shadows, with the computer turned off. Faith kept me so, humbly expecting. Each night I searched my emails, those at the Center. Nothing. During the daytime, at work, I roamed near her desk trying to reach her. But Faith would not look at me, not once, not even to let me know that my waiting was part of our secret pact.

At the end of that week, Faith entered the coffee room at the exact time I was there, taking my break. I sensed her near, but did not lift my eyes. I kept drinking my coffee as she leaned on the countertop.

"I received your email saying that you're finished with my presentation. Sorry to have taken so long to respond. I wanted to give you a rest."

"No problem."

"So, how does it look?"

"Fairly complete. However it lacks movement, and it's also short on images."

"There aren't any pictures of Xica or of Diamantina. Slave women were only photographed to be sold or if they committed a crime. And that was very late in the nineteenth century. The closest thing to a picture that I've got is the dress."

"Yeah, I saw the picture. However, it'd be great if we can compose an approximate sketch, or find an etching or something."

"You'll have to imagine them. I can send you accounts by witnesses who describe them, but they're not very convincing."

"Really? Why not?"

"Because they're taken from secondary sources, compiled by historians of the times. And they were filled with preconceptions and prejudice. You know that such accounts lack objectivity."

"Yeah, but that's all we've got."

"I know, but words are so elusive. It is better to see for oneself. To touch and find."

Then she brushed against my shoulder. It was only a slight contact, as if by mistake. But once again the hunger took hold of me. I wanted to jump upon Faith Verdejo, right then and there in the coffee room. I wanted to throw her over that counter and devour her. But I contained myself. I held my breath, cleared my throat, made sure I did not look directly into her eyes. I did not wanted her to see what was burning inside. "Fine," I answered. "But I'd still like to see them. And I imagine your colleagues in Salzburg will also wonder what they looked like."

"I don't think it would be that hard to illustrate my presentation."

"Really? What do you think they looked like?"

"Isn't it obvious? They looked like me." She said this as she was already walking out of the door of the coffee room. She was doing her usual disappearing act, but this time she did not catch me off guard. This time I read right through her.

It was close to the end of October. In a week or so, Faith was to depart for her Salzburg conference. I wanted to show her what I had designed for her, the finished multimedia presentation. But, more important, I wanted her to see the illustrations I had made of Xica, Diamantina, and the other slaves. The gift of my devotion; me a slave to her slaves.

"If you have no other engagements this Halloween night, maybe we can meet. Is my house all right?—Faith." The note was placed carefully on the center of my lonely desk.

Faith invited me to her apartment the night of the 31st to show her the whole presentation. I accepted. I could tell that the Salzburg presentation was a pretext, that something else was going on. But I convinced myself that I was imagining things. So, when I pressed the intercom button at Faith's apartment (68 Spruce Street, should anyone look for me if I happen to disappear), I was set to spend another arduous night working on Faith's presentation, pretending I couldn't feel the heat of her body next to mine. Afterward, I assumed I would head home alone, surfing the internet to find a porno site I could relieve myself to. I pressed the bell again and waited. Faith opened the door. I went in, looking for a table to set my laptop; searching for a switch. But I sensed the weight of Faith's eyes on me. It was a mistake to look directly at her.

She was wearing an impeccable white blouse and a pressed black skirt. The top three buttons of her blouse were open, exposing her deep cleavage. Her nipples were poking through her blouse. It was clear she wasn't wearing a bra. I couldn't help myself. I had to kiss her.

She was kissing, licking me all over, as she removed all my clothes. I could not keep my hands still; I panted as I touched her body at last, touching her everywhere I could. Then suddenly she stopped. Taking me by the hand, she led me to a back room with no furniture except for a weird chaise longue, a sort of antique daybed.

Beside it lay a big wooden chest filled with tissue paper. Faith sat me on the chaise and stepped away from my hands, which couldn't stop grabbing her pubis, her hips, and her breasts, as if I were a desperate animal. She took off her white blouse, her dark skirt, confirming she had nothing on underneath.

Then, she proceeded to open the chest. Out came an intricate corset made of leather and metal, and after it, yards and yards of golden silk. It was the dress. She put it on the floor. Then she fixed the corset against her bare skin. Its leather straps tightened around Faith's dark gleaming body. Faith pulled on them some more, marking her waist with the leather, which ate into it. I couldn't do anything but look and feel my hairs stand on end. She pulled again, and I saw Faith's face frown with pain and discomfort, and, yes, pleasure. I lost my breath, getting harder between my legs, as I watched Faith's skin turn even darker with pressure.

Then Faith said something. It sounded like "Menino"; I couldn't understand her very well. It was as if she was using the words of the time of Xica; the dress was speaking through her. My blood boiled. All of me wanted to be on top of her. I wanted to devour her. I saw the scratches forming on her body from the metal cutting into her, and I felt like a wolf watching its prey. My fangs sharpened, but I knew I had to stay still. Faith then bent down and picked up the dress. She put it on, and I knew that with each movement, the corset was cutting into her deeper. "Watch me, Menino," she said, or so I heard. She did not need my help to tie the ribbons that fastened the dress in front, nor the countless buttons on its sleeves. She covered her body after I had seen it all.

The yards of yellow silk billowed from her tight bodice, and she stood above me, looking down at me with a hard expression on her face. Her eyes were distant, the dress had taken over. My body shook as the silk brushed against my face, like the robes of priests who once offered me salvation. I felt out of control, I wanted to tear her apart. Then Faith conquered me, completely. She knelt down on her knees to lick my feet. I sat there, naked, while Faith licked my stomach, my hips, between my legs. She licked my penis while her flesh burned against the raw metal of her corset. She was paying in pain for the pleasure of giving me pleasure.

I could not help myself. I came in her mouth.

I have to admit that after that first encounter on the 31st of October, I intended to avoid Faith Verdejo as much as I could; I was convinced I would never put myself in a situation in which I could touch her again. I ran out of Faith's apartment no longer knowing who I was. I didn't ever want to find myself in such a place again. In short, I was afraid. But it wasn't the disguise she wore or the ritual of the corset that scared me. It was my loss of control. I was ashamed that I couldn't hold it; that I came so easily without even having penetrated her once. I was the penetrated, the one who came first. I was lower to her, I could see it in her eyes, in her silence after our game, she let me know. After I got dressed, still lying on the cold floor of our encounter, I was frantic for a means of escape. I wanted to run from the disturbing sensation of wanting to possess her completely, to mark her body and watch her bleed, to penetrate her until she hurt. Her submission had awakened a dragon within me, and I didn't recognize myself. I left her home and spent months avoiding her.

Under the glow of the computer screen my fingers are trembling, for I must reveal my true story. The one I have kept silent for many years and which I should record before I go to meet with Faith tonight. Only now do I dare tell it. My meeting with the curator had made me remember where I came from, recovering the story of my disguises along with my true face.

When I was a boy, I was fascinated by our priest's garments. We lived in a small town, my mother and I, on the eastern coast of Puerto Rico. Nothing much ever happened in our town, except for Mass. I would beg my mother to take me each Sunday morning. Watching from the pews, I could be drawn to tears, when Father Fernando walked the aisle to perform Mass in his white robes. My mother thought they were tears of devotion. She was mistaken. Those tears announced the tremors of the flesh. They were the signs of a strange obsession that consumed my childhood mind. I could not explain such obsession. I was a Catholic boy, young, yet already corrupted. Father Fernando stood at the altar, dressed in his immaculate robe and the purple chasuble of Holy Week. I watched him and a feeling of hollowness gnawed at my stomach; a heat would attack between my legs. Suddenly I wanted to press against his vestment, smell it, make it swallow all the tears of my frustration. I longed to kneel before him the way he must have prostrated himself before the cardinal, taking his vows.

I begged my mother a thousand times to let me become an altar boy. She refused. She was a believer, but not a fanatic. Her faith would take her to Mass once a week at the most; she would attend *Misa de Gallo* on Christmas Eve and do her penance on Holy Thursday and Good Friday. But she had no intention of encouraging her only son to give up his life to the Church. On Saturdays, she would send me to swimming or baseball classes; she would enroll me in basketball leagues. "Martín, how many girlfriends do you have in school?" she would ask. "Which position are you going to play in next week's game?" She wanted a one hundred percent male boy, comfortable in his skin, a hunter. She was wasting her time.

I failed at sports and lost the game of becoming popular. My body never succeeded in becoming my home. And so I grew up shy, clumsy, and lonesome. Trying to escape my mother, I would hide in my dead father's reading room, immersed in his old history books, the ones that looked similar to Father Fernando's Bible. Only there did I feel safe, from my mother, from myself, and from my body, which was always betraying me. I discovered that I had a shrewd ability to decipher codes and maps, to remember dates, the details of a battle, the names of kings, countries, and rivers. So I dedicated myself to study, to further accumulating data and uncovering the mysteries of knowledge.

All that time, cloistered in my father's library, my skin became so pale it was almost translucent, further separating me from the world of the living. Sometimes I would steal a lavender scarf from my mother's closet and put it over my shoulders, like the violet garb of the priest. In my costume I felt the power of delivering words from a pulpit. But that power scared me; it burned between my legs and shook my flesh. And so I conquered my tears, my tremors, and my treacherous body. I forgot my devotion for Father Fernando. I hid in history, where I could live unharmed.

I became obssesed with Napoleon Bonaparte and Phillip I of Spain; I read everything about Queen Isabella and the kings of the Restoration and the Second Empire. I learned by heart the lives of the colonial governors who had ravished my small country: from Juan Ponce de León to Juan Prim. I studied the life of seventeenth-century crown corsary Miguel Henríquez and of Cofresí, the pirate. I was transported by Simón Bolívar's adventures. And then I reached puberty. I became this skinny, pale boy who looked as if he had landed in someone else's body. I would bump into anything and anybody. My only companions were my books.

Then, my body betrayed me again. I had this incredible urge for something, for someone, but I did not know whom. It was neither a boy nor a girl, at any rate, no one I knew. So I turned to history again, to my father's old books. I hid in the small bathroom in his library and there, where my mother could not catch me, I touched myself for hours, pretending to read. The lust gave me goose bumps; the pleasure I experienced turned me even more secretive. By adolescence I knew that I would never become the hunter, the conqueror, a man to protagonize history. Me, Martín Tirado, a man of action. No way.

"At least I saved you from becoming a priest," my mother told me when I announced to her that I'd been accepted by the University of Puerto Rico as a world history major. "At least . . . " she said, giving me her blessing. Then I crossed the little streets of my town and landed on the asphalt seas of the city that led me to my new school, where I hid again. I spent the entire four years of my education roaming the libraries, enrolling in the most obscure classes, spending all my spare time at the computer centers. By night, alone in my dorm room, I would surf the web for history sites and porn, indiscriminately. I would touch myself and remember my mother's words, "At least I saved you . . ."

Maybe she would have changed her mind if she could have seen my perverted loneliness. But I must not exaggerate. My college years were not all loneliness and masturbation. I went to parties once or twice. The one that I remember best was a party on a Halloween night. On Holy's Eve, precisely. October 31. *Víspera de todos los Santos.*

That night I was to disguise myself as Don Juan Tenorio. I tended to the smallest detail—found the right jerkin, long-sleeved shirt with lace cuffs and ruffled collar, tights, brimmed hat, and curly mane of hair. I also went to the Sports Facility to borrow a florentine sword, with its safety cap, to make sure I would not stab anyone. I dressed myself carefully and waited for the night. Then, to top it all, I donned my black mask, giving the finishing touch to my disguise. I looked like a totally different man.

I left the dormitory and walked toward the student center. The music pulsed against the moist night air. One of those brief showers fell out of nowhere and freshened the night. Small groups of students crossed my path, also disguised. There was a pussycat, three fairly convincing superheroes, a pirate, some Playboy bunnies. It was weird the way I could glide past them, lightly, without tripping or feeling self-conscious. I walked resolutely toward the doorway and paid the entry fee.

Inside I greeted several classmates, but did not approach any groups. I wanted to remain alone. This time, however, it was not from shyness. I leaned against the bar and asked for a drink. Alcohol has never been my forte. I really cannot tell the difference between whisky and vodka, but that night I drank. I drank a lot, five or six drinks. Before my seventh drink I noticed a girl watching me insistently. I raised my plastic cup in reverence. I didn't want to get out of character.

She approached me. Her gown was an inaccurate imitation of a seventeenth-century noblewoman's dress, in the style of the court of Louis XIV. But it was made with cheap taffeta and its décolletage was from another era. The girl, who was wearing a white wig, addressed me.

"Bow before me," she said. "I am Marie Antoinette. And you?"

"Don Juan Tenorio," I answered, taking off my hat in a deep bow. I immediatedy kissed her hand. She laughed.

"The great Don Juan . . ." I responded by grabbing her firmly by the wrist and bringing her to the dance floor, where I pressed my body against her. We danced incessantly and then kissed.

"You'll make me lose my head."

"That, my dear lady, is your inevitable destiny."

I paid for her drink and afterward we walked out into the night. I took her to my dorm room, and there we spent the night in each other's flesh, biting, pushing, shoving without any tenderness. All was hunger. She was as drunk as I was; and she could not stop screaming, scratching my back. I don't know if she was screaming out of pain or pleasure. I did not care. And did not have time to ask. Exhausted and drunk, I dozed off. The next morning I could not find the girl. In her place, a big stain of blood dressed my bedsheets. "Somebody lost her virginity," I thought, but could not be certain if it was hers or mine.

I forgot the incident as fast as I could, not wanting to know any more. But my encounters with Faith made it all come back. Faith and her disguise made me remember my times of debauchery, moments in which my personality split in two.

"It happened while I was conducting an interview in the Cloister of Macaúbas convent. An old mulatta nun with green eyes gave me the key to discovering the dress."

Faith told me the story of how she found the dress in Minas Gerais one afternoon. I had finally found the nerve to approach her, consumed by fear and curiosity. I tried to explain to her, and to myself, what had happened the first time I saw her in disguise.

"I need to talk to you," I whispered in her ear, at the Center, bending near her desk. She nodded her head and invited me for lunch at an old Cuban restaurant in our neighborhood, where no one would see us.

"I cannot understand what happened," I began. "Faith, I don't know how I lost my self-control. I hurt you, and I am not that kind of a man." She brushed my comments aside with a flick of her finger. She began a confession of her own at our table in the restaurant's dark corner, where we sat for hours, forgetting our responsibilities at the Center. The sound of her own voice transported her, and the weight of her words transformed her. In those moments, Faith became for me the most beautiful woman on the face of this earth.

"The nun told Faith—*Menina*, go to the Sodality da Mercê. That is where they keep all of my great-grandmother's papers."

Faith looked as if she were possessed by the nun while talking to me. Faith paused in her confession, and along with it, the nun's. She caught her breath and the nun caught hers. Now it seemed as if the nun was the one sitting beside me, burning through me with her eyes. And Faith was more than Faith: she was reunited, doubled. The confession continued.

"My mother was a nun," the nun said to Faith, "and her mother a nun before her. She was born into the sisterhood. They all were. All nuns, who later became whores. Only I chose the habit and didn't fall to their fate, more from shame than conviction. This I honestly tell you, *menina*, because I am preparing to leave this earth. I am tired of seeing people wearing the habits of what they are not."

Faith told me how she spent entire weeks going through the Sodality's files, which were in a stiflingly hot attic. There she found letters signed by *la Xica que Manda* herself. She found account books and lists of purchases. And in that attic, behind a false wall, she found the dress. Excited, she asked for permission to display it as part of that fateful exhibit at the Research Center, which, much to her surprise, was granted. But what surprised her even further was the single condition imposed in order for her to take the dress. She must never return it to the Sodality. She must find a way to keep it, to secure a better place for its storage and care. The dress must never return to da Mercê.

The day before her departure back to Chicago, Faith returned to that attic, asking to be left alone with the dress. She caressed its soft cloth for hours, admiring its ample skirts of golden raw silk that had mysteriously stayed the passage of time. Its hard bodice was designed to refine the waistline with a braided net of strings which when tightened would hamper breathing. Faith's eyes played over its long sleeves, down to the wrist. Wings of embroidery flowed at their ends, forming the flight of a butterfly. Supporting the dress from beneath was an odd corset with a net of metal strings and leather straps. The metal was exposed, with alarming ridges of rust visible within the harness. Faith caressed these too. The metal cut her skin. Drops of blood flowed. The corset's cold dry leather sucked in each drop until it became humid and tense, as if recovering from a long drought or satiating a hunger.

"Thank you," Faith found herself saying, not entirely aware of whom she was thanking for the pleasure she felt from the scratch. She sucked on the blemish until the blood stopped flowing and then proceeded to place the dress in the box, in which it would be transported safely to the Center's keep.

The famous exhibit of emancipated slaves opened its doors at our center during the first week of November 1995. But, on October 31, while people were donning their disguises and partying in a blind celebration of that feast that the pagans left us, Faith walked alone through the hallways of the Center, attending to the final details. "Everybody was gone," she told me. With her own hands she proceeded to dress the dummy that would display the freed slave's dress. But she was unable to contain herself. The dress transformed her inexplicably. She got naked there, alone, in the cold room of the Center. She put on the embroidered hosiery, with the ribbons and undergarments. They fit her perfectly. Then she pulled the bodice over her. It was difficult to tie its braid of silk strings, but luckily they attached at the front of the dress. Down fell the leather and metal corset, which rested coldly on Faith's hips. She could not resist the temptation of wearing it bare, without any underwear on. Then she left the Center to roam the streets; and she did not return until her skin was all raw and burning. This was the first day of her ritual. This was the first night of this story that finds its end on this pale skin.

Time is a disguise, falsely convincing us that all is transitory, all perishable. But, the careful researcher is capable of discovering the continuum; of finding those small repetitions that disguise the real as passing.

Faith and I are very far from being pagans. But we work with time and its passing, the imprints it leaves in history. Now that I think about it, it is no coincidence that, before becoming a young and promising virtual researcher, I, Martín Tirado, wanted to be a priest, a shaman. Nor is it coincidence that Faith thought about dedicating her life to religion before she stumbled upon her successful career. She told me that via e-mail, after our lunch together. We are two worshippers of the past, two worshippers of the sacred and of the signs that speak of the approaching future. Through blood, *sangre*, things turn sacred. Through work, office sweat turns into sacrifice. No, it is no coincidence that both Faith and I decided to dedicate our lives to that which is sacred. I can see it clearly now. We wanted to sacrifice ourselves.

"I won a Fulbright. That is when I decided to return to the convent at Macaúbas. A year had passed since the exhibit, since the first time I wore the dress."

Faith relaxed as she told me the next part of the story, another piece of the puzzle, over our lunch. "The nun was already on her deathbed. They had taken her habit away. Her head was nearly bald with a few wispy white hairs standing up. Her coffee-colored skin was now yellow. However, her eyes were still filled with life. I wanted to tell her that I had found something miraculous. "So you saw the dress," she interrupted. "I thought they had already destroyed it. My grandmother and my mother wore that dress the day each of them was presented to society. That dress is the embodiment of sin. Arrogance. Lustfulness. It is pretty, don't you think?"

"Powerful," Faith answered.

"It is also the fastest way to lose your soul." The nun uttered her sentence, not realizing that her advice had come too late. "You should never wear it. That dress is haunted. It has drunk too much sweat and tears. They say that Xica herself wore it the day João Fernandes de Oliveira introduced her to Tejuco society. He gave a party at his estate. He invited all of the Minas Creole society. He spent hundreds of réis, all his profit of a year. He bought the yards of gold raw silk himself, sent for it from Portugal and paid three seamstresses in Rio de Janeiro to make the most wonderful dress ever seen in Brazil. An apparition in gold. João de Oliveira wanted to make a queen out of Xica, to make her luxury itself. He wanted to erase any traits of poverty and slavery. She believed in her lover and played his game. Xica learned how to walk in that dress, to wear it like a *Doña*. She believed that the dress itself would make her become accepted. But, *Menina*, you know the old saying: an ape in a cape is still an ape." The nun was drowning in her own breaths. Faith told me that a long time elapsed before the woman could resume her confession.

"Xica was João's true love, his real woman. But the laws of the times prohibited mixed marriages. No white man could marry a black slave girl. All mulatto children were therefore born slaves until their fathers recognized them, if they chose to. And João Fernandes did. Xica gave him all the children that her womb could bear, and he even accepted the children she'd born before him; they say they were from the doctor that devirginized her. He gave his name to his nine children by Xica. He took his four sons with him to Portugal and bought them titles of nobility.

But Xica remained in Minas Gerais, alone with her daughters. There were five of them, all mixed, lighter than she was, with finer features. Too beautiful to be left to Tejuco's masters and their appetites. She wanted to save them. So she hid them in convents. And that is how it all started, the story of that dress. Xica put them in convents, the girls grew up as nuns, but as they became women, Xica could not resist the temptation of presenting them to society. Times were changing, she thought. Her daughters were fair-skinned. They knew how to read and write, how to play instruments. They grew up with the fear of God. So now, maybe, a brave white Creole would dare to defy colonial laws and marry one of her daughters. And they would "pass" and be accepted into Tejuco's society. Xica's daughters would open the doors that had been shut in her face. So she organized a big party. She would take out the dress, and get it clean and lustrous again. She knew that nobody in all of Tejuco had a dress to match hers."

The nun laughed and continued. "But the very moment one of Xica's daughters wore the dress, she would go astray. They all ended up whores. Concubines; some richer, some poorer, but all illegal women. The ones whose names are never mentioned."

The nun had talked quite a lot, and she could hardly go on. Her voice was a mere murmur. "Sister, I think it is better that you rest," Faith said, wanting to comfort her. So she took the nun's hand between her own, and started stroking it, that remnant made of flesh and bones. But the nun took her hand away from Faith, with a strength that surprised her.

"Sister?"

The nun replied in fury, "I am nobody's sister. People like me had to learn how to live and die without that privilege. I am part of no family. Out there, teeth are waiting to devour me. In here, I am but the remains of a banquet of loneliness."

Faith left the convent convinced that the nun was delusional; that the story she told her about the dress was a product of her senile imagination and of an anger that had been waiting all her life to come out. She understood such anger, Faith told me, but she did not want to recognize it. "I still don't even dare to," she told me, as our lunch came to an end.

Almost a year had passed by. A year of silences, looks, and evasiveness. We had not seen each other in private since our first encounter. After that lunch date, Faith invited me to dinner. The Center had received a European grant thanks to her Salzburg presentation. She wanted to celebrate. We dined, we talked, and that was all; as if that night in her back room had never happened.

However, after that dinner, a strange thing began to happen. Faith started sending me pieces of her story—files on her—over the internet. It took me by surprise, but I could not resist reading them. Those were the only links between us. Those messages invited me to read a story from a time not so long ago. And on the nights that I found them in my email, I could do nothing but read her story, following her words on the computer screen and touching myself with my free hand. Again, I was a prisoner of that ominous hunger. Again I fell, trapped by my own curiosity. I had never felt like that for anybody else. But I knew she would free me soon.

I received a total of ten messages in three and a half weeks. Sometimes nothing came, and I would wait desperately. I would waver from desperation to patience to indifference to agony, as I waited each night in my apartment. I would savor them slowly. The one certainty is that I would never forget them. I include in this account a summary of the complete files of Faith Verdejo, the ones she sent me telling her story. Now that I reread them, I can sense that she was trying to conjure what was eating her inside, what was eating both of us, that fire.

"My mother was a novice," she wrote. "My grandmother enrolled her in a convent at twelve years of age, wanting to save her from a destiny similar to her own. So, against her only daughter's wishes, she handed her over to the nuns. At thirteen, Maria Fernanda, my mother, announced to Grandma Raquel that she wanted to take holy vows. But by the time my mother had just turned fourteen, the nuns summoned my grandmother. She had to take her daughter away from the convent under the disdainful stare of the abbess. Her daughter was pregnant, nobody knew who the father could be.

"After a great deal of effort, Mamá Raquel finally succeeded in marrying her daughter to a distant cousin, thirty years her elder. My mother moved to Caracas, from where the family had originally emigrated. I was born there, and my grandmother took care of me.

"Mamá Raquel and I lived in many places, but we ended up buying a house in Maracaibo. We settled there on my thirteenth birthday. *Abuela* decided to enroll me in a private convent school for girls. 'Let's see if you can manage to bring no shame into this house.' And she left me with the nuns. I spent the next two years following my grandmother's orders. Each time the nuns celebrated a holiday with a party or a dance, I hid in the convent. Each time a young priest came to give confession, I eluded him as best as I could. I roamed the nuns' cells.

"There I touched their habits, robes, and veils. A strange sensation came over me and, if anyone would have asked me, I could have sworn the Lord was calling upon me. But I resisted that call. I knew that if I answered, it would be the end of me.

"Other times, to escape temptations, I would hide in the school's library, to read biographies. They were my favorites, telling stories of queens and princesses trapped in monasteries where they purged their tortured souls. Or sometimes they were prisoners of their own royal families. Juana la Loca, Ana from Austria, Mary Queen of Scots, Ana de Borgoña. I would spend entire afternoons imagining their rooms, drawing maps of the chapels where they prayed, their garments, the blazons of their carriages, the colors of their flags. It was hard work, drawing those plans and maps, but it was the only way I could envision and relive those lives, be part of them and completely escape my confinement. I could have spent whole days immersed in my game. Nobody interrupted me while I was drawing.

"I wondered if anybody cared where I was, what I was doing. I lived alone in that convent for two years in my own cloistered cell — the library. I was the only black girl in the school, the only one who was not the daughter or granddaughter of a rich hacienda owner — or so I thought. I did not know of the immense fortune that my grandmother had accumulated, God only knows how.

"I wanted to be like those princesses I read about, translucent and pure, dressed in embroidered velvet and precious stones. But deep inside me I knew that such a life was not for me. I was reminded of this by my schoolmates' disdain, by the nuns' lack of interest, and by the color of my skin. That color was the map of my ancestry. And my ancestors did not wear silks or velvet. They went naked, without heralds or cloths to identify them. Their marks were worn in the bare skin — tribal scarifications, or scars from chains and branding irons of their owners. No, no cloth that covered me — no matter how sacred or profane it might be — could hide my true nature.

"Invisible, I remained at the convent. But, weeks before I turned fifteen, my grandmother sent for me. She was going to give a big party in my name.

"You have managed to become a woman, my dear Faith. And you cannot live in that nunnery forever."

"Mamá Raquel hired seamstresses, the best in Maracaibo, to sew me a dress that would surpass my wildest fantasies. I knew that dress was a prize for my loyalty. My grandmother had also thought of the best way to display it. At my party, I would be escorted by Aníbal Andrés, her best friend's godson.

"The boy's skin was the color of whole milk. He had a priest's hands, but a face unclouded and strong. He wanted to become a petroleum engineer. And just like oil, his hair was pitch black and fell against that face that exuded a sense of security and ambition. He wanted to please my grandmother, I could tell. He did not care what people said about her in Maracaibo. Aníbal Andrés danced with me the whole night of the party. He was kind and gentle.

"'That boy is going places.' Mamá Raquel whispered to me. Maybe that is why she let him walk me back to our home, without a chaperone. 'I am an old goat,' she said. 'Too tired to stay until the end of this mayhem. And besides, Faith, you have proven that you can take care of yourself.'

"However, that night I didn't know how to take care of myself in Aníbal Andrés' hands. I was the one who kissed him first. I started it, I admit it. But I was not counting on the strength of his hunger. I did not expect the forcefulness with which he grabbed at me under the dress, pulled at my underwear, and thrust in his fingers until he made me kneel down. I was not expecting the way he pinned me down to the floor while he pushed inside me, making my insides bleed and burn. I fought a little, but mainly I let him do whatever he pleased. I am not sure whether I couldn't stop him, or didn't want to.

"Aníbal Andrés didn't stop biting my nipples, scratching my thighs, and opening me wide. The worst was that I felt my body responding to each thrust of his pelvis, to each hard spank. I responded with an intense tremor that came unexpectedly from my aching vagina. I arched my back in ecstasy as I came amid the fierce bites of Aníbal Andrés the night of my fifteenth birthday."

• • •

I've taken a nap to regain my strength, but I must continue writing. I have to reveal everything, so it will finally be known. I must describe what happened between us the night of our second encounter. October 31 of last year. Again, Sam Hain.

"I am tired of emails, of this computerized confession," she wrote me, the day before Halloween. "Let me invite you to dinner. Let's talk in person. Please come tomorrow to my house. 68 Spruce. You know where it is. I'll be waiting for you."

That evening I arrived at her house at nine o'clock. Faith had prepared a lavish dinner. We sat and ate. At eleven I made the mistake of looking into her eyes again. Of kissing her. Again I ended up naked in the middle of her empty back room. Faith took out the dress. She wore its harness. I thought that this time she would not catch me off guard.

But I was not prepared for what did happen.

"Kneel before me, Martín" — I, erect, obeyed and knelt before Faith.

"Kiss my feet" — I tasted the cloth of her shoes. My tongue played with the leather straps, with its gold buttons. Then I took them off and started kissing her long, delicate toes still encased in her stockings.

"Take off my stockings" — I sat her on the chaise lounge. Suddenly I remembered how the cold corset metal would be biting into her flesh. I took my time kissing, licking every inch of her legs. I waited until the harness drew the blood it needed. Faith started showing signs of excitement. I open her legs wider, working my way up with my tongue, my fingers. I touch between her legs and find her moist and inviting. I press her legs wider apart, against the leather and metal that are hurting her, scratching

her skin and ripping it apart. I pushed
mercilessly. Then, Faith started moaning, biting her lips, holding onto the
skirt of her disguise, as if to a piece of
driftwood that will carry her ashore. I
licked between her legs, eating her up,
pressing still deeper. Then I looked up,
to see the blood oozing from her torn
flesh, I licked it too. I look at Faith,
smiling.

Faith slapped me. I grew harder, hungrier.
I was ready for the kill.

You all can imagine the rest. I went inside Faith and I pushed and
shoved until I exploded. The harness's fangs also cut into my skin. I
ended up with scratches on my legs, with my flesh torn and burning.
It was a sweet pain. As sweet as the open smile in Faith's face. That
was the last thing I saw before dozing off, Faith looking at me and
smiling. Her intense dark eyes fixed on me, on my expression of
total bliss and exhaustion. I fell next to her. The chaise lounge was
not wide enough, so we both found rest on the cold floor. I cannot
say how many hours I slept. The next thing I knew is that I woke up,
and Faith was already dressed. She was wearing a loose chemise. "It's
late," she said. "I must rest, so please, don't get me wrong, but you'd
better leave."

October is almost gone. Tonight is the 31st, the night of our third encounter. Outside, in the crisp autumn air, filling Chicago's streets,
groups of small children go from door to door dressed as pirates, superheroes, or witches and warlocks. This is what is left of the ancient
holiday of Sam Hain. These disguises made of plastic, impermeable
to any fusion of spirit and skin. The great ritual of Sam Hain, which
then mutated into Feralin and Pomona's festival, is now simply Halloween. Time has once again hidden away the connection between
death and renewal—what must be sacrificed in order to welcome a

new cycle. However, such connection endures, survives under the plastic disguises.

It endures even though the Christian Church did all it could to finish with Sam Hain. It conspired to turn October 31 into an empty holiday. After the fall of the Roman Empire, the Church, now Roman and Catholic, changed the ancient calendars. It abolished the 1st of November as the start of the New Year. Instead it turned the date into *Día de Todos los Santos*, All Saints' Day; All Martyrs Day, I should point out. And then, it came up with a new holiday. November 2 became the Day of the Dead: *Día de los Muertos*.

All Saints' Day and the Day of the Dead. That was the final turn time took to return to Halloween. But, the careful researcher knows that under the plastic disguises and the mindless parties, Sam Hain is celebrated once again. Sam Hain, Faith, and its disguises. History once again giving the impression of change and mutability, but remaining the same; repeating itself, time and time again, until it retells the sacred tale of its origins.

A bunch of kids knock at my door. I finish dressing up and rush to open it. I wear a white shirt, freshly pressed. My dark pants are neatly starched and cover my previous nakedness. I dress in Faith's attire, similar to what she wears every day for work. This is the disguise of Faith Verdejo, the museum curator. Faith the slave is dressed in another disguise. I cannot wait to see her. Outside my door, a Spiderman, a witch on her broom, a Frankenstein, and a huge Pumpkin head sing, "Trick or treat, Halloween, *tiene dulces?*"

They ask for money and sweets, half in English, half in Spanish. The two languages of our most powerful empires. Such is the ritual. The children laugh and scream in joy. Two grown-ups accompany them, making sure all is safe. I think they are two mothers who live on a lower floor of my apartment building. One of them is from apartment 6C. I am prepared for the occasion. Next to the door a huge plate filled with candy awaits them. I fill their bags and their plastic pumpkin containers with the sweet bounty they are asking for. The kids rush to unwrap my candies, eat them up. Hungrily.

"Come on kids, I told you to wait until we got home," a mother admonishes them.

"You cannot eat all that candy."

"My grandmother told me some people put needles into the bubblegum to trick kids into swallowing them. Or that they spray gummy bears with rat poison," one of them chimed in.

"Well, I don't know about that," said the mother. "but still we have to make sure. Don't you agree, sir?"

I closed the door, smiling at the kids and their mothers, but still could hear one of them: "Be patient now. There are crazy people who enjoy hurting innocent children." I cannot but ask myself, "Crazy people? Innocent people? Who is innocent and who is crazy in this world?"

I hear the kids running down the hallway, away from my door. Next to it I have put my cape, my mask, and my sword. I'll cross the city dressed as a knight. That way, I will raise no suspicion. It is said that tonight another door opens between the world of the living and the world of the dead. Present, past, and future merge into one. Our ancestors will knock at that door, coming to meet us, revealing the sacred signs. Today is the day to watch their signs flow in mid-air. To interpret and relive their stories. Only then we will be free to embody our future.

Faith waits for me. I check on the clothes that cover my naked, hungry body. The mere contact of my hands make me shiver. But I understand why. My hands belong to Faith. They are her hands, touching me, promising me more caresses, more pleasure, and more pain. It is she who tightens my leather belt, she who brushes clean the tips of my shoes. The hands of Faith the freed slave. Faith and her multiple hands: Francisca's, Diamantina's, Mariana's. It is Faith's body, which will soon welcome me, open and torn, she who will kneel before me, to kiss me, to lick me clean. I am pale and pure because Faith made me so. Faith bleeds for it and pays her tribute. Faith forgets her scars to become the Eternal Mistress, the Ancestral Seductress.

I need her to become so. My existence depends on it. So we switch roles and then I become the stained one, the humiliated one. She drives me to my knees. I offer my bleeding flesh so she can feed on it, bite me between my legs until I scream. From pleasure, from pain? Who knows and who cares? I only care to become a sibling to her flesh. To share a common ancestry with her. To carry her scars and drink her blood. To wear her and become one. Then we will both be rid of our disguises, or transcend them and reunite through time.

In short, I will close my door and walk away from my apartment, maybe forever. I will call the elevator and patiently wait until it stops at the seventh floor. Maybe this will be the last time I'll engage in such simple matters. Several days ago, I received Faith's last email.

"Please, come and meet me again. This time we will carry the ritual to its end," she wrote. Then time stood still. Days went by where I found no reason to return to the Center. Most probably I've been fired by now. But only one thing overcame me, the urge to write down this tale. To leave it all behind. It's been a week since I began awaiting October 31. "This time we'll reach the limit," she wrote. "We'll meet on All Hallows' Eve, and be together until the Day of the Dead. Please, say yes. I need you to say yes."

I accept and obey. I will enter the back room, naked, and I will lay on the antique chaise and wait until Faith appears in her disguise. The moment is here, I will say to myself, and abandon my body to its destiny.

Who will survive the ritual tonight? Who will remain by November 2? I honestly cannot tell. But I hope it will be Faith.

This is the third Halloween I spend with Faith Verdejo. She will cut me open and blend with me. I am a prisoner of her game, a slave to her disguise. I need her revelations. I am no longer afraid. I don't want it any other way. I will reach her house at nine o'clock tonight. Faith will already be wearing her dress, naked. And she will become Xica da Silva; she will be the Haitian courtesan of Henri Christophe's Court. She will become all those dark women who turned powerful through fate, but who still could not escape their place in time. I will become her Master and her catch; her slave and her sacrifice. Because she needs that open flesh to free herself from the open wound. And only I can help her do that. Only I, Martín Tirado, who submits to the horror and the bliss of sharing her scar. I will undress and await her signal.

I will wait for the sign.
Faith will slap me in the face.
I will arise from my knees and stand in front of her.

> "Be good now, *reina*, open your mouth and suck it in until you cannot breathe."

Faith will look at me smiling, daring me,
with her closed mouth.
I'll take her by the neck, pulling her curls,
pushing myself against her mouth until she opens it.
Faith licks me.

> "That's it, *bella*, do what I say. Suck me slowly."

Faith follows my orders. I have to remain calm, collected.
Allow her to enjoy my pleasure until the right moment.
When she's almost overcome with heat,

> "This is what you really like, isn't it?"

I will slap it against her face. I know that below, her harness will be cutting her deeply.

> "Now, get up from that chaise."

I'll take Faith by the arm and place her against the back of the chaise.
Faith will let herself be guided.
I'll lift her skirt and pull at the harness.
Its leather will cut deeper into her skin, restricting her breathing.
Faith's hips will be filled with tiny cuts and bruises.
With tiny scars. New ones are forming. Under the blemishes I will see blood spurting as red as anyone's; skin tissue, pale and pink, just as we all are underneath.

> "Open up, let me in."

Faith will moan gently and part her legs with her own hands.

I'll enter the sweet heat of her exposed flesh.
Go in and out of the soft maze between her legs.
In front, on her back.
Faith will tighten around me until I pour against her harness.

> We'll sleep; exhausted.
> And then we'll start again.

We will repeat this encounter time and time again. And then one of us will pull out the sword I carry. I don't know if it will be me. I hope it will be Faith. But the sacrifice must be completed so one of us will draw the sword. One of us will cut into the other's disguise. One will draw out more blood. And Faith will look at me, gratefully, lovingly.

I would look at her the same way. Flesh will open and blood will fall on the cold floor.

> And it will burn on our sacrificial fire. We will start cutting, methodically, attentively, looking for the hidden signals. The ritual requires it. Then we will be revealed.

Sensually Yours

Sofía Quintero

t hat's what I'm talking about!" said Vivacious Vicky. She stumbled to her feet and snatched The Next Best Thing out of my hand. "I need at least eight inches, baby," she slurred, waving the dildo in one hand and sloshing around her fifth glass of sangria with the other.

I took the dildo from her and handed it to her cousin, then my hostess, Lusty Liz. "That's right, Vivacious," I said, and the other dozen guests laughed. "Eight inches of SensaSkin that feels just like the real thing." Having never used it, I sneaked a glance at my inky copy of the Sensually Yours catalog. "It comes in your choice of three lifelike colors—peach, caramel, and espresso." I glanced at my manager, Wendy, who wore a tight frown on her face. What did I do wrong?

Liz grazed her fingers across the dildo's shaft and then gasped. "Oh, my God, it does feel like the real thing." She handed it to Climaxing Corrine. Or was she Cummin' Corrine? Almost three hours had inched by since we played the introductory name game, and between the heels on my leather boots and those thigh-smothering low-rise jeans, my legs were about to give. Wendy always said, "The trick is to dress sexy enough so that customers think *She can have whoever she wants*, yet not so sexy that they worry *She wants MY man*." Easier said than done. At least I allowed myself the comfort of a sage cable-knit sweater. With the exception of the jeans, the outfit was not much different than what I might have worn to school on an administrative day when the students had the day off. In fact, this was one of the reasons why I loved working for Sensually Yours; it gave me a reason to dress up, put on makeup, and actually leave the house.

I always came close to running out of sexy adjectives that start with C, M, T, and S, especially in a roomful of Black and Latina guests. Too many Tanyas and Teresas, Marias and Moniques, Sandras, Sondras, Sonyas, and Sonias. That was why I developed *The Sensually Yours Dirty Dictionary* that won me Representative of the Month within ninety days of joining the company. When The Next Best Thing reached Cherise, I remembered. She was Climaxing Cherise. Corrine was Cummin' Corrine. OK.

Cherise ran her elegant fingers along the vein of The Next Best Thing. "Oh, this is lovely," she said, as if fondling a mink stole. "How much is this again?"

"It's only seventy-nine, ninety-five," I said, finally earning a smile from Wendy, who was sitting in the corner against the wall in one of the chairs strung with red and white helium balloons. Although Valentine's Day remained several weeks away, I appreciated that Liz had chosen that motif. Valentine's Day would be tough for me, but it had to be much easier than Christmas was.

Vicky yelled, "I don't give a fuck how much it costs. I'm buying that shit." She raised her sangria glass in the air as if to seal her commitment with a toast. "I'm buying that shit and getting rid of fuckin' Johnny." Everyone laughed, and she shot the crowd a dirty look. "Y'all think I'm kidding, but I'm not."

Liz finally grabbed Vicky by the wrist and yanked her down on the sofa beside her. It was about time she reigned in her cousin. First, the party had started ridiculously late because Liz begged me to wait for Vicky. "She really needs this party," she said. She finally showed forty-five minutes later thanks to a fight with the soon-to-be-replaced Johnny. Then, even though I repeatedly told her to keep the refreshments light—chips and salsa, cheese and crackers, maybe finger sandwiches—Liz cooked a huge vat of *arroz con gandules* and even a pan of lasagna. Although I suggested to the guests that they fix themselves a plate and take their seats, Liz insisted that I let them eat, drink, and gossip before starting my presentation. I was halfway through the lingerie section of my presentation when four of her guests stood up to leave for one reason or another. Of course, they all vowed to call me with their orders. I couldn't help but think, *Where have I heard that before?*

The nightmare finally ended at a quarter after midnight, but Liz still had about ten guests who hung in there until the end. They even applauded me. A few had additional questions about the products, which was always a good sign. I said that I would be happy to answer any and all questions when they came to place their orders in the privacy of Liz's bedroom. "And remember, ladies, your fabulous hostess needs enough credit to buy the Love Swing," I added. "Don't leave her hanging." They giggled at my pun, and Wendy followed me as I retreated into the master bedroom.

Wendy was the first one to develop her own website to sell the products. She generates a thousand dollars every month from the site alone, in addition to the commission she earns on our sales. I was one of fifteen Sensually Yours consultants she managed in the Bronx-Westchester County area. Once I was working to be like Wendy, a confident, successful SY representative, instead of what I had become: a cuckolded divorcée desperate to sell well to make ends meet.

Before I could close the door and ask Wendy for her feedback on my presentation, she said, "Look, I'm going to head out now so you can take care of business, and we'll talk tomorrow when you call me with your numbers."

"Aren't you going to stay and watch me take orders?"

"No, sweetie, it's really late," she said, brushing her dirty blond bangs out of her light brown eyes. "Just call me tomorrow. At about eleven, OK?"

"As usual."

I waited for her to say more, but Wendy just gave me a hug and left the bedroom. She didn't have a single encouraging word for me? This was bad. I knew I needed to change something because after a fantastic start, I had hit a slump. A slump so bad that I had failed to meet the sales minimum in December, even though Christmastime was Sensually Yours' best season. And as easy as it would have been to blame Mike, my soon to be ex-husband, for that, I refused. If anything, I tried to use what he did to motivate me. I had no choice.

But with Valentine's Day—our second best selling opportunity—only weeks away, I had pleaded for Wendy to come to one of my January parties, watch my presentation, and give me tips for improvement. Before Valentine's Day arrived, I had to know if despite my enthusiastic delivery, my potential customers could still see the shattered heart dangling from my sleeve.

For now I had to put all that aside. I didn't know what Wendy was going to say to me the next morning when I called her, but I had this final opportunity yet to prove my worth. Nothing would soften the criticism like major sales.

I walked over to the bed and unpacked everything I needed from my duffel bag. Order forms. Booklets of X-rated coupons for customers who buy over a hundred dollars' worth of products. A small basket of cash 'n' carry items—tubes of flavored lubricant, four-ounce bottles of Chipper Dipper Erection Crème, an array of edible panties, little paddles in black and red leather, and assorted palm-sized vibrators that the company has discontinued—for those ladies who couldn't wait two weeks for their goodies and want something to take home tonight.

As I always did when I set out the tools of my trade, I felt optimistic. Every customer out there was going to whip out her credit card and order at least two hundred dollars' worth of lingerie, videos, and toys. Together they were going to give Liz and the husband she banished to the pool hall down the street for the night a Love Swing for Valentine's Day.

I hurried to the door and swung it open. "Who's my first victim?" I yelled down the corridor. Liz's drunken cousin Vicky ambled toward me, and the cash register in my head rang. "Hi, Vivacious," I teased.

Vicky stumbled into the bedroom, and I locked the door behind her. "I've been to four of these parties, Mireya, and this one was the best." She plopped herself on the bed next to me and handed me her crumpled order form. "I went to one last month at my co-worker's house, and the girl who did that party?" She hissed, and I tried to discreetly step away from the sangria-soaked spray. "She was all formal and shit. And she only played one game. And she hardly gave away anything."

Funny, I had heard about sales representatives like that before. Every time I coaxed a name out of the guest and checked into it, the same consultant always seemed to have made a killing. Maybe my recent sales slump was because I'm too much of a girlfriend, and the guests took me for granted, especially *mis hermanas*.

"Thank you, Vicky," I said as I hold out my hand for her crumpled order form. "I'm always thrilled to hear that guests had fun during my presentation."

"I had a great time." Vicky handed me the form. "I gotta question for you, Mireya."

I smoothed out the order form, and my stomach sank. I forced myself to smile as I say, "So you want the thigh-high stockings in white. One size or queen?" *That's it? After all that fuckin' talk, that's all you're going to buy? Your cousin holds up the party for almost an hour for your drunken ass, and you repay her with a buck fifty credit?*

"How do they run again?" Vicky asked as she attempted to scratch a sudden itch between her shoulder blades.

"The one size fits up to one hundred and fifty pounds."

"OK, give me those." She gave up on the itch and shimmied her shoulders, her breasts jiggling under her deep cut halter top. "And what I wanted to ask you was which of those, um, fear-moan perfumes smells like Chantilly?"

"Choice smells like Chantilly, Orgasmic smells like Opium, and Shameless smells like Shalimar," I recited. At this point, I wanted to get rid of Vicky before a guest with a *real* order decided that she, too, must leave and promise to call me over the weekend or give Liz her order at work on Monday. I just knew that Climaxing Cherise or Masturbating Melinda were fixing to plunk their credit cards down for a Love Swing or the Domme Diva Deluxe Kit. I just needed to get this cheap lush the hell out of here. *Sell, Mireya, sell.* "So which pheromone perfume do you want, Vicky?" I poised my pen over the corresponding line on her order form.

"I used to like Chantilly a lot, but mmm . . ." Vicky waved her hand as if to shoo away the impulse. "You know what? Just give me a tube of the Slide Inside." Vicky eyeballed my hand as I drew a line across the forty dollar perfume on her order form. "And how much is that?" Now she was gunning for an itch at the back of her neck.

How did I know she would ask me that? Even though Sensually Yours carried six different flavors of the Slide Inside, I just marked *Plain* on her order form. "It comes to twenty-three dollars before tax and shipping."

"Mmm . . . I don't think . . ." Vicky stood up and dug into the front pocket of her *chocha*-choking jeans, and not to tweeze out a credit card, I knew.

Damn it, I should have known she was full of shit. People who think that only men brag crudely about their sexual appetites and prowess clearly have never attended a sex-toy party filled with drunk and horny women. There was always a Vicky or two who went on and on about needing a dick the size of a small jet only to buy thigh-highs; lubricant, and all that other crap sold at any CVS.

Speak from your own experience, Wendy's voice echoed in my head. Ordinarily, this was where I would say something like, "Let me tell you, Vicky. That pheromone perfume's like a magic potion. Sensually Yours gave all us representatives samples to try before we added it to the catalog, and I swear to God, my husband jumped me the second I walked through the door."

But I didn't want to say it. When I had returned home from the sales rally in New Jersey one Saturday, I had found Mike sitting in the living room. Before I could even unpack the newest additions to my sample case to show him, he'd leaped on me and carried me to the sofa. After spending over four hours licking edible oils off my wrist and trying on vibrating panties over my jeans, I was more than ready for a vigorous fuck. As soon as Mike wrangled my jeans over my feet, I scampered onto my knees facing the back of the sofa. I felt a quick singe across my ass and heard the rip of my thong as Mike yanked it aside. With one hand on my shoulder and the other on my hip, he plunged into me grunting like a bear until I screamed so loud I thought the neighbors would call 9-1-1. And that was just my first climax of the night.

We eventually ended up on the carpet, and as I lay with my head against his sweaty chest, I asked Mike if he had noticed my new perfume. He said yes, and I laughed. "It works!"

"What works?"

"Our new pheromone perfume." I described the product to him, practicing my sales pitch.

Mike stroked his stubbly cheek as he always did when debating whether or not to speak his mind. I used to bug him to shave because I hated the way his beard hid his lopsided grin. Only when he went for the bank manager promotion did Mike finally do away with that ugly beard. "I don't need some damn hormone cologne to jump you," he said. "I jumped you because it's a Saturday, and you've been gone since seven-thirty this morning."

I gently pinched his side. "Ah, but you said you noticed my new perfume."

"That was while I was fucking you," Mike said. "That's not what made me want to fuck you." Then he got up, grabbed his T-shirt and sweatpants and started to leave. "I don't need some potion to make me want to fuck my wife." At the time I shrugged it off and, like I said, I often told that story to sell the SY pheromone perfumes. Only the first half, of course, but I don't even say that much now.

Vicky wrinkled her noise as if a foul smell had suddenly crept into the bedroom. "*Ay, no.* I don't want Johnny on me like that."

"Sounds like you might need The Next Best Thing after all," I said, hoping she would make good on her earlier declaration. "Would you like it in peach, caramel, or espresso?"

She unfolded her palm, revealing a knot of cash. "I don't got enough for that. See, that's why I was fighting with Johnny. He wouldn't give me his fuckin' credit card."

Before she could say more—because she would if I let her—I said, "With the shipping and handling and tax, that'll be twenty-five dollars and ninety-seven cents." Even if she had had twenty-five hundred dollars to spend, I didn't want to listen to that shit.

"Uh oh." Vicky unwound the knot in her hand to reveal a twenty and a five. "I'm short."

Nowhere near as much as I was right then. It took my all not to just snatch the bills from her hand. Instead I held out my hand and say, "Don't worry about it."

"You sure, Mireya? 'Cause I can just ask Liz to lend me a dollar."

"No, it's OK," I said as I tore off her copy of the order form and folded it. I handed her the order form along with my business card. "Thank you for placing an order." I stood up and walked to the door. "It should arrive in two weeks."

As Vicky was about to head out, she stopped and looked at me. "Ay, I should throw my own party, *verdad?*"

"*Pero claro que sí,*" I said. "*Tú lo mereces.*" And it's not just a sales pitch. I truly believed it. Every woman deserved sexual pleasure, and this was one reason why I came to work for Sensually Yours. Mike and I had had a fantastic sex life, and we hadn't needed the extra income so I was more taken with the opportunity to teach other women that they were entitled to skin-blushing orgasms and how to get them. But then I put Mike out, and he took two-thirds of the household income with him. Now that I *had* to do this to make ends meet, I almost forgot how much joy it used to give me to sell these products.

"Nah, I'll pass," said Vicky. "I would just invite everybody that was here tonight."

"Well . . . Johnny's gonna love you in those thigh-highs." Of course, I had a response to her excuse, but I had lost the will to sell.

A half hour later, with only about thirty-two additional dollars in massage oil sales to my name, I was ready to end the disastrous night. I asked my hostess to call me a cab.

Not only did Liz honor my request, she fixed me a heaping serving of lasagna, walked me downstairs, and gave me a hug. When my cab arrived, she said good-bye and made her way back to her apartment building. As I heaved my suitcase of samples into the back seat of the cab, I overheard her on her cell phone.

"Hey, honey . . . The party was great, Mireya rocks! . . . Yes, you can come home now." Liz giggled and said, "Now!"

The cab pulled away from the curb, and I thought back to the night when this side gig became a necessary hustle. Not that long ago, after three hours of describing how to achieve firmer erections, wetter pussies, and lasting orgasms, I myself would rush home hot, throbbing, soaked. All that changed two weeks before Christmas.

Mike had told me to cancel the party. "Look out there," he said as he pointed out the icy window. A half hour into the storm, and the snow had only dusted the street.

"Only the hostess cancels the party," I said as I stuffed a stack of the holiday edition of the Sensually Yours catalog into my duffel bag. "This is one of our busiest seasons, Mike, what with people feeling romantic and generous. A little snow's not going to keep most people away."

"It may not be bad now, but no one's going anywhere because they're to get stranded," he said. "Just call the woman and reschedule for another day."

"I'm booked solid through Valentine's Day." I had a party every Friday and Saturday night as well as Sunday afternoon. Hell, on two Saturdays in January, I had scheduled two parties—one in the afternoon and another in the evening. At that point, I booked more parties than Wendy had. "Besides, the hostess is one of your co-workers, and she's been planning this party since Halloween. No way can I call Tanisha and say I'm not coming." Tanisha was a teller at Mike's branch. Before I began selling Sensually Yours, Mike's co-workers barely remembered my name or job. Although they were never impolite, they constantly referred to me as "Michael's wife." Then I broke out my catalogs while sitting in the bleacher's during a boring softball game against Washington Mutual and became Mireya, everyone's patron sex goddess.

I zipped up the duffel and flung it over my shoulder. I planted a kiss on Mike's pout and said, "I promise I won't linger." Then I grasped the handle of my Sensually Yours suitcase and wheeled it toward our bedroom door. Mike didn't budge to pull on his sweater or boots. "You're giving me a ride, aren't you?"

"No, I'm not fuckin' going out there."

"Don't be that way." The man was acting like a teenager whose girlfriend wouldn't give him a blow job. "You know when I get home, it'll be all about you." It always was.

Mike kicked his legs onto the bed, grabbed the remote, and turned on a football game. "Just go do your party, Mia." He only called me Mia when he was horny, sorry, or pissed off.

"Fine." I grabbed my suitcase and marched out the door. He muttered something about how I'd rather go out in a blizzard to talk about fucking with a bunch of women I didn't know than to stay home than actually do it with my husband. The man was whining as if I refused him left and right when the truth was I usually initiated, waiting for him in our bedroom in the latest camisole and thong set while waving the latest gadget added to the Sensually Yours line. As if the extra cash and major discounts on all the products weren't enough benefits, Sensually Yours offered great incentives to its sales reps that I always shared with my husband. "You weren't complaining when I took us on that cruise," I shouted, referring to the prize I had earned by selling twelve thousand dollars worth of merchandise in three months.

I heard Mike stomp toward our bedroom door. He threw it open and charged down the hallway yelling, "Don't throw that in my face. I never asked you to take me on any goddamn cruise." He reaches me and says, "You spent most of the time in your so-called professional workshops anyway."

Of course, Mike was exaggerating, but I never engaged him when he acted out like this. "I'm not going to make myself late arguing with you about this," I said. "We'll discuss it when I come home." He just glared at me as I wheeled my bag out the door.

It took me almost twenty-minutes to wave down a cab. I piled my wares into the backseat, and the driver started to plow through the thickening snow. Just a few minutes and little progress later, my cell phone rang. It disappointed me for a second to learn it wasn't Mike calling to apologize and wish me a successful presentation. It was my hostess Tanisha calling to see if I was en route. I flipped open my phone and said, "Don't worry, honey, I'm on my way."

"Oh." She didn't sound relieved. "You are?"

"Of course. What? You don't want me to."

"I do, but it's just that everyone's been calling to cancel out on me."

"Everybody?"

Tanisha chuckled. "Not everybody. Only the people that have manners."

"You told them that you were thinking of canceling the party?"

"Hell, no! If it were up to me we'd have it. You know how long I've been looking forward to this, Mireya."

"Yeah, honey, I do."

"I was just going to say, OK, we'll just push it back an hour to give people time to get here. But everybody's calling me to say they can't come because their car's snowed in or whatever. So I was hoping to catch you before you left."

"Well, I'm in the cab . . ." I glance at her address in my hand and notice that her apartment number is two. "Do you live in a building?"

"No, I'm on the second floor of a private house." So much for asking her how many of her invited guests lived in her building. "I'm sorry, Mireya, I don't want you to go through all that trouble getting here, and then nobody shows, you know. I'm so sorry."

"*M'ija*, stop apologizing. You don't control the weather." I cursed Mother Nature for us both. Poor Tanisha had prepared for weeks for this party, and I had argued with my husband over it. "We'll just reschedule."

"You sure?"

"Of course! I'll save a slot for you around Mother's Day. Everyone's probably just as disappointed as you are so they won't dream of missing that one. It'll be even better than this was going to be."

"You're fantastic, Mireya."

I laughed and said, "Yeah, well, tell that to my husband." My husband who was at home lying in bed and pouting like a little boy because I wouldn't let him have his way, I thought. My adorable husband who knew how to moisten that pout and nuzzle it between my legs just right. Who would be surprised and pleased when I returned home and crawled naked under the covers next to him. Of course, Mike would pretend to still be angry with me for venturing out into the cold instead of staying home with him. But then I would seize the remote and make him wrestle me for it. Then he would lunge for the remote while winding his hips in between my thighs, rubbing his hardening cock against my moistening pussy until I flung the remote across the room, and he yanked his sweatpants down to his knees and plunged his thick rod into my pulsating cunt over and over and over again.

I apologized to Mother Nature and told the cab driver, "Never mind. Take me back home."

It took about forty-five minutes for us to slosh back through the snow and back to my building. I rushed in, ready to make peace then love with my husband. A moan hit me the second I opened the apartment door and stepped into the long hallway that ran past our living room toward the bedroom. Then I heard another. The moan of a young girl too eager to please, too easily impressed. An insincere moan. One of Mike's pornos. The one thing we didn't sell at Sensually Yours to steer clear of state obscenity laws. It made my clit tingle as I crept down the hallway. "Oh, yeah, oh, yeah . . ." When I reached our bedroom door, I stripped off my blouse and slacks and kept on my leather knee-high boots. I cracked open the door. I wanted to spy on Mike for a few moments as he watched the porno and ran his oiled fist up and down his rigid cock. I slipped one hand down the front of my panties to finger my swollen clit and planted the other on the door frame. "God, yeah, oh . . ." Only with my ear so close to the door did I realize that the moans were not coming from a porn flick playing on the TV. They were young, eager, impressed. And they were live.

I crack open the door. "Oh, God, yeah . . ." My husband was kneeling on the bed with his back to me, his caramel ass sweaty, pumping. She had one of her thin, pasty legs hiked upon his left shoulder while the other sprawled out to the side like a popsicle stick that had been sucked clean and then tossed aside. She fingered the large, rosy nipples on her floury tits as her eyes darted between gazing up at Mike with an appreciative lust and staring at his dark shaft as it slid in and out of her waxed pussy as if she couldn't believe he was fucking her. "Yeeah, oh, yeah . . ."

Lightheaded with my own disbelief, I steadied myself by leaning against the doorframe. "Uh, oh, yeah, uh." She jerked, and Mike clamped his brown hand on her white ankle. I looked at his other hand as it dangled by his sinewy thigh and saw the wire. Then I caught the glimpse of blue riding Mike's shaft as he fucked that skinny bitch, and I finally heard the whirring beneath her moans and his heavy breathing. I peered and saw the nub of the cock ring as it flicked up against her glossy clit. "Oooh, yeah, yeah . . ."

My husband was fucking the building whore. She was a skinny peroxide blonde barely into her twenties who lived in the apartment across the hall. I had seen her greet underage delivery boys in sheer undershirts and overheard her make suggestive remarks to my married neighbors in the elevator. And now Mike was fucking her in our bed. Fucking her with one of the vibrating cock rings that I sell. The same cock ring that I bought for us with my twenty-five percent discount.

If I had been dressed, I would have barged screaming into the room. I would have attacked her first simply because I knew my chance at Mike would come once she finally escaped. But I wouldn't let her leave with her clothes, snatching up her buckle-back thongs and jersey dress and flinging them out onto the snowy fire escape. And if she refused to flee without them, I would drag her scrawny, naked ass into the hallway of our floor and spike the blue vibrating cock ring into her face.

But I wasn't dressed. I was standing there in the hallway in my bra and panties. My nipples were still hard and the crotch of my panties was drenched.

"Oh, yeah, I'm cummin', oh, oh, ooooh, yeeeaah . . ."

I backed away from the door and scooped up my clothes. Just as I had undressed while creeping down the hallway, I put on my clothes again as I walked back to the front door. I grabbed my jacket and purse and left the apartment, leaving my Sensually Yours suitcase and duffel in the hallway so that Mike would know that while that slut came, his wife left.

"Mireya," my sister called through the door as she knocked. "Are you awake?" I was, but I didn't answer. I had been lying awake in the dark for hours.

I heard my sister say, "Mami, I think she's asleep. Yeah, she's been sleeping a lot." Her voice faded as she moved away from the door.

I sat up in the futon in my sister's guest room, reached for the remote and clicked on the television. The screen illuminated the darkened room. Why was it so dark already? I looked to the clock on the night table. It was only a little after five, but it seemed much closer to eight in the evening. As my eyes adjusted to the dark, the outline of my Sensually Yours suitcase materialized. I couldn't even remember when I had gone back for it or why. Then I remembered I had a party that night in East Harlem in about two hours. How was I going to get there from Central Islip? Perhaps my sister would let me borrow her car or at least give me a ride to the railroad station.

I flicked through the channels until I found a weather forecast. The forecaster was gorgeous, with deep brown eyes and broad shoulders. When he pointed to the map at the impending snowstorm, I noticed the meatiness of his palm. Why had no one investigated the possible correlation between the thickness of a man's hands and that of his dick? To think like this when I had just left Mike, maybe I wasn't so pathetic after all.

Still I clicked off the television, rolled over, and buried my face under the comforter. With only the money in my pocketbook and the clothes on my back, I had walked out of the apartment a week ago. I'd trekked through the snow to the subway station and taken the train to Grand Central. From there I'd jumped on the next train to Central Islip, only calling my sister to come get me when I arrived. On an ordinary day, the trip would have taken two and half hours from door to door. Because of the blizzard, it took me four.

Mike located me a few days later at my sister's place, and he would not stop calling. After giving up on calling me on my cell phone, he packed the voicemail box at the number I rented just for Sensually Yours. He must have found it on a stray catalog or business card. Eventually, I had to go home, so I left him a single message at the apartment while he was at the bank. "Michael? Mireya. I'm not coming back to the apartment until you leave."

I didn't want to think about him. I should have been preparing for the party I had in two hours. Release some tension. Get festive. Feel sexy. I tried to think about the weatherman with his wide shoulders and thick palms. Yeah, that was what I needed. I reached down under the covers and fingered the crotch of my fraying bikini panties. Even though I couldn't see them in the dark room, I remembered which ones they were. Instead of one of dozens of vibrantly colored thongs with jeweled buckles and boy-leg briefs with the lace panels that I had bought for myself from Sensually Yours, I was wearing a pair of old frayed bikini panties that Mike had bought for me.

I remembered when he bought them. We hadn't managed to save enough money for a long weekend in Barbados for vacation so instead we just took an overnight trip to Water Works in New Jersey. On the way back one night we decided to get a bite to eat. I had wanted to change out of my bathing suit but didn't want to head back to the hotel. So I had Mike drive us to the nearest drug store. Once we pulled into the parking lot, I begged him to go inside and buy me a tank top, shorts, and underwear. Of course, he pitched a fit. "I'm soaking wet, honey," I said, already planning our rendezvous. "The AC's going to be blasting in there, and I don't want to get sick. The last thing you want is for me to get sick, right?" Mike relented and quickly returned with a package of Hanes bikini underwear—three pairs in white, black, and red. He opened the car door to find me in the backseat. I'd move back there presumably to change my clothes. At my request, he ripped open the package of underwear and pulled out the red pair. When Mike turned to hand them to me, however, he found me with my knees splayed open and my denim miniskirt hiked around my waist. I stroked my sweaty clit and purred, "I'm still soaked." After a quick glance around the parking lot, Mike climbed over the seat. When he tried to lower himself onto me, however, I planted my bare foot against his chest. "Sit back," I ordered.

He did as I ordered and I crawled over to him. I reached down and pulled his chocolatey rod over the waistband of his swimming trunks. When I drew his cock into my watering mouth and slithered my tongue around its spongy head, I could smell the chlorine of the amusement park. This made me smile, and I said, "You'll always be my favorite ride."

Mike said, "Don't stop, Mia." And for that I teased him by only flicking circles around the tip of his dick. He growled with the pleasure of frustration, craning his hips towards my face to slide his cock deeper into my mouth. I felt his fingers graze the back of my neck than press gently down on my head. "Damn, you suck my cock just right," he said, and as if to prove him right, I tightened my grip around his shaft and bobbed my head over it like the caramel stick I had savored earlier at the water park. I felt his hand slide down the cheeks of my ass until his fingers dipped into my slippery cunt. I slowly sucked and yanked at Mike's cock, matching my pace with the rhythm of his breath, and soon my salivating lips were ramming against my knuckles. "Oh, Mia, Mia, Miaaaaa!" my husband cried as he coated my throat with his bitter jism.

"Dammit, Mike!" My sister yelled. I shot up in bed, my fingers still wedged inside my worn panties. "Mireya'll talk to you whenever she feels damned good and ready!"

I threw back the covers and rush to the bedroom door. I flung it open to see my sister's shadow swing across the floor as she pace in the kitchen. "Yeah, well, you should've talked to your wife before you started fucking the *puta* across the hallway." The loud clack of the receiver hitting the base echoed through the hallway, and I closed the door.

I walked to the night table and picked up my cell phone. As I searched for my hostess's number, I debated what plausible excuse I could give her for canceling at the last minute. There was a storm brewing, but it had yet to start. I could tell her I was stranded in Long Island where I had come to see my sister. I came out to Long Island to see my sister because of a family emergency. Or I could simply say that I had had a family emergency. Yeah, that would be the half truth I would tell.

And as I called my hostess, I cursed Mike. He had won. He'd finally made me cancel a party.

After that, I promised myself to never cancel another party for such a pathetic reason. And I kept that promise, but my sales just weren't the same. I could have sworn that I wasn't doing anything differently from before the breakup of my marriage, but my numbers indicated otherwise. After the third party where my hostess failed to sell enough to earn credit, my manager Wendy wanted to know what the hell was going on with me. Only then did I ask her to come to Liz's party to see if she couldn't tell me that very thing. I felt terrible that she had to find someone else to cover one of her own parties to make it to mine, but I had become desperate.

The morning after Liz's party, Wendy called me to receive the night's tallies. She had been in the business only two years but made almost forty grand and was considering leaving her day job as a dental receptionist to sell Sensually Yours full-time. Wendy had started selling for the company at the age of forty-one, when her husband left her for a woman young enough to be their daughter. "I did it to pay my bills and get a life," she told me when she recruited me at a co-worker's bachelorette party. "That was going to be my revenge." I wanted it to be mine, too, but I was off to a horrific start.

"So how'd it go last night?"

"Another bust."

"C'mon, you're exaggerating." I recounted the nightmare from the numerous delays to the constant disruptions of the shit-talking

Vicky. "OK, your first mistake was to give in to the hostess and not start the party on time."

"I know," I said like a reprimanded child. "But when I don't wait, the hostess always pressures me to start over again for all the people who come late."

"Well, too bad. Liz should've gotten her guests there on time. If she has to tell them it starts an hour earlier than it actually does, so be it. Did you ask her to do that?"

"Yes, and she did. We were only waiting for Vicky. And you saw when Melinda asked me to show Vicky the Tantalizer, I just handed it to her and moved on to the videos."

"That's right," said Wendy, and I sighed with appreciation at her first affirming response. "You didn't backtrack. You just gave her the product and told her you'd answer any questions after the presentation when you were taking her order. That's good, Mireya. Now when you were coaching Liz, did you remember to tell her not to make so much damned food?"

I had to laugh. "Yeah, I did."

"Look, it happens to me, too, and if they don't listen, what are you going to do?" Wendy said. "For the life of me, I don't get it. The hostess puts out more than she gets when she goes to those extremes. Yes, it's a party, but it's also a sales presentation so the rep should be the main attraction not the food."

"Try as I may, Wendy, there's just no convincing a Latina hostess to not serve up a feast at her party," I explained. "Or an African American or West Indian hostess for that matter."

Wendy laughed. "Trust me, I know. I'm Greek, remember. And I run into the same thing with my Italian hostesses, too."

"And what about my presentation?" I asked. She knew that Mike and I had split although I never shared with her why. "Is my drama showing?" I couldn't force a laugh past the lump in my throat.

"No, Mireya, it's not. You're warm and funny. You read the guests well and respond accordingly. Unless you were to tell them, they'd have no idea you were going through a divorce."

"But?"

"Here's the thing, Mireya. You've become too . . . I don't know what's the word I want. Clinical?"

"Clinical?"

"Mechanical? You describe the products as if you were a sex ed teacher."

"But you said I was warm and funny."

"You are, and that's really important in keeping their attention when giving details about the product," said Wendy. "But the guests don't want to just hear about what the product does and how it works. What they need to hear from you, Mireya, is how a product is going to make them *feel*."

Well, I haven't exactly been using them lately, I almost reminded her. The majority of Sensually Yours products like the Sexy Swing and the Come Again Board game were geared toward couples, and no weatherman, actor, or ballplayer can chase the images of Mike and that skank out of my imagination. Or Mike and me, for that matter, which was much worse. But I caught myself before I whined about this. I was already too close to being put on probation, and Wendy was only attempting to give me the help I requested. "Give me an example," I said.

"OK, like when you were describing The Next Best Thing. You said that the SensaSkin feels like the real thing . . ."

"Well, what should I have said?" I interrupted her. Even if I had used the damn thing, just how graphic did Wendy want me to get? "At the last sales rally, didn't Rosalinda strongly discourage us from being vulgar during presentations?" Rosalinda is the founder and president of Sensually Yours, the only Latina among the handful of CEOs who have started pleasure party companies in the United States. She gave us a vocabulary list of appropriate words to use during our presentations which her twelve years of experience taught her struck that balance between the clinical and vulgar. *Balls* was on the list, but *asshole* was not.

"Yes, but when you said *It feels like the real thing*, it sounded no different than when you said *It comes in peach, caramel, and espresso,*" said Wendy. "OK, you were really enthusiastic when you said *It comes in peach, caramel, and espresso.* But come on, Mireya, they can read that themselves in the catalog."

"Fine, Wendy. But, again, what was I supposed to say that wouldn't have offended the more conservative women in the room?"

Wendy sighed with exasperation. "Something like it made you miss the old boyfriend who was the first man to bring you to orgasm. Or you used it once when your husband was away on business, and for a moment, you almost believed he was actually there inside you. Whatever the damned thing actually makes you feel. You have to know these products to sell them, Mireya. I mean, really *know* them."

We both remained silent as Wendy's advice sunk into me. I heard what she was saying, and I knew it was true. Wendy finally said, "You know what else I suggest? Maybe you can ask one or two of the other gals in the crew to let you assist at one of their parties. This way you can watch them and get some pointers."

"That's a good idea," I admitted.

"Do it soon. The company likes to . . . uh . . . purge every year after Valentine's Day. Anyone who's not consistently meeting their monthly sales minimum is put on probation."

"I know."

"You're a great sales rep, Mireya. We both know what you're capable of, and that this is just a temporary funk. It happens to the best of us." Wendy sighed again. "Unfortunately, it's come at a really bad time for you, both personally and professionally."

"Well, I'm going to call Ronette and see if I can sit in on a few of her presentations," I said. Ronette was the top seller in our crew after Wendy, generating monthly sales in the thousands even when she was seven-months pregnant. She joked at our last crew meeting that she showed off her belly and told the guests. "Now if you're not trying to become a mommy, ladies, stay on top of that birth control because if you don't when you're using these products, this definitely will happen to you."

"Great idea. Ronette's not only a great saleswoman, she's a doll. I have no doubt, she'd love to have you at one of her parties," said

Wendy. "Another thing you could do is team up with someone. I just recruited two girls. The Ramos sisters. Young girls, both in college. Neither one had the money to buy the starter kit or wanted to give up her weekends so they pooled their money and signed up together. One works Fridays, the other works Saturdays, and sometimes they even work together. They do really well." Wendy stopped to chuckle. "Really well."

"Why's that funny?" I wondered if the Ramos sisters were twins, and if they did live demonstrations for horny frat boys. Of course, they didn't. Sensually Yours insisted on doing women-only parties, so allowing male guests would get the Ramos sisters tossed from the company even if they managed to keep their presentations clean. Despite what people assumed, coed parties were rarely as fun and nowhere near as lucrative. Nothing flattened a man's libido like hearing his wife or girlfriend ask about the Chipper Dipper Erection Crème in front of other couples. He only enjoyed a woman's explicit sex talk in one context—directly in his ear.

"One lives in the dormitory at her school, and the other's gay," explained Wendy. "Between the two of them, they cater to a very large population."

"Oh." I said. "Well, good for them."

"So do you want me to call any of your crew members and see if anyone wants to team up with you?"

But I wasn't ready to inject my personal pain into another professional relationship. "Let me think on it first."

"Fair enough, but, Mireya . . ."

"Yeah?"

"You can always take a break. Like I told you when you first started, you can take a hiatus and come back with no penalty. Just leave on your own accord instead of waiting until you're pushed out. Put in an official leave, and you won't have to pay the reactivation fee or buy a new starter kit."

I didn't want to tell Wendy that I couldn't afford to go on hiatus never mind get kicked out of the company. Instead I said, "Let me think on that, too." I reached for my SY portfolio for the documentation of last night's disaster. "So you ready for those numbers now?"

I heard a scratching noise and jumped from my seat. The lock on the apartment door clicked and eased open. Jesus, it was Mike.

He walked toward me fiddling his keys. I mouthed, *What the fuck are you doing here?* Mike exhaled as if he was expecting this abuse and took a seat at the dining room table. "Wendy, let me call you back in five minutes."

I hung up and turned to my ex-husband-to-be. "Why are you here?"

"I left something," Mike stammered. "Something I need for work."

So now he was a fucking liar, too. Mike knew I usually spent Sunday mornings on the telephone with Wendy to give her my tallies from the previous evening's party. He had come here with that lame excuse hoping to catch me. But I didn't care to argue with him about it. "Fine," I said. "Take the rest of your shit—all of it right now—and leave your keys."

"Mia . . ." he started

"Don't call me Mia, and hurry up." I scooped up my Sensually Yours portfolio, reached for my coat and purse, and headed for the door. "You've got an hour."

Mike grabbed my arm. "Mireya, we have to talk about this."

"No, we don't." I yanked my arm out of his grip. "Nothing you can say will change what you did to me and how I feel about it. You cheated on me, and I want a divorce. *Punto y final.*" I restrained myself from recounting the multiple ways that he had added insult to injury. By fucking a skank who I still bumped into in the building elevator, giving her the opportunity to sneer at the Sensually Yours logo on my suitcase, both of us knowing that she's thinking *All that and you still couldn't take care of you man's needs.* By fucking the same woman that on many occasions he had ridiculed, and I had pitied because she opened her legs for almost every guy in the building, and therefore, being a sexist hypocrite who could have exposed me to God only knows what diseases. By fucking that bitch and then blubbering into my voicemail about how she had come over to ask him to help her put up her Christmas tree and started crying about having no one special to spend the holidays with. I held all this back and more.

Still Mike bit his top lip as he always did when he was trying to control his temper. "Aren't you asking yourself how I could do this to you?"

"No, I'm not," I lied as I flung open the apartment door. "I could give a fuck when and why you decided to become a cheating bastard. You have an hour. Take everything you want because the rest is going to charity or the garbage. And leave your keys on the table."

I stormed out of the apartment and down the frosty street. How could he do that to me? He had no damned cause to cheat on me. I fucked Mike often, and I fucked him well. Long before I joined Sensually Yours he told me time and again that I gave him the best sex he had ever experienced, so our sex life only got better when I joined the company.

In fact, the first time we used a SY product, Mike and I said to hell with the trinkets and went straight for the swing. We couldn't stop laughing as we tried to figure out how to nail it into the high ceiling over our bed. Mike finally tried to put a slab of wood onto the bed and then a step ladder on it. Then he suggested that I climb up the ladder and nail the swing into the ceiling while he held the ladder steady for me. I stopped laughing, but Mike insisted that it was safer for me to go up while he anchored me instead of vice versa. Even though it terrified me, I couldn't argue with him. But Mike coached me through the entire ordeal. "Don't worry, baby. I got you," he said. "Nothing's going to happen to you because I'm right here." And the swing proved to be worth the trouble the second Mike eased his legs into the straps and began to sway, his hard-on flailed in the air and enticed me to leap onto it. I gripped the straps above my head then heaved myself onto Mike's lap. While I held on, Mike worked his cock into me, and soon I was grinding while flying and . . .

I had to get my mind off my cheating ex, so I called Wendy to give her my numbers as I charged down the street. When I was done, I found myself in front of a diner called Kilya's and decided to stop. The waitress led me to a huge booth where I found an abandoned weekly newspaper. I just sat there feeling like a castaway stranded on a boat in the middle of nowhere. All around me sat couples and families having Sunday brunch. Some were quite happy, and others were clearly not, but still no one was alone except me.

About ten minutes later, I had the neighborhood weekly newspaper, a half-empty cup of black coffee, and an untouched chocolate cheesecake before me. I flipped through the weekly and tried to concentrate on the stories of the latest ribbon-cutting ceremonies, high school athletic exploits, and community leader profiles to no avail. Instead my mind replayed scenes of the tragic film that had become my life. I started seeing events in my mind that had never happened but seemed inevitable. The landlord slipping an eviction notice under my door for failure to pay rent. Wendy calling me to say that the company no longer considers me a consultant in good standing and the only way to continue is to pay the three-hundred-dollar reactivation fee. I make the daily tabloid: SCHOOL AIDE SELLS SEX TOYS. I walk in on Mike again and that whore just as he dips his cock between the huge gap between her two front teeth.

A girlish laughter snatched me off this trip down anxiety lane. I looked up to see my waitress refilling my cup. "I'm sorry, I didn't mean to look over your shoulder." Then she pointed at the open weekly. "That ad caught my eye." *Come Play With Me. Attractive young lady seeks sophisticated older gentleman to explore the city with. I'm a great conversationalist who likes to try many different things. You are ambitious, successful and generous.* "I mean, who does she think she's fooling? That's an ad for a john not a date. A rich one at that!"

"Yeah," I said for lack of a better response. She left, and I pondered. In a manner of speaking, I was a sex worker, too, wasn't I?

I opened my Sensually Yours portfolio and found the matching pen. Across my napkin, I began to draft my own ad. *Get Pay for Play. Sexy entrepreneur seeks male associate to test inventory.* I went back to cross out *entrepreneur* and replaced it with *businesswoman*.

When I finally completed the ad, a half hour had passed, and Kilya's was almost empty. I flagged down my waitress, offering her a huge grin for not badgering me to order more or clear the booth. If I had, this great idea might not have come to me. She was the first person to not pressure me for anything in a long time, and I was planning on leaving her a fifty percent tip for that alone. When she reached me, I said, "You know what? I think I'm going to give that chocolate cheesecake a chance. Just make it to go." I was eager to go home and place my ad. Even though I should have been cutting corners, I left that generous tip because I was no longer worried about money.

The first thing I noticed when I entered the apartment was the empty table. Fuckin' Mike had not left his key. I had to figure out a way to get it from him. At least he was no longer staying with the hoochie down the hallway.

When he had finally accepted that I wanted nothing more to do with him, he'd packed his gym bag and crashed *over there* for a few days. When I bumped into him in the laundry room a week before Christmas, he insisted that he was sleeping on the *sucia*'s couch.

"You've got friends," I snapped when I should have just continued to ignore him. But since I had already given him an opening, I allowed myself to express my complete thought. "A sister. A mother. You couldn't go stay with one them?"

"No, because they love you," he said. "I love you, Mia. I don't want to tell them what happened until I'm sure that we can't work this out."

"You mean they don't know?" I could not believe it. "When do you plan to tell them? When you go over to your mother's house for Christmas; where are you going to tell her I am?"

Mike stuttered. Clearly, he had not thought this out. "I'm just going to tell her that you're with your family for the holiday."

"Oh, really?" I say. "And what about New Year's?" Knowing Mike has no answer, I began to add, "What about Valen—" A sob clogged my throat, and the effort it took to swallow it forced the tears I had been battling to flood my eyes. I hoisted the basket off the counter and bustled to the exit. The laundry could wait.

Mike ran past me to block the doorway. "Mia, the only reason why I'm staying across the hall is for a chance to talk to you, and she knows it. She's nothing, Mireya, and you know it."

"Nothing?" I sobbed as I rammed the basket into his stomach. "She's nothing? You destroyed our marriage for nothing?"

"She was a . . . mistake," Mike said. And as if that were the perfect answer, he rambled forward with it. "A mistake I made because I thought she would give me something that you used to. Not that she did anything that you wouldn't! She didn't. It wasn't what she did. It was how she did it. I mean, how she made me feel. I ended up in bed with her thinking that she would make feel needed the way you used to. And she didn't. She couldn't. That's why she was a mistake. A huge mistake."

I pummeled Mike again with the laundry basket. "Then take your huge mistake home for Christmas, you disgusting son of a bitch!" As I zoomed forward for another strike, Mike deflected the basket with his forearm, spiking it up and over. The basket toppled to the floor, and my Sensually Yours lingerie fluttered around us like butterflies with wings made of fuschia silk and emerald lace.

When Mike dropped to the floor to collect my underwear, I stepped over him and ran out of the laundry room. He called my name, but I refused to answer or turn. I hated Mike as much as I once loved him. I hated him for betraying me. I hated him reminding me how good—no, how much better—it had been once. And I hated Mike for reminding me this in a way that actually made me think that somehow I, too, was to blame for his betrayal.

My Sensually Yours voicemail box was choked with the responses to my ad in the neighborhood weekly. It was just like when I had first got into the pleasure party business and had been too liberal in handing out business cards with my cell phone number on it. I received countless messages from men wanting to know, "How much?" Mike thought it was hilarious until one particular sicko left me seven frantic messages when my phone was off while we were having sex. "All the home-based party businesses and this is what you had to choose," he said. "Why don't you sell makeup, candles, or something like that?" Then it was my turn to laugh. I just changed my cell phone number, rented a voicemail box, and put the number to it on my card.

I sifted through the messages, deleting them as soon as the caller revealed his inappropriate intentions.

"My name's Mandingo, and I'm an exotic male dancer available for engagements in the tri-state area . . ." Click. Good for you, buddy, but I'm not looking for some guy to steal my thunder—not too mention my loose singles—at a bachelorette party.

"Ooh, you sound so sexy, mami. Yeah, I wanna do business . . ." Click.

"How much to let me skeet on your . . ." Click.

"Hi, my name is Steven, and I have to admit that I'm not exactly sure what the nature of your business is. Why don't I tell you a little bit about myself and leave my contact info, and if I seem to have what you're looking for, please return my call at your earliest convenience."

Steven said that he was working as a stripper at a male revue in Manhattan, but that he was looking for something different, so he could spend more evenings with his daughter. However, he wasn't interested in being an escort unless it was for two or three regular clients—women only—and there were some nonsexual perks like traveling or going to the theatre or some other opportunities to grow as a person. He was single with no girlfriends and had a good relationship with his daughter's mother (not his "baby's mama") who knew what he did for a living and didn't not mind (in other words, no potential drama.) Steve offered references from his club's manager as well as women who have hired him for private parties and can testify how skilled, dependable, and respectful he is. "Women's pleasure and safety are my top priority because, like I said, I have a little girl, you know," he said before leaving his cell phone number and the best times for me to reach him.

It was of those times then so I immediately dialed his number. First, we exchanged slightly awkward introductions—it took Steve a while to register that I was "the ad lady"—followed by nerve-easing laughter. Then I said, "So, Steve, here's the deal. Have you ever performed at a pleasure party?"

"Oh, yeah, that's how I met my mother's daughter," he laughed. "She works for Spicy Delights."

I cringed at the name of SY's biggest competitor. Rumor had it that their representatives did shady things like make the hostess pay an hourly fee or make side deals with manufacturers to sell cheaper alternatives to Spicy Delight products for a cut of the profits. Sheisty. "Well, I work for Sensually Yours, the top company in the pleasure party business, and I'm looking for someone with whom I can experiment our new products."

Steve hesitated then said, "You mean, you want to demonstrate with me at the parties?"

"No! All demonstrations would happen in . . . private. And then I would incorporate the experience into my sales pitch. You know. *When I put the Turbo Ring on my boyfriend, Steve, I kept coming 'cause he kept going.*"

Steve laughed again. He had a great laugh, husky and good-natured. Even when I was head over heels with Mike, I never liked his laugh. No matter what, he always sounded like he was in on a joke, and the joke was on you. "From what I just heard, I have a hard time believing you need me to sell anything, Mireya," said Steve. "But I still want to meet you. I definitely have to meet you."

I first met Steve at Kilya's. We shared a sample platter of onion rings, buffalo wings, and mozzarella sticks. "I ordinarily don't eat like this," he said. "But sometimes it's good for the soul to be bad to the body, you know."

On sight of him, I wanted to be extremely bad to his body. Like one would expect of an exotic dancer, Steve had an amazing physique. The fact that he wasn't obsessive about his diet and fitness regimen added to his sex appeal.

We spent an hour at Kilya's. I told him about Sensually Yours although I kept my dismal sales record of late to myself. Steve described his work as a dancer at Jezebel's. We bonded as we exchanged drunk-'n'-horny women stories, but Steve impressed me when he said that he actually felt sorry for Vivacious Vicky.

Then he noticed the band of white around my ring finger. "How long have you been separated?"

"Not long enough," I said. Before he can ask me more, I added, "So, Steve, what I'm offering is a probationary period first. We see how it goes through Valentine's Day, and . . ."

"Wait, wait, wait," he interrupted me. "Don't you want to see if the chemistry we have here, you know, pans out before we start negotiating percentages and time frames and all that?"

He was absolutely right which made me want him all the more. I smiled and asked, "When would you like to come over and sample my inventory?"

When UPS delivered my shipment of the latest Sensually Yours samples hours before Steve arrived, I took it as a good sign. For the first time in weeks, I ripped open the box smiling and excited. I was rediscovering enthusiasm for my work and had no doubts that it would translate to my sales.

Steve showed up at eight o'clock, and I buzzed him into the building. I waited for him by the door in the latest addition to the Sensually Years lingerie line—a black, ankle-length lycra dress that fits like a long, fitted vest with a solitary rhinestone buckle. The neckline plunged to my navel where the buckle sat above the matching boy shorts. When I first put on the dress—which the clever minds in the SY marketing department dubbed Disco Inferno—I hated the way I looked in it. I stood in the mirror cursing *Cosmopolitan, Vogue,* and all those other waif-loving fashion magazines that repeatedly prohibited me from putting my thick thighs into boy-short panties. But when I slipped on my four-and-a-half-inch metallic heels with the gladiator straps, those same thighs went from chunky to taut, and I fell in lust with my reflection. *Whether you're thin or voluptuous, wear this dress with the highest heels you can find, and giiirl . . .* I thought practicing my sales pitch. *Never mind him. You'll want to touch yourself.*

But I didn't want to touch myself. I wanted Steve to touch me. It surprised me for a second to be so excited about sleeping with another man after years with only Mike. After all, it wasn't like Mike ever made me feel unsexy. He just rarely made an effort to make me feel like anything else. Like smart or funny the way Steve did from our first conversation. Before I first met Steve at Kilya's, I went to the salon to hack off an inch of split ends, bringing my auburn hair to my shoulders. After all, once Mike left, I had neither the money nor the desire to keep my regular appointment to freshen my fading blond highlights. Until I was back in the Sensually Yours business, I couldn't justify the expense. Nor did I want to. Auburn it was.

The second Steve appeared on the landing holding a bouquet of lilies and a bottle of wine, I knew he liked what he saw. I hoped the skeezer across the hall saw that, too. "You are so good!" I said as I reached for the wine and flowers. "This goes perfectly with what I have planned tonight. Come in and see."

I led him into the living room where I had a picnic set up on the carpet. The centerpiece was one of SY's latest additions—The Lovers Throw. It was blanket that also served as a game board. Steve and I lowered ourselves onto the blanket's silky center. I fed him strawberries while I explained the game. "It's simple," I said as I handed him the palm-sized red pillow. "You're red, and I'm white. Start here." I placed both pillows at the starting square which reads *Kiss each other good luck*. Steve gave me a loud smooch that tickled my cheek. After I stopped giggling, I said, "We take turns rolling the foam die and moving our pieces forward . . ."

"Doing whatever the square says," Steve said as he uncorked the wine.

"And whoever makes it to the end first is the winner."

"And what do I win?"

I giggled again. "The winner chooses the first position."

Steve huffed. "Hell, if we're not in the first position halfway through the game, send the damn thing back."

I loved it! I was definitely going to use that line in my presentation. *I give you my money-back guarantee.* I handed Steve the foam die. "You go first."

He rolled a four, advanced his piece forward and read the square. "Eager to please. Advance three spaces."

"My rotten luck," I teased. I sipped my wine and a little dribbled down over the glass and landed on my thigh.

Steve counted forward three spaces. "Maybe not," he said as he read the square to himself. *Kiss erogenous zone of lover's choice.* "So . . ."

I leaned back on my elbows and bent my knee, sending the wine trickling down my thigh towards my crotch. "Would you mind getting that?"

Steve leaned forward and sucked the wine off my thigh, drawing my flesh in between his puckered lips and making the skin smack in the air. As he continued to suckle his way across my thigh closer to my pussy, I slid down to meet him. Steve reached for the waistband of my briefs and wiggled them past my hips, down my thighs, and over my metallic high heels. I reached into the picnic basket for the Cumconction and peppered my clit with a few drops. It began to sizzle, making me writhe in pleasure. "Oooh," I said surprised by sensation. "They weren't kidding about this stuff."

"Really?" Steve took the bottle from my hand and read the label. "Hmmm." He leaned down and nuzzled his nose against my clit, making it hum under the pressure of the bone and the heat of his breath. "Doesn't smell like cinnamon, but that's OK by me. All I smell is fresh pussy, and that's good enough for me to eat." Steve licked his lips and pressed them against mine in a lingering kiss. His tongue slithered in between the folds, and he moaned. "Wait, I taste it!"

"Is it good?"

"Delicious."

"Shut up and show me."

Steve laughed, and the burst of breath made me grip the edge of the Lovers Throw. My eye caught the band of white flesh around my index finger. I toss my head back and jutted my hips into his face.

His tongue slid from between his moist lips, firm and wet like a lubricated cock, and he flicked it slowly up and down over the tip of my clit. "Like that, yes," I encouraged him. "Slow like that." My clit stretched for his tongue like a cat purring to be stroked. Then came the juicy pressure against the walls of my cunt as Steve slid his fingers inside me. His tongue circled my clit as his fingers glided in and out of my pussy. "Just like that." Winding my hips into Steve's face, I felt my juices oozing down the folds of my pussy and into the Lovers Throw. Thank God for the Lovers Throw. Otherwise, I would be wetting the carpet, and the smell of sex would seep into it . . . Jesus, why was I thinking of such a thing at that moment?

Steve stopped. "Are you OK?"

"More than OK," I said.

He gave me a half smile as if he was unconvinced. Then Steve got on his back. "Come sit on my face, mami."

Yes, that was right. As I sat up, I peeled off the disco-inspired lingerie so I wore nothing but my metallic heels. I got on my knees, and I lowered myself until I feel Steve's hot breath underneath my cunt. His agile fingers gently parted my sweaty petals, and then he kissed me as I imagined Mike stepping out of his parked car and activating the alarm. Steve kissed the lips of my pussy as he would those on my mouth, pressing against them, exploring their warmth with his tongue then dragging one of my lips in between his as he pulled away to catch his breath. Steve made out with my cunt, each plunge kissing more passionate than the last. "I like that, yeah, just like that." My voice strained both with excitement and from the struggle to not smother Steve's face with my hot, wet ass. I pretended to hear Mike's key in the front door.

Steve draped his tongue over my soaking mound like a warm blanket and flexed it. Its nubbly yet soft surface massaged my clit, and I started to close in. "Yeah, like that," I panted, closing my eyes and imagining Mike walk into the living room. "Oh, yeah. Yeah, yeah, yeah, ooooh!" My pussy burst, shooting heat through my chest and shattering the image of Mike's devastated face as he caught me grinding Steve's face.

I slid back to straddle Steve's chest. He grinned at me, his face wet and flushed. "I think you have a bestseller right there," he said.

I laughed. Steve was right, and I was brilliant to have thought of hiring him. This was going to be a fantastic working relationship.

It was a week before Valentine's Day, but I was already back in business. I had rocked all my parties the previous weekend, and it helped that SY offered express shipping so customers can have their merchandise in time for the holiday. As Steve and I neared the end of our trial period, I had mixed feelings about whether to continue working with him. Sales were up, and the sex was great, but I wouldn't have new products to test until the spring. Maybe I could arrange some kind of consulting arrangement with Steve. We could talk about it after Valentine's Day.

I invited Steve over to try some new products that SY was considering adding to the catalog in April. The latest company newsletter where I was featured as the Representative of the Month read, "Try these products with your sweetheart during Valentine's Day weekend then vote online the following Monday to let us know which we should add to our line." I didn't have a sweetheart this Valentine's Day. Like many single people, I would focus on work, and before I knew it, the dreaded day would have come and gone.

"Which scent do you prefer, Steve?" I asked as I straddled his muscular butt. "Mint, pear, or vanilla."

"Mmm . . . vanilla."

I squeezed a line of the sweet massage oil down his spine, and he laughed. "Ticklish, huh?" I slid my palms into the oil and rubbed it across Steve's sinewy back. "That's good to know." He moaned as I worked the oil into the crevices beneath his shoulder blades with my thumbs. Unlike the greasy concoction with the overpowering smell SY used to sell, this brand of oil felt like velvet. I enjoyed massaging it into Steve's skin as much as he did, and we moaned together as I kneaded his back, working my way further and further down.

I massaged Steve from his ass to his thighs. I poured more vanilla massage oil all over his butt, watching it pool into the small of his back and ooze down his cleavage. I stroked and squeezed his cheeks with the same vigor I liked my breasts fondled. The thought inspired me to lean forward and kiss his taut ass then trace circles across it with my tongue. Steve let out a deep breath—a mixture of moan and titter. I nibbled his ass. I nibbled and kissed and nibbled and kissed then licked and licked until Steve spread his legs.

Not wanting to stop for protection, I pulled back and pressed my thumb against his asshole. I pressed and rubbed my fingertip against the flaring nub until Steve gasped. "Lick it, mami, lick it." Ignoring his pleas, I continued to rub. "Lick it, mami."

Instead I oozed more oil along my index finger and slid it inside him. He gasped and clenched, but I still glided my finger in and out his ass. "Ah, yeah . . ." Soon Steve was up on his elbows, bumping against my fist. His buttock muscles relaxed even as his asshole clamped onto my finger, and I slid another one inside. "Fuck, yeah, aaah!" As I pumped the fingers of one hand into his hot ass, I oozed more massage oil all over the stubby dildo. I worked the oil into the firm jelly just like a real cock. For the brief second I slid my fingers out of his oily ass, Steve exhaled only to growl as I dipped the glistening dildo inside him.

"Fuck!" I pumped the dildo in and out his ass, grunting myself with every stroke. Steve bumped once, twice, three times against the dildo in my greasy palm, and then he started to buck. He bucked so wildly that he was almost on his hands and knees as if in a yoga pose. I pounded the jelly rod into him and reached around to stroke his solid cock. "Ah, fuck, yeah, aaahhhhhhh!" Within seconds, I felt his hot cum oozing down my knuckles. Steve collapsed against the bed, and I on top of him. And just before I dozed off, I thought *I'm going to get through my first Valentine's Day without Mike just fine.*

The next evening, I called Steve to propose a consulting arrangement. I launched into my pitch, offering him ten percent of my commission in exchange for ten hours per month. I recited the numbers I ran after he left the previous night so I could give a conservative yet enticing estimate of the amount of money he could make working for me. I extended my sales representative discount to him and promised to give him additional hours during peak seasons such as the holidays.

I asked, "So do we have a deal?" His response was no response at all. "Steve?" All the confidence with which I dialed his number evaporated.

"I don't think I can do this anymore, Mireya."

I couldn't believe it. First, my husband threw away our marriage over a single tryst with the trashiest woman within reach, and now a virtual stranger refused my proposition to pay him to have sex with me! Before I could say anything, Steve scrambled to explain. "It's not that I don't think you're sexy. God, you're so fuckin' sexy to me. It's so not that."

That didn't make me feel better. "Is it the fact that I want to pay you?" I asked. Then I joked, "Because money doesn't have to change hands." Now I'm no longer joking. "If it'll make you feel more comfortable just being fuck buddies, I can work with that." I hated how pathetic I sounded.

"No, it's not that. I mean, even if we had met under ordinary circumstances, and things went as they did, I'd still feel the same way."

Steve was starting to piss me off. "What did I do?" I turned him off with that butt plug, that's what I did. Then it hit me. Oh, shit, the butt plug. I fucked him up the ass with that dildo, and he loved it. Now Steve was freaking out, wondering if that meant he was gay and all that other homophobic nonsense. Mike had, too, but I eventually convinced him that he was a real man for doing whatever pleased him in the privacy of our bedroom and within the confines of our marriage, society's repressive ignorance be damned. So I said to Steve what I had told Mike and what I always conveyed to my Sensually Yours clients who were tentative about buttfucking their men. "Steve, please don't be embarrassed at all about *that*. What makes you gay or straight is not what you do in bed. It's who you do it with." I started my spiel about how the male counterpart to a woman's G-spot was his prostrate which was best stimulated through his anus.

But Steve cut me off in the middle of my explanation. "Mireya, I don't need you to tell me that," he says, his voice tight and low. "You think I would have let you do it at all if I didn't know that? My problem is that you just went and did it. How would you have felt if I had just done something to you without first getting your permission? I can't do business with you if you won't communicate with me or have so little sense of boundaries."

Before I could respond, the call waiting signal sounded. Perhaps because I realized that Steve might be right, and I needed time to think about how to make amends to him, I said, "I'm sorry, Steve, but I have to take this call. I'll call you right back, I promise." Before he could answer, I switched to the other call, "Hello." I heard nothing. "Hello, hello?" I didn't even hear breathing. Was it possible that one of those morons who responded to the ad somehow got my name and home number. "Who the hell is this?"

"It's me," said Mike.

"Oh."

"I know you don't want to talk to me, but at least be honest enough to tell me if it's on account of that guy you're seeing, and trust me, I'll leave you the hell alone."

"What are you talking about? I'm not seeing anybody. You're the adulterer, remember."

"Whatever, Mia. Maybe you overacted to what I did because you were doing the same thing all along. Or maybe that guy you were seen with at that diner is the reason you're so gung ho about divorcing me over one moment of weakness."

"You wish. That guy's just a colleague." My stomach sunk less from the blatant half truth than from the fact that Steve no longer wanted to work with me. How could I fuck the man's brains out, and he not come back for more? It made no sense to me.

"Even Wendy hasn't been in and out of our fuckin' apartment as much as this dude has in the past couple of weeks."

Goddamn neighborhood *chismosos*. Suspect Number One: the tramp across the hall. "It's not *our* apartment anymore."

"Unless that guy means something to you, I'm not giving up on us so easily," he said.

I yelled, "You gave up on us, Mike, when you fucked that bitch in our bed . . ." I almost said with *my cock ring*, but my stomach hit bottom. I hung up on him (and on Steve), turned off the ringer, and slammed the cordless back onto its base.

Then I reached over and yanked open the night table on my side of the bed. There the cock ring sat right atop the pile of bottles and gadgets. Then my entire abdomen convulsed. I couldn't believe I still had it.

I heaved the drawer into the air and dumped everything across the bed, raining containers and appliances until the little blue cock ring was buried. I reached for a tub of powder and opened it. The edible flecks with the strawberry aroma were almost gone. I sealed the tub then tossed it into the wastebasket. Then I grabbed the flattened tube of Heavenly Head. As I unscrewed the cap, the caked paste of the mint gel flaked onto the bedspread. I changed my mind, resealing the cap and throwing the tube into the garbage, too. One by one, I snatched up all the virtually empty containers and dropped them into the tin bucket next to my bed. I had no idea we had so many.

Then I reached for the Tantalizer, the motorized and beaded anal probe. No way was I going to trash a perfectly good appliance, but I had to at least remove the batteries. I always urged my clients to remove the batteries after each use so that they would not corrode and ruin the toy. I opened the battery pack to the Tantalizer expecting to find a rusty mess. But the batteries seemed as fresh as the day they were broken out of the plastic and inserted into the pack. I switched on the Tantalizer and the probe vibrated with a robust whir as if brand new. We had to have owned it for almost two years, making frequent Costco runs to feed it wholesale packs of Ever Ready batteries like a family pet.

I found myself walking around to Mike's side of the bed. I opened the bottom drawer of his night table. While my drawer had been chock-full of products, his was almost empty. In there Mike kept a stack of porno. The genuine hard-core stuff, not the educational

DVDs on erotic dancing and the Kama Sutra with only simulated intercourse that I sold for Sensually Yours. He owned a barely used tube of the Chipper Dipper Erection Crème, the remote to my wireless vibrating panties, and a few small manila envelopes. When I opened them I found photo after photo of me in provocative poses in either sexy lingerie or nothing at all. I flipped to the back of a picture of me in a cheesy leopard-print camisole that I must have bought from Frederick's of Hollywood. Sure enough, the date on the photo was a good year before I went into business and swore my loyalty to Sensually Yours.

I must have stared at that photo for fifteen minutes before I reached for the phone and called Mike. He answered, but I couldn't speak. Mike knew it was me and waited. My pain must have been audible because he finally asked, "Mireya, are you OK?" I really couldn't say I was OK, and yet I didn't want to admit I wasn't. "Mireya? Are you still there?"

"I'm still here." I took a deep breath and said, "OK, Mike. We'll talk."

Mike insisted on meeting me on Valentine's Day after work. Although I agreed to it, I refused to meet at the romantic place he suggested. Instead we met at Kilya's. That was our compromise. Although decorated with heart-shaped balloons and red-and-white crepe streamers, there were no other couples in sight. Mike brought me a box of roses and one of those watercolor greeting cards that read as if the poet wrote it specifically for our circumstances. *I know you doubt this right now, but I truly do love you . . .*

When he settled across from me, I noticed the shadow growing on his face. Mike caught me staring at him, and my disappointment must have shown because he reached up and wiped his palm across each cheek as if trying to wipe away the stubble. "Sorry about that."

"About what?"

"I know you don't like the beard. Since you left, I haven't had much of an incentive to . . . Anyway, I'm sorry. I'm sorry about a lot of things."

Then Mike rambled for twenty minutes. He went on as I had expected him to, with professions of undying love peppered with heartfelt apologies. I listened unmoved as Mike recited from the script of clichés that must be handed out to remorseful cheaters everywhere, as if it were some kind of prerequisite.

"When I was single I vowed never to get married unless I knew I could be faithful," Mike said. "And just when I had given up on finding the woman who would be all that I needed, I met you. No matter what becomes of us, I know that I'm never going to love someone as much as I do you. I didn't fuck up because I stopped loving you or loved you any less than I did the day we got married."

"Then why did you do it?"

"Because . . . because of Sensually Yours!" Mike spit out the name like an accusation, raising his voice so that the elderly man in the next booth stopped sipping his split pea soup to stare at us. Mike lowered his voice. "Believe it or not, that company hurt our marriage."

I sat back and folded my arms across my chest. "Sensually Yours did not make you cheat on me. That's a choice you made." Mike tried to interrupt me, but I wouldn't let him. "You need to admit that you stopped supporting my business when I got really good at it."

"No, Mireya, I stopped supporting your business when you brought it into our bedroom."

"So you admit it!" Now I was yelling at Mike and pointing at him. "You resented Sensually Yours."

"Yes, I admit it!" Again, Mike checked himself, leaning forward to whisper across the table. "How do you think it made me feel, Mireya, when I stopped being enough for you? When you couldn't make love to me without some gimmick."

"That's not true."

"It's not? Mireya, when was the last time we had sex without using some Sensually Yours product? With no toy or lotion or even some costume? Do you even remember?" I tried to rewind my sexual memory, zipping past my encounters with Steve and getting the mental tape stuck on catching Mike in bed with the neighborhood man-eater. "See, you can't remember, can you? Well, I can. Like it was yesterday even though it was almost a year ago today."

Last year Valentine's Day had landed on a Saturday. I had ordered my own gifts for the holiday, and the shipment had arrived the previous Thursday. Mike came home from the bank just as I was about to slice open the package with a box cutter. "What's that?" he asked as he came up behind me and pulled his arms around my waist. "Anything in there for me?"

"Baby, it's all for you." I opened the box and pulled out a package. When I tore it open, I found the policewoman costume I had ordered. It included a black vinyl minidress with a matching cap, plastic handcuffs, baton, and even a toy badge that read POLICE BABE. I held it up for Mike to read. "Look how cute!"

Mike read the badge and laughed. Then he took it from my hand and tossed it over his shoulder. "Hey, what'd you do that for?"

He pulled me to him and muttered, "You don't need no stinkin' badges."

I burst out laughing, and Mike smothered my neck with kisses. As his wet kisses traveled down my chest, my laughter turned into soft moans. Mike teased me, nibbling at my nipples through my blouse until they were stiff and aching against the soaked cotton. He straightened up to kiss me on the mouth, rubbing and squeezing breasts as he unbuttoned my blouse. As I kissed Mike back, I ran my fingers through his hair with one hand while fondling his rigid cock through his pants with the other. When I felt my blouse graze off my shoulders and down my arms, I stopped rubbing Mike only to allow my top to slide down my wrists and onto the floor. Once it was off, I surged back toward him, scooping his balls in my palm and giving them a gentle squeeze. "I love you, Mia," Mike gasped. "I love you so fuckin' much."

"I love you, too, *papi*."

Mike gripped my ass and hoisted me in the air. I wrapped my legs around his waist and waited for him to lower me onto the bed. Instead he carried me over to the dresser. With one quick swipe, he cleared away the costume jewelry and cosmetic bottles, sending a few tubes of lipstick and mascara bouncing across our bedroom floor. I planted my hands on the edges of the dresser and leaned back until my head pressed against the mirror. I kicked up my legs, and Mike guided my ankles to his shoulders. "Yeah," I said. "Fuck me like that."

"Yeah, I'm going to fuck you like that," he said, grabbing my skirt and shoving it up to my waist. "I'm going to fuck you in every way over the next seventy-two hours, you hear me?" After undoing his pants and pulling out his cock, Mike grabbed my panties and wriggled them up my thighs to air my dripping pussy. My juices trickled down toward my asshole.

"I hear you, baby," I said, lifting my hips and nudging my ass closer to his cock. "Fuck me every which way."

Mike guided his cock into me and began to pound, his shaft rubbing against my clit with every stroke. I cooed and he grunted over the muffled sweetness of his muscular hips thumping against the back of my soft thighs. With his eyes locked on mine, Mike licked and nibbled my calf as he fucked me on the dresser. Over his shoulder, I caught a glimpse of the Sensually Yours box sitting on the bed virtually unpacked. Reminiscing in the booth at Kilya's, I recalled how as I was looking at the box as Mike pummeled me to climax, I was thinking how lucky I was to have a husband who didn't need any of those things to make me cum.

"You remember now, don't you?" Mike said, and I came back to Kilya's. I realized that Mike had one hand over mine on the table while the other was stroking my thigh underneath it. He was making me wet, and I fidgeted in my seat. Mike took the hint and pulled his hands away. "Do you remember?"

"Yeah, I remember."

Mike sighed and said, "I'm not at all blaming you for what I did. There's no excuse for the terrible decision I made. I needed you to need me like she did." He paused then added, "The crazy thing is I did to her what you had been doing to me. I mean, there I was about to make the biggest mistake of my life, and I still pulled out the . . . you know. Like wearing that thing—having it between us—

somehow made the whole the thing less . . ." Mike's voice faded, and he pressed his back against the booth as if he didn't deserve to be so close to me.

"You're right," I said. "I had convinced myself that all the toys and games proved that everything was great. But you suspected that I couldn't be with you without them. That I had brought my business into our bedroom because you needed me to need you in a way I no longer did."

Mike stared at me, and I suspected that his stomach had hit bottom, too. "Why?" Then his blinking eyes bounced around the diner, looking anywhere but at me in an effort to not cry.

"I think it's because I wanted to be more to you than the best piece of ass you ever had."

"But you are, Mia."

"That's not how I felt. Soon after we got married, it was as if that's all that mattered. Your career and my . . . skills." The more I spoke, the clearer the truth became. "It was like, well, since that's what I'm really good at, why not make it a career. I'll have something to call my own and still be a good wife to Mike." When the realization sunk in that the opposite had transpired, I began to cry enough for both us. And it hadn't stopped when Mike left. I had hesitated to let Wendy partner me with another woman in our crew because I didn't want to introduce my emotional pain into another personal relationship. Then I turned around and did just that with Steve. And I had sought out Steve because when Mike left, I no longer had a human sex toy now that pleasure had become my business to an unhealthy extreme.

At the sight of my tears, Mike cleared his throat and then asked, "Does this mean that some day you might be able to forgive me?"

I nodded. I knew forgiveness wouldn't come any time soon as sure as I knew that forgiveness was inevitable. The most bizarre thing of all was that had Mike not betrayed me, I might never have realized how I had betrayed myself. "But I'm not saying I'll take you back," I said. "The way I treated you was wrong, Mike, but you said it yourself. It doesn't justify what you did. After all I've been through these past few months, I need to be alone. Make some changes."

"Like what?"

I didn't have to share this with him, but somehow despite everything, I felt feel he deserved to hear it. "For one, I'm taking a leave from Sensually Yours," I said.

"Really? Tanisha's going to be disappointed," Mike said. "She told me to tell you that she was going to call you next week to reschedule her party." It occurred to me that Mike was still hiding our separation from his colleagues if not his family.

"I'll just refer her to Wendy or Ronette or someone else in the crew."

Mike seemed to mull over my decision. Although I had made it at the spur of the moment, I instinctively knew it to be the right thing to do. "Mireya, can you afford to do that now? I mean, if you won't let me move back, how can you afford to keep that apartment without the additional income?" I was about to snap *Maybe the same way that ho across the hall does* when Mike threw his hands in the air. "I'm sorry. That's none of my business. It's just that I do care about you, Mia, and I want you to be OK."

"Maybe I'll move in with my sister and go back to school," I said. "Finish my degree. Get my teaching credentials. I don't know."

Mike smiled. "You'd make a great teacher. Everyone at the school loves you, and, well . . . You were good at selling Sensually Yours. That involves some of the same kind of skills as teaching, doesn't it?"

My eyes started to well again albeit for different reasons. "Come to think of it, that's true."

"Maybe I can help you with that. You know, with school. No strings attached. At least, think about it."

I knew he meant it. I also knew that as time passed, Mike would hope that his support would earn him a second chance. I wasn't too sure that it would. But because of the small yet significant gift he had just given me for Valentine's Day, I felt that I could honestly offer him one in return. "I will."

Don't Be Mad at Me

Adriana López

I don't usually come on to authors I interview. But the baby-fine hair peeking out of the young Spanish writer's open collar was breaking my concentration.

I had devoured his book in one lonely weekend. It was a sophisticated exploration of alienation in contemporary Barcelona. At the novel's center is an unsuccessful young author who's hired by an enigmatic older woman to write her life's story.

When I finished it, I stared at his author photo, looking for the depth in his welcoming eyes that had led to this work. I had to see him in person. I researched the controversial underground Barcelona literary journal he and his cohorts founded named *Crack*, and I found my angle. I decided he would make a good feature on the Spanish avante garde for *Publisher's Forum*.

David Canetti happened to be in New York for a few months on a writing scholarship. He responded to my email immediately. This is what I love about being the international editor at *the* book review magazine. It's "meet the author," all the time.

David and I were sitting below a Moroccan-style ceiling fan struggling through the leaden humidity of a mid-August night. I told him to meet me in the Lower East Side at a café bar called The Red Pony. Seven p.m. I'd be the girl carrying an emerald green book tote that said Reading is Radical. I told him I was tall, with short black hair, and wearing a sleeveless turtleneck dress.

After our initial Spanish two-cheek hello kiss and some nervous prattle about the similarities between New York and Barcelona, I got down to business. I asked him about his sales. I could see the creases taking center stage on his smooth forehead.

I focused on his large, hazel eyes as he attempted to save face. They were encased in a thick set of dark lashes that made him appear as if he were wearing chocolate-colored eyeliner. I furrowed my brow a little and nodded, feigning concentration.

"Few people actually read the novel today," he lamented in strained English.

"Yes, it's a problem for all authors. It's tough to keep up with the shorter attention spans."

Like a Modigliani painting, his face and nose were long. His fingers were long, too; he had them wrapped around a short glass filled with the amber-colored whiskey we both ordered.

I was as drawn to him as I am to unreadable books.

His eyes remained glued to mine. He took a sip of his whiskey and sat back in his chair and grinned at me.

"So you're family is Latin American?"

"Yes. My mother is Colombian, and my father is a Spaniard. But I was born here." My delivery was flat. I've been told that I can come off as cold, a little arrogant.

"Aha! I thought you were too attractive to be just American. Do you prefer English?"

"Spanish is fine. I need to practice."

"You have a slight accent to your Spanish. It's very cute."

"Thanks," I said, tensing at the dig.

"But it's much better than my English. Nobody in Spain worries about their English."

Of course he had the linguistic advantage. I only got to practice my Spanish with my parents and a bunch of stiffs in my prep school classes on the Upper East Side. Or on the dreaded occasions my parents dragged me to visit my humiliatingly snobbish families in Bogotá and Madrid.

"Okay then, Spanish it is," I said in the tongues of our mothers. The *r*'s rolling from my tongue gave me a whole new sexy persona. I felt like I had tapped into that dormant nineteenth-century *maja* I had in my veins.

"*Bueno,*" he concluded.

My cell phone was sitting on our table. I pretended to check it. I needed to divert my eyes from his intensity. I acted as if I didn't see him staring at me.

"I'm expecting a call from the office," I mumbled. "A never-ending edit I've been trapped in all week."

My face was getting hot. I have the kind of skin that easily reddens in the heat or when I get nervous or excited.

I downed my whiskey too fast.

"So what are you reading now?" he asked.

"Well," I begun hesitantly, "I just finished reading you."

"Thank you, that makes a whole ten people."

I smiled. If ten had read his last novel, that meant less than five poor souls in the New York literary world would have read my own pathetic attempt at experimental fiction a few years back.

"Did you hear about Samuel Reverte-Ferrante's latest novel?" I blurted, without pausing to think about the book's racy subject matter.

"About the Italian talk show host who goes to bathhouses to fuck adolescent boys?"

He said the word fuck in Spanish. I was surprised at how my nipples hardened with the release of that single word. *Follar.* Just to pronounce it forces one to clench their teeth and snarl.

"Did you read it?" I asked.

"No. Read about it. It's caused quite a stir, no? Everyone thinks Reverte-Ferrante is gay now, though he's happily married to some big-shot editor."

"Everyone is thinking: 'How could someone write about it and describe it so well if he hadn't done it himself?'"

"Men have been writing about the female orgasm for centuries, Anna. What do they know?"

It was the first time he addressed me by my first name, so soon after saying fuck. *Ah-na.* He pronounced it softly, as if he were stroking the back of my neck with his words.

"Too true," I said.

"I say good for Samuel!" David said suddenly. "What's the big deal really if he screwed some guy in the name of good research? Flesh is flesh, no?"

"Sure." I shrugged, though I didn't really agree. I decided to give him a taste of my New Yorker attitude. "But screwing your wife's brother is crossing the line, don't you think?"

"Perhaps. But haven't you ever crossed the line in a close relationship?" he asked.

"Of course, but . . ." I replied, wondering how I could change the subject.

We were coasting quickly into unchartered waters for your standard *Publisher's Forum* interview.

"Really?" he said playfully. "What, with a friend or something?"

He was as excited as I was, hanging on every careless word that flew out of my mouth. David was sitting up straight, resting his hands placidly on the tops of his spread thighs. His head was tilted low and slightly to the side. He was my captive audience.

I took a breath and told him about my roommate at Vassar, even though I couldn't believe what I was saying. I remembered the drunken night when things went too far with Natasha for the first time. The smell of Johnson's baby powder exuded from her belly button as I pulled down her panties.

Our friendship had reached that point of overwhelming curiosity. She asked if she could kiss me. I couldn't say no to a girlfriend. We were both each other's first, and we took it seriously. We left our usual fits of cackling laughter out of it.

I was larger breasted than Natasha, but just as malnourished. We both lived on cigarettes and Diet Coke. We rolled around my twin dorm bed kissing. I told David that her small pointy breasts and bony hips barely touched mine. I said that Natasha moaned too loudly and overdramatically for what I was doing beneath her perfectly manicured landing strip of a bush. (Mine in comparison was an untidy patch of overgrown ivy).

Shocked at how dirty I was talking, I stopped myself. His face had turned red.

"This conversation has gone way past any chance of professionalism, hasn't it?" I told him. But I relished the macho bravado of my words.

"I'm enjoying myself immensely," he said with an earnest smile. "Do you still talk to this Natasha?"

"No, her husband doesn't like me much."

"Fool." He tsk'd.

"So, what about you?" I shot back, downing another gulp of whiskey for support.

"My turn, huh?" he said.

"Come on. I just revealed a little too much information to you. Offer me something as good. None of this will be published, I swear."

He let out a tinny laugh. I couldn't tell if it was nervous.

"Okay then. You've heard of Sergi Canetti, right? The writer who wrote the historical novel about Hadrian, the Roman emperor?"

"Yes, you and he and some friends started *Crack*. You two related?"

"By father. We grew up together. Our father had moved us to Paris when we were boys. He was just opening his bookshop at the time. We were lonely, awkward looking, and had no friends. Our French was poor, and we felt like outsiders in that city. We spent a lot of time alone together. One day we just decided to experiment on each other."

"What do you mean, experiment?" I asked.

"We gave each other our first blow jobs."

I nodded.

"This is quite common for boys you know, at least in Europe," he said. "I don't know about American boys."

"How old were you?" I asked.

"Sixteen or so."

"Here, boys feel each other's cocks at sleep-away camp," I said. "But no one dares to talk about it. It stays in the woods, with their campfire tales."

He laughed at my attempt at being funny.

Then he suggested we try another place.

• • •

I chose this divey basement bar on Mott Street. It was called Double Happiness, and I found the name cynically comforting. The light from the hanging red paper lamp in our corner booth ruddied our sallow cheeks to a much-needed healthier glow. It seemed we both shared a dislike for healthy outdoor lifestyles.

We sat close to one another. So close that our knees kissed, though they were still separated by a hairline crack. This proximity interfered with making conversation. So I pulled my knee away slightly to concentrate on what the hell I was saying, and hopefully, to seem a little out of reach. If that was still possible.

We jump-started the dialogue by discussing new book releases we thought important (always an ice breaker for book people), when David mentioned one that I had read by a Mexican American journalist. It had just been translated into Spanish. It was about little boys in Mexico who cross the border by themselves to look for their laborer mothers in the United States. The boys leave their country with only a few pesos in their shorts and an approximate address. They try dozens of times to sneak over, only to die like stray dogs in the desert.

My heart had begun to beat faster and I felt the blood drain from my face. The mere mention of that book brought me back to that terrible time in my life.

"So you haven't read it then?" David asked.

"No, I have." I responded, sounding stiff.

"Oh. It didn't look like it registered with you." He looked confused.

I hadn't wanted to tell him about my mother. I preferred not to talk about her with anyone. But the sad man trapped in his eyes told me to. Despite his generous smiles, he had a somber look that made me think he understood the incomprehensible, like death, or why we fall in love with the wrong people.

"That book takes me back to a hard time in my life recently," I said. Then it all came out. The alcohol was making me emotional. "It's been two years since I last had sex with a guy, you know."

I was suddenly insane with an urgency to talk about it. It was like

I was a bottle of Coke he kept shaking, lifting the cap to watch me splatter. He took a sip of his scotch and placed it down slowly onto the coaster with the Chinese Double Happiness symbol.

"Wow." He paused, taking a deep breath. "Why?"

"My mother died two years ago. It closed me up to the world, made me hate it. Hate love, mistrust men, everyone."

"I'm so sorry. What she die of?"

"Oh, a bad case of sadness. She overdosed on sleeping pills. Her longtime lover announced that he was going back to Rome for a younger woman he had met while on business. She never wanted to get out of bed again."

"Oh God, Anna. I'm so, so sorry." He widened his eyes and shook his head.

"Thanks," I shot back as if he had just passed me the salt shaker. "I'm okay, don't worry."

I concentrated on carefully taking out my pack of smokes from my bag and lighting a cigarette. I inhaled and exhaled dramatically, it was a necessary release. He placed his hand on my right thigh. He didn't squeeze or press. He just rested it ever so lightly. His long fingers splayed open like a starfish.

As he rested his limb on mine, I noticed what a feminine wrist he had, despite the generous layer of fur encasing it. It was the first time he placed a hand on my body, other than to tap me on my arm, guiding me away from an oncoming waitress back at the Red Pony.

I had to explain how I got to that point from the mere mention of that book, even though his heart was coming out of his eyeballs with sympathy. I began telling David about the whole experience with a certain peace I hadn't felt in years. His whole being was an open receptacle to my feelings.

"After my mother's suicide I hadn't been able to read for pleasure, something I relied on since childhood to block out the world or my parents' high voltage fights. I showed up to the office a few days after the funeral and dove into my work as usual. It saved me. I had just recently broken off a seven-year relationship, and I hardly saw any of my friends."

"Shit."

"Yeah. It was one of those brutally cold New York winters," I explained. "I would sit on my couch curled up in a blanket desperately trying to escape into another world."

"You mean, through books, yes?"

"Exactly. But it wouldn't work. I would start to read the sentences and a voice in my head would interrupt telling me I wasn't reading. The words . . . I couldn't absorb them; they couldn't get through all the other noise in my head. I lived in a kind of panic that I would never be able to enjoy reading again. But this book broke through. It took me out of myself for once. Its words spoke a simple truth, and I could follow their trail. The pain of these abandoned little boys in the book finally allowed me to privately mourn my mother's vanishing from this earth. I mean, those little boys just wanted their mommies. And I could understand that."

"I couldn't put it down myself," David said, "That journalist really took you there, all those sordid details about eating out of garbage dumps to survive."

"I *know*; it's just terrible." I added.

I felt self-conscious again. I took another sip of whiskey, and my hand trembled as I brought it up to my mouth. I knew I was acting strangely, telling him about my mother and about not having slept with man for a while. This isn't what you're supposed to do when you first meet someone, especially an accomplished author whom you're writing about.

I let out a nervous guffaw.

"God! Doesn't talking about death just kill a mood?"

He gave me a smile more warm and generous than any I'd ever received.

"I'm not uncomfortable talking about it, Anna. Go on."

"You're probably regretting ever having mentioned that book or saying yes to me interviewing you. See what you did! You unleashed my inner monster." I was back to flirting shamelessly.

"She's a wonderful little monster," he matched, responding quickly.

"Oh yeah?" I thought for second, then went for it.

You only live once. I wanted the air, the light around him. "You want to see where I live?"

"I'd love that. But on one condition." He grabbed my thigh and gave me a serious look.

"We need to get some slices of New York City pizza first. My little monster of a stomach is growling."

He slid out of the booth and excused himself to go to the bathroom. I looked around the room to see if anyone was looking. No one was. I pocketed a darling little red ashtray that the barman had just placed on our table.

It would compliment the other souvenirs I had accumulated over the years, little mementos from places where something memorable had happened.

The Lower East Side at midnight bustled with street action from every living, breathing, walk-of-life. And something about its energy must have gotten under David's skin, making him stop short in the middle of the street.

Without warning, he grabbed my hand and pulled me into the darkness of lonely Eldridge Street. "What are you doing?" I asked even though I knew. "*Déjame,* just let me," he said like a boy who wanted to stay up later than his bedtime. He took my two hands and raised them over my head, pushed them up against the rough red bricks of the tenement building I had my back on. I was his prisoner as he breathed on my face, slowed himself down to smell me, and pressed his wet mouth onto mine.

Here was our chance to rise, to overcome the heavy gravity of respectable, dignified social interaction. We took our time exploring each others mouths, opening them slightly, then pulling back and beginning again, deeper and deeper the next time in, for anyone who cared to watch. I remember opening my eyes and seeing his closed so sweetly, tasting the booze and cigarettes on our saliva, smelling the cheese. All the pores on his naked face reeked of the slice of pizza we inhaled walking and giggling on the way to my place. On my ex, Jonathan's, face I had hated the smell of cheese, but on David it was delicious. Like a sampling of his body's baser smells to come.

We raced up the five endless flights to my apartment and panted like porno stars from severe shortness of breath. Fucking cigarettes! Still insanely aroused at just listening to his heavy breathing, I fumbled placing the key into the hole.

Once we were inside, I flicked on the dozen little lamps in my place, and David found his way into my bedroom. That's where all my books were, in disorganized piles all over the floor. I had never bothered to get book shelves or night stands, so my books became my flat surfaces for glasses and candles. Now he was sizing me up, like all book people do, by what I had or didn't have in my collection. I usually never felt self-conscious about the process but with him, I felt instantly exposed.

I took my time and slowly walked into the bedroom. He was sitting on the edge of my bed reading *Death in Venice*. He didn't acknowledge me. Looking very studious, he was either ignoring me or enthralled with the passage he was reading.

I sat next to him and stared at his perfect Roman profile, and then I leaned into him and kissed his neck. He continued to read without looking up at me, and I kissed it again.

"Can't you see I'm reading?" he said, without looking at me. The sides of his mouth twitched with abstained laughter.

"Uh, huh. I can see that."

I got on my knees and unbuttoned his shirt. I placed my hands on the center of his chest and massaged that hair I had so admired earlier. His skin was sticky from a night's worth of sweat. Without saying a word, I pulled at his left sleeve. He threw his shoulder back and held the book out with his right hand. He did the same in reverse when I was ready for the right sleeve.

Shoulders hunched over, legs spread apart, he continued to read, as I sat kneeling on the Persian rug in front of him, taking him in. He was thin but perfectly T-shaped. Bigger on top, narrower towards the waist. His trail of dark body hair mimicked his shape and thickened in the belly area. As I stared at his torso I could sense him eyeing me over the edge of the book.

He was waiting for me. I leaned forward and kissed his stomach gently. Through the hairs, his skin smelled of sweet milk. Like the sticky remnants of a summer day's ice cream cone on some sweet child's cheeks. I licked the area around his belly button. Now I tasted salt. He twitched and grunted softly. Then I inserted my tongue right into it, his inny, and he pushed me away from him. His face morphed from shock to lust in a millisecond.

"Take off that dress," he said, indignant.

"No." I said. "You."

His face bore no expression.

He lifted my dress up over my head in one smooth movement. And I was left in a pair of Gap yellow underwear. Not even the thong kind. I forgot I was wearing them.

"Are those boys' underwear?"

I shook my head no.

"Turn around," he said, still sitting on the edge of my bed.

He lowered my underwear and sat silently looking at me.

Then he grabbed my hips and pulled me closer to him, sticking his tongue right into the crack of my ass.

No man had ever gone there first.

I could hear him unbuckling his belt, unzipping his fly. Then he stuck his fingers into my sex and turned me around.

His long, thin cock was sticking out of his jeans, waiting.

"Sit down."

I lowered myself onto him.

He broke through pubic hair, tissue, blood vessels, pride, sadness, desire, me.

Then, there wasn't any room left for air in my lungs. I came pools onto his dark blue jeans.

My cigarettes called. I left him lying on my bed with one hand behind his head, the other resting on his stomach, smiling big as he caught his breath. His limp dick twitched as it rested outside his open zipper.

"Bring me one too," he said. "And that little red ashtray you stole tonight."

Later, when I had been lying there awake watching him snore, his hands clasped over his chest, like my mother in her black beaded dress the day of the funeral, I imagined his life back in Barcelona.

I thought about this half brother, Sergi Canetti. I wondered if Sergi was gay. Did David consider himself bisexual? Did it just happen once?

I got up to go to the bathroom, closed the door and placed my hands over the cold edges of the sink and pressed my face up to the mirror for a reality check. The whites around my brown eyes were blood shot and smudges of faded black eyeliner streaked the tops of my cheekbones. My lips were chapped and redder than usual. My classmates had called me bubble lips when I was a girl, but now those bubbles were extra puffy from an entire night of David's love nibbles. "I love your mouth. I love your lips," he said to me as I sucked his cock before we went at it again. He made me feel beautiful, alive again. I laughed at myself in the mirror, gave myself a wink. The man I had stared at so intently in an author's photo was now snoring loudly in my bed.

We decided that David should move in after our third date. We couldn't be without each other, and his time in New York would dwindle away fast.

When he first brought all his things over from the dingy little studio he was renting in midtown Manhattan, I was taken aback by how light the man traveled. For a four-month scholarship trip he had brought his laptop, two dress shirts, two T-shirts, one V-neck wool sweater, two pairs of shoes, a pair of dress slacks, a pair of jeans (which I had soiled), and a black blazer. The pairs of underwear and socks he had brought (less than a week's worth) he hand-washed daily in the nude and hung out neatly on the circular metallic ring around my shower to dry.

The only things that weighed him down were the seven books he intended to read or use as references for his writing. We hardly socialized or saw anyone for that first month and a half. Though I liked to blame our antisocialness on David's less-than-perfect English, I really just wanted him all to myself.

David was a social animal by nature. His mother had told him that as a child he opened his arms for everyone to hold him. He made her nervous, thinking he'd embrace a stranger *con malas intenciones* one day. Unlike most of the misanthropic writers and editors I had come to know and sympathize with over the years, David genuinely liked people.

As time went on, I got used to losing him and his attention at those publishing-world events he did eventually want to go to. In conversation, his whole being was absorbed in the plight of other people's pain, just like he had become absorbed in mine. He was a charismatic empath, and both women and men alike were taken with his boyish charm. Most hadn't heard of his work, but they pretended they had when I introduced him as one of Spain's current avant garde.

He would perk people up like wilting flowers. I even found myself feeling jealous during a genteel dinner party given by a power editor at Random House. Dressed in a low cut, very transparent blouse, Elaine Williams was just recently divorced. She had allowed her six-year-old daughter Chloe to play with the adults, and both wouldn't stop flirting with David. While Elaine told him all about her horrendous break up, the girl kept lifting up her frilly dress like a little whore trying to get his attention.

He pinched Chloe's little stomach and turned back up to Elaine's big batting eyes as she continued telling him about her loneliness. Yes, I'm ashamed to say, I felt like strangling mother and child right there.

I studied him with other people, complete strangers, new acquaintances, good friends of mine, it didn't matter. I knew his look so well, because it was the way he looked at me that first night, and thereafter, and I fell in love with him for it. I felt safe and special in that tolerant gaze of his. When he shared it with others, I began to grow resentful.

But he was all mine at home. David worked methodically on his novel while I checked into the office every day and counted the hours until I could rush home and have him again. He inspired me to kick-start my second novel, despite my first's disastrous reviews, and for the first time in years I felt confident and creative again. I wanted to write screenplays with him, edit anthologies, and coedit another literary journal with him. I was mad with creative energy.

One beautiful fall morning, David invited me to go live with him in Spain. After that, coming home to him in the evenings involved a whole new mind-set of possibilities for a future together.

When Sergi Canetti entered our lives, he shook our very foundation. I came home at around seven the night it happened, the time I usually arrived. I'd been thinking about David the whole way home. When I walked in, I immediately stripped in the vestibule, knowing he would follow my lead. We met naked in the center of my living room, under the low hanging antique chandelier with small ivory roses I took from my mother's apartment. With all our body parts saluting the other at attention, we wrestled over who would suck the other first. I won the fight, and I kneeled before him in haughty victory.

Then he regained his power, becoming serious in order to sit me down gently on the rickety wooden chair by the kitchen window. I smoked my after-work cigarette, complaining about the idiots I worked with. He kneeled at my mound, opened my lips, and suckled my clit until I felt faint. I told him to stop. He stopped his sucking and leapt up onto his feet and put on his best society lady posture. "Yes, my queen," he said, bowing before me.

With one eyebrow raised abnormally high, he pranced around the room speaking Briticisms, his hands fluttering like butterflies, while his bright red penis pointed the way. I laughed as I studied him. He was beautiful in his girlie man sort of way, and I tackled him onto the bed. He played hard to get until I mounted him, pinned him down. I could do that, we were practically the same size.

He laid helpless beneath me, eyes closed, moaning away as I squeezed and rode his dick like I had learned to ride a horse as a wannabe child jockey at our house upstate. English style, back straight, propped up on my feet, legs bent at my sides. I'd push myself up and down, up and down. I concentrated and stared at him below me, leaning back and turning around to caress his delicate balls. They felt cool to my hands, like little plastic bags of sand to play with.

I looked down and saw his feet. His long toes were curled in arthritic pleasure. It was the pleasure of being encompassed by my insides. He was my captive animal, trapped beneath my long, strong legs he loved so much, his *chaleco de salvavidas*, as he liked to call them.

Wanting to somehow participate, he lifted his upper torso to my left breast and sucked me, the saliva popping loudly in his mouth. He'd look up at me occasionally with one of my reddened nipples in between his teeth. I liked it when he did that, with that look of complete submission. At that moment I was Mother Mary giving milk to her baby Jesus. I was omnipotent and feverish, on a sort of low grade heroine haze. And then suddenly I tired and alighted off him, lying down and spreading myself out for him. I felt shaky, anemic.

He tried to eat me again but my body couldn't take any more, and I captured his eager head in between my hands like the savior and lifted it to give him my breath. We kissed furiously, mouths stretched open to their full capacity, teeth knocking, unfurling our tongues like safety ropes.

Then his cell phone rang. I hated that thing. He stiffened for a bit, as if feeling a change in the air. He looked over at it, contemplated getting it, then thought again. He looked at me instead. Then he let himself inside me elegantly, as his eyes peered into mine. It was like he was looking right through me, intuiting my life's accumulation of sadness. I tried holding my eyes right back to his like I usually did, my lioness instinct. But this time I wanted to hide. I didn't know why, but I felt shaken by the way he looked at that phone. I lowered my lashes instead.

The urge to cry was rising in me fast. I thought of my mother, her pain in love, her longtime fear of aging, of dying alone. I thought of how she finally decided to face this fear by violently making it come true. I felt myself shrinking in his sentient gaze. As he pumped me, his eyes were welling up with tears along with mine. I held back and fought the demon. I didn't want him to know how much I loved him yet or how happy I really was despite my current state. How I wanted to become part of his world and abandon mine!

Deep within me, David twisted and coiled himself, sensually taking in the texture of my inner walls. Then he stopped and said, "Let's get on our sides. But keep me inside of you."

I went with him, face-to-face, as he grabbed my left buttock, and carried me into a half turn onto our sides. Never disconnecting ourselves, David had somehow managed to go even deeper in that new position. We rocked back and forth tensely; his cock massaged my clit, our bodies aching in perfect symmetry. There was so much moisture. He pulled out, buried his head at my breasts again, allowing for us to dry off a bit.

When he re-entered me, he pulsed three times and whimpered at the sensation. That was all he could stand and I was ready too. We came in muted silence, and I allowed myself one stray tear to travel down my face as David shut his eyes and rolled over on his back. I quickly wiped it off.

"You okay?" he asked, catching his breath. He stared up at the white glare of my high antique tin ceilings. I had always thought they looked like dozens of tiny breasts lined up in quadrants. He placed a hand on my leg for reassurance. He wasn't one to touch after sex, too busy recoiling into himself.

"I thought about my mom and got emotional," I mumbled.

"You want to talk about it?"

I tried to decipher his tone before answering. Then I thought about the phone call he received during sex. Who could it have been? Why did he even consider stopping to answer?

"No, it's okay. It's passed now," I lied.

"Some water?" he asked.

"Oh yeah, parched is an understatement," I answered.

I forced myself up with him and went for a cigarette while he took his phone with him into the bathroom. It was probably Sergi. I had heard David whispering on the phone with him late at night. When he came out of the bathroom, I asked him who had called.

"It was Sergi. He likes to reminisce when he's drunk."

It was three a.m. Spain time; nine p.m. ours.

"Doesn't he have anyone else to call?"

It wasn't just the question, but the way my voice shot it out. It had a tone of desperation. I felt threatened. It was the tone that my mother had used a million times on my father when he told her he wouldn't be coming home for dinner or that he had another important business trip.

I was envious of a something I couldn't even put into words or quite understand about him and Sergi. It was just a gut feeling I had. There was nothing I wanted more than to be proven wrong.

He was calm.

"A mutual friend of ours is arriving into town tomorrow, Anna. That's what he was really calling about. Miguel Velásquez. He's an old friend of the family who's here on business. He's an art dealer."

"Great," I said, trying to keep my sanity. "Where shall we take him?"

We arranged to meet Miguel the next night at a high-end, big-chef restaurant on the newly reformed Clinton Street. We went through three bottles of South Africa's finest wines, since this was thankfully on Miguel.

It was my first time seeing David with a close friend, riding down the green, comforting path of memory lane. Miguel was jet-set handsome with perfectly styled salt-and-pepper hair. He was married to a rich *Catalana* who stayed at home and raised their two boys while he frolicked around the globe. He was cordial to me but didn't go beyond the niceties to make me feel like part of the old clan.

His attention was all on David. He had a fountain of questions about David's work and about his mother and her health. Miguel asked if she had remarried since David's father passed away. Like a pair of old women, they unearthed fresh and hardened dirt about themselves and their mutual friends.

Sergi's name was splattered over practically every adventurous tale there was to tell. *Remember when you and Sergi had that party for . . . or when Sergi and you and those girls . . . You and Sergi disappeared with those Swiss dudes . . . .Whatever happened to them!"*

It was obvious the Canettis were the life of the party.

"Yeah, what ever happened to them?" I interjected, giving him a shove and raising an eyebrow.

"Nothing!" David said and laughed. "Nice purple mouth you got there, Anna. Why don't you have some more wine?"

My teeth and lips tend to suck up the tannins. I must have looked like a fool. And he was trying to change the subject.

"Aw come on, man," Miguel egged on. "Those guys were like in love with you and Sergi. You guys were such the cock teasers!" said Miguel. He glanced over at me to try to detect a reaction.

My blood was boiling, but my face muscles were contained.

Their banter was so drenched in homoeroticisms; they might have as well been fencing with their dicks.

I changed the subject to something neutral. I asked about the art Miguel was viewing in New York. Mentally, I prepared myself to confront David when we were alone.

I knew that I was quieter than usual on our walk home.

After we saw Miguel into a cab uptown, David tried a million times to jump-start conversations about Miguel's shallow art world. But all his attempts fell flat. I was trying to breathe and shoo away the black birds of paranoia circling me. We tired from our walk and hailed a short cab ride home.

We slid into the backseat, and I gave the driver directions.

I turned to David.

"Tell me more about your experimentation with Sergi."

He was instantly defensive.

"Why are you making such a big deal about him? Do you think I'm gay or something?"

"I don't know; what the hell did happen with those Swiss guys then?"

"I told you, nothing, we just did lines together. What's wrong with you, Anna?"

"I just want you to tell me more about how you and Sergi first fooled around with each other."

We got back to my apartment and opened another bottle. I listened. I had no choice. I tried to appear calm. He delivered his words casually, like canapés swallowed with champagne. My own sepia-colored movie reel rolled in my head as he spoke.

David explained that he never believed he was a homosexual. He worshipped girls in his classes when he was young, but absolutely no one paid him or Sergi any mind. They were hideous then, he claimed, and foreigners in a xenophobic country to boot. They were simply desperately horny, pimply little bastards who only had each other for company. Sergi's mother, their father's first wife, had died during childbirth. So Sergi lived with an aunt in his early years. He became too much to handle as a preteen, and his aunt sent him back to live with his father, his father's new wife, and his half brother.

The first time Sergi and David touched each other, they'd been sitting in front of their television set in their small apartment in Paris. While David's mother smoked cigarettes in the courtyard and their father banged university students in exchange for discounted books in the back of his shop, the boys gave one another their first blow jobs.

The television had been turned to one of Europe's many soft-core porn channels, where shapely naked women lathered one another in the shower. The boys' virginal cocks pulsed and rose, begging to be set free from their pants. Through the zipper of his blue jeans, Sergi, the taller and more handsome one, released his cock and stroked it wildly to its fullness while he stared straight ahead at the telly. His bottom lip jutted out as he bit down and broke through the violet skin of chapped lips. A rebel strand of wheat-colored hair escaped from a thick mass of an overgrown pageboy haircut and dipped in and out of the pock hole on his upper cheekbone, a mark left from a severe case of the measles. David's cock swelled in sync from the excitement of seeing dozens of hardened nipples. The sound of his mother's voice giggled in the distance while Sergi worked on himself with a passionate energy that David had never witnessed before in his brother. Tense and excited David took his out too. The boys, both sixteen, sat alongside each other on a couch too small for their rapidly growing limbs. They looked over at one another, glassy-eyed and trembling as they pulled at their reddened cocks together. Sergi, who always felt he could he could control David, asked him in a desperate and unequivocally commanding voice to "kiss it, now." And David, without hesitation, leaned over and took in the warmth and mixture of perspiration and detergent smell of his best friend and half brother's manliness.

David propelled himself up and down on Sergi only a pair of times before David, overcome with emotion, prejaculated burning droplets of embarrassment at the newness of it all. Sergi pushed David off and finished himself off with his own hand, feeling overwhelmed with the sight of David's cum and now his own all over his trousers.

With a hand over his mouth, David pointed and laughed at the mess and Sergi registering what had happened, staying perfectly still. He gave David a shove and told him to go and get something to clean it up before David's mother walked in. David brought back some napkins, they cleaned themselves up, and they switched the channel to some American gangster flick.

I realized then that Sergi hadn't blown David and that in game theory, he owed him one. But I didn't want to know any more.

David left for Barcelona a day before New York had its first big snowfall. He had an important engagement to attend back home at the Círculo de Lectores. I assured him I would join him as soon as I could figure out what do about work. My first days and nights alone again were spent obsessing over Sergi and David. I imagined the wild, sexual adventures that awaited them when they reunited in Spain again.

• • •

After the reality that David had left set in, I spiraled from ecstasy to a one-lane freeway toward depression. I had been on a four-month hiatus from its dark fog, and now I was back. I began seeing my shrink again. I told Laura about my feelings of jealousy about David's experimentations and his intimate relationship with Sergi.

Sitting in front of me, on her hunter green chair, in a long, flowing khaki-colored skirt and brown riding boots, Laura was serene. She joined in the Greek chorus of those around me who pooh-poohed my irrational fear of thinking David a closet homosexual.

"This is natural behavior for men. They're just as capable of experimenting with the same sex as women are," she said.

She paused and asked, "You've been with women, right?"

"Yeah."

"Why is it different or more acceptable that you did?"

"I don't know. It's just *different*."

"It's the same. Just be grateful that he told you," she said. "This proves a wonderful aspect of his open character. He's sharing himself, his past, who he is with you."

"I guess so."

"He's chose *you*, Anna. Trust him, trust yourself. Okay?"

"Okay."

Time was up and having him so far away didn't help my overactive imagination when I *wasn't* seated in my shrink's chair.

My life in New York was no longer mine for the few months that followed. I lived in an altered state, a time-zoned paralysis as I imagined his fabulous Barcelona life six hours ahead of mine. Six hours ahead on working wonders on his novel, gallivanting with his arty friends, meeting other fascinating, brilliant women, other dashing men.

He'd send me horny one-liners in awkward email English. *I click on your clit with my dick.* I'd get them at work. He had his three p.m. siesta jerk-off while I was hitting my nine a.m. caffeine-fueled "what am I doing here?" hour.

One day I found myself completely unable to concentrate on the stories I had to edit. I *needed* to kill the throbbing between my legs.

So I decided to masturbate in the office bathroom. I watched myself in the mirror of the handicap stall, the one with the extra large sink. With my head thrown back and my mouth pleading to be filled, I let my raised nipples loose from my bra. I thought of his dick rubbing against me and touched myself, my clitoris expanding underneath my fingers. I imagined him and a strange man he'd met in a bar. I pictured him and Sergi in one of their threesomes he had told me about. I saw him and random sexy girls speaking in that castrating Spanish of theirs under the sheets.

As I looked at myself in the mirror, I didn't recognize the savage woman that looked back, the edges of her mouth sinking, her skirt hitched up under her. I was becoming like them: My lascivious parents.

High on recklessness, I resigned the next day. Without a hint of remorse I asked my publisher, Martin Powers, if he would still allow me to submit articles from Spain on the goings on in the European market. He said yes. I told Martin, who had become a father figure to me (even though at times he was overcome with visible thoughts of incest) that I was going to be working on my next novel in Barcelona.

That night I went home to buy a one-way ticket to Barcelona. I called David to tell him that I had decided to come try it for a while. I could feel his lust and longing through the receiver. He whined and told me to come right then, and I could practically come just hearing his voice, but for that we had to wait another two weeks.

Then the vibrato of that joyous conversation lulled when he told me that my arrival would coincide with Sergi's, who'd be visiting from Madrid. He was going to be there for two weeks doing a series of talks on his latest tome for Barcelona's big literary festival, Diada de Sant Jordi.

I pouted over the phone line and told him that I preferred for us to be alone, reminding him that I wasn't a quiet fuck. It didn't go down well with David at first. He insisted that he had a large flat and plenty of extra rooms and bathrooms. It took some convincing with old truisms like, three's a crowd and a woman needs her privacy.

It annoyed me that David didn't innately understand my argument of wanting alone time after such a long period of not seeing each other. He finally grunted an okay, muttering that he'd tell him to find another place to stay. He was obviously worried about Sergi's reaction. And I celebrated winning this small battle for now.

On that cold and rainy April night at JFK airport, I crossed myself. I made the four-pointed arm gestures of the crucifix slowly as I waited in line to check in. *In the name of the Father . . . the Son . . . the Holy Spirit . . . Amen.* Like I had seen old wrinkled-up women do in the face of the unknown.

It was ten a.m. Barcelona time, four a.m. mine, when my plane arrived. David was waiting for me at the airport. A lover of public transportation, he insisted we take the metro back to his apartment in the center of the city.

He was all skin and bones, wearing red unisex espadrilles as he rolled my fifty-pound suitcase over the furrows and protrusions of Barcelona's cobblestone streets. He was wearing a cream linen shirt, open to the third button from the top, exposing that pile of chest hair I so adored burrowing my face into. His skinny legs were sheathed in some army green–colored cargo pants with one leg rolled up.

Despite the tremendous weight he dragged behind him, he zigzagged like a Twyla Tharp dancer from one side of the pavement to the other, escaping la Rambla de Catalunya's undulating pedestrian traffic. Used to the daily inconveniences of living in one of the world's most enchanted cities, he parted the crowd of morning tourists with a gentle brush of his extended right hand. They obeyed like a herd of cows, letting us pass at his command.

"Almost there," he reassured me, looking back to see if I was still with him. Then he made a sudden right onto a street with an impressive Gothic church rounding its corner. Never taking my eyes off his regal back, I followed him from behind. It was impossible to walk at his side on Barcelona's truncated sidewalks with my huge suitcase in the way. I appreciated the moment alone, so I could prepare myself for reuniting with him at his apartment. "Okay," I sang back. I stared like an awed little girl at the ancient stone buildings that led to David's building, their flowers cascading over verandas and dark-shuttered doors with the promise of spreading open to mysterious lives above.

There was a morning chill in the air. My nipples rose to their points under my white shirt dress. I looked up and noticed an old man was looking down into my open neckline. I smiled, and he gave me a salacious grimace in return.

Carrer de Carme, 24. That's where my David lived. It was a busy side street off la Rambla in the Arab-dominated ghetto of el Raval. The neighborhood was a mix of strange Old-World seedy and pop bohemian artsy. It was undergoing its predictable gentrification. David had taken the inheritance his father left him and bought himself the coveted top floor of an architecturally impressive, but structurally dilapidated building. "This is it," he grinned, breathing hard through his teeth.

The building was called La India, and it had gargoyles and faces of ominous indigenous women skimming its rooftop. We walked into the cool of the building's open marbled lobby, past two sets of pillared columns and into a small metallic elevator-made-for-two hidden behind an antique glass door.

We were finally alone, nose to nose in the tiny elevator that smelled of days of accumulated sweat. I just stood there staring at him, expressionless from nerves. David shoved his hands up my dress. He slipped his hand into my underwear and cupped my wet sex. He grazed my clitoris with his fingers. I thought he was going to take me right there. His hardness was pressing up against me. We kissed furiously as the mechanical gears roared and until the elevator car jumped, signifying that we had landed. David removed his fingers from my insides and licked them clean. "We're here."

We tumbled out of the elevator into a dark, windowless hallway with a floor of large black-and-white squares of ceramic. There were only two doors on each floor, and David's apartment was behind the big wooden one on our left with an old metallic lion's head knocker in its center. Once he turned the thick golden key he took out of his pocket, I heard a click, and he pushed it open.

In an instant, all of Barcelona's splendid light poured onto us through the uncurtained windows with such grandeur, it was like we had been dosed with a bucket of golden honey. He rolled my suitcase to the side and welcomed me. "You're home."

In that light, I swear he freaking shimmered. His black waves of hair painted with rays of white light. He'd be beautiful, even old.

Light was important for David and his writing life, to psychically be away from the city's dark and noisy streets below. I squinted, feeling a headache coming on. I desired my sunglasses.

"Wow" was all I could say. Some sort of low grade aphasia had hit me with the jetlag setting in. And there was so much to absorb about David's world without me.

He took my hand and walked me through the long hallway of his railroad apartment. The floors were a swirling mosaic of salmons, browns, and greens. Their florid hues had faded and veiny cracks of time now intermixed with their patterns instead. We passed sparsely furnished parlor rooms with white-curtained French doors. There were one-person guest beds and wooden bookshelves along with antique desks with mismatched chairs scattered throughout.

In one of those rooms, a medium-sized suitcase and a pair of men's fancy dress shoes sat beside the bed. The shoes were a shiny dark brown leather, Italian, too elegant to be David's. Feeling my stomach drop, I intuited they had to have been Sergi's. I chose to remain silent. I didn't want to ruin our first moments. I decided to pretend I didn't notice them.

He showed me to our bedroom and told me to settle in. It was a large white room, with a balcony facing an interior courtyard where neighboring families hung out their underwear to dry. I stepped onto it and looked down. I noticed there was a black-haired Barbie doll, her stiff arms raised over her head, lying naked on the cement. A small child tiring of her must have tossed her out the window, wondering if she could fly.

I looked around his bedroom. His style was minimalist, mostly from lack of need. A queen-size bed, covered in white sheets and a down comforter contrasted a dark wood chest of drawers, and two matching night tables. He had a bottle of water propped up on his nightstand and book casually left open. Nothing was out of place, everything had a purpose. He must have thought my place was a tornado disaster area.

"You should eat something," he said, in a tone that seemed suddenly formal.

His words startled me. I realized I was standing there dissecting it all in silence.

"I'd rather eat you," I said playfully, turning to face him. I stepped over to him, grabbed his crotch, and kissed his neck, taking in his Mediterranean blend of olive soap and tobacco smell.

"Don't," he said, unhooking my hands and placing them at my sides. His eyes darted back and forth in thought. All the sexual energy from before had been drained from the room.

"Don't what?" I said.

"Later, Anna." He said it in the way a woman might if she had a headache.

"Fine," I said, audibly pissed.

"We have all the time in the world to make love."

He always said that. "*Hacer el amor*" instead of *follar*, fuck, which I liked to say now. Like in the Almodóvar movies. He liked to correct me on this, disapproving of my crude Spanish. "We don't *fuck* Anna, we make *love*," he'd say with a smile.

I always rolled my eyes at this. The thought of making love all the time killed the mood.

"Let's put some food into you, okay? I pre-prepared our lunch."

Though he was going through the good host's manual step-by-step, he was still acting a little weird. I started to suspect he had second thoughts about me coming.

"I'll freshen up then." My voice came out a note higher than usual.

I turned to fidget blindly with the zipper of my suitcase, his eyes still on me. And just as that feeling of exasperation of being in this unknown place was rising, the hot tears ready to roll, David came up behind me and hugged my bent body clasping his hands over my uterus. "I'm so happy you're here," he whispered in my ear.

Once he left the room, I went into the bathroom and unpacked my toiletry bag. There was a stale smell of old plumbing that turned my stomach, and I breathed through my mouth instead. Confronting my appearance in the mirror, I got back what I expected to see. I was green from a week's worth of little sleep and anxiety.

After brushing my teeth with my Tom's of Maine mint toothpaste (David teased me about it, calling me nature chica), I dabbed on some lipstick and debated which of David's fragrances to put on to liven me up. Lavander, Vetiver, Musk, Figuer. The latter was a high-end French cologne that smelled of dirt and figs. I remember thinking this was funny. *Figa*, in Italian, is slang for pussy. I hadn't known him to be a perfume wearer in New York. I went for the Figuer, in tribute to its symbolism.

Finished with my mild grooming, I went back into the hallway and walked toward the sound of banging dishes in the kitchen. On the way, I saw what seemed to be his study. I decided to dip into it before reencountering him so soon.

On an old rickety side table adjacent to a big beige comfy reading chair sat a pair of framed photographs, the only ones I had seen in the house so far. One was of a thin, bearded man in a dress shirt and high-waisted slacks. He was standing in front of a bookstore with a proud look on his face. It was almost a smirk. It had to be his father.

Then there was the other photo. Two twenty-something boys in matching white T-shirts and jeans laughed hysterically, tears running down their faces, with their arms tightly enwound around each other's waists. Sergi and David, long-haired and tan, posing with that barely perceptible femininity in their stance that only I could clearly see. Sergi towered over David, who was nestled into the crevice of his armpit. Physically, Sergi was way more striking than David had ever suggested in his descriptions. And it was obvious he held the reins.

From what I gathered, Sergi was David's ringleader, his pimp. David was always under his tutelage in writing and when it came to getting laid. Throughout their teens and twenties they'd date the same women, bed them together, and get off on the group sex. Watching the other pump. Lending a generous hand, patting each other's backsides in brotherly support. I never had the nerve to ask David if they'd engage each other during these threesomes.

An unwanted vision of David's thin lips around Sergi's cock appeared in my head. My hands clamped up around the edges of the cold wood frame, my heart beat faster in panic. I wanted to throw the photo against the wall and smash their big smiles to pieces. Why the hell was I jealous of a man? What did he have that I didn't? I thought I already knew the answer.

"Anna, come to the balcony," David called out from a distance. The balcony spread along the back end of his apartment so you could enter it from various parts of the house; from his bedroom, the study, or from the hallway. He had quite a spread of Spanish culinary clichés awaiting me: olives, jamón serrano, Manchego cheese, grilled squid, tortilla española.

"You doing okay?" He asked as I stepped out into the dry, yellow sun. A comic *vroom vroom* of a motor scooter from the side street below answered his question before I could. "Sure. Just feeling a little woozy. Probably hunger." It was somewhere in the early afternoon, and David was pouring us glasses of full-bodied Rioja. I could still feel his tension and I was grateful for the upcoming intoxication.

He dragged out a metal lawn chair for me to sit down in and slowly as if with arthritis eased himself into his seat. The sky was monochromatically blue and the sun's rays were penetrating my scalp. David had his sunglasses on so I couldn't see his eyes, but I could tell his wheels were turning; he was pushing out his mouth in thought.

It was the quiet before the storm.

"So we're not alone, huh?" I ventured first. His silence was irritating me.

He sighed a sigh that weighed half his entire body weight.

"Yes, Anna. I wanted to tell you beforehand, but I didn't want you to rearrange your plans or decide not to come or something crazy."

"Sergi's here, I know," I said.

David reached for his glass and took a swig. I reached for one of his Lucky Strikes, focusing on the bomb target symbol on its packaging. Neither of us had touched the food.

"Listen, I want you to meet him. He's part of my past. Yes, he's been a pain in the ass all his life, but he's family and I can't shut my door on him. He's harmless. God, why do you hate him so much?" His voice was whinier than usual. He looked at me, his upper lip in a curl, his mouth slightly ajar. I had never seen him look so annoyed, so nervous.

Then he put his head down, resting his elbows on his splayed knees, staring at the ground. He looked defeated. I caught a whiff of the Manchego.

I have to confess that his weakness gave me a whole new sense of strength. Sergi was obviously a touchy topic, and David was beginning to seem half the man I fell for in New York.

"Listen David," I said calmly, using my best phone operator voice. I was good at concealing the pain when I had to.

"I thought we had agreed that he was going to stay somewhere else while I was getting settled in here at least. You told me this."

He sat up in his seat, "His plans fell through with some other apartment, okay? And he has to be here for a few Diada de Sant Jordi book events. Lord knows I have enough extra space in this place. What's the big deal? What do you have against someone you've never even met?"

"I have absolutely *nothing* against him," I said. "*Really, I don't,*" I said even slower, sounding like I was gurgling under water. "I guess I just feel kind of uncomfortable, perhaps threatened is a better word . . . with all the women and all your sexual liaisons together."

I took a long drag of my cigarette.

"I'm not into being shared, you know. I just don't need that sort of juvenile shit in my life."

"He's not going to try anything, Anna. That was the past. We're adults now. Trust me. He knows that you're special, and that I'm in love with you. We're done with all that."

David was visibly trying to pull himself together. I wanted our beginning to go as smoothly as possible. I flashed him my big joker smile instead. I knew it looked natural, but it wasn't. He laughed with a gullible relief.

"You're so nutty, Anna. You're a real paranoid case." He caressed my cheek, then licked it, and with the other hand he took a piece of ham and placed it into my mouth. It was salty and warm from sitting in the sun. I think it was the best ham I've ever tasted.

"I'm taking you to a fancy party tonight."

"Really?" A shiver of excitement raced down my spine.

"It's *Libros* magazine's kick off party for Diada de Sant Jordi at the Ritz. Everyone will be there, including our friend Sergi. He's giving a brief speech, which will probably be inappropriate and sarcastic. People love to hate him here."

"Including you?" I asked.

He thought for a moment.

"Yes, sometimes, including me. Don't take this badly, but you remind me of each other. You both can be charmingly arrogant on the exterior, but viciously insecure inside. Watch, you guys are going to become wicked pals," he laughed, tears filling in his eyes.

I wanted to believe him. I wanted to believe we could all be friends.

Barcelona's springtime literary love fest, Diada de Sant Jordi, is Catalunya's take on St. Valentine's Day. The holiday takes place on April 23rd, the anniversary of Cervantes's and Shakespeare's deaths. It spotlights love's finer accompaniments: books, roses, and playing hooky from work. I loved this take on the holiday; it was a welcome switch from America's garish pink Hallmark cards, helium balloons, or the obligatory heart-shaped boxes of chocolates perfunctorily sent to one's cubicle.

Way back in the dark Middle Ages, the legendary and valiant Saint George (Sant Jordi) was said to have rescued his Catalan city and his pouty princess from a fire-breathing dragon that plagued the people. He stabbed the beast in the heart with his long sword and killed it.

Now in tribute to all that reptilian bloodshed, and the miraculous rosebush that blossomed from it, it is the custom that men give red roses to their ladies. In return, the ladies give books to their men.

Local booksellers and flower vendors cram the length of la Rambla and other streets, and everyone in Barcelona finds a good excuse not to do a stitch of work. Instead, people stroll the streets with their lovers, browse for books, crowd the plazas, and eye the fashionable authors of the day.

It is also a big day for cultural critics and the literati to see who got invited that year to sign their books around town. The high society svengalis behind the Sant Jordi events had chosen Sergi as one of the honorary invitees, while David with a new book out had been slighted in his own hometown.

David acted like it didn't bother him. He pointed out that he and Sergi had been invited previous years during the height of *Crack*'s popularity. I knew some part of him felt hurt. Could he be so above this kind of sibling rivalry? Was he already content with his literary credibility? I didn't know whether I'd ever be.

Deep down I already knew I was a better literary critic than I was a writer. I had graduated with an MFA in creative writing from a top school only to see all my friends get offered immediate high-profile book deals with their theses. I reworked my thesis over and over until I killed it. When I finally published it with some trendy indie publisher based in Brooklyn, it was so overwrought, so self-conscious, that one critic labeled it "cold and overly stylized." Somehow, this kind of criticism had never touched Sergi's dense work. His new book on Hadrian, an impenetrable thicket of pompous jargon and historical assumptions, was oddly more popular than David's last heartbreaking novel about alienation.

After David had caught me up on all the literary gossip on the terrace, we scurried into the bedroom. Talking about the book fair was our post-fight, verbal foreplay right before we finally sprang into bed and spread each other's folds open—the tension had been so ripe. We then passed out in a sun-drenched, red wine stupor, our sweaty bodies laid out naked above the sheets after a much-needed fuck.

The balcony doors were open to their full glory and I awoke to the soothing feeling of sunlight warming my bush. The sensation made me want him again, but I didn't want to wake him.

I needed water. I grabbed David's Chinese robe and straightened myself up before exiting the bedroom, thinking, perhaps *hoping*, I'd run into Sergi on my way to the kitchen. This time the room with the shoes' door was practically closed. I assumed Sergi had been here while we were napping. I tapped softly on the door and called out hello. There was no answer, so I pushed the door open.

The shoes were gone. The suitcase was now an explosion of white dress shirts, sleek belts, and identical pairs of dark denim jeans. Sergi was obviously in a rush to get in and get out fast. There were copies of his books strewn on the floor. I picked one up and stared at the black-and-white author photo. It was a more recent photo than the one I'd seen in David's study, and he was still just as stunning, having grown more distinguished with age. He had grown facial hair; and I immediately thought it was a vain attempt to look smart, less pretty boy.

White sheets of paper with elegant and scripted writing were scattered hastily over the unmade bed. They looked like drafts of his short speech for *Libros* magazine's Sant Jordi event that night. Maybe he wasn't as spontaneous as David had suggested.

While I showered before the party, I imagined what my first words to Sergi could be. I chose my outfit carefully. I didn't want to look like another literary social climber in a flowery minidress and pristine pumps. I decided to go for a black-fitted pants suit instead. I let my braless breasts hang free in their tear-drop position, rounding out the edges of my jacket. Black pointed flats provided maximum comfort while walking Barcelona's dark streets with the boys later that night.

I lined my eyes with black eyeliner and smoked them up with grey shadow. I skipped the lipstick. I wanted to be all eyes that night.

Surrounded by the unnaturally attractive Spanish publishing world, I was glad that I had fixed myself up. In the packed ballroom, the Ritz's chandeliers cast a romantic light on the wiry women in dramatically draped scarves and men impeccably dressed in dark jackets.

We were boxed into a room of wall-to-wall mirrors where violins played and enormous golden vases with long-stemmed roses for Diada de Sant Jordi lined the walls. A mighty mix of booze, nerves, and jetlag kicked in as David and I made our first rounds. I felt like Rita Hayworth's character trapped in the Hall of Mirrors in *The Lady of Shanghai*, where everything looks warped through the lens of paranoia.

I tried to spot Sergi or anybody I knew in the mirrors' reflection, but a low-lying cloud of cigarette smoke hung over our heads like a rain cloud, fogging up my view. Suddenly, David was dragged off by a pack of faceless arms in one direction. I was pulled in the opposite direction, in the liver-spotted, red-nailed clench of Catalan literary agent Silvia Riera.

I'd gotten to know Silvia well over the years through my reporting on the Spanish literary circuit. She was a *been-here-done-that* kind of woman in her late fifties, who I suspected was still up to lots of *that*. She came from a good Catalan family and got into the literary business because she liked high-brow books, cocktail parties, and sleeping with struggling writers. She was asking me why the hell had I left my high-profile editorial position to come to Barcelona—when I finally spotted Sergi. He stood five heads away from us, laughing big and showing fangs. He turned his head toward me as I eyed him up and down. I told Silvia I'd just gotten sick of New York.

It was impossible not to notice him. He was taller and blonder than most in the room. He turned his entire body to face me, even as he was still chatting up an austere, balding man, probably another veteran of Spanish letters making nice to the new lion. Silvia moved on to a woman she knew standing next to us, and Sergi kept on looking. Noticing he had lost Sergi's attention, the gentleman of letters spotted me, gave me the once over, and continued his monologue anyway.

Despite his refined looks, Sergi's smile was vulgar. He raked his eyes over me as if I were standing there naked. I blushed like a nun and soaked myself at the same time. It reminded me of why I knew I'd hate him. Did he know who I was? *How* did he know who I was? He mouthed a hello. I nodded in camaraderie and gave him a frigid politician's smile. Then he turned away to continue his conversation with the gentleman.

Silvia had seen our unspoken exchange. She turned back to me.

"Oh darling, watch out for him. Don't tell me you two have already . . . ?" She paused.

"Nooo," I said loudly. I made a hissing sound to punctuate my negation, for both of our ears.

"I'm here with David Canetti, not Sergi Canetti."

"Uuff," she said. "A *little* better, but still, the Canettis are quite the dogs around town you know." She looked at me sympathetically, reading it all so clearly on my face. She continued.

"But David has always struck me as the Abel to his Cain in that strange brotherhood. It seems they never get too far from each other, like Frack and Frick," she said in English, pumping extra gasoline into her *rrr*'s.

"Yes, they're tight," I added with an upturn in my voice. I tried to steer the conversation away from the sewage she was ready to spill.

I scanned the room, desperately looking for David. I spotted him. He was talking with Sergi and a group of Spanish literatis. He was doing a lot of double-cheeked air kissing and man-to-man back rubbing. I thought about how much more people touched in Europe.

Despite my distraction, Silvia pressed on. "Don't worry. They'll treat you well. You're with *Publisher's Forum*, and they're dying for some recognition in New York." She placed her hand on my shoulder in pity. Though I hated the gesture, I appreciated her brutal honesty, as always. In exchange, she tolerated my bad reviews of her navel-gazing authors.

I excused myself. I looked for David, who had managed to slip into the crowd again. I was hoping we could do a little public fondling. That's when I saw Sergi cutting through the crowd, quickly moving in my direction.

The bar was packed. I managed to hide myself in a group of huddled men, waiting for my chance to order a drink. Sergi slid between the men and grabbed the top of my arm. I wasn't going anywhere, his grip was too tight. He towered over me, and I was forced to look up at him.

"Anna, I'm Sergi, David's brother." He leaned in to kiss me twice, speaking to me in English, not in Spanish like everyone else did. His English was perfect, far better than David's. His voice was deep, a smoker's raspy.

"I know." I said coldly in Spanish, not wanting to look like a foreigner. As we brushed faces, I could smell the Figuer cologne on him. "When's your little talk?" I asked.

And he continued in English as if he hadn't heard my question. "What are you drinking? Let me get it for you."

He raised a long finger and one of his thick and wickedly arched brows and instantly got the busy barmen's attention. I assumed he was a man who never had to wait for much.

"*Quiero un whiskey,*" I said, insisting on speaking in Spanish.

Sergi faced the bar looking away from me, staring stone-faced into the mirror in front of us. In the mirror, I saw people around us recognize him, subtly pointing as they whispered to each other. They must have recognized him from all the pre–Sant Jordi media blitz he had done. He ran his hand through his long and wavy hair with hints of gray in it and looked down at the floor momentarily before turning back to me. He was a man used to having eyes on him. And I was stunned by how good it felt to be the woman standing next to him.

"You are an absolutely stunning creature when you're naked. Has any man ever told you that, Anna?" He was still speaking to me in English, our drinks in hand, when he turned to face me.

I felt my sex draw back into itself, tight and tense. I just stared at him.

"I watched you and David fucking this afternoon," he said. "I want you to know I really got off on it. I'm surprised you didn't sense me there on the balcony," he said, incredulously.

"No, I didn't," I said back in English, in an icy, even tone. "David didn't tell me his brother was a stalker." Sergi registered my comment by looking away. I tried to remain cool, wondering whether David had known he was watching. Our lovemaking was especially acrobatic, David taking me, turning me every which way he could onto him.

We were silent, as partygoers pushed and bumped up to us like small pesky waves out in deep water. We just stood there, feet anchored to the ground, enveloped in a sticky net of paralyzing hate for each other.

Then a young woman with a dark tan and a tight white sleeveless dress stepped between us, leaning into Sergi seductively to say something in his ear. He said okay. It was time for his speech. Before I could say a word, she pulled him away from me.

Sergi's speech was predictably stagey.

I looked for David as Sergi started his talk, his devoted listeners hanging on every word. And no one was more attentive than David, his most loyal fan, who I found standing at the corner of the stage.

"Look sweetie, it's Sergi." He giggled like a proud mother at a first dance recital. He was so proud of his conceited brother that I decided not to tell him about our conversation. He did not see him as I did, he never would. David and I had exchanged fluids. As had they. But they were flesh and blood. This was a battle between Sergi and me.

So I just stood there, next to David and imagined Sergi naked, jerking off, coming pathetically into his hand, watching us. I imagined me sucking his oversexed sanguine cock with bravado. I couldn't deny the fact I found him attractive. I imagined David walking in on us fucking secretly in the marbled men's toilet of the Ritz, staring at us with repugnance and utter joy.

When the open bar at the Ritz closed, the three of us left with a large pack of horny literary alcoholics trailing behind us. They were middle-aged and preppy, sputtering vulgarities at the end of every sentence.

On the way out, Sergi swiped two long-stemmed roses from the Ritz's vases and presented them to David and me. "To my favorite lovers on Sant Jordi," was all he said before doing a disappearing act into the crowd behind us. I caught his sleazy double meaning. We flooded the streets with a group of about fifteen, half of whom it seemed had slept with either David or Sergi (or both) at one point or another. The babbling women were eager to share their nights of asphyxiating surrender to the Canettis' charm with me. The men were more reserved, but they eyed me like a woman would her ex's new conquest.

Then, without warning, David let go of my hand and clasped his rose between his teeth to jump into a comical flamenco dance in the middle of the street. My pulse raced, and I dropped Sergi's rose to the ground, letting it slip naturally from my hands. Then I flicked my cigarette butt at it. Our group shouted olés, and some joined him, while Sergi and I stood back and watched. He looked on with feigned amusement. I knew that he had watched me drop the rose. I clapped harder, faster, as David stomped furiously for his finale. Sergi burned holes through my suit with his eyes all the while.

We moved our parade to the next place. We drank rounds of whiskey at tavern after tavern as we walked from the architecturally breathtaking streets of upper Gracia to the piss holes of lower Barrio Gótico. The night's path paralleled my degenerative transformation into a walking oral fixation. I chain-smoked, accepted drinks from strangers, chatted up the group, and made out with David wherever I could. I was mad with the newfound freedom of Barcelona's street life and being surrounded by people who didn't know me. I felt grotesquely alive.

Sergi never strayed too far away from David and me. But he avoided talking to me alone at the bars. He liked standing next to me silently, making me uneasy. I heard him breathing. I could smell his odor of perspiring figs as he'd rub his pelvis as close to my body as possible when we were standing together cramped in a group.

He also enjoyed interrupting me. I was commenting on how much I liked Spanish writer Javier Marias's long run-on sentences and closeted narrator to an editor couple in our group when Sergi cut me off in midsentence. He said that Americans couldn't possibly understand Marias's genius. He liked attacking Americans' ignorance of foreign literature, making it clear that when he said Americans, he meant me. He carried on and on, in love with the sound of his voice. But I was a snake as slick as he. When he finished, I asked him if he had been able to find an American publisher yet to translate his books into English. He smiled, his eyes said touché. But I could tell he was annoyed. He said that he hadn't found a publisher. I gave him my sympathies, excusing myself to find David.

Around three a.m., I opened my eyes in the midst of a room-spinning kiss with David and saw Sergi standing behind him, looking me directly in the eye. We were at a dive bar called Kentucky, and the group was down to a total of five, including the Canettis and me. Testing how far Sergi would go to follow us, I dragged a very drunk David to a dark corner of the bar by the bathrooms.

I had never seen him so wasted. The night's tension of having me and Sergi in a room together had driven him to it. I had watched him drink whiskey after whiskey to keep up with Sergi. But his body weight could never match his brother's. So as David got sloppier and sloppier, Sergi appeared in complete and eerie control.

David had asked me repeatedly throughout the night if I was happy, if I liked Sergi, and if we could all be friends. I lied and said yes to all his questions, assuaging his doubts. Standing by the bathrooms, he swayed like a palm tree at the mercy of a Caribbean wind storm. I held him still.

"Let's go," I said. "Let's put you to bed."

"No, I'm fine. Just touch me."

I pressed my body against his, I wanted him to feel my breasts. I began chewing on his ear and rubbing his cock over his trousers. And just as I suspected he would, Sergi appeared and leaned himself up against the wall in front of us. He was our one-member audience, standing in between two doors with the male and female gender symbols on them.

David's eyes were shut tight in ecstasy. I elongated my tongue, showing Sergi how long I could stretch it out into David's ear. I was waiting for some kind of response from Sergi. He watched without expression. It drove me mad.

David opened his eyes slowly. He saw Sergi and calmly asked, "Hey man, what's up?"

"I need another drink. Do you have any cash?" Sergi asked, balancing open a sheet of rolling paper and sprinkling in the loose tobacco.

"We'll be right there," David said, finding my hands so I'd continue.

Sergi licked the cigarette shut, exposing a long pink tongue. Then he nodded and took his time walking away. I punched David in the arm, disgusted by his passiveness.

"What?" he said.

"You're going to fucking just let him interrupt us?" He looked at me with eyes as glazed as glass marbles and began rubbing my crotch. He pushed the side of his hand in the crease of my pussy, calming me in an instant.

"Do you like it when I do this to you?"

I pushed his hand away.

"We gotta go, remember?" I said, "Sergi needs his bottle."

The bar was getting ready to shut down as we went out into the main room to look for Sergi. The other couple had gone home at this point, and we found Sergi standing outside talking to a sweet-looking woman with long black curls. We waited for him to finish and when he said goodbye to her, she looked very disappointed. I pitied her.

Sergi's hands were tucked into the pockets of his blazer, his hair pulled back now into a messy stump of a ponytail. With his head tilted to the side he looked directly at me, ignoring David. "Shall we continue this journey?"

My anger neutralized with the thought of another drink and I had liked the tone that Sergi had addressed me with. "Sure," I said nonchalantly, and we began to walk towards some underground after-hours bar that both he and David seemed to know.

It was just the three of us now. A trio, a tribe, a *tribu*. Primitive cultures knew that when there were more than two people to a group, a new set of laws had to be established to maintain order.

Nobody was walking a straight line anymore. Neither was the rest of Barcelona at that time of night. David was sputtering nonsensicals about the dragon and Sant Jordi that made us laugh. We were somehow bonding over David's amateurish inebriation and our love for him.

I kept David's step steady with my arm as Sergi lead the way to the next whiskey bar. David belted out the lyrics to an old Joy Division song in his bad British English. And I joined in. We were happy as could be.

We turned onto a dingy street in el Raval lined with African prostitutes giving us some serious come-hither looks. Sergi knocked on a nondescript rounded wooden door and a man popped out his head. After Sergi gave him some mumbled password we were let into a cavelike lair blasting eerie opera music below. We ordered some scotch, smoked the hashish that was passed to us, and all fell mute.

Sergi eventually left us to go wander in the back room while David and I zoned out to the music and to rubbing the skin on each other's arms.

Time went by; I can't say how much but I had the urge to pee and excused myself. As I walked to the back, I remember noticing that I was the only woman in the place. I climbed some rickety spiral stairs to an upper room with a cheap exposed red light bulb hanging in its corridor. Before I opened the door where the toilet was, I saw two men embracing, deep in a hungry kiss, leaning against the communal sink. The men hadn't sensed me there. But from the blazer and small ponytail, dark designer blue jeans, fine shoes, I knew it was Sergi.

I studied them, entranced by the forcefulness of the kiss. The other man was Latino looking, black shiny straight hair, olive skin, a long mestizo nose that thickened at the base and led into full bitable lips that Sergi was devouring. The other man noticed me but didn't stop what he was doing; he couldn't. Sergi now had his hand on top of the man's head and right shoulder, lowering him down to exactly where he wanted him. I suddenly thought I could do better and I was stunned to feel myself turned on. Sergi was in total control. I backed out of the hallway as fast as I could. Forewent the peeing.

I told David the bathroom was broken and that we had to go. He asked if I had seen Sergi, and I told him he'd probably gone home already. It was around five a.m. and the streets were still littered with drunken Euro hipsters. We found a dark alleyway to piss in by some old Gothic church. David took it out and aimed at the wall beside me as I squatted and pushed my crotch out towards the wall, spreading my legs so the urine wouldn't slide under my shoes.

"So I saw Sergi sucking face with some guy at the bar," I said from below, getting up to zip myself up. I was surprised by how upset I felt again. "Sergi's a full-fledged bisexual, huh? Just like Hadrian, the Roman emperor."

"No he just fucks around occasionally." He said.

"Then you could say he's gay then?"

"The man is not gay, Anna. He loves women. He just likes flesh. Flesh is flesh, right?"

"Maybe it's more like he'll fuck anything that moves, including his own brother." I shot back.

I wanted to hit him from frustration. I wanted to ask him if he fucked men on the side. But I refrained. Then he grabbed me by the hips and drew me closer.

"Stop it, Anna. Don't be mad at me, but he told me he wants to sleep with you."

I could tell David was turned on, his hands caressing my ass, his pupils huge in the night's fading moonlight.

"And what did you say?"

"I told him to go to hell and that I'd never let him. He found you fascinating. What did you think of him?"

"Honestly, I think he's an asshole."

"No, I think you like him," he drawled drunkenly, his hands had moved to the sides of my breasts.

"No I *don't*, David." But I wasn't so sure.

"Yes you do, all the girls do. But he can't have you, you're mine." He licked my neck.

"And he can't have you, either, you bastard," I said, wanting to possess him, completely.

Then a German couple walked in on us and kindly asked for directions.

We walked home in silence, still floating on a cloud of hashish. We passed minivans stocked with hoards of red roses and empty tables waiting for the books that would be displayed and bought tomorrow by idealistic, unassuming women for their seemingly perfect, Spanish men.

Our bedroom was encased by the purple glow of dawn when I awoke. We had been asleep for a half hour, maybe a deep ten minutes, when I heard Sergi's footsteps in the hallway coming in the front door. I couldn't tell if he was alone or if he had brought someone back. Aroused instantly by his presence, I sat up in bed, fully awake, and listened.

I imagined him smelling like the cheap cologne and soilings of that man from the bar. I lay back down, with a desire to touch myself as David snored peacefully beside me. I threw the white sheet off of David and reached for his cock, trying to awaken him with my touch. Now I really needed him to enter me, fuck me hard, fuck me loud. I wanted Sergi to hear it all.

David let out a cranky moan as I planted my face between his legs, lifted him up from his buttocks, like a mother lifting her child to change him. Trailing his hair-lined stretch from anus to testicles with my tongue, I took his flaccid cock in my mouth and it came to life, even before David fully came to.

"What are you doing?" he asked. Propping himself up on his elbows, blinking hard. He was startled, his heart beating fast. I didn't answer; enthralled on getting him off, I held on with my mouth, kissing, sucking as loudly as I could.

There was no sound coming from the hallway or from any part of the apartment anymore. The house was frozen in screaming silence aside from my mouth's wet popping sounds and David's gentle moaning. He was laying down again, tossing his head from side to side.

"God I love you." He said softly. And I loved him too. But maybe I hated him more right now for making me feel so vulnerable. I wanted to hurt him, to hit him. So I did. I sat on top of him and slapped his face. It was harder than I meant to. He shot up like an alarm clock had gone off under him.

I pushed him back down and laughed loudly. I splayed his arms out like Jesus on the cross and bit his neck hard, wanting to leave my marks on him for everyone to see.

"Stop it" he said. "That hurts."

And he looked hurt. I didn't feel like comforting him. "Wake up and fuck me then," I said. I got on all fours and lifted my ass to him. He obeyed like I knew he would. He licked my ass and stuck his fingers in my swelling cunt.

"Fuck me, David," I demanded.

He placed his delicate hands on my hips and positioned himself to carefully enter. And he pumped slowly, softly, as if he were nodding off on a swinging hammock. I closed my eyes and moaned for him. It felt so sweet, like being rocked in a lullaby. Holding my breath, I felt the first tinglings of an orgasm.

Then I saw a pair of strong thick legs with light brown hairs on the shapely calves and a fat, rose-colored prick being stroked happily in my peripheral vision. I didn't hear him enter the room, but I knew he'd come. I felt it.

I refused to look up at his face and concentrated on David inside of me instead. I wanted him to defend me, to scream for him to get out. He didn't. Instead, Sergi sat on the edge of the bed and cupped my left breast, weighing it, massaging it, as if he were buying a cantaloupe from the Boqueria market. He was whetting his mouth, moaning *mmmm* at the premonition of sweetness to come.

While Sergi concentrated on my torso, David's pump had gotten increasingly faster and even deeper with Sergi in the room. I could feel him spasming, becoming more erratic in his thrusts. I had become disconnected from body. I floated to the corner of the room, took a seat, and saw it all. Sergi's power, David's frailty, my complete submission. My heart pounded, so did my head, my throat, and my dripping cunt. Sergi stuck his hand in my mouth and I obediently sucked on his fingers. Where had those long and dirty fingers been all night? I caught whiffs of cigarette, semen, and garlic.

It was all beginning to hit me hard and my entire body hot flashed. Sensing this, Sergi ran his fingers through my short hair and clenched the taut skin on the back of my neck. Like you would a cat. David pinched my nipples and slapped my buttocks. I tingled and shivered, growing weaker and weaker with overwhelming pleasure. "Do you like us touching you?" David's voice was close to cracking from the excitement.

I heard a yes hissing from my throat and I wasn't sure where it had come from.

I was one of them now. Before meeting them I was woman who demanded respect. Now I'm a woman who accepts humiliation. There is a beautiful kind of strength in this kind of shame.

Sergi shoved his penis into my face. He hit my forehead, my eyelids, the bridge of my nose, with his swollen sword. He was getting back at me for the entire night, for something. Something he probably couldn't understand himself. Then he took aim and shoved his cock to the back of my throat. I gagged and coughed, unable to lift a hand.

Still on my knees, Sergi got off the bed and went somewhere behind David who had resumed fucking me. I hadn't felt Sergi get on the bed with us so I figured he was standing somewhere in the room. But where?

David put his lips to my ear and whispered, "Please don't be mad at me."

Then, as if David had just been shot in the head, he collapsed his entire weight over the curve of my back. Straightening myself, tensing my muscles, I held him up with all my strength while Sergi let out a wail and David cursed the air. Sergi was hurting him, thrusting himself gratuitously, forcing himself into David's small channel. Our interconnected motions awkward, stunted; like being connected to a long, thick, knotted sailor's rope catching, bumping, and slithering up the edge of a boat.

I fought and contorted myself trying to keep David inside of me. Caught in between us, David was falling apart, on the verge of bursting. He was snorting like Quixote's Rocinante, shouting for God, sobbing quietly, for all of us. I joined in their guttural wails. It was the holiest and saddest of choruses. And then like a crescendoing car alarm screaming at the night, it was over.

Sergi pulled out and walked out. David fell into a ball of wasted flesh in coital position beside me. At that moment, I couldn't imagine a greater pain than loving a weak man. He couldn't look at me, at least not yet. Then I thought of my mother, thought of what she would think, if anything as terrible had ever happened to her in her life.

I craved solitude and began sliding my body off the edge of the bed. My knees cracked, my joints ached. I reached for my pants suit laying in two disjointed pieces on the floor. I grabbed my shoes, my bag, and walked barefoot out of the room, down the swirling corridor of mosaic tiles, past Sergi's room with its door closed shut, and out the front door, leaving them alone in their stifling silence. My heart pounded loudly in my ears.

As I stepped out of the elevator and onto the shaded entrance of La India's outer lobby, I remember thinking that I didn't feel a single emotion. Neither happy nor sad. But I must have been wearing some kind of face, because a straight line of cheery tourists slowed down to look at me as they passed. I rummaged through my bag and found a last bent cigarette. I gave it one puff, looked right back at their innocent sun-blotched faces and had the urge to vomit.

Turning the corner off Carrer de Carme, I let it all out. The entire night's bile released onto the gray, rounded-stone streets of this Iberian port city that had witnessed so many centuries of misery.

I hung my head down for a while and watched the last string of saliva detach itself from my mouth. Holding myself up with one hand on the stone wall before me, I found its coldness provided a sobering affect. I wiped my chin with my sleeve and slicked my hair back from my face. As I straightened myself up, an old and squat Catalan couple walked by me, cautiously observing me with two sets of beady brown eyes. There was a rose in her hand and a book tucked safely under his left arm.

It was Diada de Sant Jordi. The sun felt strong. It's nice to be warm when you're feeling cold. I decided I would walk to las Ramblas and browse all those books I had yet to read. Buy a book, maybe two, maybe three. It was the new beginning I had wanted, though it was a beginning to an end. But I was good at endings.

Then a song popped into my head. It was a song that used to make my mother cry whenever she heard it in passing. *Perfidia*, Treachery, was its name. *La perfidia de tu amor.*

There was no turning back. Barcelona's morning sky was the steeliest of blues.

A Kiss From Lares

Elisha Miranda

i heard the music pumping from inside my apartment as I unlocked the door and pushed it open, carrying a camera case
that was almost bigger than me. It was Shakira's new cut, "Hips
Don't Lie." I was hoping that Jewel would just accept that I had
stayed overnight with someone from the crew on my latest film
shoot, instead of hitting me with her usual firing squad of questions.
It was going to be hard enough for me to end our four-year relationship. I may not have been in love with Jewel anymore, but I did
love her. The guilt I had over cheating on her for the past six
months with numerous women was turning me into a shameless
liar. She deserved better.

I entered to find Jewel dancing, wearing plaid boxers and a fire-
engine red muscle shirt that hugged her plum-sized breasts. She
didn't hear me come in. She was swaying her hips like an offbeat
metronome. I stopped to watch and smiled. Her ash blond hair was
tousled, like it had been gelled and then taken up in spots by the
wind. She had a severe, chiseled face. Whenever we would go out,
women would stop chattering as they noticed Jewel and her diesel-
dyke physicality, her arms as firm and streamlined as a panther's. If I
saw her walking toward me on the street, I got wet just thinking
about what she could do after lifting me onto a table.

Ironically, when it came to controlling her feelings, she was a
wuss. I was the one who sported the ruffled skirts and low-cut
blouses, but in an argument, I always kept my cool. The two of us
were quite a pair as we walked into our Chinese take-out joints or
free summer concerts: me the voluptuous Puertorriqueña cinematographer in short shorts and curly long hair that fought the sum-

mer humidity, and her, the athletic Jewish medical student, in baggy jeans and not a trace of makeup.

I hadn't touched her for two months. Her body looked as delicious as a ripe mango fresh from the tree. As I watched her dance, I remembered our first encounter on the subway.

I was racing home to view the dailies from a short film I had shot, distractedly thinking about whether or not the director would be able to touch up one of the darkly lighted frames in postproduction when the doors of the No. 4 train opened as usual, and people flooded in, racing to grab a seat. She parted the crowd forcefully, as if they all responded to her command. My eyes were instantly drawn to her highly defined cheekbones and rock solid body. I hadn't ever before been attracted to blue eyes, but she looked at me, not through me, and I felt an inexplicable ease. She sauntered toward me, and I shifted nervously in my seat, hoping that she would sit next to me. Even though I looked femmy in my black stiletto knee boots and tight skirt, I was an out lesbian. I'd come out the summer before, wildly fucking the lesbians I met at the new club, SHE BANG, with the force of my liberation. Thinking on my toes, I pulled out a copy of *The Advocate* I had stashed in my imitation Prada bag.

Little did I know that I hadn't even needed to bring her to me. She had a plan of her own. She was making her way toward the seat next to me when she tripped on her own feet and tumbled backward upon the young man across from me, sadly landing in his lap, not mine. She recovered from the fall, then proceeded to belt out a heartfelt laugh, quickly transitioning to an upright stand and then reaching for the pole. Her self-effacing sense of humor made my attraction to her even stronger.

"There's a seat next to me," I said, flashing my newspaper.

Jewel smiled as she noticed my paper. She then took the seat next to me. Her smile revealed full red lips, the color of a pomegranate. They contrasted with her even white teeth perfectly. I never knew *blanquitas* could have such delicious lips. I wanted to lean over and kiss them right there. "I was going to sit there, until, well you know," she said.

My heart pounded when her hand softly touched mine as she set-tled in her seat. It was enough to make the subway car feel as hot as summer, even though it was a bitterly cold day in February.

"Do you read *The Advocate*?" I asked, in an effort to break the awkward silence.

She nodded yes. Then leaning toward me, she said, "Hi, I'm Jewel."

She extended her hand and accidentally grazed my breast. She began to laugh loudly, with a deep snort, to cover her embarrass-ment. I didn't mind. In fact the feel of her touch made me cross my legs. I was afraid she could feel the heat rushing through me. I twisted to the left to face her more directly, but I couldn't look into her eyes. I knew if I did she would notice how turned on I now was. She leaned over, gently lifting my chin up so that our eyes could connect, and we just began to laugh and laugh like young school girls that were sharing a private joke.

"I'm also known as the klutz with chutzpah," she said.

"I like your klutziness; it's brightening up a dull morning," I said, smiling.

"What were you listening to?" Jewel asked.

I went blank. I stared at her like an utter idiot. She then touched the earphones that I was wearing around my neck. The only thing I could think about was that her touch was sending goose bumps all over my body.

"Let's see, open up, she said, nodding at the Discman resting be-tween my legs.

I gladly hit the open button. The Discman had been spinning Mary J Blige's *What's the 411*? I remembered that I was listening to "Real Love," and suddenly I just wanted to drop the subject. Jewel was making me feel goofy and out of control. I wasn't used to the feeling.

Unphased, Jewel pushed on. "Which one?"

"Uh, 'Real Love,' " I said, my heart pounding.

"Does this real love have a name?" She asked, touching my hand. Blushing and barely able to enunciate the words, I whispered,

"Yeah, it's Esperanza; it means 'hope' in Spanish. My friends call me E for short."

The subway stopped at 103rd Street. "This is my stop, nice meeting you," I said.

"All I get is a name?" said Jewel, pouting with disappointment.

And then I just did it, the unthinkable. Without even checking to see who was watching, I grabbed her hand and pulled her out of the train with me just as the doors to the subway were about to close. When the train pulled way, we simply came together in a kiss—her hands pulled me close and our bodies pressed against each other—without caring about our safety or the scene that we were making in the subway station.

"Get a room!" yelled a heavyset lady in her mid-fifties. She smiled at everyone in the station as if she were the mayor of *El Barrio*. Jewel and I unlocked lips long enough to notice that all eyes were on us. Some people smiled, and others frowned in disgust.

"I live around the corner," I said quickly, as I remembered what could happen if someone didn't like lesbians.

"Lead the way," said Jewel. She took my hand with her singular confidence.

Two minutes later we were at the door of my apartment on 104th Street between Lexington and Third Avenue. Jewel took my bag as I fumbled with the keys. I felt a jolt all the way up my arm as her hand brushed against my shoulder. Once inside, Jewel put my bag down on the floor. I almost expected us to rip our clothes off then and there. Jewel looked me in the eyes as if she could read my thoughts. She gave a sort of half laugh and walked into my small kitchen. "Do you have any tea?" she asked.

I had a huge can of fresh Puerto Rican coffee *Abuelita* had sent me, but I wasn't much of a tea drinker. I quickly searched through my cabinets and found a loose Lipton tea bag that I had snatched from some place I couldn't even remember. "Is this okay?"

Jewel nodded her head. I now know she would have preferred herbal tea with no caffeine, preferably imported. I put the kettle on the stove and waited for it to boil. Then we just sat there looking at each other in silence. I felt awkward as I waited for her to make the first move. In the past year, I had always waited for other women to pursue me just as I had when I was with men. The tea kettle began to hiss loudly for attention.

I felt lost. I stroked the kettle's handle like it was my lover and slowly poured the boiling water into a large purple mug. I then grabbed the tea bag and started brewing it slowly and tenderly, moving it in circles. Jewel just stared at me, making me realize that if something were to happen I had to make the first move. I had already stepped out of my comfort zone by dragging her off the train with me. I handed her the cup. Jewel sat there sipping her tea, playing cat and mouse. Finally, I stood up. I came around the table to where she was sitting and kissed her. She didn't respond. She let her head drop back for a moment, sweat dampening the fine hair around her temples. I had been patient long enough, so I kissed her again, looking into her open eyes.

Finally, her tongue pushed deep between my teeth and from somewhere deep inside of me came a moan. But she pulled back again. I held her head against mine. "Jewel, if this is too fast, I can stop." Her hair smelled of cinnamon.

She smiled. "No, I want this, but don't you think you should turn the water off first?" I was so nervous I had placed the kettle back on the burner after pouring Jewel her tea. Embarrassed, I walked to the stove and turned it off. Jewel slowly unbuttoned her blouse, then stripped off the rest of her clothes as she made a trail to my bathroom.

I followed her. She leaned over and turned the faucet, filling the bathtub with hot water. Her strong, rough fingers caressed my cheek, then slid down the back of my neck to hold me close to her. Her lips were cool and insistent as she kissed her way down my neck, leaving a trail of moist places along my skin—producing an even wetter place between my legs. Before the water from the tub could spill over, Jewel reached to turn off the faucet. She dipped her leg in seductively. She wanted to do it in the water. I froze for a second. I'd always avoided this; terrible childhood memories kept me avoiding being under water as much as I could. But somehow Jewel erased everything that had come before her. I shook it off. I stood across from her and stripped slowly. I pulled my sweater over my head, exposing my brown breasts and large nipples, and the tautness of my stomach.

Without a word, Jewel stepped into the tub. I followed. She cupped her hands to pour water over my hair, soaking long strands of curls that clung to my chest, neck and face as she kissed me. It felt strange to be kissed by someone I'd just met. We sat across from each other in the tub. Seconds stretched as her lips lingered on mine. Gently, she held my bottom lip between her lips. She knew how to take her time. My heart started pounding with lust and a hope for love. I couldn't believe I was feeling this with someone I barely knew. Her body moved against mine, and I touched her, kissing her neck and massaging her breasts. In the water I felt vulnerable, dependent on her as she caressed my face with her hands and kissed me again.

This time her tongue touched mine, burning me. My knees went weak. She pulled away. I leaned towards her. I reached into the water and felt the warmth between her legs. She gasped as my fingers entered her, plunging once, twice, and then again and again. We rocked against the rhythm of our bodies in the water. Jewel's body rose against mine, her hips and pelvis arching into my hand. I would not let her stop. I plunged in again, quicker and faster. Her hands were between my legs. I'd just gotten a Brazilian wax for the first time the day before, and my bare skin felt tender, more sensitive than I had ever felt before. I nearly collapsed on top of her. I regained my balance and kept kissing her, thrusting my fingers inside of her. Jewel turned and switched positions with me, so that she was on top and staring me right in the eyes as we both came.

I wasn't finished with her. I gently pushed her off me, dripping water on the red tile floor as I exited the tub and rushed towards my bedroom. Jewel followed me into my bed. I lay next to her, tracing the skin on her stomach with my fingers. My fingers ventured toward her pussy, entering her deeply. I wavered inside her and hooked my fingertips, touching her G-spot, sending her body into waves of pleasure. She started writhing on the bed as I nurtured the rough, spongy spot inside of her.

Jewel then reached over and flicked my clit with her tongue. I giggled. I couldn't help it. What she did felt so good. My limbs felt as light as feathers; my pelvis was a radiating sun of bliss. I was being transported to a place I hadn't even known existed.

She pushed deeper inside me with her fingers. "Let's see if we can make you even wetter," she said with a smiling satisfaction. Then Jewel went wild; grinding her pussy against mine, she pumped against my juicy lips. A pressure built inside of me. I held my breath. My body squirmed. My hands tried to hang on to the side of the bed. My toes curled as she now sucked my swollen clit with her lips, first fast, then slow, then fast again. My body felt flushed. Another wave of pleasure hit me. Blood raced to my head. Colors danced in my eyes. For a second I was blissfully unaware of my surroundings. Nothing existed but my orgasm.

Afternoon turned into evening, and then the night crept through my open window, lapping at our naked skin while we cuddled in each other's arms on my soaked bed. Neither of us made it to our graduate school classes the next day. Jewel was in her second year of medical school at Columbia University. She wanted to be an anesthesiologist, but the activist in her felt she could more for women's health if she were an OB/GYN. I was in my final year of film school at New York University.

Four years had now passed. She was working as a doctor in her second year of residency at New York University's gynecology program. A cinematographer, I had worked on more than ten films. I'd traveled around the world, shooting everything from music videos to feature films.

Somewhere between all my shoots and her long hours at the hospital, we grew apart. I started to desire other women. For the past two years, I had been secretly fucking other girls. Jewel and I had great sex when we had time. Otherwise, we would go through these dry spells. Psychologists call it "Lesbian Bed Death." Indeed, something had died between us. The closer Jewel got to finishing medical school, the more she changed into someone I didn't like. She wanted us to buy a house, to get married, and to have kids. The American dream. Something that was very different from my own nomadic visions of traveling the globe, discovering new things while making films and encountering new people.

As I watched my love of four years dancing by herself, I knew that I had to end it. I felt guilty for not being honest with her. I felt guilty that even though I felt this way, a wetness between my legs still desired Jewel. Early in our relationship, I named her my Dr. Feelgood, and I needed a house call. Even after all my affairs, no one could touch me like she could.

"E," Jewel said. She'd noticed me watching. "Get over here, it's time to dance!"

I broke out of my trance. Jewel was still doing her cute white girl dance; she had no idea how to make those hips work. My pussy suddenly needed some real attention. It won out against my guilt of continuing to live a lie. I moved toward her. Instead of seeing her face, I pictured myself with a long-haired, luscious Latina, with wide hips and a round *culo*. Jewel pulled me close.

"You look amazing," she said, then she kissed my neck.

I could never resist when she kissed me there. I noticed the way her jeans hugged her muscular thighs and how her bicep flexed when she ran her hands through my hair, pulling it back to kiss me a second time on the neck. I could barely get the words out, "Know what?"

She ignored my plea and began to peel away my clothes, starting with my shirt and working her way towards my tight jeans. I wore them a size too small and they could barely be separated from my skin. Jewel peeled away my winter layers carefully, as if I were a juicy mango, and she was ready to devour every ounce of my ripeness. My body hummed, desperate for the multiple orgasms only Jewel could deliver. Completely naked, I tried one last time to regain my composure, to do the right thing. "Jewel, we need to talk."

She smiled as she forcefully put her fingers over my lips. She had no intention of making this easy for me. "I need to taste you, feel you. We can talk later," she said.

She took a step closer and leaned forward just a bit. She looked deep into my eyes, and for a moment she hesitated. "What are you thinking?" she whispered.

"I think if you don't kiss me soon, I'll go crazy," I said, losing whatever backbone I had left.

"I'm hungry for you," said Jewel, putting her hands on my shoulders, drawing me closer until our bodies were touching, chest-to-chest, thigh-to-thigh. Then she kissed me, first slowly, then all over, in an almost violent frenzy. The tension of our two months apart was bursting between us. Finally, she made her way to my pussy, peeling away my panties. She had the road map of my body, brushing my ankles, my hips, and my lips with her tongue. She nibbled on my clit, then she fucked me with one, then two, then four fingers and my pussy muscles just continued to contract violently as they waited for more.

When I was thoroughly kissed from head to toe and dripping wet from her now fist working in between my thighs, she pulled away. "Feel good?"

I blinked at her, waiting until I regained some feeling in my lips to speak. "Yeah, don't stop!"

I grabbed a fistful of her T-shirt and dragged her closer. I didn't want her to stop as my orgasm was building. She wrapped her hands around my waist and backed me up against the wall. Jewel stood between my spread legs. She looked into my eyes rather than between my legs, which made me whimper with impatience.

"I love you," she said, softly in the most seductive tone.

She waited for my response. All I could muster was a whispered, "I want you." It was true.

I closed my eyes as I felt her kneel between my legs. I waited for her tongue to return, but it never came. Instead, I felt something cool against my cunt. It took a moment to register in my lust-addled brain. She had just thrown ice-cold water on me.

"What's wrong with you!" I said.

"Who the fuck is *Boricua Les!*" Jewel stepped away from me, leaving my now freezing pussy shivering.

This was the passion I'd been missing in our relationship. The fiery passion that made us so hot we couldn't wait to fuck each other into making up. It was something that I wasn't sure I could ever find in a relationship with a white woman, so I'd started looking for it in the Latinas I'd met online, then in bars. Sooner or later, I wasn't just looking.

"I couldn't access my email today, so I logged on under your name and saw an email from *Boricua Les*. I read about how she couldn't wait to finally meet you in San Juan when you go to Puerto Rico for Christmas."

"It's not Christmas, it's *Dia de los Reyes*," I said, mechanically, not answering her accusation. It bothered me that she didn't know the difference.

"Yeah, I remember. It's the same festival that you didn't want to take me to this year," she said.

I could've denied that I didn't want her to go. Instead I was silent. I didn't feel like I deserved to even defend myself. I wanted to run away without even talking about it. But I knew I had to own up to what I'd done.

"E, are you listening to me?" snapped Jewel.

"Jewel, it's been over for a while," I said. I shocked myself by saying it out loud.

"Well, at least you could have told me," said Jewel.

"I did by coming home late or not at all!" I said.

"Well, fuck you Esperanza. Fuck you!

"Fucking is all we do well, Jewel. We haven't been the same since going to Puerto Rico. And you know it," I said to Jewel, who was now crying.

I felt like a monster, as if everything that had gone wrong with our relationship was my fault. In the beginning, I thought we were soul mates. Besides my childhood love, Lares, I had never felt so deeply about someone as I did for Jewel. I thought that she may have been the one. Lares had even stopped appearing to me in dreams during the first two years of our relationship. But, after Jewel and I went to Puerto Rico together, things changed.

It took me two years to finally get up the courage to come out to my folks and to bring Jewel with me to celebrate *Los Tres Reyes* with my parents and *Abuelita* in Puerto Rico. My parents blamed Jewel for my being a lesbian, as if somehow she had turned me out. But they only had one daughter, and they were willing to accept Jewel if it meant I would spend the holidays with them. I left it to them to tell Abuelita, who my *mami* told me locked herself up in her church for four weeks to pray for my soul.

Despite my parents and Abuelita's negative reaction to news about my relationship with Jewel, it was important to me that everyone I love come together, so that I could reclaim what was once a very important day for me as a child.

I needed us to be together for *El Dia de Los Tres Reyes*. While most kids counted the days until Christmas obsessively, I saw Christmas as only a warm-up to the real big event. Once Christmas dinner was over, I'd start counting the minutes until three a.m. on January 4, when my family would fly from Newark, New Jersey, to San Juan; then by car we'd ride for two hours with my abuelita to Coamo to celebrate *Los Tres Reyes* on January 6. We would arrive at *Parador Valentín*, named by Abuelita's father and with our family surname. He had proudly built this hotel with his own hands, cement block by cement block after the *colonios* ceded land to him because our family had so loyally worked his sugarcane fields for generations. The Parador became the heartbeat of social life for our town. The nearest house was ten minutes by foot, and everyone lived in modest and sometimes unfinished cement houses. Abuelita, being the eldest daughter, carried on the tradition of running the Parador after her brother died in World War II. She and *Abuelito* raised my *mami* and her sister there too. When we arrived, the hotel would be filled with the scent of garlic and oregano. All of Abuelita's sisters would have spent the entire day making *pasteles* Puertorriqueños, preparing the *masa* by mashing green plantains and *yautia*, a root vegetable that looks like yam. Then they would fill it with boneless stewed pork and a host of delicious spices. My job was to fold the clean plantain leaves that were eventually filled with *masa* paste and then tie them together.

I was so excited to share the warmth and traditions of my family with Jewel. Even if they weren't rainbow flag–waving supporters like her family, I knew my family would be fun. I hoped once they met Jewel that they would love her too.

Jewel became nervous as we prepared to make the journey to Puerto Rico to spend *Los Tres Reyes* with my family. She started shopping compulsively, something she never did unless her clothes were ripped or didn't fit. She was making an effort. Jewel knew appearances were everything in my family, so she bought an outfit she was sure would impress them. She picked up a pair of striped flared-legged pants with a baggy, circular-shaped top with shoulder pads she found on Macy's clearance racks. Because she was trying so hard, I didn't have the heart to tell her how bad it really looked.

She even bought Abuelita one of those American fruitcakes in a tin with nuts and dried fruit that was probably over two years old. Before we left for Puerto Rico, I worried enough about my family accepting our queerness. In many ways, bringing Jewel home was my way of making them deal with me on my own terms. Jewel had been out since she was eighteen, and her parents had greeted us at the airport the first time they met me with T-shirts that said MY DAUGHTER IS A DYKE. AND THIS IS MY DAUGHTER OUT-OF-LAW. I knew her welcome to Puerto Rico would be very different, but I hoped it would bring us closer if Jewel understood more about my culture and family.

I worried about how Jewel would adjust to our family's holiday traditions. Jewel was Jewish. And these past two years since Abuelo died, Abuelita had become very involved with the Pentecostal church, what I like to call extreme Christianity. Jewel also didn't speak a lick of Spanish. I wasn't sure how they would receive her or her attitude about life.

If it were up to her, we would never eat out and only buy the bare necessities for clothes. And I disagreed. Sometimes when I was broke, a nice pair of Puma sneakers made me feel better. It's not like I would be buying a dozen pairs of Manolo Blahniks, but I did believe in treating myself occasionally. That's why I was always broke. Jewel saved every penny she got as if it were her last.

In my family, appearances were important. When we couldn't really afford that nice new car, my parents bought it to show the rest of the family that we were doing well. Jewel was raised in a hippie collective in Humboldt, California, where three families shared one used car. Her father was an environmental science professor and her mother was a psychologist, so when the car wasn't available they biked everywhere to save the world from global warming. I'd affectionately call her family "The Left-wing Cleavers."

My *papi* was a janitor, and my mami worked as a salesperson for Target. We lived check to check, and there was never any extra money. Whenever we had anything extra, we spent it because it could be gone by tomorrow.

Jewel and I finally left for Puerto Rico on January 5. Our flight was delayed due to a snow storm that caused us to arrive in the late afternoon; thus, we missed the morning ritual of preparing the meal with Abuelita for our traditional eve before *Los Tres Reyes* dinner. My parents had already arrived in Puerto Rico two days before, and they came to meet us at the Luis Muñoz Marin International Airport in San Juan with Abuelita. When Abuelita saw me, she did the customary, *telenovela* performance, tears pouring down her face and a hug that choked the living breath out of me. I joke about Puerto Rican greetings and good-byes, but I must admit, I love the *cariño* of our ways. And to my surprise, my normally loving and welcoming family pretended like Jewel wasn't there. They fussed over me, gathering all my suitcases and brushing their fingers through my freshly cut, dramatically shorter hair as they got ready to head to the door.

Finally, they looked her over. My parents stiffened, and Abuelita rolled her eyes, quickly scanning her very uncoordinated outfit of mismatched patterns and hairstyle that made her look like Sigourney Weaver in *Alien Resurrection*. There was no denying that Jewel was a dyke. I know it would have been easier for my parents to accept her if she had worn something more feminine and could pass for straight, then they could have pretended she was my friend.

"Ay, Esperanza you cut your hair, it was so pretty long," said Abuelita.

"And she needs some of your *pasteles*. Mami, she looks too *flaquita*, no?" said my papi, who referred to Abuelita as Mami since his own mami had died when he was only three years old.

"We'll take care of that; I waited to make *pasteles* till you were here. I know it's your favorite," said Abuelita.

Happy that she had waited to start the *pasteles* until I arrived, I hugged my aging Abuelita. She smelled of her own distinct fragrance of garlic and *agua florida*, a cologne extract of cinnamon and oranges that she used to bathe in or to cleanse her house of evil energy.

My parents then surrounded me with kisses and hugs, leaving Jewel outside the circle. I felt so horrible and wanted Jewel to feel at home. I grabbed Jewel's hands. I was so nervous I all but hurled Jewel at my parents and Abuelita. Jewel was now standing right in front of them, wearing the clownish makeup she had wanted to apply without my help. "Abuelita, this is Jewel," I said.

In broken English Abuelita said, "You Jew-el." Jewel just stood there. Abuelita's cold stare flustered her so much that she turned bright red. Before Jewel could think of a response, Abuelita looped her arm through mine, leading me to the car. When Jewel realized no one was stopping, she raced behind us to catch up. My papi turned and noticed she was running behind us, breathless. He offered to take one of her suitcases in his usual gentlemanly way. Jewel stubbornly pulled it back from him and decided to stumble along by herself. I felt my cheeks flush with anger. She could at least let him help a little. Then there was Abuelita. She just kept marching ahead, without even looking at Jewel. Jewel just faded in the backseat with the luggage as we drove the two-hour journey home from San Juan to where my grandmother lived in Coamo.

When we arrived at Abuelita's new tangerine orange cement-blocked home, I already felt melancholy for the *Parador Valentín*. Abuelita had been forced to sell the hotel to mainland U.S. Real Estate developers who wanted to knock it down and build a more modern gated community with cookie-cutter houses. She couldn't afford to live in the new housing development, so she purchased a modest house that was a thirty-minute car ride from her beloved Parador. Abuelita now turned her passion from the Parador to her local Pentacostal church. I guessed it both gave her community and made her feel needed.

Before we could even unpack our luggage at the house, Abuelita guided us to the feast of *pernil* and *arroz y gandules* ready for us on the table. Jewel rushed to her suitcase to get the gift she had bought for Abuelita. She handed the fruitcake to Abuelita with a sincere smile on her face. Abuelita tossed it in the far corner of the long dining room table, barely glancing at Jewel as she said, "We only eat fresh fruit here." Then Abuelita took her seat at the head of the table. She began passing the *pernil* around, and everyone scooped a serving into their plates. They all said, "*Qué rico!*" as they served themselves second and third helpings. Jewel tried to be a trooper; she even served herself a second helping of the *pernil*, even though she never ate meat. And then with her thick *Norteamericana* accent, she even tried to applaud Abuelita's cooking in Spanish. My family ignored her, speaking to each other in Spanish, not even acknowledging her effort. Jewel just sat there in silence, pushing the food on her plate around with her fork.

Jewel's picking caught Abuelita's eye. I knew it had nothing to do with Abuelita's cooking. Jewel was a vegan, and the meal was drenched in swine. Abuelita nudged my mami, leaning over. "What's wrong with this JEWel?" she asked my mami. All Jewel heard, was the word JEW; no longer able to take it, she shoved her plate away.

"Excuse me, Esperanza can I talk to you?" said Jewel, standing above me at the table, as everyone else continued to eat.

Jewel then ran out of the house. And my family kept on eating, making me even more furious. I looked to my mami, who I thought out of everyone would at least be supportive. "Mami, you said you would have my back! You lied!"

Mami couldn't look into my eyes. Instead, she stared at the wall. Then my papi stood up and pointed his very long finger at me. "Don't you EVER talk to your mami that way!"

"I just want you all to respect Jewel. I love her," I said.

My papi's eyes began to tear, and he just stood there, speechless. Abuelita then rose from her seat at the end of the table. She marched her petite five-foot-one-inch frame towards me, and in a strong, authoritative voice she said, "How can we respect someone who does such filthy things. That is not how you were raised. I dealt with her at your mami's request. But, I can no longer stand by and watch you disgrace the Lord in my house."

"Fine," I said. I left to find Jewel. I partly hoped that at least my mami would race after me, convince me to stay. But no one followed.

I went outside to find Jewel crying. "I can't take this Esperanza. I'm trying; I don't even eat pork or celebrate Christmas. They're treating me like a leper. I want to leave, now!"

I tried to reason with her. I found myself rationalizing their behavior, which even I didn't agree with. I explained that when you live in a place where people can eat the mangos off the trees for free, fruitcake is a bit foreign. I pleaded with her to stay till we at least made *pasteles* for *Los Tres Reyes*, so she could truly understand the all-day ritual I looked forward to all year.

"I'm not staying where I'm not wanted."

"I know they're difficult; it'll take time. But, they'll come around. Please, Jewel just work with me," I said, hoping to convince her to stay. I felt stuck in the middle, unable to make anyone happy. Not even myself.

"Your family has been so cold to me, I'm trying so hard, and you've been ignoring me the whole time. You didn't talk to me once during dinner. I felt invisible."

"I don't want to rub it in their face, Jewel. They're not like your family. This is new for them," I said.

Then I felt angry at Jewel. Why did she want to bail out the minute it got touchy, and she felt like an outsider? I felt like an outsider my entire life, always being too dark or too loud or, now, too gay.

"I want to leave now!" said Jewel.

"Fine. Go! Take your privileged ass back to your safety net in New York," I said, regretting it as the words left my mouth. I knew what I had said wasn't fair. I was in so much pain and I really just wanted her support. This was hard for me, to stand up to my family and to just be my authentic self, despite their objections.

Jewel ran back into the house without looking at us and grabbed her bags. Then she hurried out the door to the curb, hunting in her purse for the taxi service card she had swiped from the airport terminal. I stood frozen in my abuelita's foyer for a moment, not sure what to do. Mami and Papi looked up like they had no clue as to why she would ever want to leave. Abuelita didn't even give us the acknowledgment of a look. And it was then that I knew nothing I could say or do would keep Jewel in Puerto Rico or force my family to love her the way I did. The hardest part was telling them I was leaving before *Los Tres Reyes*.

"Why is she leaving?" asked my mami.

"Do you have to ask? And she's not the only one leaving," I announced.

All Abuelita could say was, *"Pero mi'jita* who will crush the *yautias* and *plátanos* in the *pilón?"* She acted like those mean words before had never parted from her lips.

Speaking directly to Abuelita. "Well, it won't be me," I said. "I just wanted you all to be nice. That's all I asked!"

Abuelita looked shocked that I would raise my voice to her. Papi didn't say anything. And Mami started to rage. "You're the one who brought someone like that into your abuelita's home. You're lucky she didn't throw her out."

I wanted to cry but no tears came. Instead, my heart just became frozen. I couldn't feel a thing. *"Yo soy una* LESBIANA," I said, loudly enough for all the neighbors in the barrio to hear.

"Enough! *Si te quieres ir, véte,* but I didn't raise you to disrespect us like that," said Papi.

Mami looked at me with tears streaming down her face. *"Te vas con esa loca, en ves de quedarte con tu familia?"*

"Whatever!" I said, then I grabbed my suitcases and joined Jewel outside. I apologized to her, and then we waited for the car service together.

My family just stood there peeking at us from behind the window curtains. I know they were shocked that I would leave them to return home with a stranger. But in my heart I knew that had Jewel been a Jaime or even a Jim, they would have bent over backward to make him feel at home.

I did the right thing. I flew back to New York with Jewel, even though I was fuming inside at everyone for not being able to spend the holiday with my family. We spent January 6 shopping at Fairway in New York, buying nonfat cinnamon scones, and hanging out in Central Park, where no one even knew about *El Dia de Los Tres Reyes*. That was the first time I ever began to question whether Jewel and I could ever survive despite our differences. It took over a year for me to want to patch things up with my family. I finally bit the bullet and called my parents and then Abuelita. Of course, I apologized. We all cried, but in the end we agreed to disagree.

Though I was angry at my family for shutting Jewel out, over time my resentment settled on Jewel. Making me leave my family was unforgivable. She should have stayed, even if they were rude and unwelcoming out of misplaced love for me. Her solidly upper-middle-class family, English-dominant, and overeducated, allotted her a certain individualism that I still have yet to claim in my own family. I didn't know if I ever wanted the kind of separation shoving my sexuality in my family's face would bring. It's Americanized and selfish to expect them to understand. I thought I had loved Jewel, but I loved my family even more. I had been searching for something that was missing for a while, and I just didn't know how to say good-bye to Jewel before all this drama erupted.

Remembering everything that happened between Jewel and my family in Puerto Rico gave me a dose of reality. Two years later, nothing had really changed. Since then we both just went our separate ways during the holidays; she flew to California, and I stayed with my parents. We never spoke of that fiasco again.

"Esperanza, hello! I'm talking to you!" said Jewel. I snapped back into reality and knew that I had to deal with her.

Jewel, not satisfied by my lack of attention to her question, now began to rip her shirt like the incredible Hulk.

I rushed to her, "What are you doing?"

"I just want you to see me," said Jewel.

I did what she asked. She was staring at me, naked, her sultry nipples exposed, which made her even more raw and vulnerable. It was like the first day I met her; I was at a loss for words. I wanted to be with a woman that got me, whom I didn't have to explain everything to all the time. Who could speak Spanish to me when we were having sex, and who could move with me as if we were one on the dance floor. When Jewel and I were first dating I thought those things were irrelevant, but now I knew in my heart that they were critical to my happiness.

She looked at me with her piercing blue eyes. I'd grown to love them, despite the torment I'd received by girls that looked just like Jewel. I was one of the few brown-skinned, brown-eyed *Boricuas* at Wadsworth Academy, the private boarding school I had attended on scholarship in southern New Jersey, and girls with bright blue eyes had loved to inflict their cruel remarks on me on a regular basis. But Jewel's eyes were sincere, and I wished in that moment I could will myself to be in love with her again.

"It's not you, it's me," I said, owning up to my part as I delivered that cliché line. I couldn't find the strength to explain it all to her now.

"I don't want to hear it, E, just admit that you cheated on me with her."

Jewel deserved the truth.

"Yes, I cheated," I said. I felt both relief and panic at the same time.

"Do you love her?" asked Jewel

"No."

"How long have you been sleeping together?"

"A few months," I said, remembering that less is more. I hoped that if Jewel thought there was only one person, we might be able to remain friends. I would miss her support.

But Jewel would never settle for anything less the raw truth. "Does she make love to you the way I do?" she asked.

"Never."

I had never connected with anyone in bed the way I had with Jewel. She made me feel so alive. She now grabbed my hand and pulled me close. I could feel her hard nipples pressed against my chest, through the torn shards of her shirt. We were pressed so close I not only felt her wetness, but I could smell her hot cunt on my hands. I took a deep breath and stepped behind her. I grabbed her ass as we stood together. I started to finger fuck her from behind.

Before I knew it, Jewel's arms flew up and over me with one swift movement, she flipped me over her head and on to her bed. She knelt over me, forcing me to bury my face in her overgrown sweet, pungent bush, then she moved down as her own juicy lips began gnawing at my naked cunt. Pilates and self-defense class could not have prepared me for the powerful Ms. Jewel. She was sheer muscle from years of doing judo. My legs kicked for a short time as I tried to avoid letting her mouth near my cunt, fighting for a second for fear that I would not be able to leave her if I let her work her heavenly magic. She knew how to please a woman. Jewel had mastered over fifteen different oral sex techniques, when most women were lucky to know three. The harder I fought, the more luscious her tongue felt between my legs, between my swelling lips, right on my clit. Her arms were strong enough that she could hold my whole body off the floor and rub me against her, up and down, slow and steady, her arms wrapped so tight around me that I knew I would be bruised, her fingers firmly gripping my limbs while she moved me against her mouth and tongue like a naked rag doll. My own arousal betrayed me as I became hot liquid against her, my thighs quivering, my sex moving to her offbeat white-girl rhythm that she created, and for the first time I followed.

I came quickly, with a shout of surprise. It usually took me at least an hour to reach this level of orgasm. But she didn't let it end there. She kept flicking my clit over and over again till my orgasm became a fountainlike ejaculation, a rain bath for us both.

Gently, she lowered me right side up onto her lap, allowing me to disengage from her muscular, sweaty, viselike grip. Speechless and angry at myself for not being strong enough to walk away before our final fuck, I walked over to my clothing and began to dress. Jewel followed, pressing her index and middle finger between her sated lips to indicate that she wanted more. I gathered some clothes and then headed to the door.

"You're just going to leave me hanging?" Jewel shouted at my retreating back. "You're the one that had the orgasm. Not me." Jewel then started to cry, tears pouring down her face.

"Fine. Get out, go to Puerto Rico, be with your lover." she said.

Jewel raced to the side of the couch and hurled a small box at me. I didn't want to take it, so I pushed it back towards her.

"I can't return it." she said. "I got you something for Christmas."

"But you don't celebrate Christmas."

"But you do, just take it."

So, I opened it and inside was a necklace with five charms. There was a Star of David, a movie camera, a subway car, the three kings, and a rainbow flag. "There's a charm for each year of our relationship plus one more, the rainbow flag signified endless possibilities."

Then she opened the clasp of the necklace and put it around my neck.

It would have been so much easier if she just called me a bitch and we parted ways. But Jewel started to cry, completely comfortable with her emotions. I, on the other hand, couldn't. I opened the door and closed our life together. I felt like the biggest *pendeja* in the world. And I wondered if, somehow, I would regret this moment for the rest of my life.

I woke up suddenly from a bad dream. They had been haunting me again, ever since I broke up with Jewel four weeks ago. I was now lying awake in bed, in an unfamiliar apartment in Puerto Rico, with a woman I had picked up in a bar the night before. She was snoring beside me, and I couldn't remember her name. The bedroom smelled like sweetly stale sex, empty beer bottles, and cigarettes. I could feel tears drying on my cheeks.

I remembered every detail of the dream instantly; I've been having it since I was ten years old. It first happened when I was in Puerto Rico for the holidays, my favorite time of year. *El Dia de los Reyes* was special for two reasons—one, I would see Lares Lébron, and two, I would visit Abuelita. Our flight would always arrive in the early morning; the red-eye's were always the cheapest. Abuelita would be waiting for us at the airport with her arms wide open and a car full of relatives to give us a proper welcome.

The visit we made in 1986 didn't start out any differently. We were in our homeland and staying at *Parador Valentín* in the beautiful mountainous town of Coamo, a township filled with the life of people mixed with African, Taíno, and Spaniard blood, along with vibrant magenta and turquoise flowers. On the day after we landed, Abuelita had me picking grass from the front yard of the Parador, so the camels the three kings rode in on would have something to eat. Before I went to bed, I wrote a "wish list" for *Los Tres Reyes* and put it under my bed in a shoebox. My mami told me *Los Reyes* would only come if I'd been good all year. If the *Reyes* saw that I was awake, they would pass right by *Parador Valentín*. When I woke up on the sixth, there would be a gift from *Los Reyes* in the box. Usually the gift would be something small or practical, like a new skirt *hecho* by Abuelita or a new pair of *chancletas*. And in the evening, we would have a huge dinner of *pasteles, lechón asado, arroz dulce, tembleque,* and *coquito.* Abuelita adopted the entire *barrio,* and our parador would be packed with family and friends for a true *parranda* of eating, drinking, and dancing to *musica jíbara* or salsa. I learned to dance salsa at those vibrant community *fiestas,* stepping on my Abuelo's toes to learn the right steps. As I grew older my ability to follow more complex dances with my young male partners became a sign of my *Puertoricanidad* to my island-born *familia,* partying as we took the *parranda* from *casa à casa*. It always made sense celebrating with modest gifts from *Los Reyes Magos*, after all, how would Santa ever had made it to the tropics in his hot wool suit with cap and reindeer?

On that evening in 1986, my parents decided to go to the *parrandas* with the Lebrón family. The Lebrones lived in the ruby red clapboard house about a fifteen-minute walk from Abuelita's. My parent's loved hanging out with the Lebrones, a laid-back family that was always down for a good time. I loved them too, for a different reason. The Lebrones arrived around eight at night to leave Lares with Abuelita, so she and I could keep each other company while they were gone. When they arrived, I raced to open the door, quickly hugging Mr. and Mrs. Lebrón out of respect, then squeezing Lares as hard as I could as I secretly inhaled her freesia-scented hair. Lares had long flowing curls that fell to the middle of her back and black coal eyes that pierced my heart. Once both our parents gave us their long Puerto Rican good-byes, I'd set my sights on Lares. I was intoxicated by her energy. Lares was named after the first and only Puerto Rican battle cry for independence against Spain's colonial rule—*El Grito de Lares*. Though she may not have led us in battle, her charisma and beauty made all the kids follow her. Usually Abuelita would make up stories until Lares and I fell asleep, always holding hands. But this year, Abuelita drank too much *coquito*, and she fell into a deep slumber on the couch while Lares and I were watching TV. This is where my dream begins.

"You wanna go swim at the hot springs? C'mon," pleaded Lares.

"But, I can't swim," I said, afraid that Abuelita would wake up and be terrified when she found us gone. We had been warned many times before to not go there without adult supervision. I knew my parents would be furious, and *Los Reyes* would not leave me my present in the morning if we were caught.

"Sergio and Manuel are coming, and they know where a hot spring is where you can see the moon in the water," she said. Lares had been crushed out on Sergio, a boy who lived down the street from her house since we were young enough to crawl. Whenever he was around, Lares would focus all her attention on him. Manuel was his sidekick. The two boys literally looked like a young Puerto Rican Laurel and Hardy. Sergio of course was the handsome *flaquito* and Manuel was the *gordito*. They both loved Lares. Whenever the four of us played house, Sergio and Manuel would fight over who got to be Lares's husband. Sergio always won. Defeated, Manuel would then refuse to play my husband. We would both walk home angrily to our separate houses, leaving the two lovebirds alone to flirt. On this night, I ignored Lares's plea to go to the springs at first, since I was not willing to share her with Sergio. Lares then fixed her eyes on me, and I couldn't say no.

I smiled, not because I wanted to see either of the boys. I was curious to see what my reflection with Lares would look like in the moonlight. But Abuelita would never let me go to the hot springs unaccompanied. I felt guilty as I covered Abuelita up with the peach-colored crocheted blanket hanging over the side of the couch. Lares and I found a towel big enough to wrap around us both and tiptoed out of the house, afraid to even giggle for fear that Abuelita would wake. Safely outside, I followed the fearless Lares around the corner and across the street to a windy path that lead us through the park and to *Los Baños de Coamo*, the hot springs that Abuelita had told me had magical rejuvenating powers. I heard later that even *El Presidente* Franklin D. Roosevelt used to come to Puerto Rico just to experience the healing powers of *Los Baños*.

A full moon loomed over us when we arrived at *Los Baños*. I stopped for a moment to stare; in Newark I never saw the stars. As we walked through the dark park to a fence that separated the public springs from the gated private one, Lares and I were alone. The boys were supposed to have been there already, but she didn't seem disappointed. She climbed onto the giant boulder that rose above the springs by herself, while I remained at the bottom. Once atop the boulder, she stood up and started to howl like a *lobo* at the moon. She reached for my hand, but I was too scared to join her for fear of falling into the water.

"C'mon, howl like this," she said, as she stood above me.

She looked like the most beautiful alpha *lobo* as she serenaded the moon, her nose pointed toward the sky and her head tilted back, Her hair poured over the rock like a waterfall. I wished she would serenade me. I was jealous of the moon as I stood below. I didn't understand it then, but I was falling in love with her.

She stopped howling. The only sound was the coquis' chirping. Lares kneeled down and reached for both my hands. I allowed myself to be lured up onto the boulder, forgetting my fear of water as she smiled and showed me her dimples. We both stood tall, and she began to move her hips perfectly to a clave rhythm, her interpretation of the sounds of the hot springs flowing from the mountain, the rustling in the night air.

"Dance with me, Esperanza," she demanded.

"We can't dance—there's no music," I said.

"There's music if you listen real hard."

I listened. As she reached for my hand again to join her, I just followed. I heard the bewitching sound of the coquis' chirping and moved to their siren call. I danced on the rock with Lares, while the moon became our spotlight. We twirled and laughed as we jumped, using the rock as a trampoline. I tripped and fell with Lares, but we recovered, now safely on top of each other on the rock. We rolled around wrestling and tickling each other till finally her hair brushed upon my cheek and our virgin lips kissed. We both became still as statues, not really understanding what had just happened or who initiated the kiss. I took a mental picture of that moment. I've unfairly compared every kiss I've received since then to that magical moment.

Footsteps started to crash through the springs, accompanied by loud laughter. It was Sergio and Manuel releasing their unbridled energy after being on best behavior all day out of respect for the adults. Lares gently pulled away from me. Not from shame, but to protect our sacred sister cipher from being invaded. The boys stripped down to their shorts and dove into the pond that was adjacent to the springs. Sergio pulled himself out of the water long enough to reach for Lares's hand as he helped her down from the rock.

"Sergio, hurry up! I think I found something," said Manuel. Then he held up a scuba fin.

"That's mine," yelled Lares. " I left it there when I was here yesterday. Maybe the other one is there too." She looked back towards me, alone on the rock for a second. Then Sergio pulled her with him, and she joined the boys in the search for her other fin. And I was left alone on the rock.

My legs locked, I couldn't move. I was stuck up there alone as they all jumped into the water. Like a lovesick puppy, I just waited for what seemed to be an eternity. I knew she would come back for me.

Sergio and Manuel raced to see who could find Lares's fin first. Neither was successful. Lares began to search for it herself as she swam to the other end of the pond away from the boys. "I think I feel something," she said, diving under the water. All three of them were diving, then splashing, then laughing. Suddenly, Lares attempted to come up and then was pulled down, the boys thought she was playing. Then she screamed as she surfaced for a second, splashed, and then went down under. From what I could see in the dark moonlight, Sergio and Manuel were panicked as they swam to save her. But it was too late, the screaming and splashing just stopped, and both boys ran for help in their bare feet. Afraid and overwhelmed by guilt, I couldn't move myself to do anything.

Lares' parents came running with my parents, all dressed in their finest with the boys in tow. The only thing I remember after that was Mr. Lébron swimming out of the pond with an unconscious Lares in his arms. I wailed hysterically as my papi carried me from the rock. When I woke up the next day, *Los Tres Reyes* bore no gifts for our family.

The dream always ended with an adult version of Lares, with full breasts and long legs, standing naked above me on the rock. She'd be reaching her hand out to me, ready to pull me up. Twenty years later, the dream still haunted me. I woke up in the stranger's apartment with a horrible headache. I turned to the nameless Puerto Rican beauty that I had picked up the night before and covered her naked body with her comforter, which had fallen to the floor. I got dressed and didn't look back as I walked out the door.

"*M'ija*," my Abuelita said as she seized the sheet that covered my entire body, which allowed the light from the sun to blind me. "I don't understand you, out all hours of the night and when you're not working, you sleep all day. You're hardly here. And it's the eve of *Los Tres Reyes* tonight."

I'd escaped to work in Puerto Rico after Jewel and I split, deciding to stay with Abuelita. I had practically slept through Christmas, and I knew I couldn't miss the eve of *Los Tres Reyes*. But, I didn't want to be there. I was sleeping in the guest bedroom at Abuelita's, and I was trying to think of a way out, even though missing the celebration would be an unforgivable sin. Especially since my parents wouldn't be there this year because they were trying to save more money for their retirement to Puerto Rico. I hadn't really spent a real holiday with Abuelita since the Jewel incident years before. And Abuelita was now too old to have any kind of fiesta at her house.

I'd just been throwing myself into shooting *Island of Lesbos*, a reality show for Lifetime television. I woke up every day at six a.m., and worked till ten p.m. Days on a film shoot were long, and we couldn't finish until the director made her shot list for the day. And when I wasn't shooting, I was usually partying it up with the crew or sleeping with some new hottie.

I didn't respond to Abuelita. I just kept my eyes tightly shut and pretended to be asleep. I wasn't ready to face anyone, even myself. I just wanted to forget Jewel. And I was afraid if I opened my eyes that I would see Lares. If that happened, I didn't want to scare Abuelita with the weight of my unhappiness.

Abuelita sat on the bed. She had her new cordless phone tightly wound in her hand. I could hear my mami's deep voice vibrating in her hand. "Elena, she's not depressed, just Americanized. I would've never put up with *you* coming home so late." She tapped me with her free hand, then finally gave up. She became more interested in gossiping to my mami. Her footsteps grew more distant as she walked down the hall to her bedroom, so she could tell my mami what she really thought of me these days.

Sadly, the only day I've really spent any time with Abuelita since I arrived was the day she picked me up from the airport. She greeted me with a huge smile and *un abrazo* that would make anyone else feel instantly loved and healed. But I feared being so close to her, as if she could feel the root of my sadness with her magical hands. Abuelita and I had spoken only by phone these past two years. She and my parents have just acted like my love for Jewel was a passing phase, like any first love. They figured it would end and I'd move on. Or so they hoped. It hurt that I needed my family support, and they had no basis for understanding my pain.

"*Nena*, you'll find another love," said Abuelita as we stood outside the baggage claim, waiting for our ride. I was startled. I hadn't told her about breaking up with Jewel. I hadn't told anyone in the family, so even my mami couldn't have spilled the *habichuelas*. Plus, we all knew that she never approved of my relationship with Jewel, or any relationship I had that wasn't sanctified by the church. I squeezed her close. I hoped somehow she would protect me. My eyes started to tear in the corners, but I wasn't able to cry. She pulled me closer and rubbed the back of my head, making me feel safe and happy for the first time in years. Then, she said, "I promise, some handsome man will come along and sweep you off your feet like your Abuelo did for me!"

As we waited for the porter to bring my suitcases—I broke the embrace abruptly and looked down at the crusty gum stuck to the cold cement floor. I sucked in my tears. I stared at Abuelita for only a second, any longer would have been disrespectful. I wasn't sure yet how I was feeling. One moment I felt totally at home. Another, and I felt totally out of it. In some ways, nothing much had changed.

"Abuelita, I'm *still* a LESBIAN!" I said.

"I know it's not you *mi'jita*, it's that evil woman, she has the devil inside her. You have the chance to embrace the holy spirit now." Abuelita said, raising her arms to the sky as if she were talking directly to God.

"God and I are fine, Abuelita. It's you who has issues." I said.

Thankfully, she didn't hear my sarcastic comment over the roar of cars passing us by as she looked for her neighbor's 1986 Chevrolet.

The horn honked like it was dying a slow death. Happy to break the tension, Abuelita raced to Señora Quintero's car, her new neighbor and fellow holy roller. I followed in tow with my luggage. She sat in the front with Señora Quintero—her eldest and dearest friend of over sixty-five years—chatting her up like a regular social butterfly while they quoted Bible scriptures. I, on the other hand, gave her only my perfunctory *saludo*, a kiss on the cheek, a nod to her questions, and then I slunk back into the backseat with my luggage pressed against me. Driving in from the airport to Abuelita's, I had the sense of being suspended in the air. I hadn't landed on the ground anywhere.

Besides the customary kisses hello and good-bye, Abuelita and I have not spoken deeply since that moment at the airport.

Back in her guest room, I pulled the blanket off my head. I opened one eye squinting, my attempt to face the world slowly. My partying had at least managed to numb me out enough to stop dreaming and having visions of her. Then I reached for my cell phone that I had tossed messily onto the nightstand during my drunken stupor last night. The time read: eleven-fifty a.m. Shit, I was late to work. I was scheduled to be there at eight a.m. My reckless behavior had already ended my relationship with Jewel; now I might lose my job. So much had happened in this past month, so many new people and old relationships to mend. Find your mind, I told myself.

I opened my phone and began to check my messages. There were two. One from Jewel, and one was a message from my segment producer and boss, Maribel Medina aka *Boricua Les*. Things have been a whirlwind since Maribel appeared in my life four months ago. Her essence is pure sin, and every time she's near me I feel pure intoxication. We began communicating for work over email; a previous employer referred me to her. She wanted a female cinematographer for this shoot she was doing for Lifetime, and a friend recommended me. It all started with a yellow smiley-faced icon wink on email. Then before I knew it we were IMing each other every day to check in and about our days. We started ending our IMs with "I like you's." The "I like you's" became "I want you badly's." We even had our web cams hooked up, and we had started to create our own porn archive of each other. We did this for three months without ever meeting in person. Then, Jewel found our email. What they both didn't know was that Maribel wasn't the first. Women had become an addiction for me for the past two years, and it always started online. I needed to feel wanted and desired. I loved the freshness of making a new woman fall in love with me. It made me feel good about myself. It made me feel loved.

Maribel was wise to my email cruising style, so I knew she'd realize pretty quickly that she wasn't the only one. But I wasn't sure she'd be cool with it. After all, things got intimate really fast among women. "*Nena*, tell you what, I'll excuse you if you come over to my house later today. "*Llámame*," she whispered into the phone.

I wasn't ready to call anyone, but I knew that Maribel's message was more of an ultimatum than a suggestion. If I wanted to keep my job, I had to call her. I was prepared to lie about where I had been after leaving the previous night. I paced back and forth. She would never forgive me if she knew I had slept with Raquel, the production assistant.

I dialed Maribel's number quickly. "Hi, it's me!"

"Back from your drunken stupor?" Maribel said sarcastically.

"I wasn't that bad." I said. Truthfully, I only remembered getting into bed. But from the smell on my hands, I knew I had at least dipped into Raquel's honey pot. Maribel snorted on the phone. "You only did a lap dance for the very cute production assistant who is totally enamored with you."

I was fucked. "For real?" I said, trying to play it off.

"Well, she, unlike you, was at work today," said Maribel.

"Seriously?" I blurted. "I mean, of course, she was at work. She dropped me off so I could spend the rest of *Los Tres Reyes* with my abuelita."

"Glad to hear your life isn't becoming like the reality show we're shooting," said Maribel. "But you still have to make it up to me. How about dinner?"

I needed to spend some time alone. On the other hand, the after parties and beach scene had their own rewards—one curvy *chula* after another kept slipping me their phone numbers. If I wanted my Puerto Rican *Mami chula*, this was the place. Yet I felt like an empty shell at a beautiful beach. And no matter how much fun or sex I had, inside I was dying a slow death that had started even before Jewel. It started with Lares, and being in Puerto Rico made it harder each day for me to deny. I felt like there was nowhere to go.

"Sure, how about six p.m.?" I said. Then I hung up the phone, unsure if I had made the right decision.

I checked my final remaining message. Jewel's number was also on my caller ID. I hesitantly pushed the number one to listen to her first message. "Esperanza," said Jewel, crying. "I love you no matter what, but just remember no one will love you better than me." I deleted her message; when I got back to New York I'd do my best to be friends. I then unfastened the clasp to the charm bracelet Jewel had given me and I had worn religiously since we broke up. I lovingly wrapped it in one of her old workout shirts that I kept and put it under my pillow. For now, I didn't want to look back. I quickly flipped the phone shut. I felt haunted by this feeling that someone was in room with me, but there wasn't even a breeze coming in from the window. I walked to the door and stood on one knee as I peaked through the keyhole to make sure Abuelita wasn't spying upon me. The hallway was empty. I scanned the room once more. I looked underneath the bed, but not even the cat was hiding under there. I was surprised to find a box under my bed, the day before *Los Tres Reyes.* Abuelita never gave me my gift on the eve of the holiday; I always had to wait till the sixth. I pulled out the shoebox. I opened it quickly, in anticipation as I did as girl. Inside the box was a wooden, handcrafted framed picture of Lares and me sitting in front of Abuelita's house as girls. I felt a tightness in my chest. I thought I was about to have a heart attack. I knew if I just cried everything would be fine, but I haven't been able to cry since the day I lost Lares. I willed the tears to come, pushing deeply from within, but for some reason the tear well always remained dry. I was alone. Abuelita was in the backyard tending to her chickens, and I was still too afraid to rush up to her and just ask for a hug.

At first, it bothered me that I was forced to meet Maribel for dinner and not be with Abuelita, but another part of me didn't want to face an evening that was filled with such pain. I told Abuelita that my job would require me to work that day, but I would do my best to make it back to her house by midnight. She gave me this I know your not telling me the truth look, but said nothing. Instead, Abuelita just left me alone and joined Señora Quintero next door to make *pasteles*. I knew not being invited was my punishment for lying, even though Abuelita never confronted me.

After being alone all afternoon, I welcomed any company that would keep me from mentally masturbating about my problems. I arrived at the penthouse of Maribel's übertrendy condo in the Condado district. The Condado houses a chic cluster of clubs, shops, and Sex-and-the-City wannabe bars, both queer and straight. It's east of Old San Juan, where tourists sip their cocktails and speak English only over their twelve-dollar *Mojitos*. Working and sleeping with Maribel these past weeks, I discovered a bourgeoisie reality I'd never experienced in my *patria* as a little girl. I was almost embarrassed. Here I had my Puerto Rican dream girl, and she was more materialistic and bourgeois than Jewel.

I rang the doorbell. Maribel opened the door dressed in a pair of designer Joe jeans and a skintight tank top. I liked the way her jeans hugged her muscular thighs and her biceps flexed when she ran her hand through her long curly hair. As she turned to lead me to her chic living room, I took in her ample booty. She had a shake that would make Beyoncé jealous.

Maribel had what I needed physically. I just doubted whether she would challenge my mind. Always dressed in sexy power suits in her big corporate chairs at the office, she exuded capitalist. She worked her way through college studying business and marketing without the support of any family. She was self-made and never settled for the safe way out. Aside from my detour with Raquel and few other nameless *chicas*, when I haven't been at work, I've usually been locked up with Maribel drinking her favorite—a *guayaba* and *quenepa* martini with Grey Goose Vodka. As I gazed at my sexy Puerto [EM1]Rican would-be *novia*, I thought, "Be careful what you ask for." Maribel grabbed my hand, leading me toward her dining room table.

She greeted me with a kiss on the cheek and a fresh martini, which was beautifully surrounded by several mango slices, and served on a silver serving tray. I downed the drink like I hadn't had a glass of water in weeks. Maribel just watched and then flashed me her dimples as she poured me another and I downed it, too. Suddenly, I forgot about wanting to be alone. I was at her command.

"Sit, she said.

I did. I thought I was hallucinating. The sexiest dyke alive was telling me what to do. Before I could utter a word, she placed the tray on the corner of the table and leaned down to press her sensual lips against mine.

Her hair grazed my face and the smell of mangos intoxicated my senses, and I kissed her back. Her tongue pushed between my teeth and from somewhere deep inside of me came a moan. Her fingers, feminine and long, caressed my cheek and slid down to the back of my neck to hold me close against her. Her lips were wet and ripe as she kissed her way down to the back of my neck, leaving a trail of moist places along my skin—and producing an ever wetter place between my legs.

She gently pushed away from me. She then stood up and reached for a mango on the tray. She began to peel the fruit slowly with her teeth, and then she motioned for me to stand with her.

All I could see was an older Lares. I looked away. "Sorry," I said, suddenly embarrassed. Abuelita's photo of her somehow reminded me that I needed to let go.

"Don't be." She picked up my hand without any notice to my distance. She began kissing my palm and then pulled me up to stand facing her. Lares finally disappeared, which made me feel brave and that I could do anything with Maribel, uncensored. I grabbed the slice of mango now dangling from her lips and turned her around to face the door; I pushed her up against it, holding her there while the mango held between my lips followed the line of her jaw and then continued down to her neck. Along the way pieces of mango blended with her flesh till there was nothing remaining between my teeth but my tongue.

"*Me fascinan los mangos,*" she said, softly.

In her strong Spanish accent, the mangos rolled off her tongue. It was the sexiest thing I'd ever heard a woman say. I should have been bringing in the eve of *Los Tres Reyes* with Abuelita; but she in this room was the one—for the first time since I'd arrived on *La Isla del Encanto*—who made me feel connected to home. And something just took over as my teeth pressed into her tanned shoulder, biting hard until she let out a cry of pain and surprise. I stopped only long enough to lift her tank top over her head and use the material to loosely bind her arms behind her. My breath coming faster now, I leaned in and asked, "Is this okay?"

"Yes," Maribel panted. "I want it hard."

My thumbs pressed roughly into the flesh on her back, squeezing and pinching, and then sliding around to pull on her hard nipples. My hands slid over her smooth sides, moved around to her curvy belly. I kissed the large scar she had from a past surgery, and she smiled at my acknowledgment of her journey. I cupped her double-D breasts, then held her nipples tightly between my fingers together to pinch and twist them, which made her squirm quietly. I pinched harder and she cried out. "*Ay Mamita* what will I ever do with you?" I murmured in her ear just before my teeth pressed her earlobe.

"Anything, please, something. Whatever you want. Please!" said Maribel.

I stepped back, taking hold of the waistband on her panties, and pulled that down. She stepped out of the fallen undergarment. Her ass cheeks, high and round, were beige compared to the rest of her cocoa-colored body. Using my fingers to follow the crack of her *culito*, I slipped my hand between the legs and found Maribel to be wanting this almost more than I did. Her lips were wet and swollen and her clit was like a marble under my finger.

"Ay *Mamita*, *Sí!*" she whispered, as I used my foot to slide her legs apart, Maribel leaned her cheek on the door and pushed her *culito* out towards me. I squatted on my knees, running my hands down one leg to the top of her other side. Her *culito* now stuck out in my face, and I breathed deep the scene of her excitement. With one hand on her thigh and the other holding on to her hip, I took a mouthful of cheek and bit down gently. Maribel pulled her ass back in far enough to press her stomach to the table.

"Now Maribel," I said sternly as I stood up again, "are you going to pull away every time it hurts a little?" Her *culito* moved backwards again and I smiled. My hands, rough with calluses from holding my video camera for my job, traced her arms up to her shoulders. I turned her to face me, and her nipples puckered when I took each in my mouth, my tongue flicking over and over. Maribel's eyes closed as she learned awkwardly on the door, her arms still bound behind her. She whispered something too quietly for me to hear. I stopped my gentle sucking and stood to look in her eyes, now open and pleading.

"What did you say?"

Maribel's eyes closed again, and in a tiny voice she said, "I want you to hurt me. I know you know how."

I wondered how she could possibly know, but that didn't stop me from walking her to a clear place on the bed and pushing her down on her back. It was then as the light from the morning peeked in through the curtain that she looked like a goddess with her flowing curls cascading like ripples of water upon the bed. Not unleashing her bound hands, I kneeled between her legs and opened them. I then made her watch me as I peeled away the rest of the mango and rubbed it like body butter all over her body with my tongue. Flicking then kissing then sucking her clit.

"Close your eyes, and don't peek," I said.

No more mango to be had, I reached the mango core that still had enough meat around it to make it hard, but malleable. I placed the core between my lips and used it as a lip extension. I then began to push it inside of her, in and out.

"*Mami*, what is that?" she said, then attempted to open her eyes.

"Close your eyes!" I commanded.

"I don't think that's a—"

"Sshh," I murmured, sliding the mango in deeper. "Don't think, just relax."

It seemed silly to argue while the mango and now my fingers were in her cunt so she layed back against the chair and relaxed.

"The mango tickles," she giggled.

I couldn't tell what it was, but I know that she was aroused as I braced my hands on her thighs and breathed against her cunt, I could see her own juices oozing. "Mmm, you smell like mango," I said.

I then dove into her cunt with my own tongue deeper and deeper. Her moans encouraged me to continue. I then worked my fingers, then my fist inside her while I continued to stroke her clit with long tongue kisses, then short tongue flicks and finally I would suck her clit with my lips and tongue at the same time. As her cunt contracted around my fingers, her juices began to squirt everywhere like a water fountain in five different directions.

I then sat on her face and she then sucked my clit between her lips, and I gripped her head with my legs. In a rush of juices, I came. Hard. I gasped as the odor of fresh mangos filled my senses. She sighed and lapped gently at my cunt as my cunt dripped juices on her face as the ripples of my orgasm faded.

I unleashed her hands from the tied negligee, and we fell in a heap upon the floor, making it creak with relief. I laughed, then she laughed, stroking any part of my body she could reach. I could feel the mangos remnants still trickling out of her, and I couldn't stop giggling.

She pulled my mango-scented mouth down to hers for a kiss, "That was pretty fucking intense," she murmured against my lips.

She sucked my bottom lip into her mouth, and I could taste the juice from my own cunt. "I think I love you. I want to meet your *abuelita*," said Maribel.

I sat up against the wall, going from this satisfied Zen state to one of utter horror. After all, I've only known her for four months, three of which were online, and I'd just got out of a four-year relationship. I struggled with how honest to be. I didn't break up with Jewel to be with her. I needed time to explore and to figure out what I wanted, not be harnessed into another long-term relationship. I started to see a pattern. I had never learned how to fuck someone and not get romantically involved. My weakness was sex. Once I crossed that line it was like I confused it with love. "It's too early," I said.

"What, you don't love me? You still love her, the *blanquita* you broke up with in New York! The one you kept complaining about over email?"

"It's only been four months. And three of those were over the Internet." She had no idea it wasn't just about getting over Jewel. I still had to face Lares.

"You sounded pretty committed when you were emailing me from your ex's house!"

"I was confused," I said.

Maribel jumped up, of course, looking sexy as all hell. "I'm not some *blanquita* you can just fuck and then toss away. *Malagradecida, tu crees que lo sabes todo, puta de mierda.*"

I retreated back into myself. Maybe Maribel was right; I was an ungrateful whore who thought I knew what I wanted but didn't. That's not a literal translation of what she said but it is what I took from her statement. I'm really beginning to think I suck at this thing called commitment, and maybe it's not meant for me to find happiness since I just seem to hurt whomever I love.

"You aren't going to make this easy, are you?" she asked, quietly. Then she walked toward a pitcher of martinis and poured me a drink. And for the first time, as much as she had accused me of using her, I felt used too. I was a trophy for Maribel, being ten years younger. I'm sure me being a baby dyke fed her ego. As much as I had self-medicated with alcohol, Maribel and all the other women always handed me the bottle.

"What you think you'll do better than me? You're lucky to have this job! You know the only reason I gave you the Lifetime job is because I wanted to fuck you!" said Maribel. Her words stung for a second as she looked at me with her just been fucked hair. But, the one thing I did know in my life was that I was one hell of a cinematographer and I worked hard.

Then I grabbed the martini and threw it against the wall. The glass crashed against the table, almost hitting Maribel.

"What the fuck are you doing you slutty bitch? You could have hurt me!" said Maribel. Suddenly, I didn't care about Maribel or Jewel or any of the nameless faces that I had fucked. I only saw pieces of Lares in the broken glass, and finally I knew that I had to face her before I could ever love anyone again, especially myself.

I gritted my teeth and ran to her.

"That'll be seventy dollars," said the cab driver.

The drive from San Juan to Los Baños was a blur, and now I rummaged through my purse searching for enough money to pay the driver. After having barely scrounged the fare together, I paid the driver. He looked at me funny, perhaps expecting a tip. Or maybe he noticed how red my eyes were and took pity on me. Tears had just kept flowing after I left Maribel's, but I still couldn't utter a whimper. Alone in the backseat I'd sat teary-eyed as I'd looked out the window toward the star-filled night, which filled me with a déjà vu connected with what I had felt over twenty years ago.

"Want me to stay?" asked the driver, sounding concerned.

"Do you mind, my abuelita's house is over an hour walk from here? We could stop at an ATM inside El Pueblo supermarket en route to her house."

"How could I resist such a beautiful woman?"

"*Gracias*," I said, thankful for once that chivalrous men still existed. Then I began the half-mile hike up the hill toward *Los Baños de Coamo*.

"*Cuidao nena!*" said the driver, yelling out his car window. "Women traveling alone have been known to disappear."

"Yeah, I know," I said, turning towards him, sadly thinking of Lares. I should have been more afraid of being alone with a strange man, but the driver was only being parental as he looked out for my safety. Our eyes connected and he intuitively knew that the trek was mine alone to make. And, going against his old school upbringing, he parked his cab and waited inside. I wanted to race back to the car and request the driver drop me off at some bar. But, I took a deep breath, and step-by-step made my way toward the entrance of *Los Baños de Coamo*, which I hadn't visited since Lares died.

I arrived at the entrance. Over twenty different *dichos* were now painted on wood slats that were nailed to the two fifteen-foot palm trees that served as a natural guardian to *Los Baños*. One *dicho* stood out and gave me the courage to enter: *Si quiero arreglar el mundo, lo mejor será que empiece por mi misma.* So, I wandered into my child-hood playground determined to change myself. The moon was full and tonight she decided to bless me with her light as I searched for our rock among the many that were scattered upon the small hill that stood above *Los Baños*. An old palm tree branch hovered over one of the rocks. I gently moved it aside, which allowed the moon to serve as a spotlight over our rock. I wanted to dance upon the rock without a care in the world. To have the grace that Lares exuded even as a child. The courage to be out and love myself.

My heart started pounding faster as I easily leaped upon the rock; in my youth I had had to climb. My feet were cemented to the rock as I caught sight of *Los Baños*, which flowed ten feet in front of me, and to my right was an Olympic-sized pool which replaced the pond in which Lares had drowned. The pool was surrounded by a twenty-foot-tall barbed wired fence that guarded it from people who did not live in the newly developed gated community with the sprawling golf course. They would have captured *Los Baños* too, but years ago, the people of Coamo fought to have them protected by making it a public park.

Besides the gated community, everything else about *Los Baños* felt familiar, it was just smaller viewing it with my adult eyes. The sound of the coquis serenaded me, but now I was too big to dance upon the rock. Instead, I followed the moonlight as she moved from our rock to *Los Baños*. I looked into the hot springs, and I saw my reflection. Lares and I never had time to find the moon in the hot springs as she had promised. But, instead, the moon led me to myself. I took off my shoes and rolled up my pants. I danced to the sound of the coquis as I splashed through the warm springs and howled as loud as my lungs could bear. I closed my eyes, "*Dame la bendición*," I yelled. I'm not sure to whom or what. I figured we all needed some type of higher power during difficult moments in our lives. I wrapped my arms tenderly around myself, and I blew a kiss to Lares. In that moment, I too felt the rejuvenating powers of *Los Baños*. And I really needed a blessing to take home with me.

The taxi driver dropped me off at Abuelita's house fifteen minutes before midnight, just in time to bring in *Los Tres Reyes*. I entered to find Abuelita standing at the table, with two plates filled with freshly prepared *pasteles y arroz con gandules* in her hands. I silently sat in the chair beside her, and let her place the food in front of me. I was ready to celebrate the holiday with her, putting the tension of the last few months behind us. The framed picture of Lares and me now stood upright on the dinner table, next to two goblets. It was as if Abuelita had summoned me home. I reached to grab the picture. But not before Abuelita sat in the seat across from me at the table.

"Esperanza, I knew you'd be home before midnight." She calmly reached for the goblets, and filled them both with *coquito*. She handed me one, and then left the other next to the picture. "Let's make a toast," she said.

"Abuelita, I don't want to drink," I said, pushing the goblet away. I felt like I needed to be sober in that moment. But she pushed the glass toward me again, and I knew her offering was more than just a drink. She was serving me her acceptance. Abuelita didn't pick the other glass up to join me. Confused, I searched her aging face for an answer. She sat waiting for me to lift my glass. I didn't know whom or what to toast. But I decided to do as I was told. I owed her that. I lifted the glass. Abuelita raised her empty hand and said the toast for me.

"To Lares, may she finally be able to rest in peace knowing that you have forgiven yourself, *mi'jita!*" Abuelita then stood up and planted a kiss on my cheek. She grabbed my hand, moving my arm upwards to meet hers. She grasped my hand in her own. Abuelita then lit a white candle that had been decorated with flowers using a colorful glitter. I pressed my lips together, unable to utter a word. I had let Lares go, but I still needed my family. Years of repressed tears streamed down my face, turning what had been perfectly painted mascara into a messy painter's palette. I couldn't bring myself to release the cry stuck in my throat until Abuelita wrapped her arms around me and I yelled so loud, I'm sure it was heard for miles. I fell to the ground, and I cried for what seemed to be hours.

Abuelita continued to hug me as she used her apron to wipe my tears away. Once I had calmed, the candle had burned down to half its original size. I took a deep breath and I raised my glass. "To Lares my first love. I release you," I said, taking a sip of my *coquito*. Then I turned to Abuelita, "And to Abuelita thank you for all the love you've given me through the years, no matter what." I caught her eye and held it for a moment. I knew she understood. "Your love is healing."

Abuelita began to cry. This was only the second time in my life I had ever seen her shed tears since Abuelo died. I wanted to believe otherwise, but deep inside my heart, I knew she wept for my soul. My lifestyle went against her beliefs, and I refused to hate myself anymore for being a lesbian. And yet here we were together, accepting each other completely. We sat there, both sobbing, and in our silence we found a peaceful place.

The Lunalía

Yxta Maya Murray

December 23, 2005. 9:30 a.m. Studio City, California.

this is my first confession in this diary. I bought it just this morning, after clutching it in the Long's Drugs stationery aisle like some unmedicated Sylvia Plath. Journaling, I've read, is good for a girl's psychology. Excellent for times like this, as I've just had a tiny . . . episode. That is, I've only now taken up this diary to write down the events of last night. Something very queer happened to me.

I was literally *moonstruck*.

Here is how it happened:

After I returned home from the library, I sat on our garden's stone bench, looking out at our frosty lawn and the half-dead hydrangea bushes circling the property. My watch showed seven o'clock. Patrick hadn't come home from the hospital yet.

I drank wine, wrapped in a flannel robe and my husband's old down parka. I'd had a difficult day spent with a disrespectful librarian-in-training named Steven, whose education has fallen to me since my promotion to head of the Studio City branch of the Los Angeles Public Library. I was so cranky it seemed a better idea to withstand the chill outside rather than go inside, where I'd have to tidy our house, an embarrassing calamity of Christmas tinsel. Our cat, a sexist orange tabby called La Chupacabra, purred and yawned as she sat at my feet, not so much keeping me company as waiting impatiently for my spouse. The full moon hurried through the black sky like a school of gilded fish; I once studied moons in an almanac, and I think this December *luna* is called the Long Nights Moon by farmers, as it marks the Winter Solstice. This is the longest night of the year.

The Long Night's Moon breathed its light down on us, pale and faint. I placed my glass of chardonnay on the bench, feeling randy on account of my power struggles with the aforementioned novice-boy-librarian, who's about as sexy as he is colossally irritating. I looked around at the grass, the hedges, and the fence. I remained perfectly alone. Pressing my fingers to my tongue, I parted my robe, bared my legs.

I began to touch myself.

I lightly petted the swell of my thighs, then the sweet, tense little bridge of muscle leading to my sex. My skin was warm. I grew bolder. Within the lips, the hidden flesh felt wet and lovely. As I pressed my fingers deeper into the cleft, red whorls and veins flickered across my closed lids, as if I could see inside my body. I could see other marvels, as well: images of women. The pleasure of my caresses released into my imagination underwater pictures of rose-colored lips and glistening feet. These night-ladies were like goddesses, or harpies, and in my fantasy they reached out their moon-drenched hands to pinch and tickle me. Just behind them, I could make out an old crone with black looks and silver hair, who watched their happy defilements with an approving expression on her haughty face.

I fucked myself like a banshee. Guided by those daydream harlots, my hand found the hot spot. I reached my slick index finger until I hit that rough-skinned key, the little zone that's a hooked-finger's breadth from the furred entrance of the lips. Sliding off the bench, teetering but not spilling the wine glass, I writhed *nastily* on the ground. And as I lay in the grass with my eyes still closed, I didn't notice the moonlight slowly grow brighter, streaming down in a white flood on my half-naked body.

La Chupacabra yowled, and I opened one eye to see the garden brimming with an unearthly light. It transformed our little lawn into a Versailles inhabited by alabaster bushes and mother-of-pearl trees. The grass billowed beneath me like a white tapestry.

I didn't know at the time what was happening—that I was being possessed. Overtaken by an exotic impulse, I grasped the glass of wine and poured it on the grass as an offering to the moon, the same way the ancient Aztecs and the Greeks once made libations to their pagan gods.

"*Salud*," I said.

Then everything changed.

The hydrangea bushes rustled. The flowers instantly grew as lush as hothouse blooms. I smelled narcissus. The scent of myrrh filled the air. The bushes heaved, shook back and forth, and trembled.

A young woman's face appeared between the flowers.

"She heard you." The phantasm laughed, pressing easily through the hedge, revealing that she was nude from the waist up. "She's waiting for you."

"What?" I managed to blurt out.

"Your prayer has been accepted, Imogen."

She had high bones, long black eyes, mink-dark skin. Her tiny breasts thrust out at me. She was a *nymph*.

"I don't understand," I whispered.

Her hair sprang out of its twist as she jumped with glee. "My name's Selena. *Hello?* You just saw me in your vision, silly. All those girls who were tickling you? The old woman with the silver hair? That wasn't just a fantasy, you know. It was a summons."

La Chupacabra scrambled away, her tail as big as a bush. I felt myself floating over the moon-burning garden toward this Selena-fairy, stopping short of crossing the blossoming hedge. Perfume wafted from the flowers like a sweet drug.

One by one, women appeared in the hydrangea bush alongside her. White and black and tawny fingers poked through the flowered hedge. Their faces pressed past the leaves. They were of all races; I marveled at blue eyes, at hooked noses. Like the flower fairies Victorian madmen once painted, here were blossom-spangled ladies with wolfish teeth and freckled or onyx skin. Some had heavy breasts with dark mauve nipples. Others had small breasts with delicate points like the petals of African violets. Their glossy hair fell over these treasures. They had plump and shining bellies.

"Hello," they sang in a chorus, as they reached out to pet my limbs in a frenzy.

I understood suddenly that these were the women from my fantasy.

"Oh, take *this off*," they squealed, ripping my parka and robe with terrifying ferocity. "Kiss us, hold us, squeeze us tight!"

But when they stroked their dozen hands from my throat to my thighs, the sensation was so gentle, so languid, that I sighed.

With Amazon strength they ripped away the hedge as if it were made of tissue paper. Beyond the edge of our yard, I saw that our neighbor's house and Studio City itself, with its chain stores, boulevards, and suburbs, had disappeared.

In its place unfolded the strangest of forests. The old woman I'd spied in my vision, with the pale hair and astonishing eyes, was robed in black. She stood before me and slowly smiled.

She didn't speak, but I understood that she invited me into this mythical grove. Three moons careened in its sky, and blood red oak trees burst from its indigo grass. The firmament looked carved of diamonds, and within its glittering facets and sparkling black helixes hung gold stars and green clouds that stared down like eyes. The very *air* was different here. It was a substance like both wine and water, sweet to the taste and agile as a snake as it curved around my throat and hips.

The women swarmed around me, murmuring, whispering.

> Come along.
> There's no need to be afraid.
> Mother, can we have her?
> If she's good.

I hovered on the brink between my house and this carnival land, swaying slightly as their hands on my thighs and breasts grew more insistent. This was not real. I had stumbled onto some occult magic show; I was being hypnotized and instructed in the ancient art of levitation as six tender mouths licked and bit at my skin. My knees buckled. I was ready to *leap* into that dreamscape.

But then I saw . . . it.

A naked snow-white man with a face like a hawk's and a long, pointed penis skulked behind the crone. He darted between the red trees and grinned at me with a crimson mouth. I recognized him. He looked like one of the devils painted by the lunatic Hieronymus Bosch.

The sirens huddled closer to me when they felt me stiffen.

"Oh, don't mind *him*—he's just jealous," the girl called Selena said.

"Hello, Imogen," he growled out to me from the trees. "López, is it?"

I screamed.

Turning, I bolted over my little lawn, my stone bench, the assorted snares of watering hoses and littered garden equipment. As La Chupacabra began caterwauling, I skidded in through the French doors connecting the yard to our bedroom, glancing back over my shoulder. Now I only saw our same withered garden, with its dying flowers and watery moonlight. Still, I kept whirligigging my legs in a Charlie Chaplin hysteria so that I banged through the hallway, shouting, nearly slamming into the wall before hurtling into the Christmas-littered living room.

I stood naked in the middle of the den, chest heaving for more air. La Chupacabra had scratched her way up the curtains and was shredding away the fabric. I stared wildly at the Christmas tree. It was half-toppled from its smothering cover of tinsels and deviant-looking papier-mâché *putti*. Everything appeared the same in the house, our afghan-covered sofa, the suspicion of dust, and profusion of books stacked haphazardly on the floor and tables. I crept over to the south windows, which looked out onto the garden. Nothing. My parka remained strewn on the lawn and my robe was wadded up in the hydrangeas.

Had I just seen what I had seen?

I blinked. I coughed. I blinked again at the flashing lights of the tree.

Then the front door rattled and Patrick came home.

"Where are my babies!" he bellowed. "Hooo, it's good to be home. Hospital was an asylum today. I did the surgery on Mrs. Flanagan—the patient I was telling you about? The really nasty one? She took me *seven hours . . .*"

I could hear him banging about in the hallway as he chattered. La Chupacabra fell from the curtains and scratched across the floor to go greet him. Patrick stomped into the living room with the cat now latched to his chest and his strawberry hair flaming around his head, a medieval saint's halo. My husband has blue eyes, a robust nose, and wore one of his polyblend remaindered Land's End suits. ". . . I swear, I thought I was going to lose the old bird. I was putting in the prosthetic—that negative pressure device I was telling you about? And she started fibrillating. They rang the bell, and I'm shouting at her, 'Mrs. Flanagan, you old bat, you're not dying on me! Come on! You're just doing this to *piss me off'*—and then, it was like I got her mad again, because her heart starts whacking away. But it was a near miss. I swear, I thought I was going to have an embolism . . ."

"Hi, honey!" I attempted to rearrange my nudity from its spastic pose into something more normal-looking.

Patrick wobbled his head hilariously when he saw me. He stopped describing his workplace near tragedy in midbreath. "Why are you buck naked, baby?"

Because I just crossed over to Hades, like Odysseus.

"Imogen?"

My arms involuntarily flung themselves above my head. "Christmas surprise."

"Christmas surprise?" He bugged out his eyes so he looked like the biological father of the goggling cat, whom he still cradled. "Aren't you cold?"

We smiled confusedly at each other. I never feel awkward with Patrick but had to admit that my living-room bare-assedness was uncharacteristic, as I generally scamper about the house in my jeans and his old *Adam Ant Live!* T-shirt. A simple explanation of my Lady Godiva condition rose to my lips but a delirious-sounding laughter bubbled out from them instead. He still looked bewildered as the seconds ticked away. I realized I had to do something to show him I wasn't crazy.

So I jumped him.

"Hold on! Wow! What a welcome! I just hope I can—agh—" I'd already removed the cat from its viselike grip on his chest, and was working on simultaneously disrobing Patrick and knocking him to the ground by softly kicking at the insides of his knee joints. I ripped his shirt off his shoulders so that the buttons pinged and ponged off, and bounced on the floor. The shirt shredded in my hands. This effect was actually more difficult to get than would seem from the movies. The buttons skittered beneath my bare feet. The pants and briefs came down in a twisted mass around his ankles. My husband stumbled forward with one arm outstretched to embrace me, while also squeezing his eyes shut and attempting to achieve an instant and heroic erection; but he admittedly had some trouble because he had started laughing so hard at this unexpected homecoming.

"This is awesome," he blathered.

I clutched onto his stupendous broad chest, with its freckled upright pecs and covering of a kind of pre-Raphaelite red fuzz, this thinning to a little arrowy line as it traveled over his rodeo-cowboy's six-pack and down to his supersized yet still zippy penis, which had now grown to a full and impatient height. Digging my heels harder into his knees, I sent us tumbling to the floor, me on top. I fandangoed over him with such energy that it amounted to a kind of wild erotic flailing, and on account of the spasms of my hips, we had not quite yet inserted said zippiness into my raging *vagina dentata*. Patrick clung on for the ride, laughing less now and more cheering me on. His jackhammer belly bumped under my thighs while he licked my pebbly nipples.

He pulled my head next to his to whisper in my ear. "You're a big crazy slut! I'm a football player and you're a wicked cheerleader who's tempting me. I'm going to fuck you with my big meaty cock— when you let me get it in—I'm going to take you in the ass and you're going to suck me and then I'm going to lick you and bite you really, really, hard, right on the clit."

"Ah—ah—"

"How's the dirty talk?"

"Be worse!"

With his right hand, he put his fingers in my pussy, and with his left, he directed his penis at the target, which was still moving ecstatically in the air above him. "You're a cunt!"

"Yes! Yes!"

"You're a big raving—"

"Whore!"

"Okay!"

"Fuck me, oh my God!"

But then he asked: "You ovulating, sweetie?"

I paused for a second. I felt the heat start to drain out of me. I had to cut him off. "I don't know. God, I don't *care*—"

He pushed himself in. "Didn't you take your temperature?"

"I'm fucking *hot*—"

"Okay, sorry, yes, you're so, so, so hot—"

I yelled, "Bitch, fuck me!"

"Come, come!"

His dick was completely inside of me at this point. It was whacking away at a good fast clip, and I balanced my G-spot directly over the head.

I rampaged my hips over his. While the papier-mâché angels flung around the branches in a seeming fit of bacchic raptures, I smoothed my thighs across his waist and thumped my feet against the floor. Patrick's freckles floated like stars over his pale, pointed face, and his springy pubic hair scrubbed up against my bottom. He whacked my cheeks with the flat of his hand just hard enough so that the pain was delicious.

"Fuck it fuck it fuck it, fuck it."

There we were, humping in the glory of holy, possibly procreative, Christmas-time matrimony. We were just two ordinary humans in love, carnally romping with our typical wildebeest abandon.

But for one second, I had an image of that White Man I'd seen standing behind the old woman, and that vision made me terrified. I saw his hawk face and his pointed penis. Fear shot down from my mind to my slit, and I can't understand why, but that mortal dread made me buck and hoola-hoop over the shivery stiff loins of an enchanted Patrick.

"Shake it! Shake it, crazy!" he called out before madly orgasming himself.

Afterward, we gathered our flung clothes and sprawled together on the sofa. Patrick almost immediately began talking again about his medical case, and though I tried to pay attention to his elaborate descriptions of urological prostheses, my mind was admittedly more absorbed with the incredible events that had passed in the backyard.

I quickly decided that these were *not* events that I should share with my husband, because he was so Spock that he wouldn't react well to the idea of fairy portals in the hydrangeas. Patrick is a urologist-oncologist. He's Dr. Patrick Weston, and thirty-six years old (I'm thirty-four). He's of Finnish extraction. *Not* Mexican, like me. We're totally different. While he's red-haired and white and pointed, I'm round and dark, with nice, slim hips, but also with an almost too-large mouth and breasts so extravagant that my colleagues have had to train themselves to look me in the eye rather than in the nipple. This "nipple test," in fact, quickly proved to me that Patrick was a good man the day I met him. On a Saturday, in 2001, I first saw his red hair bobbing up and down in the library. His akimbo arms were struggling with multiple tomes on bladder cancer while he skidded toward me like Gene Kelly's uncoordinated cousin. As the books tumbled onto the check-out counter, he impeccably kept his small, minty eyes on mine and laughing, asked questions about the book I had opened before me, *When God Was a Woman.* Right in the middle of my lengthy explanation of ancient Mesopotamian goddess rituals, he suddenly exclaimed: "I don't believe God was ever either a man or a woman or anything at all—except, a girl as beautiful as you are *must* be some kind of miracle." Then he blushed burgundy and said, "I'm sorry, that just came out." And I said, "That's okay by me."

Six hours later, the direct-eye-contact courtesy was well and truly over, as Patrick was by then treating me to Herculean oral sex in his apartment. Seven weeks after that, we were married. For the past four years we've been undeservedly happy in almost every crucial marital category: sex, laughing, nonsense, finances, cats, and housework (both of us are lousy at this last one). The one area that we've floundered in is childbearing, which used to seem like the most important one of all. We've been "officially" trying since '03 to make me pregnant. But I haven't even had a skipped period. My fertility game plan has thus far consisted of me lighting a thousand church candles and praying to God so forcefully I *sweat*. Patrick deals with the crisis by persistently reminding me to check my egg-receptivity by taking my temperature before coitus, as well as shuttling me to female-fertility experts who have subjected me to one unsuccessful IVF cycle (the problem is me; his swimmers are fine) after another.

Our different reactions to our babymaking imbroglio give a quick picture of the difference in our natures: I'm "spiritual" and Patrick is a godless heathen. And as I flopped with him there on the tinsel-speckled sofa, it was this philosophical divide that prevented me from breathlessly admitting I'd just fornicated with angels in the backyard. He'd chalk it up to a chemical imbalance, or some sort of neural hiccup.

And maybe, I thought, *he'd be right.*

"I think Mrs. Flanagan's going to make it," he continued, "and when she gets in remission, she's going to kick my ass, because she is the damn meanest patient I've ever had . . ."

"Well, maybe . . . I need to go on Xanax," I muttered to myself.

"What?"

"Nothing. Just thinking about Mrs. Flanagan, maybe she needs a prescription."

I was lying. For as I nodded distractedly at his complaints about Mrs. Flanagan, I concluded that I hadn't just had a very Close Encounter with the Other Side. Rather, it suddenly seemed clear that my nasty bouts of baby-fever had so damaged me that I must have *hallucinated* that coven of moon fairies who lived in our hydrangea hedge.

• • •

I always thought I knew exactly what I wanted. I wanted what every woman wanted: a baby.

This makes me sound normal, I suppose. It makes me sound like a regular, biological-clock-ticking woman who is born with the instinct to give birth. But I'd have to say that the genesis of my *very* early infant-craving is less organic and natural than literary, as well as symptomatic of a weirdly overheated imagination. In other words, I'm trying to convince myself that my long-standing, bookish, and flamingly quirky "baby brain" gives a reasonable explanation for why last night I dreamed that I partied with supernatural strippers in the backyard.

I decided that I wanted a child when I was seven years old, and my mother scared the hell out of me by reciting a Keats poem. It was *Ode to a Nightingale*.

The year: 1977; the setting: the shadowy and cool basement of my parent's three-bedroom ranch house in far-flung Galveston, Texas. My mother, Carolina, a then-pony-tailed, Indian-faced lover of all overripe literature, from biblical to British (which is why my christian name sounds as if it's been plucked from the pages of a Bram Stoker novel), sat next to me on our futon sofa and cracked open a book. She said, "I'm going to read you something really pretty, Imogen," then proceeded to incant the timeless lines that describe Keats listening to a bird singing outside his window:

> Thou wast not born for death, immortal Bird!
> No hungry generations tread thee down;
> The voice I hear this passing night was heard
> In ancient days by emperor and clown.

I didn't react in the way that she expected. As Mom had recited the ode, I'd heard the nightingale sing; I'd seen the hordes of hungry generations. But I was not reassured by this account of eternal beauty. Instead, I sat there on the futon, frozen and terrified with eyes expanding ever wider because I knew that Keats was telling us something awful: the reason why the bird's song was eternal, and heard not only by the tubercular poet but also by clowns and emperors, was because it kept being born, again and again, and that while old nightingales grew old and doddery and plummeted from the sky to screaming bird-death, they also kept making baby birds who carried with them some still-warm DNA crumb of said croaked birds. So giving birth to your own biological chick was the only way you could cheat the Reaper.

"Imogen, it's just a nice poem, calm down," my mother had said.

Ever since then, I'd wanted to make a nightingale. I realize that this dream of biological stasis is in conflict with my religious faith, which traffics in cherubic and nonstop afterlives. Nevertheless. I wanted to be sweating and heaving in the OR while squeezing out the head of a squalling babe. The nurse would then hand over the creature to me so that I could hold it in my arms, and faint dead away, assured that my doddering DNA would be carried forward in perpetuity.

Twenty years later, when I met Patrick, it was settled: I was *going to have his baby*. The process was very fun at first. But what was frisky Kama Sutra sex in the inaugural year of our marriage, in the second turned into orgies consisting of me holding a bobbing thermometer in my mouth while rigorously raping him. My mental scrapbook of year three is filled mostly with pictures of me strenuously urinating over a blinding succession of EPT pregnancy-test sticks. In the fourth, I recall blubbering hysterically while watching a rerun of *Rosemary's Baby*, and actually wishing that I would be as lucky as Mia Farrow cooing at her devil-spawn.

But then, around the beginning of 2005, I . . . lost interest.

It started to happen last year, after my promotion to head of the S. C. branch. On the day I'd received the ambiguous but very not positive results of my fertility tests, I distracted myself by hunching around our Women's Interest section, which needed reorganizing. Beneath *Our Bodies, Ourselves*, I found a crazy volume detailing the burnings of Renaissance midwives, which had perverted woodcuts illustrating the supposed crimes of these "witches." The ladies' crimes looked far more fun than my spirit-crushing hobby of pissing on preg-test cocktail stirrers. They mostly had to do with sex. I squatted down on the library's green-gray Berber rug and peered at an etching of a gorgeous European succubus, who with sharp-clawed hands dandled the colossal erection of a shocked-looking priest as a massive moon beamed through the monastery's window. On the next page a big-bottomed Incan moon goddess lasciviously embraced some sort of possibly Asian devil-lady with booming bosoms and webbed toes. On the page after that, sexy African midwives ecstatically tortured bishops with hot brands beneath the horned *luna*.

I found these pictures very interesting.

My desires began to change soon after. I am not yet precisely sure what it is exactly that I want—it remains something as dangerous as Keats's nightingale—but I can say that since my first taste of sixteenth-century porn, I've become less fascinated by babies, and more by occult sex. I've begun to very covertly purchase smut for the library, usually in the undercover forms of academic treatises that detail Renaissance sex-sorcery, as well as dissertations on the orgasmic moon-goddess cults of the ancient Americas. At the S.C. branch, we have a basement (shadowy and cool like the one of mortal memory in Galveston), and I've stocked it with these rare, first-edition sodomy manuals. I've attempted to reenact some of their more exciting historical sex rituals with Patrick, but we experienced one humiliating failure on the night when I began ravening around our bedroom with a dildo and tickling his anus with it. He had the flailing "that-is-too-gay-for-me" straight man's response, and since then, I've been trying to come up with less threatening ways to ravage him, like some terrifying and big-dicked snake goddess.

But it seems I should probably cut down on the dirty books. I think this "research" might have backfired on me. With my subconscious so primed by infertility and lurid literature, I've apparently snapped, and last night had a psychotic break that reads like an X-rated Book of Shadows . . .

"Imogen," Patrick was saying. "Did you hear me?"

We were still on the sofa, and I realized that Patrick's surgery story had tailed off into disgruntled mumbles. He was staring at me.

"What's that, sweetie?"

"You spacing a little bit?"

"You wore me out."

"I WAS incredible."

"The dirty talk was good."

"I was trying to make it really bad."

"You *did*."

"Okay. Excellent. But I was asking—want dinner?"

"Um . . . yeah."

He peered down at me, frowning a little. "Honey, are you okay? You seem a little—zoned out, or something."

"I'm fine—"

"You sure?"

"Yes, yes. I just have post-O brain. Can't think straight."

"Oh, well, that's okay."

"But—I didn't cook."

"Well, get to it right now, woman," he boomed, slapping me on the bottom.

"Forget it!" I chuckled.

"So when you were shimmying around here naked, you didn't think to make me some macaroni?"

"No."

"You are a bad girl. You're objectifying me. You just *used* me like I'm just some sexual stallion instead of a sensitive and overeducated white guy—which I actually don't mind."

"Will you just please order out?"

"I wish I could tell them at work. My patients just *laugh* at me when they see my dented collars and wrinkled pants and all your pictures on my desk. They start telling me how whipped I am and make that *whut-choo* noise when I walk by—"

"Go—go."

"Okay."

Before he raised himself from the sofa, Patrick leaned over, lifted the afghan covering me, and kissed me on the stomach, very tenderly, for good luck in babymaking. He's mostly been very Buddha on the baby front despite my recent reluctance to start the IVF rodeo again, but lately he's starting to get antsy.

"I think Chinese," he said.

And so, we had dinner. I still didn't raise the subject of amorous elves. After that, I gave him a massage and we went to bed.

I'm now writing this account in the kitchen the next morning, now that Patrick's gone off to the hospital.

I have no marks on my skin where the supposed sylphs touched me. There is no trace of my encounter with those fairy women.

Of course not.

But I can't help but wonder about other fairy-sightings like mine. I think they were common in the European Middle Ages and during the Mexican Inquisition, when women would divulge gothic sexual rhapsodies to the titillated father-confessors, who then ordered them to be burned alive.

I would like to know that I am not clinically crazy.

Even if I am, I'd like to know that I'm not entirely alone.

January 2. Moon in Aquarius. Second Day of the New Year.

The research that I've done is very exciting.

I'm trembling now as I sit in the basement of the library, with the cache of rare books and papers I had that novice librarian Steven Montalbán get for me on a recent whirlwind of interlibrary loans, as our bulked-up Women's Studies section still doesn't have quite enough material on obscene fairy-sightings. Just an hour ago, I looked up to see Steven standing in the doorway, holding a pile of tomes, which were heavy enough to make the sinews in his annoyingly shapely arms bulge even larger. I could see from the puzzled look on his dark-eyed face that he was intrigued by my work. The boy is twenty-two, I think, a mixture of Mayan Indian and Pennsylvania Dutch. He is also sullen, intelligent, and slovenly in his baggy jeans and his indecent rock-concert T-shirts that seem shrink-wrapped to his *too*-muscular torso. While I used to find him a bother

because he expressed his antiauthoritarianism through sloth (prone
to talking to girls on the phone when he should be cataloging or
servicing customers, he was hired for his University of Chicago pedi-
gree and not for his industry), as well as the tacky sex fantasies he inspired, I now wish that he were a little less diligent when it came to
my personal project.

"These folios have some interesting . . . pictures," he said in the
doorway, posing with the books. "I thought we already had a bunch
of women's studies things in the library."

"I'm making a survey of the literature for an annual report
to . . . Sacramento."

"Oh, *really*?"

"What do you need again?"

"I'm not complaining. Personally, my favorites are the Dührer
woodcuts of girl-on-girl—"

"Put them down, please, Steven."

He walked over and placed the volumes on my desk. "Just offering an opinion, Ms. López. Why *are* you reading all this stuff?"

"I told you, I'm writing an article."

"On what, sex?"

I looked up at him. He has a very wide mouth. The shape of his
lips inspired in me two different ideas, one of which was obvious and
unfaithful, and the other concerned a muzzle and a sharp little whip.

"You're not dressed appropriately for work," I said. Since he is a
repeated failure at the Nipple Test, I always take care to cover my
décolletage in the most conservative of skirt-suits purchased on
sale from Coldwater Creek. Steven's wardrobe choices cleave less
faithfully to the librarian-neuter archetype. I gestured at his shirt,
which seemed intentionally shredded and bore a portrait of some
ghastly gaggle of boys who call themselves *Green Day*. "This is
ripped."

He smiled and looked down at himself. "Where?"

I pointed at the delicate little hole gaping over his left rib.
"There."

"I'm sorry, where? I don't know what you're talking about."

"*Right here.*" I stupidly touched my finger to the skin revealed by the hole, which sparked an electric current between my body and his.

He smiled wider. "Oh, you're right, Ms. López. Would you like me to—"

"No." I knew *exactly* what the minx was going to say.

"—take it off?"

"Steven, go up to the main floor. I don't know if anyone is manning the desk."

"You sure?"

"Do you want to be fired? *Go up to the main floor.*"

Up he went.

I'm not surprised that Sir Cocksman was tantalized by my bookhaul. What I have here before me are sixteenth-century witchhunting manuals, erotic woodcuts by Dutch Masters, and brochures on demonology and *the moon-rites of bad women.*

I am getting the spooky feeling that the moon has been hunting me since I first cracked open that book on midwives last year.

My palms are sweating. Look what I found in Dr. Edvard Murillo's *Daemonologia* (1882)! Murillo was a Victorian-era folklorist-scientist who trekked into the wilds of the Americas and published a book about its magical cultures. He writes briefly of a particular moon cult that he heard rumors of in Cuzco, Peru, which revolved around the worship of a lunar goddess called La Chusa.

It is said that in Cuzco, certain Indian women gather beneath the full moon to pour wine into the earth and dance, burn special herbs or stones, and sing the praises of the moon goddess known as La Chusa.

These festivals, which are called "The Lunalía" are intended to persuade the goddess to allow her priestesses entry into some sort of mythical paradise, which the women claim is nothing less than God's lost Eden. Yet these women worship La Chusa not only for her access to Zion, but also because of her stupendous powers of creation and healing, which she wields by virtue of her mystic Laughter—this, as opposed to the genius of her consort, Satan, who appears to his faithful after they call his Name three times, and destroys life by virtue of his Tears. . . .

La Chusa's story is most titillating: The priests say that she was once a wicked woman, the first woman, who disobeyed God and dishonored her husband. What was the cause of her sin, which was to garner her such unholy power? Her Imagination, which was Lecherous. That is, she imagined herself better than her design, as she sinfully refused to take the passive role in sex, insisting on riding her husband as if he were a horse! Cast out of Paradise, she flew on her dark wings to the moon, where she lived in shame for a thousand years. La Chusa is thus none other than Lilith, the Apocrypha's first wife of Adam, and the precursor of Eve.

La Chusa—or Lilith—has found her way back to Eden by virtue of a mysterious Key. In turn, she allows her most loyal followers into that Otherworld, where they are able to harness superhuman energies, and experience unmatched sensual Pleasure. According to the Tales I have studied, the Goddess's gift of Paradise is given to her worshipers (after their making to her of some Sacrifice) during an orgiastic Rite that is the apex, and purpose, of their profane holiday: the Lunalía . . .

I have just locked the basement door, so none of my librarians can see me prance around in joy over this book.

The Lunalía. The Lunalía! It *was* a full moon the night I was seduced by imps!

I am trying so hard to remember what I did to conjure those mermaids, but I only remember drinking some wine and some self-diddling mischief that I indulged in on the garden's stone bench.

What was the cause of her sin, which was to garner her such unholy power? Murillo writes. *Her* Imagination, *which was Lecherous.*

That must have been what drew them to me.

The next full moon is in twenty days.

January 14

They are not fairies but flesh and blood women.

I am *not crazy*: The midnight pixies, lunar succubi, starlit earth goddesses, and moon-eyed devil-girls that I have studied and hallucinated are real. Everything I've imagined is true.

I know this evening that the January moon is called the Wolf Moon. It appeared in the sky this morning at 1:48 a.m. The thistle is holy to the January moon, and its flower is the crocus. Its tree is birch and it colors are white and black.

This is what the insane women who worship the Luna have told me.

I am at the kitchen table at two a.m. My body shakes with fear and joy as I write this. I began the night as myself, and ended it as another kind of creature, if such things are possible—that is, if I'm still in the possession of my senses and haven't lost my mind.

Patrick and I sat down to dinner at our ordinary hour, eight-thirty. A bottle of wine cast a garnet shadow on the table, and the candlelight gentled the icy air cast by the huge moon outside. Nat King Cole's melancholy but beautiful *Smile* crooned on the new stereo, which we had purchased as a New Year's gift to ourselves:

> Smile though your heart is aching
> Smile even though it's breaking

Despite these little comforts of the evening, my husband's face was paler than usual as he sat with me at the table; it contrasted badly with his red hair that flashed around him like an aura.

"She's not doing that well," he said, meaning Mrs. Flanagan, the surgery patient he nearly lost in December.

"I'm listening."

"It's age, I think. Or loneliness—her husband died last year, after bringing her here from Ireland. That can weaken you, loneliness. The procedure was too hard on her."

"What can you do?"

"Drugs. Maybe another operation. I just hate to see her—"

"Suffer."

"I'm trying to get used to it."

I touched his hand. Though he's had plenty of successes, sixteen of his patients have passed away since his residency and practice, began eight years ago. His ensuing grief and flattening depression have been a "weakness" that the chief of his unit has talked to him about. He's visited the hospital therapist; he's also done bio-feedback, and even coerced himself to watch a numbing array of war movies. By this internal, forced discipline, he's been trying to train himself to deal with death, which is a mental process I understand about as well as the theory of relativity.

He suddenly burst out: "Imogen, I worked *so* fucking hard on that surgery—I thought I could fix her—"

"I know."

Silence, here.

"Patrick. Don't lose confidence."

He played with his fork. "What do you mean?"

"Maybe she won't die, you've become such a great surgeon."

I'd thought that my words might help him. But he looked at me strangely.

"Of course she's going to die, sweetheart." His voice was serious.

"Well—"

"It's natural. Dying. That's what I'm saying. What I have to deal with. It's inevitable."

"Honestly? I don't see death as being very *natural*—"

A blue vein pulsed in Patrick's forehead. He gave me a searching look. "What's going on with you, lately?"

"What?"

"I just—"

" 'Going on' with me?"

"You're just so funny—recently. You're sort of—I don't know. Different."

This frightened me, as I didn't want my adulterous pixie-dreams to leak into my life with him. "How?"

"Distracted." He looked befuddled. "Happier? But like you're somewhere else—"

I swallowed. "I'm happier with you, Patrick."

"Ugh, I don't know what I mean. But, to say that—that death isn't . . . natural. When I'm trying so hard to deal with them dying! It feels like you're not listening."

"I'm sorry. Seriously. You're right, I shouldn't have said that—"

"Are you angry? Or—is it the baby? The not having the baby?"

I could feel something open and close inside of me. "No. I'm okay about that."

He stared down at his dinner plate. "What do you mean, you're okay?"

"That I'm okay with it. Right now. I'm hanging in there."

"Oh, Jesus, for a second there I thought you were telling me you didn't want to have kids."

Is that what I meant? I said, *"No."*

He stammered, "But if you did feel that way you could tell me. And that would be all right." We let his lie drift in the air between us. Then he coughed. "Look. Bagh. I just have to adjust myself. That's what I'm talking about. I'll do my best, but at some point— goddamn. There just won't be anything else I can do! For Mrs. Flanagan. I'm teaching myself that. She'll go or she won't go."

I felt a chill; my tongue flumbered in my mouth in an unaccustomed loss for words. But at least I knew that my husband did not want sentimentality, so I said, "look, the only thing I know is that old bitch needs you."

He rewarded me by laughing. "God, she does give me hell. The cow! She's going to kill me! If I got close enough she'd bite me. Calls me filthy Irish names. She's got me so desperate, I've started to sing to her—anything, pop songs. It clams her up, anyway."

"You said she was the worst patient you ever had."

"She terrorizes the nurses. The cuss. I like her, though, you know. She reminds me of Dad."

"Well, there you have it then!"

He laughed harder, getting my private joke. "What, because mean old farts don't die?"

"Look at your father. Ninety-three years old. And vicious."

"Yes, all right." He reached down and snatched La Chupacabra into his arms. "All right, then. *Wife.*" He looked at me over the tips of La Chupacabra's ears while the beast purred at a thunderous and ecstatic pitch. "You know, look. You're a good one, old lady. You're a good catch."

I picked up the bottle of wine. "Get up and shut up. Let's get drunk and have some sex."

His eyebrows raised. "Are you . . ."

Ovulating.

"I don't *know*, Patrick. But come *on*. Screw all that. Let's go get wild."

He began to look cheerier. He stood up to waltz with La Chupacabra around the table. "Fine! That sounds like a good idea! I obey!"

I turned on bedroom heat, stripped Patrick naked, and blew him on the bed. I fairly gobbled him, having taught myself through scads of trial and error how not to gag or at least how to hide the gag. His penis is as big as Paul Bunyan's and it wiggles when it's excited. Its delicate veined staff was illuminated by that monstrous moon that peered in through our bedroom window like a stalker. I pressed my tongue against the base of its head, as I had read about in a self-help book called *Sexual Ecstasy.* He began to squirm so happily under my ministrations that I half-chuckled my way through the fellatio until he came. "No, no, your turn," he insisted soon after. He reached into our bed-stand drawer and pulled out "The Rabbit," which is a bionic phallus capable of filling me with a violent and helpless orgasm. I saw his rust-haired arm thrusting from under my bottom as he inserted the convulsing plastic beastie into my sex; I eased back my shoulders on the bed and shouted, twisting to see the pale moon waver in the sky.

After I'd come again, I hugged myself tightly in the bed. Patrick immediately fell asleep, with the cat draped over his neck.

I, however, did *not* sleep. I lay next to him in pajamas made of blue Polartech and stared at that white winter moon.

I felt—*wonderful.*

I felt like I do when I go to church: On Sundays, I can get really emotional, shivering in the pew and barking fiercely at God in my mind. I almost yell out my petitions for babies—that is, I once prayed for babies, and now more inchoately holler at God to help me satisfy this probably profane erotic longing of mine.

And there, as I remained cuddled in bed by my husband, and looking at that moon, I found myself shivering once again even though I understood that this excitement was somehow heretical.

I waited and I waited. At one-thirty in the morning, when I saw the moon begin to burgeon and billow with even more fiery intensity in the black sky, I left our bed, poured the last of the wine in a glass, and went outside.

It was cold in the garden. The moon bore down upon me, filling my eyes. It was as white as a polar bear, as an iceberg. I stepped onto the grass while a shaft of light shuddered down, scribbling on the lawn, veering this way and that. I drank a sip of the wine before pouring the remainder out as a libation. The moonlight began to *dance*, sparkling and skiddering over the ruins of the garden and the crumbled stone bench. It slowed down to crawl across the lawn, brightening the hedge. It lit up the hydrangea bush, which had begun to bloom unseasonably again.

"Hello, Imogen."

Between the flowers, I saw the glossy face of the Nefertiti woman. She spoke an African language, I think, though I understood her perfectly as she extended her hand to me, pressing through the foliage so that I could see her sculpted collarbone and her tiny breasts.

"Selena," I said.

"Yes, yes, it's me! So good to see you, you're looking well. *She's* waiting, you know, I hope you won't run away this time. She gets awfully angry when she's rejected, which is *not* a state I recommend you get her in."

"Who gets angry when she's rejected?"

"Don't be ridiculous—you know. Oh, hurry up, Imogen, up go you. You'll *love* it!"

I took her hand and with extreme force, she hurled me inside the hedge. When I stood up (I had fallen to the ground), I looked up, and didn't see a moon, but instead a dark and tangled wood spiraling above me in an intricate lace of leaf and vine and branch.

"Quickly, quickly," Selena said, leading me through the forest. The trees surrounding us glowed blood red and smelled like narcissus. The air was black and full of those colossal burning stars.

"Where's the city? Where are we?"

"That's all gone. We're Home."

"Home." Beyond the red trees, I could see what appeared to be spectacular white-spired buildings with an architecture simultaneously Arthurian and Arabian. "What are those?"

"Never mind. That's for much later; those are the schools. You'll be trained, you know, if you pass—I know you *will*—though you shouldn't worry about that now, should you? This is your first *real* time; it's so thrilling! Spectacular! You've never been to a Revel before, have you? No, I suppose not. Remember not to be afraid; just dive in. You won't get hurt by our girls, at least not for long."

She was running like a four-legged creature, but I found that in that magical atmosphere my own limbs moved with a jaguarlike alacrity, and I kept pace without hyperventilating.

"I'm so excited," she went on. "That's why I'm chattering so much; you'll have to forgive me. It's just that I've heard so much about you, and I knew we would *instantly* become friends. Because you're kind of like me. You're the *librarian*. We have so much to talk about. The other girls aren't much for reading, so when I say, 'don't you think that Milton got it *so* wrong in *Paradise Lost*,' or, when we're having a particularly good party, I happen to quote from Neruda or Senghor, they have absolutely no idea what I'm talking about. When I try to explain, they start *teasing* me and *tormenting* me with the most fantastic little gadgets they design here."

"Who are you?"

"A woman, just like you are." She wore a little skirt of deerskin and ran with high, quirky leaps, like a coyote, ducking under the tree branches and the jungle fronds. The wood rustled and crowded around us as she took an invisible path though the shadows. "Perhaps the question you mean is who *was* I?"

I was flying past the burgundy trees. "Then who were you?"

"A frightful little obedient schoolteacher in Kumasi."

"Kumasi?"

"Ghana. And I have a family. A beautiful mother. Two children. And—right—a husband. I see them all the time. And, back in Kumasi, I remain the most faithful of women." She began to slow down, tracking into a thick and tangled grove of birch. I could just see the faintest blush of gold light through the leaves. "But I was a bold girl. Like I said, you're just like me. I wanted what you want."

My face was covered with sweat, and I was scared. "What do I want?"

She grinned. " 'What do I want?' That's a good one."

I only continued gawking at her.

"Oh, you're not joking."

"No."

"Well. Imogen! You want *too much*, of course! That's how you *got* here, silly!"

Then she pulled back the bush, revealing a fantastical world that I thought only existed in my beloved books.

The Clearing was illuminated by three blue moons and a magnificent bonfire, which revealed a fairy-tale forest. Vivid black violets covered the ground with their blood-dark petals, and the clouds in the copper sky were as green as sea creatures. A leopard vanished into the red woods; a silver horse with a scarlet horn upon its head shook its mane by a large apple tree, from which hung golden fruit.

There before the bonfire at the Clearing's center was the older woman with silver hair, sitting on a huge sculptural throne that appeared to be carved of ivory or human bone. She wore a green robe made of some silken stuff that looked finer than any earthly fiber, and a bloodstone around her neck. Her eyes were pale blue and heavy-lidded; her skin flashed black and bronze. Around her, and the fire, circled a mob of those audacious women, some dressed in deerskin, like Selena. Others were completely naked, or wearing gowns embroidered in the Arabian or Grecian styles. Many of them wore some little badge of a craft or art. These included daggers hung on their belts, and bronze rings of occult design on their fingers. A number had vials of some potion strung around their necks.

One of the women, in particular, struck me: she didn't wear a badge, but had lavender ribbons woven through her yellow hair; and on her otherwise nude body she wore wreaths of flowers, voluptuously twined around her hips and across her large, hanging breasts. She looked like she'd been prepared for some celebration, or ritual.

"I brought her, Lady," Selena said as she bowed to the old woman on the throne.

"Yes, you have," the crone replied, indicating with a minute gesture that Selena should move to the side, which my guide promptly did. She critically surveilled my Polartech pajamas. "You don't *appear* to be pregnant."

I touched my stomach. "No."

"Strange. I thought you might be. Selena, did she seem in any way—"

"Unusual, my Lady?"

"Yes."

"Not in the way that you described, no."

I stood there, just freaking out and hugging myself.

The Lady now smiled kindly at me. "Do you know who I am?"

"I think I do," I stammered. She tilted her head at me, waiting. "La Chusa," I said, in a stronger voice.

The crowd of women murmured encouragingly when I said that.

"Yes!" She tilted her head and signaled to me to draw closer, and so I did, growing brave enough to add a detail I'd learned from my studies of Murillo's *Daemonology*: "But you have an older name than that."

"Do I?"

"Lilith."

At the sound of this title, the priestesses around me sang out a diabolical chant of *Lilith, Mother, La Chusa, Lilith, the Lady*, their throats shining in the moons' light. They drank wine and fed each other ripe fruit, even kissing and fondling each other's breasts. The mood was high-strung and rock-and-roll; the girls seemed ready to break at any moment into a crazed riot.

"What happened to Lilith?" she asked.

"Lilith was married to Adam," I answered, "but then was expelled from Paradise for disobedience. She flew away to the moon, and vanished."

"That's right, she did! She was disfavored, and replaced with a tiresome harlot who wasn't fit to lick her feet."

"Eve."

"Dead and gone, her. But this first wife of whom we speak, this first bad and *wicked* wife . . ."

I suddenly heard a seductive male voice behind me.

"Was the most clever girl in the whole world," it growled, finishing La Chusa's sentence.

I turned around and to see the White Man, the one with the hawk's face that I'd seen in my previous vision. He wasn't naked anymore but wore a black robe made of fur.

"Lilith found a back door to Eden, didn't she Lady?" he went on, staring at me as he walked forward.

Around us, the women hissed at him like snakes and laughed, chattering among themselves. Their obvious hatred of him, though, didn't stop them from swaying and leaping into the air like circus dancers.

"Yes, she found her *back door*," he repeated.

"Don't be vulgar," interrupted La Chusa. "He's making a joke about sex."

"And once she got back in, she hung on for grim death." The hawk-man thrust out his hips and squeezed his arms around his shoulders as if he were fucking an imaginary girl. "Can you imagine it? La Chusa a squatter in Paradise? It's the best trick that was ever played on God! Because she can be a *bitch* and still live in a state of grace!" He approached closer, looking at me with casual interest. "So this is the new one? You always stock up when you're about to initiate one of the older girls."

"Leave her alone, Pan."

"No."

"Lord, I wish I could kill you."

"*Isn't* this the one I heard those strange stories about?" In a flash, he had appeared by my side and stroked his face against mine. I screamed. "That's right. *You're* supposed to be different, somehow. Still, you look just the same as the others, don't you? And I suppose you *are* just the same as the rest of these grasping sluts. Ready to make your trade, then? Hand your heart over to the Great Holy Cow?"

"Are you a Goddess?" I stuttered.

"Yes." La Chusa scrutinized me with her pallid eyes. "I'm self-made."

"Self-made?"

"I was born a human, but transformed myself into the Divine after forty nights of unimaginable suffering." She gestured at the White Man, who smiled.

"I don't understand."

"Oh, I can see you're not a very good Buddhist. What do they say? Only the divine can worship the divine? Or is that the Hindus?"

"Are you the—the—*Buddha*?"

"Oh, good Gracious no. What dreck old Siddhartha talks. As if sitting under a Lotus tree can catapult you to Nirvana! As if transcendence can be achieved by wanting nothing. It's the absolute *opposite*, isn't it? And even to become priestesses like my girls, here, is a far more difficult process than the Bodhisattvas or the good Krishna would ever admit."

"As you shall see now, I suppose," said the White Man menacingly.

La Chusa turned from me, scoping out the crowd of women, who grew quiet immediately and bowed their heads in obeisance. "*Isn't* it hard, darling?" she called out. "Though you've already paid your share of pain, haven't you? My dearest, Françoise? Are you ready, child?"

Circled by that throng of women, the flower-strung girl said, "Yes, Lady."

"So then, we begin."

La Chusa clapped her hands, which sounded like silver chimes, and the priestesses exploded into a frenzied revelry.

Women with unbound hair flung their arms up to the sky, and their friends crawled over them, panting and laughing and suckling at their breasts. Sweating, dancing, the wine spilling over their cheeks in the example of the crazed bacchantes, they pushed each other to the ground and gleefully fucked. Girls lying in the beds of black violets, with their hair spread wild across the ground and their beautiful faces shimmering with sweat and oil, spread their legs so that others could plunge wooden phalluses or their fingers into their large red sexes, which were blooming from their legs like surreal flowers. Their hips collided. Their veins stuck out on their throats so they had the violent, half-animal looks of Picasso's Algerian whores, as if those girl satyrs had jumped from the canvases and were seeking revenge. The hawk-faced man skittered on the edge of this party, grabbing at a girl here, stroking a woman there. Every time he was violently pushed away, and his face twisted with rage. He ran away into the woods, just as one black-haired Valkyrie, her naked body streaked with ocher paint and cobalt stain, stood on one leg, lifting the other like the most extreme of Martha Graham dancers, so that her freckled, braided-haired lover could hunker before her and bury her face in her wild-haired vagina. In the midst of it all stood the flower-bedecked Françoise; she clearly waited for something.

I was knocked down in the melee. I was trampled. Spying between the frenzied legs of dancers, I ogled at four intertwined women moving together sinuously, sweetly, even as blood flowed from their scratched backs. A maenad kicked me. They were *barking* and howling! Reaching up, I grabbed hold of a haunch, an oil-slick leg, before I was thrown down again by one of those harpies.

I saw Selena gazing down at me in the throng. She bent down and lifted me to my feet.

"There's no need to be afraid," she laughed. "I told you, you can't get hurt here."

"I'm terrified!"

She caressed my face and kissed my mouth. "You'll be fine—relax—let go."

"Let go of what?"

"You're a monster, don't you see that? You're a *beast*. That's why you were chosen. And only these women are strong enough to take you."

"A monster." I began to laugh like a human hyena.

"Obviously! Look at yourself! You're an animal, my love. You're a *creature*."

"I like that," I shouted above the din. "I love that, what you just said."

"Of course you do!"

And then I, too, was dancing.

The women's hands clawed away my clothes and pulled at my hair. Blossoms were strung across my brow, and a girl with blue woad-stained skin painted me with circles of diamond dust and cinnabar. Selena kissed me again, and this time her lips lingered, pressing rudely and beautifully down my chin and my throat, to my breasts. This was adultery; in my forbidden-fruit schizophrenia *I did not care*. More of these rabid girls joined her, and one hundred fingers stroked me, lightly, lightly, then harder. All at once, a wood staff was plunged up my legs. A dildo, if that's what that dragon-cock can be called. It slammed into me, fabulously hurting, and too big to fit. I was Catherine the Great, fucking horses! My feet rose to my ears—I was more limber than in the mundane world—and a huge rush of amber came flowing down from my slit. It was a flood, sticky, juicing down my thighs, which would have embarrassed me with anyone but Patrick or these gorgons.

I fucked, and fucked, and came, and came six times, ten times, until I was bleeding and covered with bruises.

When I woke up from that haze I opened my eyes. The women bounded away from me, and I heard again that they were howling.

I sat up. La Chusa watched the scene from her bone chair, as Françoise looked to the far side of the wood, into which the White Man had disappeared.

Another man emerged from the trees, but not that demon.

This was an ordinary, small fellow, dressed in jeans and an Oxford shirt. He had sand-colored hair and a chiseled, awestruck face. A baffled smile played across his features when he saw Françoise.

"Who is this?" La Chusa asked.

The girl's brow darkened. "My cousin. Charles."

"Françoise?" said the man.

"What must you do?" the crone asked.

"You've made this one easy for me, Lady. When this is done, I want to learn the art of war."

"First," La Chusa said, "this task."

The priestesses, wet from their labors and shiny-skinned crowded around them. Selena grabbed me again and pushed me through the throng, so that we stood nearly at its front, with a clear view of this bloodcurdling comedy.

"It's the Test," Selena whispered in my ear. "There's no way of telling what it'll be. Sometimes it's simple, sometimes it's very hard. She teaches us that you have to suffer loss to be a good priestess. That you're useless to her unless you've felt the worst pain. And she tailors her test to make sure you know the cost of human life."

In my dreamlike state I accepted this without further explanation.

"What *must you do?*" La Chusa asked again.

"Choose," said Francoise.

"*Choose! Choose!*" the rest of the women screamed. I found myself shrilling out that word, too, with only the slimmest idea of what it might mean.

"What did Charles do to you?" the Lady asked.

"He raped me. He used me. He did not love me." The girl said this very calmly, as if she'd rehearsed the answer.

"And that is why your test is simple, darling. You have already paid the price. You have suffered; and so you have the crucial knowledge that will make you wise."

"I have."

La Chusa flourished a hand in the air. "Show them. Show them how this man schooled you."

The girl bent down to snatch a blade of grass springing up between the black violets. She turned, blew on the blade, and threw it at us.

Somehow, we saw what she'd endured. I saw the girl raped by this man in the basement of a damp and ugly house in Dordogne. I saw her beaten by him in a field. I saw her begging him for love, even as he ran off with other women, only to return and brag of his conquests to her.

All of us were shrieking. I wasn't myself. I wasn't Imogen. I bellowed out obscenities and curses, and I clawed at the ground, gnashing my teeth. I was bloodthirsty at the condition of women. At the crimes against women. I've had a small taste of that pain myself. Not all men are like my tender Patrick.

Then the vision cleared.

Françoise approached the man. He still looked passive and confused. Bending down again, she plucked one of the black violets from the lawn. She removed one of the petals of these flowers, lifted it to his face. Without her saying a word, he somehow knew to open his mouth, and the dark petal was pressed onto his tongue.

He swallowed the flower; his eyes glazed into an opal color as his breathing turned quick and rough.

"What did you do to me?" he asked.

He shredded his clothes with frenzied hands, the buttons falling from the shirt. He moaned. Naked, he stood there, shaking, and his penis grew twice, three times its original size. It *burst* from his hips, magenta-red, strung with beating veins.

With both hands he began to violently stroke himself, but Françoise said, "No, *no*."

He obeyed.

She touched him lightly on the shoulder with the palm of her hand, which flung him to the ground as if he had been thrown by a giant. Writhing in the grass, groaning louder, he sang her name as if haunted.

"Françoise!"

She stood over him. She parted the lips of her vulva with her fingers, whispering a chant or a prayer, or curses, as she kneeled down and impaled herself on him.

I had never seen a man and woman fuck like that before. The girl was a Titan—strong, like a gorilla, or an ox. She thrust herself over him fast and so crushingly hard that the earth shook. He was screaming with pleasure and terror. Her hips swelled, Venus-like, covering his hips, flowing over his legs. He hung onto her arms and blithered, and wept, until she'd had enough, and fell back from him.

Françoise stood up, wiped off her face and said, "I choose you, Lady."

Something happened then that I didn't really understand. I only have an animal's memory of it. I saw the girl's face lengthen into a muzzle; her ears elongated and grew fur. She fell to the ground again, but this time to land on four paws, and her pale skin sprouted with dark, wiry hairs.

Charles shouted out something I couldn't hear. By now my ears had also lost the capacity to understand human words. He shrank, he turned red. He scurried across the ground.

He was a fox. When I heard the howl rip from my throat, I felt that I was a wolf in the company of my pack.

A horde of hell-dogs transformed in honor of the Wolf Moon circled the fox, gnashing, drooling, yelping. One wolf leapt forward to nip the cringing victim on the side. Another scurried toward it, batting it with her paw. I smelled blood. It was salty and raw-tasting.

We all barreled forward, biting and scratching and wounding each other to get to the fox.

Within seconds we shredded it to pieces with our red teeth, and it was dead.

The rest of my idyll in the forest passed in a blur. I remember looking down and seeing that I was a woman again, though unrecognizable from my wounds.

"Those won't last," Selena murmured to me as she touched my scratches and deep cuts. She was also running with blood and looked extremely happy.

"I don't feel any pain," I shouted.

She looked up. "The moon's waning now. You can leave when you like."

"What happened to me tonight?"

"I think we're going to get along," she said. "I think we are going to be friends. You were *fierce*."

And after that there's nothing but blankness. I opened my eyes to find myself in the garden again, sprawled beneath the stone bench, flat on my back on the lawn.

I was unwounded. There wasn't a single mark on me. When I crawled back into bed beside muttering Patrick, the clock read 1:51.

I'm trembling with joy now, or maybe I'm in a state of grace. I sinned in Heaven. I sinned against Patrick.

I am bad, I am bad, I am bad—but only in the other world.

Here, in ordinary time, it never really happened.

God—*right?*

January 28. Moon is void-of-course.

Selena said that I was like her, and that I wanted "too much."

I think I might discover my secret desires in that forest, if it really exists.

My betraying Patrick wasn't my worst crime.

Did I kill a fox two weeks ago? Did I howl and gnash while a man was murdered?

No. Impossible.

February 7. Moon in Gemini.

Since the miracle of January 14, I haven't felt normal. When I talk to God in church, I don't yell out to him like I used to. I mutter bamboozled questions. Work also suffers. At the library, I ignore the larger bulk of my administrative duties to glut myself on old, smutty, splendid books in the basement, and I've ordered Steven to get me an ever-filthier assortment of pornographic treatises. He sort of *hovers* while I give him my instructions, which he knows to be so ludicrous and so professionally inappropriate that he allows himself the reciprocal luxury of commenting on the tighter and sluttier Urban Outfitters dresses I've recently taken to wearing to work, since I can't bear trapping the animal body that ran through La Chusa's Forest in my old drab suits anymore. ("That neckline looks . . . *good* on you, but you should wear your hair down.") He even once made me admire the white oxford shirt he'd bought for work, going as far as to gently take my hand and run it across the starched cotton covering his arm. ("See there, Ms. López? No holes.") I can barely look at the boy. He *sweats* sex. But he's an excellent researcher when he has good enough motivation. So I bat him away after he's brought me the latest haul, and lock myself in the basement to binge on these books on witch burnings; on wise women; on Diana, the goddess of war; on the night-hawk La Chusa; on Kali Ma, who made the world with the sound of her laughter, a mantra known as the Logos, or the Supreme Word *Om*.

I read my books in bed, too. I read way too much these days.

The biggest cost of my distraction has been my time with Patrick. For his part, my husband has also been preoccupied, spending long hours at the hospital and bringing files and studies home to read before he falls asleep. We still have sex, though it's more perfunctory than usual. I put down my books (Patrick rolls his eyes when he sees their titles), and force myself to put all images of Selena and orgiastic wolves and homicidal cultists out of my head. Patrick puts down his reports. He's the more ambitious baby-maker these days. He helps me take my temperature, digs out various pharmaceutical potions from the bed stand's top drawer, and then we don't so much pleasure each other as *will* our personal orgasms with the concentrated intensities of hard-laboring western pioneers.

Despite this sexual work ethic, however, I'm no closer to getting pregnant.

"We could try IVF again," he said last week. We were both wearing pajamas and floundering on the bed; it was late, around eleven p.m. Patrick had a big sex-induced raspberry on his chin and was tortoise-eyed from insomnia, but he still rubbed my feet and kissed my toes with his nibbling lips. "The tests you took showed the possibility that . . ."

I shook my head while reciprocally foot-massaging. "No, not yet."

"Why? There's a decent success rate."

I hesitated. "Side effects."

I could hear him thinking, *but the risks aren't that bad.*

He said, "Of course. That's okay. It just feels like we don't talk— enough—these days. You're—"

Different.

"Distracted," I said.

"I know that I am, too."

"You *are*—you've got Mrs. Flanagan—you're busy—"

"And you're-you've been working on . . . what was it again? I haven't been able to figure out what it is—"

"Just library stuff."

"Library stuff."

"Cataloging."

He hesitated, his hands still on my feet, then said, "Anyway, we're always at the office or, when we do see each other we're—"

"Grimly fucking?"

He laughed hysterically at that. "That's a really nice way of putting it!"

"It's true!"

"I know. I *know*. Agh. You want to just cuddle tonight?"

"I'm about two days away from my window. We probably won't have any luck."

He brought his hand to his face. "And I'm getting a rash from giving you orals. Not that I mind. Maybe I just need some lotion."

"Poor *baby*." I exhaustedly got up on all fours and tried to growl at him playfully. "Look. Why not? Maybe I'll do you. Here. Come on. Let's go. I'll do you. You'll like it."

He leaned back and smiled. "Really?"

"Yeah."

"Actually, I was really was hoping that we could try again tonight. I'll try to make it really good."

"Just lie down."

"I'll lie down."

"I'm going to pleasure you." I tried to growl out *pleasure*.

"*Wow*. Bonus. Do you want me to get the Rabbit?"

"No. This is Patrick time."

We rambled around the bed; we huffed and puffed and talked dirty. But I was distracted. After I slipped his penis into my mouth, he seemed to get concerned about my excitement levels, and so he flipped me on my back and tickled me and spanked me and bent his mouth onto my cunt and ate me, and then he rubbed his penis to make it hard again and put it in and banged me.

As he loomed above me, his penis rapidly hammering in and out, a worried look passed over his face.

"You okay? You okay? Can you come? You just tell me. Sweetie. What you need."

I dredged up all my energy and said, almost automatically, "Fuck me, bitch, in the ass, do it hard, rape me, rape me."

Finally, he came.

After, he reached out his hand and wiggled his fingers. "Here, here, let me diddle you, just a little one."

I rolled over and kissed him. "Honey, honey. Go to sleep."

His mouth was already open and his eyes rolling back in his head. His chin was very red.

"Okay," he muttered.

And that was our spontaneous sexcapade. We slept.

I suppose what I'm really saying here is that ever since I wandered into La Chusa's Eden, I have been dreamy and abstracted and not the wife I used to be, which is probably because I've had illicit sex with demon-girls, and have also been hungering after a half-Mayan, half–Pennsylvania Dutch frat boy.

In other words, I miss my husband. I miss my old sweet habits with Patrick.

And that's why I visited him at work today.

I drove to the Center. The nurse at the front desk told me he'd be in his office on the fourteenth floor. I knocked twice on his door, heard him babble out something incomprehensible, and opened it to find him working at his paper-trashed desk.

He looked haggard, which I hadn't noticed earlier this morning. Skin the color of paste hung beneath his eyes. Here we bumbled through a bit of a confused greeting and even awkward hugs. "Sweetie." "What's wrong?" "Is everything all right?" "You're pale." "Did you come because there's a problem?" "No, just lunch." "Lunch?"

I stood back from him and studied his ravaged face.

"Mrs. Flanagan," I said. "That's what's the matter."

"Yes." He cleared his throat, rustled the lunch bags with his fingers. "It's not good."

"Patrick."

He put his head on my shoulder. "Oh, I can't have lunch. I have to go see her."

"No, you're going to eat something. You're going to go outside with me and sit in the sun."

"Sunbathing? Nah. Looking like a mole rat is so chic right now." He delicately touched his cheek. "Come on, you have to admit that I'm just scorchingly handsome."

"Well. Dracula was handsome."

"Oh, good. So I look like the undead?"

"Just a *tiny* bit."

"You need to work on your pep talks."

I kissed him all over his face. "Come on. I brought ham sandwiches. And pickles. And ice cream sandwiches."

His eyes bulged, making him suddenly look like a shocked if cheerful fish. "Woman, are you trying to tell me something?"

I showed him the lunch bags I'd packed. "Just about some snacks—"

"Ice cream and pickles?"

"And ham sand—"

"*Are you pregnant?*"

"What?"

He took me by the arms and began to smile. "Imogen, is this a pregnancy lunch? Did you come down here to tell me you tested positive?"

"No, honey."

"Oh."

"Agh. I. Am. Not. Pregnant."

His face kind of . . . collapsed.

"Patrick, your face looks like it's literally falling off your head."

He touched his cheeks and tugged them upward. "Damn. Oh. God. Really sensitive."

"Calm down."

"I'm pressuring you, aren't I? I'm sorry. I'm an asshole."

"No, you're not. It's all right."

He yanked on his bangs. "Okay! Husband of the year! In a minute I'm going to be pushing a Baby Alive around in a carriage and telling everybody it's my son, while you come to your senses and start up some scorching affair with a hot guy." He put his head on my shoulder again. "And, anyway, having a kid won't make it any easier for me that this old bat—Flanagan—isn't going to make it. Right? Right? Tell me that's right."

I lifted his hand and kissed his knuckles. "Look, hey. All I want is that you don't crack up."

"Um, I'll put that on my list. And I'm *not*, by the way. Having a crack up. Not a big one, anyway. I'm just a little pale. I need a tan. Or that man-bronzer stuff. Or something."

"And a bottle of Scotch."

He hugged me before gathering his stethoscope and files together. "Sounds great. But right now I do have to go and check on her."

"Then we'll eat."

"Yes. Then we'll eat."

We went. He led me out of the office by the hand. We were whisked down by the elevator and wandered down an intricate com-

plex of white, shining halls until we found ourselves in the vinegar-
and-carrion-smelling room of Mrs. Flanagan.

The old woman looked like a parrot as she lay there shriveling in
her hospital cot. She had a large, shining forehead and portruding
colorless eyes. Her steep cheekbones perched on her face, collapsing
into a little mouth and raspberry-shaped nose.

"That the kid," she rasped, though I could hear her lilt.

"Yes, Mrs. Flanagan," Patrick answered.

"Told you to bugger off, doc."

He led me over to the bed. "Brought my wife this time."

"Let me look at her," said Mrs. Flanagan, munching her eyes up
as I bent over her mummified face. "Strange dark one, aren't you.
Pixie. Oooh, she's a bad one, doc."

"Maybe," I said. "But I've heard a lot about you, too, Mrs. Flanagan."

"Not much to know. I'm a good old Irish broad, followed her husband to the end of the world. Don't know what I'm doing *here*. I
should be in the land of the fairies, like me mum used to tell me.
But you have to be truly wicked to get there. And me, hell, I never
had th'nuts."

"It's the drugs," whispered Patrick. "Doesn't know what she's saying."

"It's run by a Lady . . . *This* one, though"—she tweaked her head
over to Patrick—"he's going to heaven. Aren't ya, ya little git?"

"Enough of that, quiet down," said Patrick. He rustled in his coat
pocket for his stethoscope. "I'm going to take your vitals."

"Mrs. Flanagan, tell me about the place where they send wicked
women." I was trying to divert her.

She gave me a good, long stare with her murky eyes. "Called her
Brigid. Beautiful lady. She was bad. Dangerous, see. But all us gels,
we love her. We love her. We can't help ourselves."

"What do you mean?"

But even as I had my flash of recognition at her words, I saw that
her thoughts had instantly shifted away from that curious subject
onto something far more excruciating.

"You'll have to leave him some day, you know, like my Francis left me," she said suddenly, in a frightening voice.

"The husband," whispered Patrick, and I remembered how hers had died.

"That's what hurts, lass. That's what's the killer. Not even God himself can stop it hurting."

"No, no no," I said uselessly and falsely.

She closed her eyes. "Boy, I'm dying," she wailed.

"Sssshhh." Patrick darted a gaunt look at me before bending over her. "Listen. Here, Sssshhh. It's all right. It's okay. Mrs. Flanagan."

She kept weeping.

Patrick pressed the stethoscope to her chest and his lips hardened. He removed it from his neck before taking her hand, whispering to her. She began to calm down.

I saw him flick his fingers around his eyes, but his head was turned, and I couldn't see his tears. He began to hum, or mutter something. I didn't understand at first what he was doing. My heart clenched when I heard his words more clearly.

In an uneven voice, he murmured to her that tune of Nat King Cole's that we played last month, around Christmas. "Smile" is a rough song, actually, because Cole tells us that suffering is inevitable, but that we have to be happy anyway. And when I heard the lyrics, I realized that Patrick really was changing his views on death because he never would have sung a patient that good-bye lullaby before:

Smile though your heart is aching, my husband sang. *Smile even though it's breaking.*

Mrs. Flanagan's eyes closed. Her mouth relaxed. It had worked.

"You're a good boy," she whispered.

The woman's head tossed back in her pillow at an awkward angle, and she looked like a fragile sculpture made of paper.

"I think she'll sleep now," is all Patrick said.

After that, he summoned a nurse, and we left Mrs. Flanagan to her care.

• • •

Ten minutes later, Patrick and I stood in front of his desk, holding the lunch sacks I'd brought.

"No," he said, taking the lunches and putting them on a stack of papers.

We began to kiss, hard, roughly, even a little painfully.

I untucked his shirt and gripped onto his ribs. He had his hands in my hair and bit my neck.

We unzipped my pants, his. We stumbled toward the desk. The fluorescent lights turned us white and yellow, and I could see the shadows under his eyes as I took his penis, coaxed it, and half-slipped, half-forced it into me as I balanced precariously across his lap.

It hurt at first, the little delicate fibers of my sex snagging roughly on the cock. I spit on my hand and rubbed it between our legs. We were utterly silent. Voices in the hall accompanied the dark shapes passing by the frosted glass window on Patrick's door.

"There, there, there," he said, very gently fucking me. "I love you."

His hair smelled like antiseptic, earth, oil. His hands pressed onto the desk, the fingertips turning white as he struggled to keep from toppling over. I kissed those shadows under his eyes. My orgasm came quick and bumpy, and made my legs shake. He came very fast. I was wet on the inside from his sperm and it covered my thighs, making spots on my slacks when I pulled them up.

"Imogen," he said.

Both of us instantly began laughing. I kissed him again. "You're a wreck."

"Do you want me to—" He touched my thigh.

"No, no. I did fine. I had a good one. I'll see you when we get home tonight."

"Okay—" He did look better.

"Honey, eat your lunch. Eat both the sandwiches."

I smoothed my shirt and waved at him with both hands as I moved out the door.

• • •

The trees bristled in the wind as I drove through the streets, on my way back to the library, and all my books.

That's where I am now; I write this in the basement, surrounded by my stacks of penny dreadfuls and witch-hunting manuals. Only Steven dares to interrupt me while I work.

Just now he popped his head in, his white cotton shirt straining against his shoulders. "Need anything else, Ms. López?"

"No."

Ooooh, she's a bad one, doc.

In a seventeenth-century book I have here on fairyism, it says that the Brigid Mrs. Flanagan mentioned is a Celtic lunar Goddess, who was born from the moon, and as an infant was blessed with the gift of speech that she used to sing Gaelic lays of indescribable beauty.

La Chusa, Lilith, Brigid.

Those are the names of the Lady I followed into the forest.

When I was in the wood, I saw and did things I didn't even know I desired. Even as I write, I have momentary images of a red fox, which I push away.

And there is another fox outside my door now. Better push him away as well.

I'm shaking again.

I know what Mrs. Flanagan told me was true. We all have to eventually leave each other; it's the natural law. But somehow, I just can't believe that Patrick and I could ever be apart.

February 12. Storm Moon. 8:44 p.m.

I am in the kitchen, nauseous from exhaustion, but I need to get tonight's events down on paper, so that tomorrow I don't attribute them to a nervous breakdown catalyzed by my whorish and sacrilegious daydreams.

What has happened? Mrs. Flanagan has dropped into a coma. This happened two days ago.

Patrick wept very hard on the night it happened, though has otherwise taken her downturn much better than I expected. While he shaved this morning, he was still pale, but running the blade under the water he said: "I think I'm doing it. Kind of. I'm getting the hang of it. Maybe, the patients dying. *There's nothing I can do.* And I've got another patient now."

"That new girl," I said. Two days ago Patrick did a surgery on a teenager, an advanced case.

"Yes. The kid, Gloria, she's terminal. I have to focus on *her*. And I'll beat that bastard cancer off for as long as I can, but I still can't help that— that— we're all going to just— *die*— at some point—"

"Even you," I said, querulously.

"Even me, of course."

"Even me."

"Even you, baby," he said after a minute's pause. "Even you, sweetie."

He smiled until his new toughness wavered, then one or two tears flew down his face.

I think that Patrick might be better than me, where death's concerned. He'd *made* himself better and isn't so tempted by fantasies. He's remained calm and mostly clear-eyed. I'm trying to be supportive as he gets through this hard time.

I can't tell him my own reaction, obviously.

When I learned that Mrs. Flanagan was fading, I felt scared. My parents are both alive and living in Texas. I haven't had to deal much with death, yet. But here it is—I had touched that old, sick woman and she told me secret things, and now she's losing her grip on life.

Patrick told me the news about Mrs. Flanagan on the phone, last Friday, on the tenth.

The second I heard I wanted to go to the forest.

At 8:40 Patrick was combing La Chupacabra. The damned cat looked like a blowfish on account of its static-sprung fur, and it purred indecently; when I poked my head in to see what they were up to, it gave me a snarky look, snatching at Patrick's sleeve with her claw.

"Are you two all right?" I asked.

"Fine, fine." He's just in love with that animal. "Doesn't she look great?"

"Do you want something to eat?"

"What? No thanks." He waved me off; he says I've been fussing and clucking around him lately.

Maybe so, but I was glad La Chupacabra kept him so distracted.

In the kitchen, I poured a glass of wine. Bringing with me a polished jasper stone that I'd bought at a notions store nearby, I also unwrapped a clump of sage fresh from the supermarket—as this stone and herb are sacred to the Storm Moon. The last thing I needed was matches.

I stole out to the garden.

The *luna* formed into a white dragon in the sky. It sent me a blast of pale fire from its mouth. The moonlight poured all over my body; it had seen me.

I took a sip of the wine, tipped the rest out onto the grass. I said a short, nervous prayer. The sage burned while I buried the jasper in the ground. The bushes encircling the garden began to shudder, as if they were being shaken by invisible leprechauns, causing dead petals to whip into the air. I screwed up my eyes, wrapping my arms around my chest. It grew colder, and colder—soon I could see the blurs of my breath, which melted into the turbulence of the sky, itself thickening and quickly whitening into a whirlwind.

The maelstrom soon surrounded me with its shrieks and celestial blindness. The shutters banged against the windows; the gates of our neighbors' houses buckled; while the beech trees in their gardens raised their dark arms and danced.

Lightning spilled down from the sky and set everything on fire. The hedges encircling our property quaked as the wind ripped and tore at them. I shouted in disbelief as they were lifted whole by one huge slash by the wind, spinning into the zephyrs and the white-dark sky.

On the other side of the stripped property, I saw the red-black grove of La Chusa.

Selena wasn't there to greet me. But I knew my way. I didn't look back in Patrick's direction from fear that I might turn into a salt-girl like Lot's wife, and ran across the shredded lawn, passing over the periphery of our home, to find myself in the cool shadowy lair of the forest.

Peering down, I saw that I was suddenly wearing a white cotton robe, and my bare feet stumbled down a path faintly shining in the darkness. This little trail was like an arrow painted with ocean phosphorous; I knew it must have been the passage that Selena had followed the month before. As my eyes adjusted I made out the blue snakes twining through the tree branches like vines, the green flicker of basilisks' eyes, hand-shaped leaves fluttering down from the red oaks, and the giant silver moths darting to and from a growing incandescence.

Before me, through the bush, swam a golden light. I hurtled through lilac and a tangle of cedar trees.

Then I was in the Clearing. I had stumbled into a wild festival. Priestesses whirled around a man, whose face I couldn't see because he wore a hooded linen cloak. He'd been tied to one of the trees.

La Chusa presided on her white throne. Her hair was uncovered, and her face lined and beautiful, particularly in the light of the huge bonfire her priestesses had made out of cinnabar branches and moss. She nodded to me when I appeared, and I was so excited by the gleaming girl limbs shuddering in front of the fire and the captive man that I could barely think to make a gesture of obeisance. Women were everywhere, kissing, fondling, dancing, pouring wine into each others mouths, or onto their breasts and bellies. Dressed again in deerskin or Grecian-style robes, with their hair caught up in gold diadems, some of them fought with one another, but nimbly, pinning and throwing each other down onto the beds of black violet in the same way I've seen Greco-Roman boys wrestle each other in the Olympics. Some of them were talking—what was it, about philosophy? The craft of war? The White Man with the hawk face circled them with a starved expression and an erect penis, but they slapped him away. He reached out to touch the haunch of Françoise, who now wore a bronze dagger at her waist, and he licked the arm of Selena, who scratched and bit at him. Once she'd rejected the White Man, Selena turned and ran happily toward me, even as Françoise approached La Chusa, bowed, and suddenly began to sing

> The young girls wear flowers on their breasts as they dance.
> They cast the blooms in the air, their arms glistening.
> Do not wait, my daughter, to embrace your lover.

Selena grasped my hands. Her hair was tightly curled and spun down to her hips; her eyes were very beautiful and dark and shining.

"I've been waiting for you," she said rapidly.

I hugged her. "I've been thinking about you, too. Have you been here the whole time?"

"The whole time?" She frowned.

"The whole time I've been away?"

She rubbed her face, smiling. "I think so!"

"You haven't gone back to your husband. Your family?"

"I've seen my *mother*, yes. But let's not talk about her. Imogen! Let's talk about . . . let's talk about . . . this place! Can you imagine it! Isn't it ridiculous? It's like—did you ever read Swift? It's like Gulliver's Travels, don't you think? Fantastic, and terrible—but nicer—and it's *better* than the paintings of Michelangelo, the Sistine Chapel. Because it's *all women*."

"But who's the man in the robe?" I pointed to the hooded victim tied to the tree.

"Never mind him yet. Listen—I'm telling you that you can do anything you like here . . . and there are books!"

"Books?" I laughed.

"Did you hear what Françoise was singing?" Selena hooked her arm into mine to pull me toward the bonfire, and La Chusa. "That was Sappho. Françoise is in the first years of her training. She gets to read, you know, the lost books? The collections of Alexandria, of Aztlán, the poetry burned in the Cultural Revolution? It's all here. There are *libraries*."

We'd moved closer to the bonfire and the Goddess, passing by the White Man, who leaned toward us.

"Ah, the girl who was supposed to be special. Hello again," he purred.

"Hello," I answered.

"Come keep me company, sweetheart. Come be my daughter, Imogen. I'm barren, you see . . . without a soul in the whole universe to love." He waggled his talons at me. "Perhaps I could love *you*, even if you've turned out to be an ordinary slag like the others."

Selena pulled me back. "Watch out for him. He's disgusting. He tries to trick you. And he can hurt you."

"What do you mean?"

"We're not supposed to talk about it," she muttered. "He was very hard on the Lady. Before she earned the Key to this place."

"How?"

But my question withered away under the force of La Chusa's voice, as we heard her calling out:

"And my husband left me. *And* he loved me, I know it. *That's* the sin, you see. That was the crime. They tossed me out, I had to claw my way back here on a path of pain. Which Adam never had the balls to do, I'll tell you that much."

She was talking to Françoise, who replied: "But Lady, in one of the books I've studied, I learned that you found your way back here because you outsmarted—"

"Who, God?" brayed La Chusa. "You needn't believe everything you read, no? That's just *superstition*. The story I was some shabby little wench who tricked the Yahweh of Abraham by seducing Satan? That I conned the *Alpha and Omega*? You must know that things are more complicated than that."

"She lies, the reason why she got here *was* me," said the White Man, who came scrambling up to Françoise and started molesting her again. "She *romanced* me. Because she knew I had the Key to the garden! And I was stupid enough to brag to her that I'd been given hunting rights here, my favorite quarry being ladies and their perky little *apples*. She was so impressed. And then I couldn't get rid of her!"

"Enough of your whining," La Chusa answered. "And stop pawing my girls."

He crept closer to me. "So you've decided on this one, then?"

"I don't know yet." She began looking me up and down. "Would you like to be with us?"

"Yes," I said, without hesitation.

She tilted her head. "Do you think I should let you?"

"Yes, yes *yes*," Selena insisted.

"That's not for you to say, is it?" La Chusa asked. "You haven't passed your test yet."

Selena beamed. "I will!"

"For now, let's just see what we've got. *Imogen*. I can see you do like it here. Though, again, I thought you would be different. I thought you'd be . . ."

"Pregnant?" I asked. "That's what you said before."

"Yes, I prophesized you would be with child."

"She had a vision," Françoise explained, giving the White Man a hell-bitch look as he retreated to skulk around the perimeter of the forest. "She saw you holding a pomegranate."

"A . . . pomegranate."

They laughed at my stupidity. "It's the harbinger of fertility," Françoise went on.

"It's a good sign," said Selena.

I shook my head; years of trying and still no pregnancy. "But I can't get—"

"Yes, yes, so I've come to learn," La Chusa interrupted. "Though, you don't *want* to be pregnant, do you, darling?"

I was shocked at this, but even more at my own answer. "I don't know any more."

"Then again, Mary didn't want to get knocked up, either, did she? Poor old girl. So, I suppose you should count yourself lucky. You do seem to have a dry womb. *And* signs can lie, you know. Even Goddesses can make mistakes. And that doesn't mean that I won't love you. I would adore you even if you were the most sterile of hags. That is, if you were faithful to me. In fact, I've planned something today to prove how much I do care for you, as I care for all my good girls."

"What do you mean?"

"I thought that I would give you a treat. That I'd give you what you *wanted*, that is. And you know you can have that here, what you want. You've been in something of a muddle, haven't you? It will free up your mind, so you can think of more important matters than beautiful boys."

"What I want . . ."

Images from the pages of my perverse books ran through my mind—hot brands on skin, young pretty men, fetters, chains, delicate tortures.

Her gaze directed me to the tied man at the edge of the clearing, as the crowd of women began singing in high clangorous voices while parting a path between him and me.

"Go." Selena bent down to pluck one of the black violets from the ground, thrusting them into my hands before pushing me forward. "Just give him one. They're aphrodisiacs! But they're potent little things."

Slow and *fucking* scared I walked down that gauntlet of buzzing women to the man. The linen cloak draped against the outlines of his tall, broadly shouldered body. A thick rope ran around his waist, tying him helplessly to the tree. His face remained shielded by that hood.

The women breathed loudly behind me. My arms and legs quavered as I lightly touched the man on the chest, through the linen. I could hear him gasp even as I felt he had a round, hard body. The thin cloth covered his thighs, which were tight and strong.

I lifted the edge of the cowl and softly smoothed it down the man's head. Disbelieving what I saw, I still didn't hesitate to touch his wide mouth. His dark eyes stared back at me.

It was Steven.

"How did you know?" I asked back over my shoulder. Neither the women nor the White Man answered, but somehow I understood that in this place there was an omniscience, that my other life wasn't

invisible to those here. My life with Patrick. And this revelation reminded me that *I am a married lady*. I voiced a question I'll admit
didn't occur to me when I rode these witches like a cowgirl under
the Wolf Moon: "Will this hurt my husband?"

"No," came the answer.

I turned back to the boy.

"Do you know me?"

Steven stared at the women and the uncanny forest, glaring also
at the White Man who prowled among the trees.

"Do you know who I am?" I asked again. When he didn't answer,
I knew what to do by instinct. I plucked one of the petals of the
black violets so that I could eat it. It burned down my throat like
whiskey. As Selena had instructed me, I put only one on his tongue,
as if it were a communion wafer.

Steven stared at me. "You? I don't know. Or, wait—I know that
you're a bitch." He began breathing hard. "I know that you smell
like sex. You walk like a slut. I'm in love with you."

"You're not very nice to me." The violet-drug was having its effect
on my body. It was Spanish fly and heroin and champagne. I was hot
between the legs and suddenly read to get down on all fours to finally fuck him like a dog. I peeled the robe away from his shoulders,
which rippled, and his swelling chest. "You have no respect,
Steven."

"Get me out of this." He strained against the ropes. His throat was
purple with lust. "I'm going to eat you."

The rope strung around his waist, and I lifted the folds of the robe
from his thighs. He was barefoot. His sex was long and monster-
thick. Sweet moisture—I swear it was honey—began to drip down
my legs.

"Do it," he begged. His penis grew larger and flame-colored. "It's
going to kill me."

The women behind me started to dance again. Their feet
pounded, they were shouting and singing. Selena moaned while she
made love to another girl. When I looked over, I saw the White Man
slinking back up to Françoise.

I undid the rope.

Steven untangled himself and walked toward me slowly, stealth-ily. I backed away, and swiped at him with my nails. Three deep scratches appeared in his right forearm, which pooled with blood. His mouth opened so I could see the sharpness of his teeth.

I kissed him, hard, and teeth clashing, and hot, the way I kissed Patrick that first night we met, after we'd talked about God and books in the library. Steven had his hands on my shoulders and he threw me to the ground, pressing open my legs with the flats of his palms. He bent down and put his mouth to my pussy, and I shouted and cheered to see the women tumbling around me like wicked balleri-nas. His fingers were inside me. He bit me—hard—on my thigh, breaking the skin in two places. His cock went inside, smooth, long, ramming me so roughly I would have been sick back home, but here I loved it and I could have taken three of him. His torso shimmered in the firelight, the gold glancing off the blood that streaked his skin.

So we fucked like animals, and when it was done, he fell back from me into the beds of violet, stunned.

"Steven," I said.

He looked suddenly ill and began to claw at his throat. "What did you do to me? Who are you?"

"It's all right. You're fine."

He glared up at me, then down to the blood on his arm. "Oh my God." His face crumpled; he jumped up. "Oh, no."

He ran into the grove, but I couldn't run after and take care of him because right then I witnessed something else so fiendish it rooted me to my place.

I turned to call for help. Through the crowd of unhearing women, past the sight of Selena's avid face, I saw the White Man abusing Françoise for her rejection of him. He bent over her, mur-muring threats in her ear while his features changed shape, spas-ming into a dragon's face, a girl's, a demon's.

"Stop it," she screamed. She reached for the bronze dagger at her waist and with one hard thrust, she plunged the blade deep into his pearly stomach.

But he only raised his arms and let her see that the gory wound flooding gold blood down his hips meant nothing to him.

"Lady," she shouted. "Help me."

The White Man was crying.

He stared at her as thick glistening tears ran down his pallid cheeks, which warped like a mask of Tragedy. It was here that I knew the White Man was a nightmare version of Keats's nightingale. He wept death instead of sang life, and somehow, his grief *hurt* Françoise. He *was* death. She stumbled away from him. She clutched at her chest.

The priestesses screamed. Selena was bellowing. She separated from her lovers to race toward me, wrapping her arms around me and weeping. "No."

Françoise fell to the ground, dead-faced, and La Chusa instantly ran to her with arms outstretched.

"You know that I protect them, Pan," the Goddess said in a quiet and vicious voice.

"And you know *that I am lonely*," he spat back. "I am barren—I cannot have children."

"That is your burden, not mine. And you forget yourself, Pan. Our truce is fragile. Do not tempt me to war."

The White Man stared her down, cursing, even as La Chusa stroked the gray cheek of Françoise, threw back her head, and laughed.

This laughter tore from her throat like thunder. It was a gong in a holy temple. I knew immediately that this was the sound of the Goddess's laughter, the mantra that made the world, which was the only power that could save Françoise from the killing power of the White Man's woe.

It was a creation sound. Françoise's cheek grew rosy again and she opened her eyes, even as the rest of the priestesses screeched at the White Man like Furies and drove him from the clearing.

Selena and I were gripping tightly to each other.

"Selena, I have to know something. *Can we die here?*" I hissed.

"Die here?"

"Yes."

"You have to pass the test."

"I don't understand."

"You have to pass the test, Imogen." She clung onto me ferociously. "Like you saw Françoise pass hers. Mine will be coming soon. And there's no way I will fail it. If you fail, then no one will protect you. If *you* failed, I would have to become your enemy. But if you pass, nothing can hurt you. Not even death. Not even *him*."

So then I knew. I knew what I suspected and wished for when I watched Patrick sing Mrs. Flanagan to sleep.

If I am very smart, or very good, *I can have what I want.* I used to be confused, but all at once, I knew exactly what that was.

What I want most of all is more forbidden than babies or black magic sex. It's a sin, too, I think, and of the imagination.

I want what I have.

It was an epiphany: I don't want anyone but Patrick, and I need him to be alive forever, and me too, so that I never suffer like that old widow dying in the hospital.

Does it seem strange that my thoughts would turn to my husband after screwing Steven, and making love to these women?

No, I'm writing about desire, not loyalty. And after tasting Steven, I knew the likes of him are sweet, but I was suddenly very clear that they aren't what I wish for most in my secret heart.

His hair like the halos of the medieval saints; the shadows under his eyes.

In that forest, death would never separate me from Patrick.

February 14. Valentine's day

No miracles. But excellent sex. With my husband.

March 11. Moon in Leo.

Mrs. Flanagan died two days ago.

Patrick has resolved himself. He cried a little more, letting me hold onto him. After that, he went back to work. "This is the *job*," he said. He is now devoted to that sixteen-year-old girl patient, who is terminal, and dying very painfully in the ICU.

There is something else.

Steven didn't return to the library for two weeks after the Storm Moon, and when he did come back to work, I saw that he wasn't doing very well.

"Help me with these," I said to him yesterday morning as I crouched in the stacks, putting back the dictionaries. He wore a tight, ripped, concert T-shirt but did not otherwise seem like his old swinging self. His eyes were shielded in his thin face as he talked to me.

"Yes, ma'am."

He stooped next to me, picking up the English-Italian dictionary. It didn't take long for me to see that he could barely speak.

"What's wrong?"

"Nothing." He wiped sweat off his face. "I don't know. Bad dreams."

I gripped hold of his arm, and he did look at me then. His face was sharp and naked with love.

"Ms. López."

I glared down. "Steven, what happened to you?"

There were three pearly scars on the skin of his forearm, like scratch marks.

"Got these fixing my car." I could tell he lied, but didn't remember the exact truth about the cause of his wound, either.

I stumbled up and ran away from him to the bathroom.

In the stall, I raised my skirt. I peered down at the skin on my thighs.

There were two tiny puncture scars across the tendon, as pearly as those on his arm. There was no mistake that they were from his bite. I was wrong. I didn't come out of the forest unscathed. There was no other way I could have been marked like this.

I received these wounds when Steven was drugged and wild with the black violet.

March 14. The Crow Moon. 3:35 p.m. The Lunar Eclipse. 3:49 pm.
Purim.

Everything has changed. Something terrible has happened. I swear, God. *Eden is dangerous.*

It must have been the eclipse.

I stayed home from work today. At 3:35, I walked outside with my glass of wine, my bloodstone, honeysuckle, and moss, which are sacred to the Crow Moon. I poured the wine, buried the herb and flower. I kissed the stone. I said a prayer.

Above me, the moon was just visible, appearing faint and ghostly among the blue clouds like an afterimage on a closed eye.

A black crow appeared in the sky. I was happy because the damage to Steven, which I am guilty of, hasn't deterred me from my secret hopes of a long, long life spent with Patrick. I watched with joy as the bird flew down to the yard to land on the hedge, singing and squalling.

"Let's go," I said impatiently. "Take me."

It hopped to the grass and pecked on my hand so that blood seeped through the skin. This didn't hurt. It nuzzled through the hedge and disappeared. I followed the animal, finding that I was easily able to pass through the dead hydrangea bushes and melt into the black and red forest.

I flew into the Clearing.

Another lady festival raged beneath three shivering silver moons: this time the women circled Selena.

Priestesses in red, blue, gold gowns whirled around her like dervishes as La Chusa sat back in that gleaming white chair and smiled. Selena was dressed in white silk, with black violets in her hair, and pearls on her feet. Her little breasts were visible, and lacquered with sapphire pigment and diamond dust, which also hooped her arms and throat.

I pummeled through the crush of women to reach her. "This is it! Your Test."

She yelped at me like a bride. "Do you know what I'm going to do when I'm initiated? I'm going to become a bard. I'm going to memorize all the secret books, Imogen. Like Merlin. And I'm going to write everything down. I'm going to write love poems and epics and spells. People will recite my songs as their vows when they get married. And I'm going to write laws. Kings will consult me. Presidents will call on me—"

"Concentrate, Selena," warned Françoise, who had just come tearing up from the storm of Amazons twirling and howling even more furiously around us. "I told you to be quiet. To *focus*. None of this is settled yet."

"Right, right, you're right," Selena said excitedly. "I'm going to focus. So I can be a poet." She squeezed her eyes shut. "I *am* concentrating. I know this will be hard."

"Let's go—we have to leave her alone." Françoise pulled on my arm and led me back to the throng. I shuddered at the calamity of vaulting, high-jumping women, and was tossed from girl to girl. One blonde, named Sarah; one imposing tall lady, named Tameka; a short, square-hipped girl named Deepa—I had met them all, and many were warriors or magicians of formidable talents. But none of them meant to me as much as Selena; and now I don't care to record their particular stories.

We danced and danced. Astral moonlight stained my body amethyst and pearl. The girls plucked black violets from the ground to string them in my hair, around my throat, around my breasts, and I was drunk from their fragrance.

I opened my eyes. I looked to the far side of the clearing.

In the periphery of the woods, I saw Patrick.

It was my husband. He was pale and his red unkempt hair flared out from his head. He wore the beige pants and white shirt and blue tie that I had seen him leave home in this morning. He didn't understand where he was and looked nervous.

"Imogen?"

I raced to him.

"Patrick! Patrick!" I ranted and clung on to him. "Let's stay here. Let's not go back. This is a good place for us."

He didn't answer.

"Sweetie?"

His eyes were very tender, though they were circled by those dark shadows again. Raising my hand, he saw the wound given to me by the crow.

"Oh, that's just . . ." I shook my head. "It'll go away."

Still, he said nothing. He didn't seem quite the same.

"Pat?"

He touched my breasts and fingered the black violets around my throat; he kissed my mouth. He began to unbutton his shirt, and now I was laughing again, and helping him, wrestling with his belt buckle and his zipper.

When Patrick was naked, he grasped me on the shoulders.

"Ready?" he asked.

"For what?"

He flipped me over and grasped onto my breasts, almost too brutally. He bit my shoulder with sharp fanglike teeth. His mouth was hot. Grasping between my legs, he used his fingers to spread me as wide as my lips would extend, and then he slipped inside of me, ramming his penis nearly to my womb.

I was calling out in a trance. He came, bouncing inside of me. *Was* that his penis? I was bucking back and felt a piratical and colossally large cock boosting itself to my throat. I was all warm juice, and even urine flowed down my legs. I lost such control over myself. He climaxed again, two more times, and slipped out. I fell onto the ground. When I turned around, I saw him sitting above me; he was smiling.

I was unsure. "You've never done me like that before." I pressed my hand to his face. "Where did you learn that?"

"You're very beautiful," he answered in a shifting voice. "I could love you. And it is just possible that I could give you what you want. What you *really* want. Your Patrick! Because you don't *care* about being some twiddly soldier or poet or wizard, or living here forever with these bitches, do you?"

As I had my hand on his cheek, it paled to a shade far more livid than the dying face of Mrs. Flanagan. The eyes changed. The lovely mouth of my husband bulged into a hawklike mask. The rest of the body drained of color. The creature's sex was long and pointed. And then I remember what Selena had said:

"Watch out for him. He's disgusting. He tries to trick you. And he can hurt you. He was very hard on the Lady. Before she earned the Key to this place."

It was the White Man.

"Oh my God."

"No, of course you don't want to stay here with these tiresome whores," he said in his natural growl. "But, remember that *I* can be nice to you. I can give you what you want. And it's quite easy to get my attention. You merely need to call my name."

I tore at my hair, and violets came away in my hands as I howled, "What did you do to me?"

"I only have a thousand of them, names that is. You do need a *key* to this place, you know, if you want to enter it on your own terms. La Chusa earned her Key from me, after much hard work. And I would put you through your paces, too. But remember, I'd never put you through *that*."

He pointed toward the clearing, then slapped my face so I would turn and see. Selena wriggled in the center of the dancing women, glowing like the Madonna. La Chusa remained on her bone chair; the Lady watched her charge.

There was a rustling among the priestesses. Two of them separated from the crowd and made for the trees on the side opposite where I lay. They vanished between the red cedars and returned guiding a bedazzled-looking older woman, who had dark skin, a tidy coif of hair, and wore a housedress. She looked just like my friend, with the same high cheeks and long eyes.

"Ah," Selena gasped. She brought her hands to her laughing face. "Is she here to watch?"

No one answered; it was suddenly very quiet in the wood.

"Selena," the woman said.

"Mama, you're going to be proud."

"What's happening?"

"You're here to watch me do this! Right, Lady?" Selena gestured toward La Chusa. "My mother's here as a guest. As my honored guest."

"That is one way of describing her presence here," answered La Chusa.

Selena's smile wavered.

"What's my test?" she asked.

La Chusa kept silent on her chair. Her hair spilled over her shoulders as black as the bird that had led me here.

"You're going to ask me to choose you over my husband," said Selena.

"No."

"You'll ask me to choose you over my children, then."

"No."

"I would do that! I would do that for you!"

"But that's not your test."

"You've never brought a *mother* here before."

"Choose."

The priestesses began wailing and twisting in agony. Françoise threw her head back and cried as they all continued dancing, but mournfully, hideously.

"*Choose,*" they echoed.

"No, not *her*," called out Selena.

"What in the *holy* hell is going on here?" the mother hollered. She began kicking at the priestesses who tightly held her.

"Of *course* it's her, darling. Because you haven't yet paid the price for Eden, have you?" said La Chusa to Selena. "You know of what I speak . . . that really, you are, right now, the stupidest of women! Oh, don't gawk at me like that, dearest. You must admit that you have *no idea* what your unhappy human race has endured. Earthquakes, floods, wars, plagues, death, rapes?" The other priestesses chanted this litany of world suffering in tandem with their queen, like a Greek chorus. "You *have* been lucky. You've suffered only the pettiest of woes! But the loss of your mother would teach you the pain of men and women. *As you must be taught.* For an ignorant girl is an evil girl. A wicked, wicked, girl. And if you remain an idiot and stay here, you would be a wicked *powerful* girl. We can't have that. And I can't let you go home, can I? So here we are: Choose!"

Selena shrieked: "I would give you my children. I would give you my husband."

But already it was too late, and my friend's chance passed in a twinkling; the spell was broken. La Chusa raised her hand as the priestesses shrank, blackened, developed wings. Dozens of gleaming crows flew up from the ground and whisked away into the trees.

"Look, look," said the White Man, next to me. Above us, the three moons had disappeared in the eclipse.

Selena ran to her mother, who spat out: "We're getting out of here. Are you taking drugs with these people?"

"Goodbye, Selena," said La Chusa.

Selena clasped her mother, and I could hear her teeth chattering. "Just one minute. Just one minute," she kept shouting.

Now the White Man curled himself up from the ground and began to move over to the women.

"What the *fuck*," said the mother at the sight of the monster.

"Do you still think I'm disgusting?" he growled at Selena.

The mother made the sign of the cross while shouting obscenities. Then she switched theologies, brandishing her thumb between her first two fingers, in an ancient hexing gesture.

"Run, Mama," said Selena. She looked over at me with a nightmare look on her face.

"Jesus," whispered the mother when she saw the White Man had begun crying.

The tears poured down his cheeks. He sobbed.

Selena closed her eyes.

The White Man made a screaming sound like a hawk, and his terrible sadness infected them like a magic disease, just the way it had poisoned Françoise. But no one would cure them of his grief. The two women's bodies shuddered. Their eyes turned white. They exploded in a satanic bomb so full of blood and flames that their torsos and legs blew apart like leaves.

I ran.

I bolted insanely through the woods, tearing the skin of my neck and shoulders on the branches of the red trees. It was black. The moons were still eclipsed. Nearly blind, I could barely make out the flickering arrow that would lead me from the forest.

But I was chanting Patrick's name, and I said, "I want to go home. I want to go home."

Soon enough, I found myself, bloodless, naked, and crying like a stabbed animal in my sunlit back yard.

The eclipse ended at 4:02 p.m.

I am writing this in my bedroom now.

Besides the scars on my thigh, the only sign that I've been to the forest is this: I found two black violet petals in my hair.

I put these in my bureau drawer, and I locked it. Other than that, every single thing in my life is going back to the ways it used to be. I *swear*.

Selena.

She's dead. I know it was real.

Like her, I haven't suffered. Not really. I've lived a beautiful life full of my husband and my books, and so I, too, am the stupidest of women. I can't even face the agonies of Mrs. Flanagan, who died in a clean white hospital surrounded by doctors and soothed by morphine. I haven't yet paid the price of admission to Eden.

I know La Chusa would make me sacrifice Patrick.

And that *is impossible*. The one thing I've learned in forest is that my husband remains the only person in the whole world who I can never, never surrender.

[Later]

What did he say?

He tempted me.

What did the White Man promise me?

March 15.

I returned to Mass.

The light was lovely as it drifted through the red and blue stained glass. I sat in the pew and prayed very loudly in my head. I was again *yelling* to God. I now knew what I was asking for: life everlasting, with my husband.

Jesus promised I could have that. I think.

Can I be sure I'll see Patrick after I die? Would I recognize him in Heaven?

I want to know there's a Heaven, and that I'll still be admitted.

So I asked, yelling in my mind. But there was no answer.

The naked body of Christ graced the church altar. I stared at the pierced ribs, the thin stomach, the long, Grecian feet of the Savior. He's beautiful, he is sexual. What happened to him during those forty nights he starved in the desert, I wonder.

I prayed, and I prayed, and I prayed.

But I'm so afraid that God won't help Selena, or me.

March 17

Once I was in Eden, and I discovered that if I brought Patrick there, we'd never lie dying in a hospital, crying, and lonely.

But now I can't go back.

La Chusa is a bitch-goddess, and I know she won't let me have both Patrick and the forest.

Except . . . the White Man isn't so harsh. He said he'd make me a bargain.

I've just read the portion from Dr. Edvard Murillo's book that I transcribed in this diary.

Satan . . . appears to his faithful after they call his Name three times.

I shouldn't be reading that.

I shouldn't be thinking this.

[Later]

The White Man said I could call his name to get the Key. That he would give me my wish.

What *would* I call him, if I were foolish enough?

El Diablo
Old Nick
Mephistopheles

Patrick is working very hard on his lost cause with the sixteen-year-old girl, Gloria, who will be dead within the year, he says.

I could just whisper it, like a secret. The name.
What could happen?

the white man the white man the white man
I hear a noise

What day?

The young girls wear flowers on their breasts as they dance.
They cast the blooms in the air, their arms glistening.
Do not wait, my daughter, to embrace your lover.

Never, never, never, never

March?

I called his name three times.

There was fire, and I danced for forty nights that lasted many, many, many years.
There was a cold, cold lake and the sound of laughter.
The White Man is made of steel and has hands of red hot iron.

April
Easter

When I came back from Hell, I saw Patrick and I didn't recognize him.
When did that happen?

I don't know, exactly. It was *After*. I was in the house. I don't know how I got there. I was in bed and it was dark, and I understood that I was on earth again, and should be asleep, because it was night, and that's what human beings do. But next to me lay a man with red hair and a nice face that looked ugly to me after the incandescent monsters who had tortured me in the underworld.

I stared at that skinny mortal man beside me. I didn't know his name. He had a small furred animal wrapped around its neck.

This human flesh is poor and thin and measly, and I don't know why the White Man wants it. And I can't understand why he sent me back here, after marrying me in a ritual of flame. He burned his body onto mine in a glittering bed, sucking out my spirit with his mouth—then laughing, and exhaling it back into me. I'm so ruined that I'll never, ever get over it.

I don't want to be me any more.

Here in Patrick's bed, I began to scratch at my chest and my arms so that golden jagged wounds tore my breasts before they disappeared into my virgin skin.

The noise half-woke Patrick up.

He turned and, without opening his eyes, said, "Hi sweetie, have a bad dream?"

And then I recognized his voice. It crept inside of me. Sweetheart voice. I remembered that the man was Patrick and that I loved him.

Or the measly thing I used to be, the human being, loved him.

I used to hold him and tease him and fuck him. I met him in the library and we talked about books and God. I visited him at the hospital. He sang Mrs. Flanagan to sleep.

But for forty nights, I betrayed my husband, and became a stinking bride to a hawk-faced man, who is a terrible nightingale, who is the Beast.

Patrick rolled over and fell back asleep. I crept out of bed, naked and shivering, and went to the kitchen. I drew out a knife from a drawer. I went outside to the garden, under a horned moon. The grass was silver, the sky black, the trees white.

No more dreams of immortality for the thing that used to be Imogen López. I so long to forge my corruption that the death of atheists would be a pleasure. I scratched myself again, deep, deep, deep, with my sharp nails, on my thighs and my throat. I jabbered songs, obscene nonsense, while I took the knife. It was a sharp, long, silver knife, and I tucked the tip into my side. Gold blood ran down my hip. I aimed it at my heart, and with my unnatural strength plunged it into my ribs up to the hilt, so that I could hear the liquid ripping sound it made.

But I am such a bitch that the steel melted inside of my body, and the scratches closed up tight. I am such a devil's whore and vampire that I can't die.

There's not a mark on me.

May 2

"The library called, Imogen. They say one of your kids has disappeared. A boy named Steven."

. . .

"Imogen?"

. . .

"Honey, I think we need to take you to the hospital. Jesus."

May 13

Yesterday I fell down in the garden, screaming, and where my hand touched the grass, red hyacinth bloomed.

The White Man made me terrible. He murdered me. He called me his wife.

Patrick can tell that I have changed, though I try desperately to hide it. I can still move and talk and shape my mouth into a smile like the other human women I have observed on the streets, outside the windows.

He says I am depressed because "we can't get pregnant."

I am taking little pills that burn away like ether inside my hot and perfect mouth. My breath smells like flowers and my teeth can do the damage of a shark's.

My body is too strong for earthly drugs and there is no medicine for my condition, anyway.

• • •

"Honey, you're going too fast. What's wrong? Why are you touching me like that?"

"I'm sorry—I'm just—"

"What?"

"Nothing. *Leave me alone.*"

June 11. Strong Sun Moon. 10:05 p.m.

I wonder if my nightmare with the White Man purified me or destroyed me.

For forty days and forty nights I was in a long, stark, burning desert, and I begged *him* to love me, though I hated him so bitterly, so insanely, that I hoped to die.

Hell is very beautiful except for the pain.

I am trying hard to forget it.

[later]

death runs from me
[illegible]
[illegible]
[ripped-out pages]

June 30

I have been psychotic for the past four months.

When no one's looking, I've been crazy. The symptoms, I've looked it up. My condition's not unheard of. Dionysus, I think, was insane.

Still, things might be getting better, now.

Maybe there's hope.

Two weeks ago, I tried to kill myself again. Frankenstein's Bride should be put down—but, as I can't seem to overdose on booze, sleeping pills, or Xanax, I've devoted myself to knives and razor blades, despite my initial failure at suicide the night I returned from hell.

I was in the garden, sitting on the grass by the stone bench. La Chupacabra drowsed next to me, blinking in the sun. It was ten in the morning. I took a thin little blade of Patrick's and cut deeply into my wrists (though he's stuffed me full of pills and forced me to a psychiatrist, he still has no idea what I've been doing; either because of his denial or because I've been so careful to hide my death-trips from him, he doesn't know how far my "depression" has taken me).

I cut into my vein. My hand was upturned, and I watched a drop of golden blood—ichor, I think is the proper name for it now—fall on the grass and turn into a hard, bright jewel.

Then my wound gathered back in on itself without the trace of a scar, as if my flesh were made of lava instead of carbon and water.

But here's where I saw something strange in my hand. My palm was golden and glowing. It *shone*. It pulsed with light. I sobbed as I stared down at this miracle. My hands glistened like stars. And in the next second, I knew that I'd seen that kind of radiance before, in the old paintings of prophets. It's said that when Moses came down from Mount Sinai after talking to God, his face glittered with that same color, from his exposure to grace. Paintings of Moses show white beams strobing from his head, as if his eyes were made of diamonds catching the sun. The same marvel is said to have happened to Muhammad, who had to wear a veil after conversations with Allah. There's also the tale of Jesus and his bright fingers, touching the eyes of a blind man and filling them with light.

I was in the garden, staring at my angel's hands. The day was light and windy as I wept for the majesty of Hades. I cried because I wanted to die, like I used to want sex and children. But when I touched my golden fingers to my lips, it was like I tasted a beautiful drug. I felt some kind of relief, like morphine's, like hash's. I touched my tongue. I tasted . . . *health*. So I took my bright hands and put them on my face. I stroked them over my mind.

I took my hands and pressed them to my heart.

And from my white-shining palms seeped an elixir, which somehow cured me of my memories of my torments in hell.

It was as if I'd been touched by a miracle-working preacher who handles snakes, walks on water, and cures cancer from a tent in a fundamentalist Christian revival.

• • •

I'm healing myself.

As a result of my unlikely therapies, I've stopped secretly and use-lessly attempting suicide. I've also ceased screaming obscenities and prayers to God when I'm alone. I can now speak to people again. I even returned to the library yesterday, for the first time since the White Man released his hot grasp on me.

But when I picked up a book on birds, a red starling flew out of the pages, and my glistening hand trembled so hard that I nearly threw the volume across the room.

I should also write here that my glowing hands and my horror are not the only difference in me. My body is marked. I was right to fear the scars on my thigh, from Steven's teeth. What happened in the underworld is also felt here.

My body—

My only solace is Patrick, whom I have grown to love with a new, horrible and carnivorous hunger, which I can barely control.

July 12. Blessing Moon. 10:02 p.m.

I love my husband and I have to be careful.

I want to devour Patrick.

The moon shone like the sun through the window tonight. I reached for him. That cat hissed at me, and I poured it tenderly it off the bed, the more gently to keep from killing it.

"Now?" he asked.

I rolled him over. I pulled off his shirt. I was panting.

"Patrick."

I kissed and bit at his back. I scratched at his skin. Between my legs I was burning and the honey was pouring out of me.

His pale ass was toward me. Patrick, still groggy, was on his knees and his elbows, and didn't know what I was doing.

I wanted to fuck him like a man, like a minotaur.

I touched myself with one hand, and with the other, pushed my fingers onto his anus.

He immediately leaped.

"Honey. Honey, you know I *don't like that,*" he said, revolted and confused.

"I do, I do, I do," I wept.

"You're just going through some changes. It's because you're pregnant," he said, trying to understand.

What he said is true. I have to admit it. I'm going to have a baby.

There was no angelic Annunciation, like when Jesus was conceived, and the oceans didn't boil, and the sun didn't turn to blood, which I hope is a good sign.

I hadn't had a period all spring. Then my belly began to swell. My skills at denial have been so effective that it's only two weeks ago that I urinated on a stick and gave it to Patrick.

"It's blue, it's blue, it's blue."

He ran outside to the garden and did a funky, chicken-winged, knock-kneed dance like football players do when they score a goal.

But I didn't dance. I stayed very still in the bathroom. I didn't move, on the toilet seat. I didn't know if I was happy.

And then, I stood up, and washed my hands. I was terrified.

I heard the baby inside of me singing, and she sounded like a nightingale.

I'm going to burn this book.

August 9. Moon When Cherries Turn Black. 3:54 a.m.

This Moon's bird is the falcon, and its stone is the carnelian. Its tree is the hazel and its flower the marigold.

The moon came to me again, and it killed my husband. No, I'm lying when I write that. This morning *I* killed Patrick.

And I learned this morning also that I have become an unnatural and gifted woman; I am not really Imogen López any more.

Today was a beautiful Sunday. Patrick and I were in bed. I couldn't control my appetites again. I'd served us wine, despite the early hour. We'd locked the cat out. The sun flowed through the window, turning me the color of honey, and my hair into bronze. Patrick's freckles stood out on his shoulders and his stomach.

I poured wine onto his chest and drank it off.

"You're wearing me out today," he laughed. "You have to watch out for the baby."

"The baby will be fine," I said, unnaturally sure. "Touch me again. Touch me."

"Let's relax."

I don't know when I thought of the two black violet petals in my bureau drawer. But the idea came to my mind like the Still Small Voice: *If he takes both, maybe he'll be even stronger than Steven was—he'll be like me. He'll be a monster.* Selena once warned me about the violet's potency, but in my extreme state I didn't think of any possible dangers.

"Do you want to try something different?" I asked.

"Like, sleeping?"

"No," I said. "This will be great."

I stood up from the bed. I retrieved the key to the top drawer from my nightstand table, which was cluttered with our half-finished wine glasses. I unlocked the bureau and found the black petals there, beneath some tissue paper.

"Here," I said.

"What's that?"

"Mexican ju ju."

"What is that, drugs?"

And before he could object, I slipped both petals onto his tongue.

"It tastes . . . Imogen."

He didn't finish the sentence. His head eased back, his face darkening against the whiteness of the pillow. His chest began to flush, bright red, like the gold and red hearts of Christ in Renaissance paintings.

He looked up at me and his face was different. His eyes had turned entirely black, and were tilted like a tiger's.

His penis rose, stiffened, lengthened. It began to shiver; sperm foamed and pearled around the head.

Wordlessly, brutally, my husband began to fuck me.

I loved it. I was on top. He pulled my hips down, shaking them fast, fast, fast, so my lips rasped over his skin. He was shouting. His eyes widened; and the most infernal, delicious profanities spewed from his wet lips.

"You're a *bitch*. You want it. You are going to take it. You're going to take my cock, and you're going to scream for it."

Animal noises came from my throat. From outside the door the cat shrieked and raged.

I scratched him; he didn't bleed. I slapped him, and I was pulling him up, and I bit him through the flesh. I shouted to him that I loved him, and I loved him, and I loved him.

Looking up, I saw his hand jerk to the side. It smashed the wine glasses to the ground as I screamed words that were like prayers.

"Christ, Oh Lord it's good, Oh Lady, help me."

And here is where the world contracted and turned upside down.

It was an accident, but She heard my supplication. I didn't mean to call her, but I have a suspicion that intent, like the imagination, is uncontrollable. From outside, I detected a cracking sound and a roaring.

"Hold on, Patrick."

He didn't hear me. His eyes were now opal-colored and his hips moved in an epilepsy.

Looking outside the window, I could see the hedges fly away from the perimeter of the house. The lawn filled with marigold, whose perfume poured into the room. The full moon appeared like a barn on fire, drowning out the sun, making a holocaust of the earth. All the mist-colored Otherworld flooded into the yard, eating away the grass, the garden tools, the stone bench, the concrete path. It burned down the French doors and the side of the house, and red trees sprang up as if born from the dragon's teeth of Greek myth.

We were in the Clearing.

La Chusa sat on her bone chair with a melancholy look on her face. The brightly clad priestesses gathered around her. Françoise, majestic in deerskin and her bronze dagger, danced and keened with grief while leading them in a dirge. At the edge of the wood the White Man capered like a hideous marionette.

Patrick and I were naked in front of them. My husband had gone feral from the drug and didn't notice our unworldly travel. He lay there, quieter now, with his eyes closed and touching me.

"I heard you call," La Chusa said.

"I didn't call you. I don't want you." Terror strangled me. "Let my husband go home." Before she could even ask me, I shouted, "I choose him. I choose him. Go away."

"You choose *him?*" she asked unbelievingly. "You *poisoned* him."

"What?"

"You gave him too much black violet!"

I snatched my head back toward Patrick. He was very still and pale, and I knew then that he wasn't strong enough for the two petals I'd foolishly put on his tongue.

"I would have made you a healer," La Chusa seethed, as the White Man skittered among the trees, inching his way closer to us. "That's what you want, isn't it?" Eerily and horribly, she began to speak in the lilting voice of Mrs. Flanagan: *"You'll have to leave him some day, you know. That's what hurts, lass. That's what's the killer. Not even God himself can stop it hurting."*

"Make me a healer now." I pulled Patrick up toward me. His irises were huge and white and he was limp in my hands.

"No, there's something wrong with you. You want too, *too* much." She narrowed her gaze, studying me, then it seemed as if a word came into her head with the spontaneity of prophecy. "You want *nightingales*, yes? You want you and your husband to live forever *and* without misery."

I shook so hard I nearly convulsed. "Yes. But you said I could have everything here!"

"Not even Adam got what you want, dearest. And as I told Selena, we all have to make a sacrifice." She pointed at the White Man. "That agony made me into a god—and it taught me things you can't know, which is how others suffer."

"But I have suffered," I cried, remembering my own anguish at the hot hands of the White Man.

She narrowed her eyes, then blanched at her first glimpse of my swelling belly; I saw that the White Man had hidden from her the knowledge of my time in Hades, and the burden I carried. "Whatever it was, it wasn't enough. Nothing would hurt you as much as your husband dead. Not even the murder of that child in your womb. And without that lesson you cannot be gentle. You cannot wield power." Her eyes glittered. "Isn't that fox blood on your mouth?"

I brought my hand up to my lips and gasped: it came away red. This was gore from the killing of Françoise's lover.

"So you see," La Chusa said. "Already you have forgotten poor Charles, the fox. You *Wolf!* If I let you go back now, without my blessing, you will destroy everyone you encounter to get back to this place."

"Lady, I thought you said she was special," I heard Françoise whisper.

"No, I know now that she's dangerous."

The White Man now crept toward us, quietly.

"Go away." I clutched Patrick closer to me.

But La Chusa didn't stop his progress.

"Hello again." He gently ran his clawed hand over my belly, whispering, "You *do* have the Key now, you know. I'm so very, very intrigued by this new development."

"You said you would give me what I want," I raved to him. "My husband!"

"Oh—that. I *lied.* I'm not at all interested in keeping *him* around! I really hate any kind of competition. Don't I, Daddy?"

The White Man glared down at Patrick, making a woeful mouth. I saw a droplet form at the corner of his eye. The tears poured like wine down his face.

"Stop it. Stop it."

But he began singing:

Smile though your heart is aching
Smile even though it's breaking

I looked down at Patrick in my arms. Because of my poison, and the White Man's curse, he had collapsed backward. His mouth was open, gaping over on one side of his face. He was the color of a dolphin.

He was dead.

I don't know how I knew what to do next but I did. And I had paid for that wisdom in pain.

I threw my head back and I *laughed*. Like Kali Ma, like La Chusa. The sound came out of my throat like a typhoon, whipping its winds and throwing the trees back and forth. The laughter came out of me like a cyclone, golden and blue, and filled with stars. This breeze that I think I stole from heaven sifted down on Patrick, whose color came back, and whose heart started beating again.

"Yes, damn, I thought you might try that," muttered the White Man.

Patrick opened his eyes, blinking, and frowning up at the unnatural women, the red trees, the three eclipsed moons. "This is weird."

I was too scared to cry.

A grave and deathly silence filled the forest. The priestesses peered at me with shock-sharp eyes. Françoise whispered to one of them, and I could tell from their excited gesticulations that they were both astonished and impressed at my miracle.

As for La Chusa, her face twisted with anger. And fear.

She raised her hand and shouted a word I couldn't understand.

Then suddenly they all rose into the sky, the Lady, the girls, the trees, the White Man, the trinity of moons, spinning and twisting like a white tornado into the cosmos, even as the shabby lawn, the dead hydrangeas, the stone bench, the French doors, our bed, our bureau, and the smashed wine glasses collected together like heads of mercury, and reformed our life back around us.

Patrick lay in our bed, and I still held onto him.

He blinked again. His eyes were normal. He continued gaping at the sunlight with the sound of La Chupacabra's tigerlike scratching at our door.

Finally, as the good rationalist that he is, he said decisively, "I fell asleep."

I threw myself on top of him, and now I did start crying hysterically.

He said it was the hormones.

"Honey, let the cat in."

February 23, 2007. The Storm Moon. 6:35 p.m.

It's peaceful and gloomy outside as I write this at the kitchen table, while Patrick waltzes our fat and giggling baby around the house, ignoring La Chupacabra. The cat's been cast aside in favor of the child, and these days clings to me; the poor pet is thinner than I've ever seen her, and her usually luxurious marmalade fur has grown matted.

"Have a cookie," I say, feeding her a piece of kibble, which she gratefully takes in her jaws. La Chupacabra is starved from heartbreak over my husband's total, over-the-top passion for our daughter, so I take her up on my lap while I write.

I see from my last entry that it's been nearly seven months since my last confession, which would explain these abrupt changes in my life, as well as indicate the time it's taken for me to return to some pretence of normalcy.

It was a hard birth. I thought the baby, named Selena, would kill me.

She was born exactly nine months after the eclipse of the Crow Moon. The sky rained blood that night. There were also global sea storms that took the lives of over two hundred people off the coasts of Florida and Casablanca, and an earthquake that killed seven thousand in Cuba.

All this I learned later. On the night she was born, she crawled out of me with her sharp hands as if she were a sapper hacking through a tunnel in a war. And when my daughter flung herself out of me into the dazzle of the hospital room, I saw that she was red-brown, intact, with tiny feet and arms and only the smallest suggestion of a tail. But the doctor and nurses weren't so much flabbergasted at this stigma of hers, nor at the gilded blood that had flowed out of me, as at the peculiar sounds she made.

"That's a strange cry."

"It sounds like she's singing. Words."

"Except, like a—"

Bird.

"She's beautiful," Patrick cried, holding out his arms and taking her.

But when she looked over at me, in his arms, her lips began to move in articulate ways that were not normal for a newborn, and I knew what she could do.

"Give her to me," I shouted so they wouldn't hear her, my voice still strong even though throughout the birth I'd been screaming so loud that the lights had shattered, and the hospital pipes had burst, and many of the children born that night, I know, are going to be deaf.

I pressed her to my chest and whispered, "Sssshhh, ssssssh, sssssh." She obeyed.

So that was the birth. Ten weeks ago.

It seems like longer. We're all fine now, and all my scars have vanished. That is, we're all fine except for Steven, who's disappeared despite my efforts to find and cure him of the insanity he contracted from me. I *will* have to find that poor, sick boy. Some day soon, I'm going to have to save him. He's my guilt. I know that his chapter in my story isn't finished, and that I've done him a terrible wrong.

But . . . I don't want to be melancholy right now. Not about Steven or the birth or the moon.

It's gloomy enough this evening, anyhow, as I've already written here; the sky's the color of a judge's robe and there's an omen of a breeze. In accordance with the name of this month's moon, there's going to be a storm tonight, but it won't be caused by any act or will of mine. Though my interlude with the White Man has given me certain skills that I desire over nearly all other things in the world, the moon remains closed to me. No amount of chanting and libations and burning of skullcap or sage will let me sneak back into the forest. The hydrangea bush is brown and thick and dry, and when I look over it, I see our neighbor's amply fertilized backyard.

There's only one key to Eden that remains available to me, and I'm afraid to use it.

That is, I'm afraid to use her.

A pot of chicken stew bubbles on the stove as I scribble this; all the lamps are on; the room is bright and warm, and a faint, powerless *luna* shines through the window. Patrick sings to the baby, and as he dances around with her, Selena laughs in that cackly way of infants. My husband has good color now, with ruddiness in his skin and no shadows under his eyes; his hair flames around his good, full-cheeked face. There haven't been any more deaths, which makes him very happy—I visited that patient of his, the now seventeen-year-old girl named Gloria, the terminal case. I touched her with my glowing hands, and then the girl lived.

It seems that I *have* become a healer, though I think probably one more powerful than La Chusa would have allowed. And even if my skeptical Patrick has no idea of the cause of his patient's cure, he admits that the girl's remission is a "miracle." Gloria has made a total recovery with due credit going to his hard work; and I think he's found a new faith in his chosen vocation. He's still a good and virtuous atheist; he faces death with a clinical calm. But that didn't stop him from jumping and leaping like a teenager on Ecstasy when he came home with the news of his success.

Still, I know that it's our daughter that makes Patrick happiest of all.

"We did it," he likes to say to me about Selena's conception, and the healthy delivery—he's blocked how horrible that last part was.

And now he sings, absentmindedly, as though he's absolutely forgotten other painful things, too:

> Smile though your heart is aching
> Smile even though it's breaking

My daughter and I glance knowingly at each other as he warbles to us.

You can't tell. Selena looks just like me. Dark-eyed, dark-haired, round-faced. There's only the faintest cast to her skin that marks her as belonging to someone else, a pearliness, an opalescence, which hints at the pale shades that run through her blood. In this, as might be obvious, Patrick thinks he sees himself.

"That's the Finn in her," he brags.

Neither of us wants to disabuse him of that misconception.

"Are you wet?" he asks her now. He's feeling her bottom. "No."

I look up from my journal. Selena is still the size of a dictionary, and her hot black eyes stare at me from over his shoulder. "Do you want me to take her?"

He laughs, gripping harder onto her. "She's fine. She's always wonderful."

"Is that the phone?" I can hear it ringing. "Here, just give her to me. Go get it. You can have her right back."

"All right." Patrick moodily pours the baby into my arms, as La Chupacabra scats off, hissing. It is difficult to write like this, but I can still manage.

Selena burbles up at me while he is still in the room. I named her after my friend, but she's decided, with a dark humor that I hope is not harbinger of future bad behavior, that her *real* name is Salomé. My daughter is remarkably, strangely gorgeous in ways that she didn't inherit from me. It's like there's this candle burning inside of her translucent little body. Patrick is so distracted by her that we have had very little sex, which is all right. I understand, for the time being. I love her and am also obsessed with her, though I must admit that I am less maternal than I thought. It turns out that my baby desire was nothing more than a diverted greed for Nightingale-life, that is, my own and Patrick's immortality, because I don't want to smile when *my heart is breaking*. Patrick, on the other hand, is a more modest person, and also a much more talented parent, as our daughter well knows.

She knows, too, that this mundane earth-place is not really where she belongs.

"I like him very much," Selena just said in her musical voice when she was sure Patrick was out of earshot. This is because *she can already talk*, just like the baby-goddess Brigid.

"I do, too," I answer.

"You did a good job, picking that one for a husband," she adds. "Will my real father be that nice, Mother?"

"No," I say.

"The White Man wants to see me soon, though, you know."

"I know."

"Don't you want to go back, Mother?" She is talking about the forest.

I don't answer. I try to breastfeed her, but she's being finicky, so I put my pen back to this page.

Selena is my Key to Eden, so there it is in plain writing. Whereas La Chusa used her sensuality to persuade the White Man into allowing her a back door into the forest, I have in Selena something much more attractive, much more needful to him than a warm hurting body and hellish sex. The White Man thought he was barren, remember. And La Chusa had that vision about pomegranates when dreaming about me. The White Man is lonely. I hear him whispering in the night; he's desperate for his child. But I can't forget what La Chusa said about me: *I know now that she's dangerous.* I've taken that as a possibly accurate description about me, as well as my daughter; so I'm in no rush for the White Man's desired family reunion, which I know would open the Pandora's box of our natures.

"You *know* we have to go back," my daughter presses. "They're breaking Eden's law, and that can't last forever. And there's going to be a war between them, Lilith and my father. We have to go and play our parts."

"What parts are those?"

"We don't know yet."

I grip her, hard, but she can take it. I begin kissing her hands and feet. "I have to protect you."

"Oh, but you *will*."

"Sweetie, are you good or bad?"

"I have no idea!" she laughs.

"Am I good or bad?"

"You're *perfect*." She takes a couple of nipple-sips, burps, then asks: "Mother, don't you miss it? The Forest?"

"No."

She smiles at my lie, touching me on the forehead so that I have a vision of the red woods. Even as it floats across my mind, I try to put it down in this journal, to give it some form, some reality:

I see the burgundy trees and the bonfire. The clouds in the copper sky are like green eyes, and underfoot, the wild grasses are the shade of chameleons. The violets are like black pearls, the thistles like diamonds, and the air is made of grace. A leopard emerges from a purple forest; a silver horse with a scarlet horn stands by a large apple tree, from which hangs golden fruit.

I see the long, tiny-breasted body of my friend Selena. I remember her chattering, and the soft way that she kissed me. I remember how she talked to me of secret libraries.

"Honey?"

(I'm hiding my face in this diary because I'm crying.)

"Imogen? It was just the office—"

Patrick is back in the room. I chose him. I still do. But somehow, I'm getting the feeling that my choices won't determine everything that happens to us in the near future. I don't know yet if I'm a Goddess on account of my purification through the agonies of the White Man; I'm only sure that my shining hands and humor can bring the dead back to life.

"Baby, give her to me. You're getting tired."

Patrick whisks Selena away, perking me up again by singing more of his nonsense songs.

I know now that sin and happiness reside in the imagination. And I know also that the moon calls to wicked women. In a month, it will be the Crow Moon, whose flower is honeysuckle, whose stone is blood-colored, whose herb is Irish Moss.

But I will not bring my daughter to bask under its rays. I will wait until Patrick is very, very old, kept alive by the sound of my magic laughter. I will tend the books in my care, culling every tale of witches, Satan, Paradise, and Merlin (whose father was the Devil) to learn all I can about our perilous future. I will not touch any more boys with glistening skin or girls with fabulous breasts and eyes. I will go to church. I will kiss my husband's body and perform upon him my restrained seductions. I will tend to my daughter, whose voice sounds like birdsong, and teach her all the wisdom I can from my own life and that which I've learned in the library.

And only if and when death threatens Patrick will I succumb again to the Lunalía. Only if I see the shadow on his face will I bring her under the moon and tempt the White Man with the girl he loves, so that I can bring my husband to the undead forest.

I think that means my sin, after all, is Patrick, because I'd sacrifice everyone for him, and it's my fantasy that he live forever.

Maybe that also means that La Chusa was right about me, and that I *am* dangerous.

"Will you put that pen down?" Patrick asks, carefully squeezing the baby and trying not to crush her with his adoration. "Let's sit down to dinner, so we can have an early night."

Selena looks at me impatiently, and not about the chicken stew.

"No need to rush," I say, laughing, so that the air around us turns slightly green and gold and fills with infinitesimal stars. "There's all the time in the world."

Outside, the dark trees sway and turn in a gathering storm, and I swear I can hear the dancing footsteps of pallid, webbed feet as they prance in the Otherworld, which is not far away. The leaves blow crazily across the window pane; the priestesses murmur secrets to me from beyond the pale. And as I stare up at the sky, I see that La Chusa's fury turns her holy moon a dark and warning red.

Acknowledgments
From the Authors

For many of us, writing *this* intimately was like getting naked in front of another for the first time. We never could have found the strength to do it without the love and support of those who nourish our work and our lives.

My eternal gratitude goes to Tsaurah Litsky, for her months of diligent attention to making my story sing; Sofía and Adriana for their close reads; my agent, Joy Tutela, for her infinite supply of moral support; Anjali Bhargava for taking the first pictures of me that I love; Johanna Castillo and Amy Tannenbaum for giving me the time and space to create work I can be proud of; and all our contributors, who were never too tired for more editing. Lastly, I'd like to thank Bryan Vargas, for the love he gives me every day, and for all the inspiration I need.
— Michelle Herrera Mulligan

My story goes out to all the *jotas* who learned to love themselves even when there was no love to be found; and to G.G., who remains forever in my heart, *gracias por tus cuentos*. I'd also like to thank Sofí, Jose y Pura who blessed me with home and food in Puerto Rico while I finished this story; Johanna who had the courage to put these stories forward; Jennifer my agent and fierce sista; Michelle, for her loving but tough editorial guidance; and Alex, my forever love.
— Elisha Miranda

I dedicate my story to all the women who made my stint with Fantasia Home Parties so wonderful, especially Rosalinda Alvira. *Eres diosa, hermana!*

—Sofía Quintero

To my husband, Andrew.

—Yxta Maya Murray.

I'd first like to thank Johanna Castillo for inviting me to do the most courageous act in my writing, so far. The brilliant Michelle Herrera Mulligan, for her unwavering vision and keen eye. I'm so lucky to have been able to find a playmate like you for my writing head. Thanks to my loyal support team throughout the process: my mother Victoria Vargas; my agent Joy Tutela; my partners in crime, Deborah Kreisman Title and Carmen Ospina; and *mi amor*, Rafael López. And to my friends and family in New York and Spain, for always being there whenever I came out of the cave.

—Adriana López.

To Mario Santana Ortiz.

—Mayra Santos-Febres

Contributors

Mayra Montero was born in Havana and has lived in Puerto Rico for the last thirty-five years. She is the author of a collection of short stories and nine novels, most of them translated into English. Her most recent book is *Dancing to Almendra* (Farrar, Straus and Giroux, 2007). She is also a journalist who writes, among other things, a weekly column in *El Nuevo Dia* newspaper.

Michelle Herrera Mulligan is an editor and a writer based in Brooklyn, New York. She coedited *Border-Line Personalities: A New Generation of Latinas Dish on Sex, Sass, and Cultural Shifting*, an anthology of essays on the contemporary American Latina experience. She received an American Association of Teachers of Spanish and Portuguese (AATSP) Ruth Bennett Outstanding Contributions to Hispanic Studies Award in spring 2006. She has contributed to *Time Latin America*, *Woman's Day*, *Latina*, *Teen People*, and *Publishers Weekly*, among many other publications, and is currently at work on her first novel.

Mayra Santos-Febres is a Puerto Rican professor of literature, poet, novelist, and critic who has garnered fame at home and abroad. Santos-Febres holds an MA and PhD (1991) from Cornell University. Her work has been translated into French, English, German, and Italian, and is presented in many universities in the United States by college teachers. She is currently teaching at the University of Puerto Rico, Rio Piedras Campus. Her last novel, *Our Lady of Night* was a finalist at the *Premio Primavera de Novela 2006*.

Sofía Quintero is the author of several novels, including *Divas Don't Yield*. Under the pen name Black Artemis, she wrote three hip-hop novels, including *Explicit Content* and *Picture Me Rollin'*. As an activist and entrepreneur, Sofia also cofounded Chica Luna Productions and Sister Outsider Entertainment. To contact Sofia and to read excerpts of her forthcoming projects, visit www.sofiaquintero.com or www.myspace.com/sofiaquintero.

Adriana López is a writer and editor based in New York City and Spain. López is the editor of the anthology *Fifteen Candles: 15 Tales of Taffetta, Hairspray, Drunk Uncles and other Quinceañera Stories* (HarperCollins, 2007) and was the founding editor of *Críticas* magazine, *Publishers Weekly's* sister publication on the Spanish-language publishing world. Her work has appeared in *The New York Times*, *Los Angeles Times*, *The Washington Post*, *Time Out*, *Black Book*, *Latina*, among other publications. She is at work on her first novel and is a member of PEN international.

Elisha Miranda
Under her pen name E-Fierce, Elisha wrote her debut novel, *The Sista Hood: On the Mic*. She received her MFA in film from Columbia University. Also an activist, film director, entrepreneur, and writer of television and film, she is the cofounder of Chica Luna Productions, a nonprofit arts company for young women of color, and a creative partner of Sister Outsider Entertainment, which seeks to create quality urban media. She can be visited at www.elishamiranda.com.

Yxta Maya Murray is the author of four novels, including her most recent, *The Queen Jade*. She's a professor of law at Loyola Law School in Los Angeles. A winner of the 1999 Whiting Writers' Award, she lives in Los Angeles with her husband and two dogs.